Convoy North
&
Convoy Homeward

PHILIP McCUTCHAN

Convoy North
&
Convoy Homeward

PAN BOOKS

Convoy North first published 1987 by George Weidenfeld & Nicolson.
Convoy Homeward first published 1992 by George Weidenfeld & Nicolson.

First published in paperback in this omnibus 2005 by Pan Books
an imprint of Pan Macmillan Ltd
Pan Macmillan, 20 New Wharf Road, London N1 9RR
Basingstoke and Oxford
Associated companies throughout the world
www.panmacmillan.com

ISBN 0 330 44380 1

Copyright © Philip McCutchan 1987, 1992

The right of Philip McCutchan to be identified as the
author of this work has been asserted by him in accordance
with the Copyright, Designs and Patents Act 1988.

1 3 5 7 9 8 6 4 2

A CIP catalogue record for this book is available from
the British Library.

Printed and bound in Great Britain by
Mackays of Chatham plc, Chatham, Kent

Convoy North

ONE

The cold was bitter; men's breath crackled from their lips. As yet, no ice had formed on the fo'c'sles of the ships in convoy or on the decks and lifeboats; but that would come soon enough, even before they raised the North Cape at the tip of Norway and headed into the Barents Sea and the terrible conditions of the Arctic winter. Commodore John Mason Kemp paced the bridge of the ss *Hardraw Falls*, a heavy duffel coat covering the bridge coat with the thick gold stripe and the interlaced 'curl' of the Royal Naval Reserve on the shoulders, thinking ahead, planning in advance what his moves should be in any imaginable situation, prepared so that every vital second should be saved when trouble came. As Commodore of the convoy he was responsible for the conduct of the merchant ships, eighteen of them all told, shepherded along the route to Russia by an escort of two cruisers and four destroyers plus a group of anti-submarine trawlers and corvettes. Not a very strong escort; but the best that could be mustered by an overstretched British fleet against the might of the German Navy that would stand between them and the port of Archangel – or Murmansk if the big winter freeze, predicted by the Met men to be coming later this winter than was usual, should in the event confound the forecasts – and between Kemp's duty to deliver vital war supplies to the embattled Russian armies that were trying to block the eastward thrust of Hitler's Panzer divisions.

In the fading light, Kemp looked astern. Moving out from Hvalfiord in the early morning, they had steamed north about past Ondverdharnes and Bjargtangar to take their final departure from Norway from Straumnes. Now they were standing

1

clear for the northern ocean wastes behind the A/S group, with the heavy cruisers *Nottingham* and *Neath* out on either beam, the destroyers moving astern to form the rearguard.

'Commodore, sir?'

Kemp turned. 'Yes, Cutler?'

'All clear ahead, sir.'

'In what respect?'

'Situation report from the Admiralty,' Cutler said.

'Say so, then. An incomplete report's worse than none at all, Cutler. All clear ahead – that could mean anything.'

'Sorry, sir.'

Kemp nodded and grinned. 'All right, Cutler.' The Commodore's assistant tore off a salute, a curious one that Kemp had not yet acclimatized himself to: it was a movement of a vertically-held hand across the face, the fingers almost touching the nose, a parody of an American style salute. Thomas B. Cutler was in fact an American, from Texas of all places, cow country, not a wave in sight. But Cutler had been dead keen to join the war in which his country was not yet involved, and he'd seen that the best way of doing so was to join the Royal Canadian Naval Volunteer Reserve. A thrustful young man, he had achieved this against many difficulties. Kemp admired his courage in joining in the war when he had no need to. Kemp believed he had got himself a very useful assistant, but Cutler had a thing or two to learn yet. However, it was good news that the Admiralty had nothing on the plot.

So far.

Kemp glanced across at the *Hardraw Falls'* master. Captain Ezekiel Theakston was a Yorkshireman and looked it. A strong, square face, not truculent but determined and forming the window of a mind very much its own. Theakston had already told Kemp, back at the convoy conference some while before, that he came from Whitby, the birthplace of Captain Cook, who had been his boyhood hero. Kemp believed that Captain Theakston had told him this because the Commodore had been a peacetime master in the Mediterranean-Australia Line, which he wouldn't have been, presumably, if Cook had never discovered Australia. . . . Theakston had spoken of his hero in such a way that he had managed to sound as though he himself in some former existence had been jointly responsible for the voyage of

2

exploration. Perhaps, Kemp thought, this was a manifestation of being a Yorkshireman.

The PQ convoy had assembled off the island of Mull at the northern end of the Firth of Lorne ten days earlier, and the convoy conference had been held in the port of Oban. Captain Theakston had come to this conference by train from Whitby, the *Hardraw Falls* having been sailed north from Liverpool by his chief officer, Ben Amory. Captain Theakston had obtained compassionate leave because his wife, Dora, had been seriously ill; he believed she had now turned the corner but in any case he had had to leave her to rejoin his ship before the convoy finally sailed from the United Kingdom. War was all-consuming and didn't wait for mariners' wives to recover. Dora Theakston didn't carry much weight in the scales against the munitions requirements of Marshal Stalin, and Captain Theakston was a man who took his duty seriously. He looked down at his wife as she lay in bed, as he might into an open hold to ensure that his chief officer had been attentive to the stowing of the cargo; and he saw that indeed she carried very little weight and never mind Marshal Stalin. She was all skin and bone, but he didn't mention this to her.

'You'll do, lass,' he said.

'Yes, Ezekiel. You're not to worry.'

'You know I will.' Dora was fifty-three and currently looked twenty years older. 'I'll be back the moment we dock. Amory's a good man, and can be left in charge again.' He bent and kissed her and left immediately. A backward glance from the door, a brief pause, showed him a grieving woman and a lonely one who would worry about him without cease, all the time he was gone. No children – a pity, now. Not that they hadn't tried, but Dora wasn't a childbearing woman it seemed, even though she came of a big family herself, one of eleven offspring of a dales farmer – oddly enough from Cotterdale near Hardraw Falls. A coincidence, that, and Theakston thought it could even have some significance; he wished he could read the mind of God.

Grim-faced, Captain Theakston embarked on the long journey

north, taking the train from Whitby to York where he caught the express for Edinburgh and then travelled on to Perth and thence via Kinross to Oban, and the convoy conference where he and the other assembled masters were addressed by an officer of the Naval Control Service staff, a lieutenant-commander RNR who had given them their route and detailed convoy orders. Theakston had listened attentively, as he had done when Commodore Kemp had taken over and introduced himself, an informal talk and a welcome to the man he was to sail with. Captain Theakston, who knew already that his ship was to wear the broad pennant of the convoy Commodore, had been pleased to learn at the same time that the Commodore was genuine RNR: Theakston had no love for the RN, and with foul luck might have drawn a retired admiral serving in the rank of Commodore RNR for the duration. There were plenty such officers with much experience of bull but none of the ways of the merchant ships and the men who sailed them in peace and war.

After the conference, Theakston found himself alongside Kemp, a man built like a bear, a big bear with a kindly face. Theakston said, 'I reckon we'll get on.'

'I hope so, Captain.'

'Aye. I'm told you're a liner man, Mediterranean-Australia.'

'Yes.' That was when Kemp heard about Whitby; and learned that Captain Theakston, whose uniform jacket, like that of Kemp himself, bore a row of medal ribbons from the previous war, had been with Bricker Dockett Steamships of Hull from third officer to master, a matter of twenty-nine years now.

'A long time,' Kemp said pleasantly.

'Aye, it's been that.' Captain Theakston gave him a look that said he'd made a trite remark and might have saved his breath. Kemp grinned to himself: he'd always heard that Yorkshiremen were blunt in speech. Now he knew this one was blunt in facial expression as well.

iii

Sub-Lieutenant Thomas B. Cutler, RCNVR – 'Tex' to a wide variety of friends – had spent the night before the conference ashore in Oban's Station Hotel. He had spent it with a girl he'd

4

met the previous day in the Central Hotel in Glasgow. He'd bumped into her, literally, soon after he'd got off the train from Euston. Right in the hotel entrance he'd almost knocked her over with his grip. He'd swept off his cap with a flourish and apologized handsomely.

'My fault, ma'am. I'm an oaf.'

'An American oaf by the sound. What's that uniform?'

He sang it to her. 'If you ask us who we are, We're the RCNVR ...' The tune was 'Roll Along, Covered Wagon'. 'But don't let it worry you. Just call me Tex.'

The girl giggled, a friendly sound. They looked at each other. She appeared to be at a loose end. Cutler spotted the bar.

'How's about a drink?' he asked.

She nodded, and he put a hand on her elbow and guided her into the bar. They sat at a table for two, in a corner. He saw she was wearing a wedding ring and noted also that she already had a drink or two inside her.

He asked, 'What's it to be?'

'Scotch, please.'

At the bar he ordered two doubles and carried them back to the table. He knew he was lucky to get whisky so easily in wartime Britain, but this after all was Scotland and probably the Scots saw to it that not too much of their life-blood crossed the border when it was scarce.

He said interrogatively, 'Well?'

'Well, what?'

'I've told you I'm Tex. You?'

She shrugged. 'Roz,' she said, sounding indifferent.

'Two nice single syllables. Roz anything else?' Cutler lifted an eyebrow. She didn't answer; he laid a finger on her left hand, on the wedding ring. 'Ma'am,' he said earnestly, very American now, 'I don't reckon to drink with women whose husbands might show at any moment. Not drink too long, that is. Some husbands might not like it.'

'It's all right,' she said. Her fingers shook a little, the voice became clipped. She drank the double Scotch quickly and then confided. Her husband had been in the RAF, a squadron leader, and two months earlier he'd been shot down in his Spitfire over the eastern counties. Roz had drifted since then. No children, not married long, no parents living ... currently she was staying in Glasgow with an aunt who was something in the wvs and was often away, as she was now. They had more drinks and Roz became tearful. They had dinner but she had no appetite. That night she went up with him to his room and next day, since she had nowhere else to go other than her aunt's flat, the empty flat, she went with him on the train to Oban and they booked into the Station Hotel.

iv

Aboard the *Hardraw Falls* lying at anchor in the Firth of Lorne Chief Officer Amory looked across the water at the hard outline of Mull to port, at the Argyll hills to starboard, hills that ran down easterly towards Loch Awe and a slice of Scottish history – Campbell country, and Amory's mother had been a Campbell from Portsonachan. Amory had spent summer holidays there in his schooldays; he wished he was there now, looking across the summer blue of a loch that could grow grey and angry in winter, across towards the ancient stronghold of Kilchurn Castle. But wishing would get him nowhere. He smacked a horny palm against the teak rail of the bridge and went below to his cabin to go once again through his cargo manifests, wondering if the Old Man would ever wring a proper signature of receipt from the Russians. The manifest *in toto* ran to many pages and each entry concerned materials of war – ammunition, explosives, guns and gun parts. The *Hardraw Falls* was loaded to her marks, ten thousand tons of mostly HE, a fine place, Amory thought, to put the Convoy Commodore. One unlucky hit by the Nazis and it would be a case of finito. But then almost all the rest of the convoy would be carrying similar cargoes. You didn't take toys to Russia in wartime . . . some of the ships carried foodstuffs, grain and so on, but they weren't fitted out to take the Commodore and his staff. There was a tanker, but she would be equally at risk, and in any case she was a Royal Fleet Auxiliary and thus officially part of the naval escort, no direct concern of the Commodore.

After a while Amory gathered up his papers and shoved them away in a drawer. He lit a cigarette and drew in a lungful of smoke, pushing himself back at arm's length from his desk. His glance fell on three photographs in silver frames: his mother and father, taken some years before – his father was wearing the uniform of a police superintendent. Amory grinned to himself: his father had always been a copper, on and off duty, never let up, do this, do that, get your hair cut, don't come home late, where have you been . . . no doubt it had been good training and had helped the young Ben Amory through a tough sea apprenticeship lasting four years plus. But it hadn't made home life easy and it had worn his mother out, worn her literally to death.

The third photograph was of a young woman. She, too, was dead: a Nazi bomb on London, back in the days of the Battle of Britain, more than a year ago now. Ben Amory had considered himself a confirmed bachelor until he had met Felicity, who was some years younger than himself and had captivated him from his first sight of her. They hadn't married: Hitler had beaten the banns. So bachelordom was back. Amory knew there would never be anybody else. He had picked up the silver frame when a knock came at his door.

He put the frame down as though caught out in some guilty act. 'Yes?'

It was the watchman from the gangway. 'Boat coming off from Oban, sir.'

'Approaching us?'

'Yes, sir. Could be the Captain.'

'I'll be down.' Amory got to his feet and reached for his cap. He followed the watchman down to the starboard accommodation ladder, arriving at the upper platform just as the boat came alongside. A bulky figure stepped out first and climbed fast to the upper platform, followed by Captain Theakston. There was a naval cap badge and a row of brass oak leaves on the cap's peak: the Commodore. Amory saluted awkwardly. Theakston made the introductions, including in them a young officer wearing wavy stripes who had come up behind him.

'All ready, Mr Amory?'

'Yes, sir.'

'Good.' Captain Theakston looked briefly fore and aft along the embarkation deck. 'The convoy leaves at 0100 hours. Be ready to shorten-in at half an hour after midnight, Mr Amory.'

'Aye, aye, sir.'

The sky was darkening already, the early northern evening setting in. The last of the sun glinted from the snow-clad Scottish hillsides, shafted across dull grey water between the arms of the land. The water was still, no wind at all, and there was a hint of fog about to come down to make the outward passage tricky. The ships lay ghostlike, the naval escort taking on a sinister look, lean and grey and with their guns neatly trained to the fore-and-aft line. They wouldn't stay that way for long. The Russian convoys had started quietly enough but the Nazis were known by now to have built up their destroyer and U-boat strength in the northern waters.

Theakston stumped up the ladders to his quarters below the bridge, accompanied by the Commodore and Sub-Lieutenant Cutler. Entering his cabin he pressed a bell for his steward.

'My compliments to Mr Paget and I'd like to see him at once. And Mr Buckle.'

'Yes, sir.' The steward left the master's cabin. Kemp looked around, feeling in need of a short drink. No offer was forthcoming, and no apology. Captain Theakston, Kemp reflected, had the look of a teetotaller. No bad thing, of course, and not to be faulted. But teetotallers tended to make prickly shipmates. Kemp caught Cutler's eye and refrained from winking back at the grin he saw on his assistant's face. Cutler evidently had the same thought. Until Paget and Buckle had reported, Theakston said little other than to indicate chairs for Kemp and Cutler. Paget, the second officer and thus responsible for navigation, was told to lay off a course through the Minch for Hvalfiord in Norway.

'We call in there, Mr Paget.'

'Yes, sir.'

'Go and get on with it, then.' Next came Buckle, the ship's chief steward. The accommodation for the Commodore and his staff was ready, he said. He would show Commodore Kemp to the master's spare cabin. Theakston grunted and waved a hand: Kemp gathered he was dismissed, and took his departure.

v

In addition to Cutler, Kemp's staff consisted of a leading signalman and an ordinary signalman, a telegraphist and a number of gunnery rates – a petty officer with the non-substantive rate of

8

seaman gunner in charge of a leading seaman and ten hands to man the ship's armament, which wasn't much: close-range AA weapons – Bofors, Lewis guns, Oerlikons, mounted in the bridge wings, on monkey's island above the wheelhouse and chart room, and aft above the engineers' accommodation. The other ships in convoy carried similar armament; the main defence would be the escort. Aboard the Commodore's ship, Petty Officer Napper was the man in charge of the weaponry and his sour, horse-like face said he didn't go much on it. No use complaining though; it was the best that could be allocated, no doubt of that. There were always shortages. In fact PO Napper was inclined to be sour about taking valuable war material to Russia when Britain herself stood in need of it.

'Bloody bolshies,' he said to Leading Signalman Corrigan in the compartment allocated as the naval messdeck. 'Hitler's allies, not long since. Probably change again before long.'

Corrigan didn't waste breath answering. Hitler's hordes advancing like Attila the Hun across the Russian land mass had put paid to any thoughts of another Nazi–Communist get-together, and now Russia had to be treated as a full member of the Allies against the Axis powers. Napper went on chuntering away to himself, a regular old woman Corrigan thought, though they'd met for the first time only in RNB Pompey when they'd been detailed by the drafting master-at-arms to form the party for the *Hardraw Falls*. Napper was an RFR man, a Fleet Reservist, and looked it, grey-faced and wrinkled, not far off fifty, too old to be still at sea. Napper's bunk was piled high with home comforts extracted from his kit-bag: mufflers, balaclavas, seaboot stockings – fair enough, of course. But the rest! There was a tea-cosy, currently filled with an assortment of medicines. Corrigan had seen Enos, Carter's Little Liver Pills, a packet of senna pods, aspirins, a tin of Germoline, corn plasters and a small corn knife, and a bottle of Dr J. Collis Browne's Chlorodyne, presumably in case the senna pods worked too well.

Napper saw Corrigan looking at it all.

'What's up?'

'Nothing, PO. Just hope you won't be needing it, that's all.'

'It's the wife,' Napper said defensively.

'Looks after you, does she?'

'That's her job, isn't it?' Napper began to push things

straight, looked round and found a drawer beneath the bunk. He opened it and began stowing away his medicine chest. He gave a sudden cough, and stopped to feel his chest. Buggeration – his weak point! And sod the war. He rooted about, found some camphorated oil. Better not rub it in now, the air up top was enough to freeze the balls off a brass monkey and he couldn't turn in yet, not until the convoy had weighed and the ships' companies had been fallen out to take up cruising stations. After midnight, that would be. Napper stood there uncertainly, with the camphorated oil in his hand, and coughed again. His face looked hollow with anxiety.

Corrigan grinned. He said, 'Big decision, eh, PO?'

'What d'you mean?'

'To rub or not to rub.'

Napper glared. 'What do you know about it?'

'More than you think, PO.'

Napper shoved the bottle out of sight. That Corrigan . . . there was a posh accent. The wartime navy had brought in all manner of different people, not a bit like peacetime. Corrigan, a hostilities-only rating, was a convoy signalman, something a shade different from a proper naval bunting tosser, a shorter qualifying course, and some of them were posh, so he'd been told, aiming for commissions as sub-lieutenants RNVR. 'You a college boy?' he asked.

'That depends on what you mean by college, PO.'

'I don't want any of your lip.'

'It wasn't meant to be lip, PO, just a statement of fact. It so happens I was a medical student . . . I wanted to get into the war so I chucked it, anyway till the war's over.'

Napper's lips framed a whistle. 'Makee-learn doctor, was you?'

'That's right.'

'Then you know all about camphorated oil.'

'A little,' Corrigan answered modestly. Petty Officer Napper rubbed reflectively at a blue-shaded jowl. This bunting tosser was a find and he'd never had such luck before. His own medical adviser, right on the spot! Worth keeping in with, worth buttering up in fact. Free advice. . . .

'What do you advise?' he asked anxiously. 'It's me chest, you see. Got a cough.' He lit a fag and coughed some more. 'I had pleurisy, once. Don't want to get it again. Then there's the bowels, see. Not reg'lar . . .'

vi

'Escort taking up station, sir.'

'Thank you, Corrigan.' Kemp turned to Captain Theakston, a thickset shadow in the dim light from the binnacle behind. 'All ready, Captain?'

'Aye, all ready. Mr Paget?'

'Yes, sir – '

'Pass to the fo'c'sle, shorten-in to three shackles.'

Paget passed the order down and the sound of the windlass, steam driven, came back to the men on the bridge, a rackety, clanking sound as the links of the cable came home up the hawse-pipe to drop down into the cable locker beneath the fo'c'sle accommodation. The senior officer of the escort, with his de-gaussing gear switched on, like all the other ships, against the possibility of magnetic mines, and paravanes ready to be streamed from either bow to deflect and cut the mooring cables that would attach any conventional mines to their sinkers, moved past to take up station ahead for moving out the convoy; when they were clear of the firth the cruisers would move out to the beam and leave the A/S group to sweep ahead of the merchant ships.

The windlass stopped and a shout came from Amory in the eyes of the ship: 'Shortened-in, sir, third shackle on deck.'

'Right.'

They waited. The darkness was thick but the fog was holding off, had not after all come down with the dark, thanks to a breeze that had come up to blow it away before it had properly formed. If that wind dropped, then the fog might come back. The water's surface was slightly ruffled and the breeze was a cold one – but the sea was cold too, otherwise the wind would have brought its own fog. Kemp sent up a prayer that it would hold off: no joke, navigating blind or by radar in pilotage waters, those of western Scotland in particular.

'Executive, sir.' This was Corrigan, watching the flagship's signal bridge.

11

'Thank you. Executive to all ships.'

'Aye, aye, sir.' Corrigan used his blue-shaded Aldis to flash the brief signal to the merchantmen in company, the signal that told the masters to proceed in execution of previous orders. Theakston gave the order to weigh anchor and once again the windlass started up, the wash-deck hoses in action to clean down the cable as it came slowly inboard under the eagle eye of Jock Tawney, the bosun, once again saying his farewells to Scotland ... he'd long since forgotten how many times he'd done that, though in the past it had been mainly the Clyde he'd sailed from.

Amory's voice came again from the fo'c'sle. 'Anchor's aweigh, sir.'

'Heave to the waterline, Mr Amory. Hold it on the brake.'

'Aye, aye, sir.' Until the ship was clear of the firth, the anchor would remain veered ready for letting go in an emergency: Theakston was a careful master.

Kemp said, 'We'll move to the head of the centre column, Captain.'

'I know that. I know the orders and this isn't my first convoy.'

'My apologies,' Kemp said. He cursed himself for a lack of tact. He would have to watch his step with Captain Theakston. The master, after all, commanded the ship, the Commodore of the convoy was a mere passenger until it fell to him to order the movements and manoeuvres of the convoy as a whole. As the *Hardraw Falls* began to move in response to the engine-room telegraph the other ships fell in astern on a sou'-sou'-westerly course to take them down towards Colonsay and the turn to starboard for the Dubh Artach light which they would leave away to port when they turned up for the Minch on passage north to Iceland.

The PQ convoy was away.

TWO

Always at the start of a convoy, of any sailing across the seas, there were the thoughts of home, many and varied. John Mason Kemp, by long experience of the sea life, was able to switch off the moment his ship was under way. The job needed concentration and so he concentrated. Before sailing he was as bad, as nostalgic as anyone else. He always hated leaving the cottage in Meopham, way down in Kent. He always had, even in peacetime, but it was that much worse with Hitler sending his *Luftwaffe* over to blast London and its environs – Meopham was scarcely an environ but was in the flight path from the airfields in occupied France and not all that far from targets such as RAF Biggin Hill. Then there were the simple facts of wartime life: the shortages; the queues; the making do; the difficult lot of a wife left to cope on her own, not that Mary was unique in that respect, nor unique in having two sons as well as a husband involved in the war at sea. But she also had Kemp's aged grandmother to look after. No joke that, Kemp knew. Just before sailing from the Firth of Lorne, Kemp had reflected, as he had done many times before, that it was a curious situation for a middle-aged convoy commodore still to have someone to call granny. A pernicketty one of well over ninety, not far off a hundred in fact, one of life's trials but a very game old bird.

Before going aboard the *Hardraw Falls* Kemp had rung his wife from the Station Hotel, a circumspect conversation with no places or ships mentioned since Hitler's ears were said to be everywhere, though a German agent in wartime Oban would have stood out like a bishop entering a brothel. Mary had seemed somewhat down and he'd chivvied her a little.

13

'It won't last for ever, Mary. Chin up!'

'It's not that,' she'd said.

'Ah! Granny?'

'Yes. She's been complaining – '

'She always does. What is it this time?'

'Oh ... the cold, for one thing.' Kent could be cold and, like Scotland, often suffered snow problems, but not quite yet. 'She seems to feel it more and more.'

'Age,' Kemp said. He knew Mary had fuel problems: everyone was supposed to save gas and coal and electricity. 'Try not to worry ... my shilling's run out,' he added as the pips went, 'and I haven't another. Sorry.'

'All right. Take care of yourself, John.'

'I'll do that,' he said, and the line went dead before he'd actually said goodbye. It was rather like an omen. He'd half a mind to ring back on a transferred charge call but it could take up to half an hour to be passed through all the exchanges that stood between Oban and Meopham and time was short. Leaving the telephone box, Kemp caught sight of his assistant, a new one whom he had met for the first time at the convoy conference. His assistant was doing two things: waiting for his lord and master and trying to disengage himself from a young woman with deep, dark rings under her eyes and an unsteady gait.

'All set, Cutler?' Kemp asked as he came up.

'All set, sir, Commodore.' He didn't look it by any means. Given any encouragement at all the girl would embark with him. 'Drifter's at the quay, sir.'

'Let's go, then.' Kemp felt he'd sounded like an American film: the rub-off already, just from knowing he had an American assistant? He fixed the young woman with his eye. 'Make short work of it,' he said, and headed for the hotel entrance that gave on to the quay, not far to go. He saw the drifter waiting and Captain Theakston, beneath a harbour lamp, holding an old-fashioned pocket-watch ostentatiously in front of his face. From behind he heard the girl's voice, quite loud and very clear, something about an old fuddy-duddy who was jealous because he was past it. A moment later Cutler caught him up.

'Cleared away?' Kemp asked sardonically.

'Cleared away?'

Kemp said, 'The young woman.'

'Oh – yes, sir, Commodore, I guess so. All aboard, I told her
. . . and stand well clear of the bubble-gum chutes.'

'*What*?'

'US Navy pipe, sir. Boats' crews keep out from under the
chewed gobs coming down the chute – '

'This isn't the US Navy, Cutler. Do you chew gum?'

'Why, yes, sir, Commodore, I guess I – '

'Not any more you don't.'

'Sir?'

'You heard.' Kemp's tone was harsher than he'd intended:
he'd once sat on some gum in a railway carriage. He believed
Cutler had taken umbrage; there was a hurt silence as they
embarked aboard the drifter to be greeted by Captain Theakston's upraised timepiece. That watch looked as though it might
have belonged to Theakston's grandfather; it had an uncompro-
mising Yorkshire aspect.

ii

Tex Cutler was one of the home-thinkers as the *Hardraw Falls*
dropped south towards Colonsay, but not of the USA: Oban
with the girl in residence was currently his idea of home, though
he doubted if he would ever see either again. The return convoy,
the QP out of Archangel – or if the freeze did in fact come sooner
than expected, then out of Murmansk – wasn't likely to sail for
Oban. More likely Liverpool, possibly the Clyde. Not that the
girl would be around anyway, of course. She was going back to
Glasgow, true, but only for a few days. She was fed up with the
Glasgow scene, the cold and the wet. The aunt would be back
soon and she was fed up with the aunt as well. Once you'd been
married, you didn't settle easily to aunts and their ways, however well-intentioned. She was heading back to London for a
while and after that God knew where. She might join the WAAF.
One thing was certain in Cutler's mind and that was that it
wouldn't be long before she found another serviceman passing
through and then she'd hitch her wagon to his temporary star.

Which was a pity. Cutler liked the girl a lot and wished he
could have stayed near to help her through. And he hoped she
wasn't going to get pregnant. . . .

'Cutler?'

'Yes, sir, Commodore?'

Kemp felt a twinge of irritation at being addressed as it were twice. 'I'd like the close-range weapons exercised before the hands stand down.' He paused. 'That's if it's all right with you, Captain Theakston?'

There was a brief nod. 'Aye. So long as there's no interference with the ship-handling in the firth.'

'There won't be. All right, Cutler, carry on, please.'

Cutler executed one of his salutes. 'Yes, sir, Commodore.'

Kemp said, 'That's not necessary, at night particularly – and not every time I open my mouth.'

'What's not –'

'The salute. Everything in its time and place, Cutler. Meanwhile, exercise close-range weapons.'

There was no Tannoy system aboard the *Hardraw Falls*: Cutler went to the bridge wing and shouted aft.

'Petty Officer of the close-range crews!'

The return shout came from the darkness. 'Here, sir.'

'What's your name, bloke?' Bloke was a term Cutler had picked up along the way, not realizing it was strictly an Australianism. Napper didn't like being called bloke in full hearing of junior ratings and he shouted back with a touch of truculence that his name was Petty Officer Napper.

'Okay. Report to the bridge, pronto.'

Pronto, was it? Petty Officer Napper moved for'ard at a fairly leisurely gait as befitted his rate and age. He climbed the starboard ladder and approached Cutler.

'Wanted me, sir?'

'Napper?'

'*Petty Officer* Napper, sir, yes.'

'Okay. Exercise action. All the way through from the word go. Get me? All guns' crews to fall out and go below and wait for the order, and I'll be timing how long it takes for all guns to be manned and ready to open fire – all right?'

'All right, sir, yes.' Napper's voice had a long-suffering backing to it. 'No Tannoy, sir. Going to press the tit, sir, sound the action alarm, are you, sir?'

It was Theakston who answered. 'No, he's not. Do that when there's no call for it, and what happens when an attack comes? I'll have no crying wolf aboard my ship.'

16

'But, sir, Captain Theakston – '

'I've nowt more to say and that's final.'

Kemp listened but didn't interfere. He was intrigued to know how Cutler would handle this. He hadn't long to wait. Cutler said, 'Okay. Petty Officer Napper'll be the alarm. All right, Napper?'

Napper's mouth fell open. 'Me, sir?'

'Yes. Stand by somewhere near the guns' crews' quarters. When I'm ready I'll pass the order down to you, exercise action, all right? When you get that, why, you just holler.'

There was an indeterminate sound from Petty Officer Napper. Kemp turned away, hiding a grin. Napper hadn't liked it and Kemp could appreciate his feelings but it showed one thing, and that was that Cutler could think on his feet. An assistant who could come up with something fast was welcome enough to Kemp. Improvisation was an essential attribute in anyone who went to sea but it wasn't often found among the inexperienced. Kemp paced the bridge, scanning the convoy and escorts through his binoculars, the dark, unlit shapes standing out in the loom from the water, and kept his ears cocked for Cutler's orders and the 'holler' from Petty Officer Napper. The resulting exercise was good in patches: the gunnery rates hadn't exercised together before and the turn-out wasn't as fast as Kemp would have liked, but once again he didn't interfere. He liked to trust his officers and there was something about Cutler that said he could take charge. He did, and in the process he made rings round Napper, who largely stood about with a look of bewilderment. It was plain to Kemp that Cutler knew his gun drill, at any rate so far as the close-range weapons side of it was concerned, and aboard the *Hardraw Falls* that was what counted.

iii

As the convoy made the turn off the Dubh Artach light and headed up for the Minch the wind came. A bitter wind from the north, from Iceland and the Arctic wastes, funnelling down on the ships between Tiree and Mull. The convoy altered again when Skerryvore was abeam to starboard, to head up between Barra and Rhum, and then they met the blow head on. The bows dipped to a roughening sea and, with the guns' crews by this time stood down, Petty Officer Napper turned into his bunk after rubbing some camphorated oil on his chest, now shrouded in a woollen scarf pulled tight about his ribs. Napper would have liked to strangle the drafting jaunty down in Pompey barracks, and a certain surgeon lieutenant as well. Napper had reported to the sick bay when he'd got his draft chit, spinning a yarn about vague pains here and there, principally in his chest. The sick bay tiffy had passed him on to the doctor because he'd insisted, and the doctor hadn't been interested beyond a brief bit of play-acting with a stethoscope, after which he'd said Napper was as fit as a fiddle, which Napper knew was a load of codswallop and proved the doctor, like all seagoing doctors, didn't know his job. To have said as much would have been to chance his arm too far, so he had to put up with it and now look where he was: Russia-bound with a dickey chest, the sods, a chest made worse by having to hang about in the open and bloody holler. Strike a light, Napper thought, Yanks!

Napper thought about home. The missus would be worried about him: she knew all about his chest. He wasn't too worried about her; home was in a Hampshire village behind Portsdown Hill, far enough away from Pompey and Gosport to be safe, nothing nearby to attract the Nazi bombers. Napper was more inclined to worry about his daughter, who at nineteen was man mad, go out with anything in uniform, even airmen. Marleen was a constant worry, liable at any moment to get a bun in the oven and destroy Napper's respectability. At his age, it wasn't fair.

Napper's last leave stuck in his mind like a bad go of tooth-ache. On his last night, Marleen had announced she was catch-ing the bus into Pompey. There was a dance at Clarence Pier.

'Not on your nelly,' Napper had said.

'Why not?'

'Cos I say so.'

Marleen's nostrils had flared and her mother had made a bid to defuse the situation. 'It's not just that. Your dad's worried about the bombs.'

'What bombs?'

'Oh, for God's sake,' Napper said wearily. 'Don't you know there's a war on? It's me last night, too. Anyway, you're not

18

going, so that's that.' He took up a poker and thrust angrily at the fire, or what there was of it. The Napper household was a patriotic one, even in the bath: like the King in Buckingham Palace, they never exceeded four inches of hot water.

'I *am* going! I'm bloody *going* so there!' A foot was stamped and Marleen's eyes flashed. 'I'm meeting Danny – '

'Not that wet weekend – '

'I don't care what you say. You never say anything good about any of my boyfriends – '

'That's cos there's nothing good to say.'

'Oh! You – you – ' Words had seemed to fail Marleen after that; there was too much head of steam inside. She whirled about and stormed out of the parlour, slamming the door with a crash that shook the whole house. A second later the door opened again and Marleen delivered her parting shot: '*Go and get stuffed, you rotten old fool!*'

Old fool eh? Napper could hear the shrill yell still. When Marleen had gone he'd stormed about the room, he remembered, talking about a taste of the belt when she got back, but Ethel had gone to Marleen's defence, saying that if he laid a hand on her she would walk out of the house. In the end he'd calmed down, though the scene had had an effect on his stomach and he felt quite sick and had to go to bed with some milk of magnesia and two aspirins, and even then hadn't slept a wink, lying there beside an unresponsive Ethel waiting for the sounds of Marleen's return and fearing the worst, not just the possibility of bombs but also Danny, even though he doubted if Danny was capable of putting a bun in anyone's oven. Thinking back now from somewhere north of Rhum, Napper began to sweat. At first he thought it was the effect of his own thoughts and bitter memories but after a while realized that it was the tightness of the wound scarf and too liberal a hand with the camphorated oil that was making his vest stick.

iv

By 1600 hours next day the convoy had left Cape Wrath on its starboard quarter and was heading into what had become a full gale. Out now from the narrows, out from the land's shelter, they moved into the danger zone that stood between Cape Wrath and their Iceland landfall, as yet some two days' steaming ahead. The convoy was now larger: two ammunition ships had joined out of Loch Ewe, tagging on astern of the centre column after an exchange of signals with the senior officer of the escort and the Commodore. The ships moved on into the night and the gathering storm, their fo'c'sles swept by the heavy seas that dropped back aft to swill over the hatches and against the midship superstructures, pouring in white cascades from the hawsepipes and washports while the wind sang through the steel-wire rigging and buffeted the watchkeepers. No weather for U-boats; but Hitler had other methods and the first alarm came early next day as the morning watchmen were about to be relieved. Leading Signalman Corrigan made the report to Captain Theakston, wedged in a corner of the wheelhouse, grey with lack of sleep.

'Senior officer calling, sir. Aircraft bearing green two oh, hostile, closing.'

Theakston spoke to the officer of the watch. 'Call the Commodore, Mr Amory.' As he spoke he moved across the wheelhouse and brought a heavy hand down on the action alarm.

THREE

'Unexpected,' Kemp said. Up to now, the Luftwaffe had left the
PQS alone, as he remarked to Theakston.

Theakston gave him a sideways look. 'There's always a first
time,' he stated flatly. Kemp scanned the skies, which were a
clear blue with a scud of white cloud racing before the wind. The
attacking aircraft were at first hard to pick up ; they were coming
out of the sunrise. The cruiser *Nottingham*, away to starboard,
was already in action, her ack-ack sending up shells that burst in
puffs of smoke to dot the sky. Soon the Germans were in sight
from the *Hardraw Falls*, keeping high, sweeping right over the
convoy before coming back in for their bombing run.

'Buggers are well out of range,' Kemp said, referring to their
height.

'Aye, they are that.' Captain Theakston was phlegmatic,
almost indifferent. You did what you could, you handled your
ship in accordance with your training and experience, and you
hoped for the best. No use worrying. If you got hit, you got hit
and that was all about it. Aboard the *Hardraw Falls* you'd go fast
enough if you did get hit, blown straight up into the heavens to
sit somewhere on God's right hand and look down on it all happening.

All the ships of the escort were firing now, all except those of
the A/S screen who were forming the guard against U-boats and
whose depth-charges would be vulnerable in the racks and
throwers. The sky above the convoy seemed filled with the shell
bursts, a shrapnel curtain to keep the attack high and hinder the
bomb-aimers.

'Here they come,' Kemp said suddenly. 'Laying eggs. . . .'

They watched as the bombs dropped from the bays, clusters of them that spread wider as they fell. The sea became dappled with waterspouts. A ragged cheer went up from the decks of the Commodore's ship as the convoy steamed on unscathed: not one hit. The next bombing run came in at reduced height, the Germans taking a chance on the ack-ack fire, zooming across with a roar of engines and this time to better effect: three ships, two in the port column and one in the starboard, were hit. Those in the port column, not badly damaged apparently, moved on. The starboard one had carried a cargo of cased oil and had taken a bomb on her fore hatch. There was a brilliant flash and a spreading column of smoke that spiralled and billowed for hundreds of feet into the sky. More explosions came, and more thick, oily smoke, as the fire took charge below and the shattered ship settled lower in the water.

'Not many'll come out of that,' Theakston said in a flat voice. There was no response from the Commodore: these were the times that Kemp detested with every part of his mind. A seaman's instinct was to stop and help, and all he could do was to steam on and make sure that all the other ships steamed on as well. The overall business of the war came first, and you didn't hazard more cargoes and more lives in the middle of an attack. But it still left a nasty taste and a certain knowledge that however long your life lasted there would be no forgetting.

This time, it was to be pointed up cruelly.

Leading Signalman Corrigan reported. 'Signal from ss *Wicksteed Park,* sir – request permission to stand by for any survivors.' Corrigan added, '*Wicksteed Park*'s next astern of the one that went up, sir.'

'Yes. Answer: "You are not repeat not to stop engines but may lower nets".'

'Aye, aye, sir.' Corrigan flashed the answer with his Aldis, voice and face expressionless. Kemp wondered what he was thinking – probably the same as himself: that in such desperately cold sea, men would die within the minute, that to lower nets and hope to catch anything would be as forlorn as looking for a sixpence in the Sahara? Just a sop to Kemp's own conscience, better than a flat refusal order. A ship sweeping past, the shocked survivors, if any were alive, too dazed and broken to reach out a hand for the trailing nets – he might just as well have sent that refusal.

Cutler was on the bridge now, come up from aft where he'd been with the close-range weapons above the after island, yelling words of encouragement as the gunners pumped away, sitting in their harness as the guns swivelled after the enemy to no effect.

Kemp faced him. 'I gave no order to open fire, Cutler.'

'No, sir.'

'You know the general order, given at the convoy conference: no firing from the merchant ships except when under individual attack or when aircraft are clearly within range.'

'Yes, sir, Commodore – '

'God damn it, the country's desperately short of all kinds of ammunition! So is the ship. We're going to need to make every round count. Remember that, all right?'

'Yes, sir. It was just that I wanted to have a crack at them, that's all.'

Kemp nodded, understanding only too well. 'All right, Cutler. Just bear in mind what I said. See that the order from the bridge is awaited in future.'

'Yes, sir, Commodore.' A hand started to go into one of Cutler's odd salutes, but wavered before its manoeuvre had been completed. Two minutes later the attack was broken off, very suddenly. Soon after that the reason became apparent: the RAF had arrived, presumably from Shetland.

Theakston said, 'Better late than never.'

ii

With just the one loss to report, the PQ convoy reached the shelter of Iceland and the anchors were let go in Hvalfiord. Shelter was not quite the word, except as regards the enemy: the wind was bitter, the cold intense. A naval motor-cutter came off to fetch the Commodore and his assistant and Mason Kemp made his report to the Naval Officer in Charge while the escort vessels and merchant ships topped up their fuel tanks for the long run to Archangel. The damage to the two ships, Kemp reported, was not enough for them to be taken out of the convoy provided the base had facilities to effect temporary repairs. This, NOIC said, would be attended to so far as possible in the time available.

'Can you delay our sailing if necessary?' Kemp asked.

NOIC shrugged. 'My scope for that is limited, Commodore. The Russians are said to be bellyaching for supplies ... but of course they won't be wanting a short delivery. There's another angle, though: we're not so far off the winter freeze-up around Archangel. It's going to come *early* this year, so the Met boys say now. An unexpected shift in the weather charts. You might get in, but you might not get out again after discharging cargo if we cut it too fine.'

'Murmansk instead?'

'Yes, we may have to ask the Russians to approve a re-routeing – you'll be kept informed while at sea, of course.' NOIC, a captain RN named Frobisher, seemed, Kemp thought, to have something else on his mind but if so was either keeping it to himself or hadn't yet got around to it. Frobisher asked abruptly, 'Gin?'

'Thank you. Just a small one.'

'That's all you'll get. It's not easy to keep Iceland properly supplied with all the essentials! You don't know how lucky you are to have a sea appointment.'

Kemp smiled politely but was thinking of the ship that had blown up. Lucky to be at sea? Perhaps the dead had thought so too, until they'd stopped thinking altogether in the instant of disintegration. But Frobisher, whilst pouring two small gins with plain water, was speaking again. . . .

'I'm sorry,' Kemp said. 'My thoughts were – somewhere else. I'm not convinced that there's much luck about the sea. Not for some.'

Forbisher looked at him keenly. 'Yes, I think I understand. That ship. Rotten – I know that. Goes against the grain, just leaving them to it. But there wouldn't have been many left – *any* left most likely.'

'I still hate my own guts.'

'Well – don't. You know perfectly well you had no choice. Here, drink this.' Frobisher put the gin glass in Kemp's hand. 'I can rake up another if you feel you need it, and you'll be more than welcome. And a word of advice if I may offer it: when you get back aboard, relax and have a bloody good skinful!'

24

'I've a damn good mind to,' Kemp said.

He did have a second gin and while he was drinking it NOIC relieved his mind of its burden.

iii

Returned aboard, Kemp went to his cabin, looking grim and upset. He poured himself a whisky : like any other ship, naval or merchant service, the *Hardraw Falls* carried a plentiful supply of spirits and tobacco and Kemp had ordered cigarettes and a bottle of whisky from the chief steward's stores. The drink, a short one, poured, there was a tap at the door and Sub-Lieutenant Cutler came in.

'Well, Cutler ?'

'Request, sir, Commodore – '

'I have one of my own, Cutler. A request.'

'Sir ?'

Kemp said, 'Aboard a ship I may be God, but I'm not the Holy Trinity nor even the holy couple, if there is such a thing. Get me ?'

'Why, no, sir, Commodore, not – '

'There you go again ! I'm sir or I'm Commodore, but not both at once. Let's settle for the unadorned sir, shall we ?'

'Why, sure, sir, Commodore . . . sir. If that's what you want.'

'I do. Like a whisky ?'

'Thank you, sir.'

Kemp poured, the broad gold band on his cuff catching a shaft of sunlight striking through the scuttle. 'You had a request. What is it ?'

'Not me personally, sir. Petty Officer Napper. To see the doctor ashore, if there is one. If not, then the doctor aboard the *Nottingham*, sir.'

'Reason ?'

'Chest pains, sir. And a few more elsewhere.' Cutler paused. 'If I may offer an opinion, sir, I reckon Napper doesn't want to go to Russia.'

'No more do I, Sub. But you may be right. Whether you are or not, he'll have to be allowed to see the doctor. Make a signal to the Flag . . . ask for a medical appointment soonest possible.

25

Better ask them to send a boat, too. They've got more spare hands and boats than the *Hardraw Falls*.'

'Very good, sir.' Cutler finished the whisky. 'Sir, the orders from NOIC – '

'I have them in mind. I'll be talking to Captain Theakston shortly, Cutler. For now, keep the orders under your hat.'

'I'll do that thing, sir, Commodore ... sorry, sir.' Cutler left the cabin. Kemp went over to the square port beside his bunk and looked out across the fore well-deck and the battened-down cargo hatches to the shore beyond. Iceland in midwinter was a cheerless, grim place, snow and mostly iron-hard skies, rock-like mountains, sea-worn ships with rust marks drooling from the hawse-pipes and the engine-room outfall and along the sides, the odd small boat pushing through leaden water, and overall the terrible, biting cold made worse when the wind blew up. Turning away from a depressing scene, Kemp poured himself another whisky. NOIC had been right: one or two over the odds often helped when it was safe and prudent to take them, as it was now. The *Hardraw Falls* was not his responsibility and Theakston was well capable of dealing with anything that might arise in that direction. In port the Commodore was a spare number for most of the time.

The Commodore might as well enjoy his respite and kill the pain of memory. Kemp seldom drank alone but by this time he had ascertained that his initial belief had been correct: Captain Theakston was a teetotaller.

The whisky went down and he felt better. He had one more, a small one and the last, and was about to put the bottle back in the cupboard over his washbasin when there was another knock and Theakston came in.

iv

Petty Officer Napper disembarked on to the bottom platform of the flagship's port accommodation ladder and ascended to the quarterdeck, which he saluted punctiliously. A starchy looking lieutenant RN strode the deck complete with looped sword-belt straps of black patent leather dangling empty of any sword in indication of his current duty as officer of the watch. He looked Napper up and down, and Napper saluted again.

'Petty Officer Napper, sir, from *Hardraw Falls* to see the qu – medical officer, sir.'

The lieutenant made no reply but lifted a hand to the corporal of the gangway, a Royal Marine. Napper was taken in hand and led by a sideboy along pipe-lined alleyways with corticened decks, over coamings in the watertight sections, the well-remembered ambience of a warship, not experienced for quite a while; until his draft to the *Hardraw Falls*, Napper had served ashore ever since his recall on mobilization in 1939, a nice soft number in Pompey barracks as petty officer i/c cleanliness in the seamen's blocks. It was a rotten shame he'd been propelled out of it at his age.

He reached the sick bay: it was a funny thing but it was like when you'd gone to the expense of buying a new washer and when you came to fit it the bloody tap had stopped dripping . . . the pains had gone from his chest. He gave a racking cough to stir them up but without success. His long, mournful face lengthened still further: the quack would go and say he was swinging the lead, malingering, but he wouldn't say that if he could only see Napper's stock of medicines aboard the *Hardraw Falls*: if you were just a lead-swinger you didn't go to that sort of expense, not on a PO's rate of pay. Stood to reason, did that. As he waited for the quack he felt a little twinge in his chest and hope returned, but not for long. In the first place he was seen by a surgeon lieutenant, which was a disappointment. As, in a sense, a guest patient from a merchant ship he'd expected the surgeon commander. No such luck, and the surgeon lieutenant was brief and preoccupied. Preoccupied with bugger all, Napper thought, naval quacks hadn't much to do normally.

Napper was told to remove his upper clothing.

'Been using camphorated oil,' the surgeon lieutenant remarked.

'Yessir.'

'Quite a stench. Good stuff though, camphorated oil.'

'Yessir. I – '

The inevitable stethoscope interrupted Napper's discourse but his time came when the quack asked what his symptoms had

27

been. There had been many and Napper detailed them at some length, interspersing them with nasty coughs.

'Yes, yes, I see. There's nothing to worry about, just a touch of fibrositis.'

'I smokes a lot, sir –'

'So do we all.' The quack's fingers, Napper had noticed, were yellow with nicotine. Napper, thinking he might as well make the most of his visit, began to go through his ailment list. He spoke of his bowels, which was a mistake brought on by nervousness and the feeling that he was on a loser as usual. Given an opening on bowels, the quack cut him short, told him to get dressed and nodded at the leading sick-berth attendant, who seemed to understand without a word being said. When Napper was once again dressed, the LSBA handed him a glass of dark liquid.

He said unnecessarily, since Napper knew it of old, 'Black Draught, PO. Number Nines in liquid form you might say.'

Mutinously, Napper drank it up: bowel mixture! In the Andrew, so long as your bowels were regular, you were fighting fit. Regularity cured even chests.

v

Captain Theakston had seen the whisky bottle: Kemp had made no attempt to hide it, seeing no reason why he should act like a maiden caught being chastely kissed.

'I know you don't drink, Captain – but you'd be welcome enough to join me, of course.'

'Thank you, no. Life-long abstinence has suited me well enough. You were in the liners, of course.' Theakston said that as though the liners were the iniquitous jaws of hell, leading inevitably to the everlasting fires. In some respects that would have been a fair assessment, Kemp knew. Too much cheap liquor, too much time on one's hands, and always the temptations provided by the passengers. Women and drink: parties always going in the cabins, in the many bars, ship's officers very welcome. Many had fallen by the wayside and Theakston would be aware of this. There was a stiffness about the master's manner, more so than usual, and Kemp hoped he wasn't in for a sermon: Theakston had a somewhat pulpitish look about him. But it appeared that that was not his current mission. He said, 'Your visit to the shore, Commodore. I was wondering, are there any orders?'

'As a matter of fact, yes, there are. I was intending to tell you, Captain.' A grin came to Kemp's face along with a sudden wicked desire to shock. 'I'm afraid the bottle intervened briefly.'

'Aye. . . .'

That expressive face of Theakston's was off-putting: one look from the Captain of the *Hardraw Falls* was the equivalent of a speech in Parliament and much more to the point. Kemp knew he should not have given way to an impulse to tease; he felt almost as though he were back again to his apprentice days, hauled up before the master for some omission – or for smuggling a flask of whisky aboard. He had to rehabilitate himself somehow, not an easy task under the stare of Theakston's formidable eyes. Best leave it. . . .

He said, 'There's a special job for us, Captain.'

'For the *Hardraw Falls*, or for the convoy?'

'The *Hardraw Falls*. NOIC – '

'Because you're aboard, because my ship carries the Commodore?'

Straight to the point, like any Yorkshireman. Theakston hadn't come down with the last shower. Kemp said, 'Yes, that is so. We're to rendezvous with a British submarine coming south, round the North Cape from Murmansk – '

'Position?'

'68°10' north, 12°40' east. Off the Lofotens.'

'Close to the Norwegian coast. Too close.'

'It has to be accepted, Captain – '

'Is there a Norwegian involvement?'

Kemp nodded. 'Yes. The submarine will have picked up a man coming out in a fishing boat from the Norwegian coast north of the rendezvous position, too close inshore to divert a ship from the convoy safely – too close navigationally and as regards the Germans. The man is obviously regarded as important, and – '

'Do you know his identity, Commodore?'

Kemp hesitated for a moment, then said quietly, 'Yes, as it happens I do. I know him personally . . . that's why we've been landed with the job. He travelled frequently to and from Australia before the war, in my company's ships – '

'Do I take it he's British, not Norwegian – a British agent?'

Kemp said crisply, 'Neither. He's German. This is strictly between the two of us, Captain – us and Cutler. I'm under the strictest orders.'

Theakston nodded, his eyes never leaving Kemp's face. 'I understand. I'll ask one thing only: this man, this German – I take it he knows you are aboard the *Hardraw Falls* and because you have sailed together he trusts you, and has asked to be brought aboard to join you.'

Kemp gave a heavy sigh and shook his head. 'Wrong, Captain. He knows nothing of my appointment. *I*'ve been chosen by Whitehall because *they* know we'd become good friends – this man's pre-war business interests in Australia are known to Intelligence, and naturally, when asked, the company's London offices co-operated in making passenger lists, pre-war ones, available.'

'Yes, I see. Then – '

'When he boards, yes, he will know me, of course. That's going to be the hard part.'

Theakston looked at him critically for a few moments, then said, 'I'm going to make a guess or two. This German, now. For some reason he's to be landed in Archangel – else, they'd have waited for the QP homeward. Again for some reason – I'll not ask *what* in either case – he's to give you his trust. It's your job to encourage that.' When there was no response from Kemp, Theakston leaned forward and put a heavy hand on the Commodore's shoulder. 'And now I think I know the reason for the whisky bottle. And I don't blame you.'

vi

The facts were simple enough once a straight line was drawn through the intrigue and skulduggery that were part and parcel of the Intelligence services on both sides. Simple but dirty: again, part of Intelligence. NOIC hadn't liked it any more than Kemp, but the excuse was, of course, that the man was an enemy agent and nothing else could be allowed to count. Truth, decency, honesty were out for the duration. Kemp felt it was going to be like the massacre of Glencoe all over again, the hospitable MacDonalds as it were to fall again to the Campbell treachery. He remembered Gunther von Hagen very well indeed, had always been pleased to see his name in the passenger list, had always, once he'd gained command as master, had the German seated at his table in the saloon. Many an afterdinner drink they'd taken together in his quarters. Von Hagen was a chess player, so was Kemp, and they had been of about equal standard. Von Hagen had worked for a firm of London wool importers, and had much business at the Australian end. It seemed that shortly before the outbreak of war von Hagen had returned to his country and had been co-opted into German Military Intelligence, in which he was now a colonel. His sphere of operations, NOIC had told Kemp, had been Norway – digging out the Resistance groups, a dirty game certainly, but he had never so far as was known operated against the British themselves. Kemp had been able to confirm that von Hagen, at any rate before the war, had been very much an Anglophile and had felt at home in England.

Kemp also knew that the German's *bête noir* had been the Russians. Communism he had detested; he and Kemp had had many discussions as to the way the world had been going. Kemp had never concealed his own hatred of the Nazis and their regime, but von Hagen had been non-committal; he was, Kemp believed, a Nazi but a lukewarm one, one who merely accepted rather than fully supported, except as regards his loathing of communists. But all that was unimportant now. Von Hagen had done his duty, NOIC had said, quoting British Intelligence, and had done well – or bloodily – in Norway. That was, until he'd slipped up and had been taken prisoner by the Resistance, who were now handing him over to the British.

Or so he believed. In fact he was to be taken on to Russia once the transfer from the submarine had been made. In Archangel he was to be handed over to the security police: the men in the Kremlin had a use for his knowledge of Norway and the German defences there. Kemp's job was the simple part: he was under orders to talk to an old friend and find out all he could about German Intelligence, on a basis of the old pals' act, before von Hagen was handed over to whatever awaited him after his interrogation by the Russians: probably Siberia, possibly death. His lever was to be a promise that von Hagen would not in fact be handed over to the Russians. A promise that was not to be kept.

No job for a convoy Commodore; but the orders had been very strict and were to be carried out to the letter. No jiggery-pokery on Kemp's part, no back-tracking for an old friend. Whitehall had no wish to upset the Kremlin.

FOUR

So now Iceland lay behind as the PQ convoy headed on its course for the rendezvous behind the busily sweeping A/s screen. The commanding officers of the escorting warships had been put in the picture only to the extent of being informed at the departure conference of the British submarine's presence ahead of the convoy, and this had added a new dimension of danger: the submarine would proceed on the surface whenever possible but might have to submerge at any time; no Asdic contacts in the relevant area were to be attacked until the identity had been positively established, which in effect meant that no contacts at all could be attacked whilst submerged. The submarine's human cargo was not to be put at risk.

The senior officer of the escort, Rear-Admiral Fellowes, had been informed in Hvalfiord of the full facts, the only one apart from Kemp who had, and he had been livid. 'It's damn lunacy! Putting the whole convoy at risk for a blasted Nazi! Who the hell dreamed this one up, can you tell me that?'

NOIC had shrugged. 'It comes from high up, I believe, sir. But enough said – I can't exceed my brief or my guts'll go for garters.'

'I'd like someone's guts laid bare,' Fellowes said in a voice like ice. 'I'll tell you one thing – I'll be putting my representations to Their Lordships in very plain language once this is over. Too late, I know – but good for the blood pressure just to have it to look forward to!'

ii

Kemp, who normally liked to take a ship's company into his confidence when it was safe to do so, letting them know the risks

33

and chances, knew that this time it would not be safe even if the orders for silence had not been so rigid. At any moment the convoy could come under attack, the Commodore's ship could be sunk, conceivably some men could be picked up by a U-boat or a German destroyer – unlikely perhaps but the possibility couldn't be disregarded – and they might be made to talk. The presence off Norway of the submarine must not become known. So nothing at all was said; even so, by some curious alchemy of ship life, it was known even before the *Hardraw Falls* had cleared away from Hvalfiord that something was in the wind and that this was no ordinary Russian convoy.

As so often happened aboard ship, the source had been the Captain's steward, a plump man named Torrence who reckoned he could tell from Theakston's mood what the future held. Not just Theakston – any captain, and that included Commodore Kemp, upon whom also he was attending. Little bits of preoccupation, a show of irritation over trifles, the gesture of a hand and the expression of a face, they all told their story to Torrence, who was a great putter together of two and two.

'Something up,' he remarked to the chief steward in the latter's office.

Buckle cocked an eye at him. 'Oh, yes, and what, may I ask?'

'Don't know that, not yet. But Kemp . . . he came back from the shore looking pretty sick. Had some nasty news I reckon, Chief.' Torrence wiped the back of a hand across his nose. 'Went on the bottle an' all.'

'Measured, did you?'

'I always keeps a check.'

Buckle nodded; it was a steward's duty to see that an officer's stock was kept up, not an onerous duty in the case of Captain Theakston, but Buckle also knew that Torrence was not above helping himself to the odd tot, a steward's perks in Torrence's view. He asked sardonically, 'How much, eh?'

'Not a lot, but enough, seeing as it was morning.'

'Doesn't signify. . . .'

'Not on its own, no, maybe not. But when the Old Man come out of Kemp's cabin . . . well, *he* looked sick an' all and got stuck into me just because there was a speck of dust on his desk. Relieving his feelings, like.'

'So what's your deduction, eh?'

Torrence blew out his cheeks and looked like a pale pink balloon. 'Dunno. Early to say. But if I might hazard a guess, like . . . I reckon Kemp was given word of the bloody Jerries being out in strength.'

Buckle rubbed reflectively at his jaw and looked at Torrence through narrowed eyes. Torrence often had the buzz dead to rights and that was a fact not to be disregarded. A kind of clairvoyance, or more likely a big ear to the keyhole. Thoughts of the cargo beneath the hatches went through Buckle's mind: they were all sitting on sudden death. You didn't usually think much about it, you got used to it, and if you did think too much you'd go round the bend sharpish. You always hoped for the best, confident that it wasn't you that was going to get it. All the same, it was human nature to be curious, which was why the buzz-mongers always had an avid audience. This time, Torrence's buzz wasn't all that much.

Buckle said, 'That wouldn't be news, would it?' He pursed his lips as a sudden thought struck. 'Think it's anything to do with that Yank?'

'Cutler? Maybe it is but I dunno yet.'

Torrence went about his business, which currently was seeing to Theakston's and Kemp's laundry, also Cutler's: Torrence, accustomed to wait upon the master only, was now a busy man, as busy as the steward who attended on the other deck officers single-handed. Buckle sat on at his desk, staring at a calendar depicting a frozen-looking semi-nude girl against a backdrop of December snow with compliments of one of the ship's suppliers. Buckle stared without seeing. That American. Canadian uniform, odd in itself. He knew Cutler wasn't a Canadian: the Texas accent was unmistakable. For a period of his life Buckle had served in a tanker that made frequent use of the port of Galveston on the Gulf of Mexico and he'd known many Texans. So why an American – an American on the Commodore's staff of all things?

It could tie up.

Some US angle, but what?

Buckle felt a prickle of fear run up and down his spine: there was the tang of special operations, and such could mean extra danger. Special operations, and the destination Russia. Buckle, a

35

divorced man who had not remarried, thought of his mother, a widow living alone in Bermondsey. If anything happened to him, it would be curtains for the old lady. He was her life, and now he was moving towards some US conspiracy with the Russians, and the States not yet even in the war themselves.

Not yet.

The day was 7 December; and next morning's BBC News brought the word to the *Hardraw Falls* and the world at large that the Japanese had shattered the United States Pacific Fleet at Pearl Harbor.

iii

'Bastards!' Tex Cutler spoke through clenched teeth, his face white with shock. Two waves of aircraft, a total of forty torpedo-bombers, a hundred high-level bombers, a hundred and thirty dive-bombers, escorted by around eighty fighter aircraft. *Arizona, Oklahoma, West Virginia, California* – all gone. The *Tennessee* and the *Nevada* had been put out of commission. That was the big stuff and it wasn't the full tally. There were tears in Cutler's eyes.

Kemp put a hand on his shoulder. 'I'm desperately sorry, Cutler.'

'All those ships. Jesus, I lived for the Navy! If we'd gone into the war sooner, I'd have joined.'

'And I'd have lost a good officer. I'm glad I didn't, Cutler, very glad.'

'So I'm glad you're glad.' Cutler spoke with an intense fierceness, staring unseeingly across the cold grey of the sea.

Kemp said, 'Go below to my cabin, Cutler. You'll find whisky in the cupboard. Help yourself.'

Cutler seemed to take a grip. He said, 'Thanks, sir. I guess I feel like getting stewed.'

'Don't overdo it.'

Cutler went below. In the Commodore's cabin he found Torrence, who was polishing around. Torrence said, 'Good morning, sir.'

'The Commodore's Scotch, and fast.'

'Coming right up, sir.' Torrence went to the cupboard and brought out the bottle. 'Bad news on the wireless, sir.'

'Right.'

Torrence shoved his polishing cloth into his trouser pocket, from which it dangled like a yellow pennant. 'Reckon the US'll have to come in now, sir.' There was something of a gloat in his voice.

Cutler stared at him, a reddish fleck in his eyes. 'Fuck off,' he said tightly. 'Just for Christ's sake fuck off out of it.'

iv

Two days later, by which time the convoy was not so far off the rendezvous position and steaming unattacked through bitter but calm seas, the BBC brought more news: Germany and Italy had declared war on the United States. The feeling throughout the *Hardraw Falls* was one of relief tinged with guilt: America had proved a good friend short of actual war and it was not up to British seamen to wish the agony of war upon her, but the fact that America and Britain would henceforward stand together was immensely heartening.

According to Petty Officer Napper, Adolf Hitler would now be wetting his pants in large quantities. 'Have the bugger on the run soon,' he said with satisfaction to Leading Signalman Corrigan.

'Well, let's hope so, PO. He's far from finished yet.'

'Ho! Know so, do you?'

'No.'

'Then don't shoot your mouth orf, son. Think of all those Yankee troops that'll be coming over any minute!'

'Poor sods. Why should they pull our chestnuts out of the fire?'

Napper glared. 'That's a fine thing to say! We're all white, aren't we?'

'So's Hitler – Aryan white. So's Musso, so's Stalin . . . what's colour got to do with it, PO?'

Napper knew Corrigan was a superior bugger. Angrily he said, 'Don't be bloody cheeky, all right? I just don't like blacks, that's all.' He turned and walked aft along the well-deck, past the after hatches towards the superstructure above the engine-room and the engineers' accommodation, realizing he'd said something daft that would make Corrigan even more superior in his attitude. There was something about Corrigan that made Napper say daft things; he'd tried to be matey since Corrigan was not only something of a medic but also a leading hand and those in authority had to stick together. But maybe that had been a mistake: Corrigan's lofty tones were reacting on his state of health and the chest pains had returned to plague him, together with a vague unrest in his stomach, a churning feel. He wished he could diagnose it, but wishing was vain, and in fact Corrigan hadn't been much help. Napper thought of the seaman's bible, the Admiralty Seamanship Manual: by rights there ought to be an issue to all hands of an Admiralty Medical Manual, then they'd all know what was up with them and be able to keep a check on the quack.

Petty Officer Napper had his own checks to make, on the ship's armament. He'd done his stuff on the bridge and monkey's island before encountering Corrigan; now he climbed the ladder to go through the drill on the close-range weapons mounted on the after superstructure, first chivvying the AB sitting in the straps and dreaming of home. Or looking as if he was. And half-frozen with it.

'Come on then, lad.'

Able-Seaman Grove looked round. 'Come on where, PO?'

'Bloody look lively!' Napper snapped.

'How?' Grove looked blank.

'Don't give me any lip, lad. I said, look lively, look as if you *belonged*.'

Napper, in Grove's view, was a right old tit, a dug-out from very deep down who even now hadn't yet quite surfaced. What Napper knew about modern weapons could be written on a half-farthing. And what the sod did 'look lively' mean when you were all ready at your gun and all that was missing was the enemy? Grove had a sudden impulse: he gripped the gun, swung it in a circle and made loud phut-phut noises at imaginary Nazi aircraft swooping in from all directions.

Napper stared, his long grey face reddening. 'What's all that in aid of? Going round the bend, are you? Or being bloody cheeky?'

'No, PO. Looking lively, that's all. Dealing with the Luftwaffe –'

'That's enough o' that, sonny boy. Moment you come orf

watch, you'll be on the bridge, one-one-two, up before Mr Cutler, all right?'

'You putting me in the rattle, PO?'

'Got it in one. Charged with insolence to your superior officer.' Napper turned away, seething and feeling more unwell than ever, his check on the rest of the after close-range weapons left undone. As his cap disappeared down the ladder Grove made a rude gesture towards where he had been standing. The PO was totally impossible: nag, nag, nag. Maybe he was missing his sex life, but so were they all ... and in point of fact, Grove reckoned, Napper didn't get any anyway. He didn't look the sort: to Napper, the word 'fanny' would mean nothing more than a mess kettle.

v

Still ahead of the PQ convoy, the pick-up submarine had remained submerged as close in to the Norwegian coast as was navigationally possible. Now, under cover of the darkness, she had come to the surface. With his navigator and a signalman the lieutenant in command scanned the surrounding water through his binoculars. He was a shade early on his ETA as notified to the local Resistance command by a coded broadcast from London. No need for anxiety yet; but the tension was there already. Fortunately there was no moon: the sky was nicely overcast, the night pitch dark. But that wasn't a hundred per cent protection. The Nazis could be waiting: the Resistance had reported that there were no surface radar stations in this part of the coast so there were no worries on that score. But there could be other things: there could have been a leak. Even in the Resistance there were Quislings, and the man to be picked up wouldn't have been operating entirely on his own.

The minutes passed, agonizingly slow. The terrible cold encroached, penetrating duffel coats and oilskins, scarves, mittens and balaclavas. It was cold enough almost to freeze thought. The hills, the rocks of the coast, were aloom with snow and ice, making men aware of them even through the thick dark: high, impregnable, threatening.

They all knew they could have entered a trap.

The lieutenant turned as the scrape of feet was heard on the ladder leading up to the conning-tower. A voice said, 'Kye up, sir.'

'Keep your bloody voice down!' The Lieutenant spoke in a hiss.

'Sorry, sir.' A seaman emerged from the hatch, miraculously carrying a tin tray with three mugs of thick, sweet cocoa which he handed round. 'Not a drop spilt, sir.'

'Congratulations!'

'Watch out for cockroaches, sir.'

'If I find just one, you'll need to watch out for yourself.'

The man grinned and vanished back down the ladder to the boat's interior. The watch, the seemingly interminable wait, went on. The lieutenant looked continually at the luminous dial of his wrist-watch: he had a deadline after which he was under orders to extricate his submarine to sea. But there had been something underlying those orders: a hint that failure to bring off the German agent would make the submarine's co an unpopular officer in high Whitehall circles. A whiff of cigar smoke, perhaps ... Mr Churchill was said to be often irrational and impetuous and blame didn't always end up in the right quarter. A lieutenant in command of a submarine was in no position to control the actions and movements of the Norwegian Resistance or to ensure the security of their communications. But to tell Mr Churchill that would be to risk personal disaster. The lieutenant, as the minutes ticked past towards the deadline, was on tenterhooks. A nasty decision was coming up. Did he obey orders and scarper out to sea? Or did he heed that hint, and hang on in defiance of the orders? Typical Admiralty, he thought. Whatever you did, they could have you by the short hairs. If blood, the lieutenant thought, was the price of Admiralty, then ambiguity was its watchword.

When it happened the suddenness caught them all on the hop and the lieutenant literally felt the pause in his heartbeat: a voice came from the darkness on the port quarter of the submarine.

'Captain, we are here.'

The lieutenant turned quickly. He could see nothing. No one had seen anything. There had been no sound, just nothing, no sound of oars or paddles, no swish of water. A moment later, as the lieutenant climbed down to the after casing, a hand appeared and made a grab for the triatic stay. A body heaved itself up, followed by another and then another. The lieutenant saw a black inflatable dinghy being held alongside.

'Thank God you got here,' he said, finding nothing else to say.

'Yes. God is good and is on our side – with a little help from us! A case of Schnapps carelessly left . . . there is drunkenness in a certain German mess tonight, and tomorrow more than heads will be sore. But now you are in a hurry –'

'You can say that again!'

'Therefore I will stop.' The Norwegian was a big man, built like a bear and almost as hair-covered as to his face. He turned to the man who had come aboard behind him, a man with a revolver held against his spine by the other Norwegian behind again. 'Here is your cargo, Captain.'

The lieutenenat saw the outline of a tall man, slim and upright. He was aware of a heel click and a stiff bow. He asked, 'Colonel von Hagen?'

'At your service, Captain.' The English was faultless, no trace of an accent. Presumably his command of Norwegian was as good. A hand was extended and the German said, 'How d'you do.' As he spoke, the bear-like Resistance man smashed down hard on his wrist.

'There was no need for that,' the lieutenant said.

'Captain, that hand is not for shaking by us or you. It has killed . . . innocent people, patriots. Remember that. Now we shall go. And God go with all of us.' He and his companion dropped back into the dinghy and moved away as soundlessly as they had come. The lieutenant nodded at an armed seaman who had followed him down from the conning-tower and the German was led for'ard towards a hatch in the casing, a hatch that was clipped down behind him as he descended. The moment this had been done the submarine moved out, her motors going dead slow.

'Cutler?'

'Sir?'

'How far to the rendezvous?'

Cutler had just taken a look at the chart and had the answer ready. 'Seventy miles, sir.'

'Five hours' steaming,' Kemp said. 'Let's hope that submarine's on time. I don't want to have to hang about. Nor will the Rear-Admiral.'

'Out of our control, sir.'

'I know.' Kemp turned and paced the bridge wing, backwards and forwards, feeling caged – or feeling that he might become caged in a sense if he had to lie without way on the ship, or had to steam around in circles, waiting for the submarine to show. The German U-boats loved such a situation, and if a contact was found by the A/S screen there would be nothing they could do about it immediately in case it was the pick-up. In any case, if the wait was a long one, Kemp was going to endure it almost on his own. That had been thrashed out back in Hvalfiord: Kemp would not risk the main convoy. If the submarine was thirty minutes late he would fall out in company with one destroyer while the convoy steamed on, leaving him to catch up later. If the distance was great, then the chief engineer of the *Hardraw Falls* was going to have to give him everything he'd got in the way of power. The nearer they approached the North Cape, the greater would become the danger of attack. It would not be possible to reduce the convoy's speed, and never mind that it would be the Commodore who was arse-end Charlie. But all this was speculation, the crossing of bridges in advance that was a vital part of a commodore's job so that one was not caught with one's pants down. With any luck that submarine would be dead on time and dead in position. If she was not . . . like the submarine CO, Kemp had been aware of the pressures, the unspoken urgings of Whitehall, and he, too, would face dilemma: did he give it so long, and then chase up the convoy? Or did he risk the men aboard the *Hardraw Falls*, and wait? Again there was the similarity: any convoy commodore who frustrated the will of the Prime Minister would soon find himself on the beach.

As he paced, Kemp became aware of Petty Officer Napper

approaching Cutler together with a rating from the guns' crews. The rating had a mutinous look: Kemp kept his distance when he heard Napper say, 'Defaulter, sir. Will you see him, sir, please?'

Some niggling trouble. Napper was a real old woman. But of course discipline had to be maintained. Once again, Kemp wondered how Cutler would handle it.

Cutler said, 'Oh, Jesus. Yes, all right, Napper.'

'Thank you, sir.' There was a pause then Napper's nagging voice. 'Off cap! Able Seaman Grove, sir, official number P/JX 004399 ... was insolent towards his superior officer, to wit, myself, sir, in that he – '

'You representing your own case yourself, Napper?'

'The ship, being a merchant ship, sir, has no regulating staff as such. Just me, as you – '

'All right, all right. Well? What are the grounds?'

Napper said, 'Made daft noises, sir. Phut-phut-phut, like. Shooting at imaginary aircraft, sir. After I'd give 'im an order.'

'What order?'

'To look lively, sir. 'Is response was like I said. Phut-phut-phut.'

'Aha.' Cutler kept a straight face. 'How many phuts?'

'How many –?' Napper's face was scandalized: he was having the mickey taken. He said stiffly, 'Didn't count, sir.'

'*Didn't count?* Well, never mind, perhaps it's not all that important.' Cutler turned to Grove. 'What have you to say, Grove?'

'Nothing, sir.'

'Nothing? Then you admit the charge?'

'Yessir. Or rather no, sir. I was obeying orders.'

'To look lively?'

'That's right, sir. On'y way I saw of doing it.'

'Yes, I see. Don't do it again, Grove, or you'll be in trouble. No one's going to put up with insolent behaviour. So watch it, all right?'

'Yessir, thank you, sir.'

'Don't thank me, you've had a ticking off. Case dismissed.'

Napper looked as though he couldn't believe his ears. His eyes almost popped from his face and his mouth opened. But he met Cutler's cool stare and shut it again. He shouted, 'On cap!

Salute the officer! 'Bout turn – double march! Down the bleedin' ladder.'

Grinning, Cutler moved to the extremity of the bridge wing and joined Kemp. 'Did I do right, sir?'

'Yes, very right. I'd have done the same myself.'

'Napper's not pleased, sir. He wanted Commodore's Report.'

'Yes. Petty Officer Napper ... a word of advice, young Cutler: use his rate when speaking to him in front of junior ratings. It's only his due.'

Cutler said, 'Okay, sir.' Then, looking past the Commodore towards the van of the convoy, he stiffened. 'Flag's calling up, sir.'

Kemp turned. The signalman on watch was reading off the flashing light. He began calling out as he read. 'Commodore from Flag, sir: "RDF contact two surface vessels bearing red four five. Am investigating."'

Kemp saw the flagship heel over to port and increase speed even as the signal was coming through. 'RDF's a handy thing to have,' he said. 'One day, perhaps the merchant ships'll be fitted with it.'

Cutler asked, 'Think the enemy's out, sir?'

'I've no idea but I'll take no chances.' Kemp turned to the signalman, 'Pass the bearing to all ships by flag hoist.' He took up his binoculars. *Nottingham* was coming up now to her maximum speed of thirty-two knots and was being followed by the second cruiser now threading through the convoy columns on a dash across from her steaming position on the starboard beam. Ten minutes later the flagship signalled again across the widening gap of water: 'Two enemy destroyers in sight.'

Almost on the heels of the signal the *Nottingham* and the *Neath* had engaged. The sound of the big guns rolled back on the wind and Kemp saw the distant orange flashes and the smoke as the eight-inch batteries opened.

FIVE

The voice-pipe from the engine-room whistled in the wheel-house and Captain Theakston answered. 'Bridge, Captain speaking.'

'Chief here, Captain. What's up?'

'Enemy destroyers ahead. Two of them.'

'What are we going to do?'

'The convoy's opening formation. Stand by for engine altera-tions. And maybe bumps.' Theakston banged down the voice-pipe cover and concentrated on handling his ship. He'd seen bumps, and more than bumps, when a convoy was changing its formation – or barging freely about the ocean would often have been a more apt description. Kemp had a similar anxiety. Ships of different sizes and shapes and speeds, each with its own handling characteristics in the way it answered its helm – it was a far cry from warships of a single class responding to fleet ma-noeuvres on the executive from the Flag, carrying out red turns, white turns, blue turns, the colour being the indication of the particular manoeuvre to be carried out . . . currently it would be a case of each ship for itself and never mind the rule of the road. Kemp, who had had no option but to spread the ships out so far as possible – short of an actual scatter order, which might be given under much heavier attack – so as to disperse the target, felt like shutting his eyes and asking Cutler to tell him when something hit. The *Hardraw Falls* was maintaining her own course and speed, acting as some kind of lode star while the others altered around her, but Theakston was having to watch it pretty carefully. When a ship came slap across his bows, Theak-ston caused a flurry in the engine-room: the telegraph rang

45

down for emergency full astern and Mr Sparrow, chief engineer, gritted his teeth hard. Engines never liked going from full ahead to full astern without a pause in between, but the bridge had spoken and that was that. The engine-room shook and shuddered and the plating of the starting platform, where Sparrow was standing, vibrated beneath his feet. He used his imagination as to what was going on up top: some silly bugger getting in their way and any moment they might be in collision. Then the engines were eased and put ahead again.

Sparrow let out a long breath of relief. It was cold outside and he didn't want to know, didn't want the cold to come through broken plates into his engine-room, nor seawater either. Sparrow didn't like the sea, not after thirty-odd years of it. He'd spent much of those thirty years wishing he hadn't gone to sea at all. It was an unsettling life, here today and gone tomorrow, and not overpaid although there were the perks of duty-free fags and whisky plus free living and a steward to wait on you. It had been all right when he was a younger man, in fact it had been fine, but not after he'd got married. By that time it was hard to find a job ashore; he'd become too set in the ways of a ship's engineer and then he'd come up for chief and had settled for it. He would never have got an equivalent status anywhere other than aboard a ship.

He was joined on the starting platform by his second engineer, Bob Weller, who gave him what Sparrow considered a careful look as he did each time they came into contact. Sparrow knew why: Weller was next in seniority for chief of one of the Bricker Dockett Line's ships and Sparrow was getting long in the tooth, although he still had two years to go to retirement – unless the war went on that long and kept him at it. Bob Weller was impatient for promotion, and a man of Sparrow's age might well kick the bucket at any time, so Weller was always on the lookout for signs of illness, like a stroke or a heart malfunction. Mr Sparrow knew this perfectly well and occasionally played up. He did this time.

'Sudden flaps,' he said, sounding breathless. 'Don't like 'em.'

'Don't blame you, Chief.'

'Flutters the heart.' They were having to shout over the engine sounds, and Sparrow, for the sake of ageing bones, was hanging on tight as the *Hardraw Falls* rolled heavily to an alteration of course. The starting platform was a slippery place. Sparrow sometimes wondered if Weller sprayed oil on to the plates when he knew his chief would be down.

'You should take it easier, Chief.'

'Maybe I should.' Sparrow put a hand on his chest and managed to make his cheeks look hollow. He didn't miss the sudden look of hope in Weller's eye. There was no surer way to promotion than to have the chief engineer die at sea: the second stepped automatically into his shoes, at any rate for the rest of the voyage, and then with Weller's seniority it would be equally automatically confirmed on arrival back in UK. But Sparrow felt as fit as a fiddle and Weller was going to have a long wait yet.

ii

'*Nottingham* and *Neath* returning, sir!'

'Thank you, Corrigan.' Kemp, his binoculars levelled towards the port bow where the firing had been heard, had already seen the cruisers reappearing over the horizon. Once again a light was flashing from the Flag. Corrigan reported: 'Commodore from Flag, sir. "Interception successful. Both destroyers sunk. Have sustained superficial damage only." Message ends, sir.'

That was all: no indication of casualties, no indication of whether or not anyone had survived those terrible sea temperatures. Kemp said, 'Make to all ships, resume formation, course and speed.'

'Aye, aye, sir.'

Kemp looked at the clock on the wheelhouse bulkhead: an hour had passed, four more to go to the rendezvous. And the wind was increasing now, coming up to around Force Five on the Beaufort Scale, and it was filled with the threat of snow, bitterly cold and bringing the sea up in white horses that blew icily from the wave crests. Not bad enough to inhibit the operation of the U-boats, however; and Kemp was surprised that no attack had developed. Of course there was plenty of time yet: the U-boats and surface vessels and aircraft could be waiting for the convoy to make its landfall off the North Cape, and come round it into the Barents Sea. Why cover the whole ruddy ocean, Kemp thought, when you knew the convoys had to close towards the

North Cape whatever happened, whatever their courses up from Scotland or Iceland?

With the ship now secured from action stations, Cutler came back from the after gun positions: the routine had to be gone through, the close-range weapons manned however useless they might be in some situations.

'All correct, Cutler?'

'All correct, sir, Commodore.'

Kemp clicked his tongue. 'You don't give up easily, Cutler.'

The American grinned tightly, more of a baring of teeth. 'My apologies, sir. Guess I'm thick at times. Or just a Yank.'

Kemp gave him a sharp look. 'You sound bitter.'

'Maybe I am. That Napper, he doesn't like Yanks.'

'He said so?'

'Sure he said so. Loud and clear – but not meant to be heard. Correction – meant to be heard but not meant to be addressed directly. If you get me, sir.'

Kemp grunted. 'Don't take it to heart, and don't hear – if *you* get *me*.'

'I get you all right, sir, and I agree. But I keep thinking of Pearl Harbor.'

'Of course you do. I think we all do, probably even Napper. But try to remember that the British Navy's been fighting the Atlantic war a long time now – '

'Not Napper. Not sitting on his ass in Portsmouth barracks till now. I'd like to have been there, to kick that ass of his all around the parade ground till he got prised loose – '

'All right, Cutler, I appreciate your feelings, but for God's sake and the convoy's don't let them show any more. You've let off steam. Let's leave it at that.'

'That an order?'

Kemp nodded briskly. 'It's an order, Cutler. I'm not having friction of that sort.'

'Yes, *sir*,' Cutler said, and tore off his weird salute, his face set. Then he turned about and went into the chartroom behind the wheelhouse. One of a commodore's assistant's jobs was to keep the chart corrections up to date on the Commodore's folio, and a whole batch of Notices to Mariners, incorporating the latest corrections, had come aboard in Hvalfiord. They would take time to enter in red ink on the relevant charts. But Kemp knew that

Cutler's main preoccupation currently was to keep out of range until he'd simmered down.

By now the snow had started, thin so far, but the sky spoke of a really heavy fall to come. That sky was bleak, dark and heavy and foreboding as the day stretched into the afternoon. No sun at all, just that grey overcast and the spray being blown back over the bridge and wheelhouse and monkey's island, over the decks and the watchkeepers, over the reduced guns' crews of the watch, soaking into duffel coats and down the collars of oilskins to bring discomfort and piercing cold. Spindrift came, blown along the wind to search out every nook and cranny, and now the snow was blown with it, all the way, as it seemed, from the North Polar regions. The visibility was already coming down with the snow. Captain Theakston stood huddled in the port wing of the bridge, along with his chief officer, Amory. No use taking the easy way and keeping in the comparative warmth of the wheelhouse and trying to peer through the Kent clear-view screens as they whirled electrically at a speed that anyway in theory kept them clear of rain and snow. That was in Theakston's view the pansy way, the way that led to accidents in convoy. And because the master was on the bridge, Amory was also out in the open. The Old Man expected that and would have said so had Amory not come out into the biting cold. . . .

'You look frozen, Mr Amory.'

'I am frozen, sir.'

Theakston was sardonic. 'A little bit of snow! Come now. We don't complain about it in the North Riding, you know. Shepherds . . . do you think they aren't out in it continually, seeing to the sheep? Lambs get born in this sort of weather, in the dales.' Theakston flapped his arms about his body and his breath went like steam into the wind. 'You're a good chief officer, Mr Amory, but you'd make a poor shepherd, very poor.'

Amory laughed. 'I'm not much bothered about my qualities as a shepherd.' He looked around the convoy, at the warships of the escort, lean and hard but with their outlines blurred by the different shades of grey-blue of the camouflage paint, cutting through the waves with bones in their teeth and the water flinging back. The little ships of the A/S screen were having, as ever, the worst of it. Amory knew that those small ships were manned mainly by hostilities-only ratings and officered largely by the RNVR, what used to be called the Saturday-afternoon sailors until they'd proved themselves through two long, hard years of war at sea, never out of uniform, often enough watch on, stop on when the weather was bad or the enemy was out. And they and their mates in the cruisers and destroyers were the shepherds now, tending the convoys along the world's trade routes, keeping Britain fed, ensuring she and her allies were armed and supplied with troops. ... Theakston was going on about his favourite subject: Yorkshire and its dales and fells and great stretches of moorland. The road that wound through Wensleydale from Leyburn to Hawes, through the little villages, Wensley, West Witton, Aysgarth, Bainbridge, and off the main road the tiny, isolated communities of Thoralby, Thornton Rust, Stalling Busk, Countersett ... Amory had never seen any of them but he knew them intimately by now. There, Theakston said, was where the snow bit hard. You could be cut off for weeks, no movement except on horseback. And the winds blew strong too. Amory wondered why Theakston hadn't become a farmer instead of a seaman. There was, in fact, a lot of similarity between the two callings. Each was deeply committed to facing the weather in all its moods, facing it and beating it. And now, in wartime, even that shepherd simile was apt.

Theakston fell silent. Not a man of many words normally, he had talked in spasms, with long gaps. Amory, who knew about Theakston's wife, guessed he had been talking to stop himself thinking. There were times when Amory was glad enough not to have married: the fact that Felicity was dead meant that now he had nothing in the world to worry about. Had she lived, had she married him as had been intended, she would have been his constant worry as well as a brief delight every now and again when he had leave from the sea. He would never have stopped worrying about her; in a sense, like children, wives were hostages to fortune. They could fall ill like the Old Man's wife. Amory was saved all that, now. Or anyway he kidded himself he was: he couldn't forget the bad nights, thinking of what might have been, tossing and turning, flicking on the light over his bunk and smoking one cigarette after another. Or the hours on watch in fair weather and safe water, pacing the bridge with nothing to do but keep an eye on the course and the occasional avoidance of another ship coming up on his starboard bow. That was when a man's thoughts, like the snow in Wensleydale, bit hard. So he could understand Theakston.

'I'll take a look at the chart, Mr Amory.' Captain Theakston came away from the bridge rail and walked into the wheelhouse and then the chartroom. When he came back after a minute he said, 'We're closing the rendezvous position.' He had told Amory, as he was bound to, of the rendezvous but had not gone into any details. 'Half an hour I'd say. Call the Commodore, Mr Amory.'

'Aye, aye, sir.' Amory went to the voice-pipe to Kemp's cabin and blew down it, activating the whistle. Kemp was on the bridge within the minute. After a word with the master he scanned the seas ahead through his binoculars. The light was fading fast now, it would soon be full dark, and the sky was heavily overcast though as yet the snow was still falling only thinly.

'Plenty more up there,' Theakston said.

Kemp nodded. 'Let's hope it holds off for a while.'

'Aye. . . .'

There was no sign of a submarine and no reports had come back from the escort. Fifteen minutes later a blue-shaded lamp started flashing from the Flag: not a contact report, but the expected order to reduce the speed of the convoy. Theakston passed the order down to the engine-room on a nod from Kemp, and the speed of advance came down to seven knots as the ships butted into the sea and the wind and the whirling snowflakes. That snow was already building up on the decks, thin as it was, and the *Hardraw Falls* was mantled in ghostly white, like a shroud, Kemp thought. Sub-Lieutenant Cutler came to the bridge, carrying his own white covering: he had been checking around the guns once again and he looked like an animated snowman.

Kemp caught his eye. 'Almost there, Cutler.' He turned to Theakston. 'What d'you make it now, Captain?'

'Within a mile or two. Mr Amory, have the hands ready with

the jacob's ladder now. Mr Paget to be in charge, with the bosun.' He added, 'Port side amidships.'

Amory passed the word. Below the bridge, shadowy figures moved and there was a clatter as the rolled-up jacob's ladder, rope and wire and wooden treads, was hoisted to the rail ready to be sent down the ship's side along with heavy fenders.

Cutler asked, 'Any contact yet, sir?'

'Not a bloody murmur,' Kemp answered, sounding on edge. He drummed his fingers, half frozen already despite thick gloves, on the teak of the bridge rail. By now they were as near as dammit in position; *Portree* should have picked up the submarine on the Asdics quite a while ago. But there was just nothing. Kemp could not take the *Hardraw Falls* too far beyond the rendezvous. He would in fact very much have liked to do so: if he failed to take off the German agent he would be relieved of a very dirty job.

Now was the time for decision: Theakston reported the ship had reached the rendezvous. Kemp said, 'Very well. No contact. Signalman?'

'Sir?'

'Call up the Flag. Make, "In the absence of contact propose breaking off now in accordance with earlier planning. Request destroyer be detached."'

The signal was flashed across on the blue-shaded Aldis and quickly the reply came back: 'Commodore from Flag, concur. *Portree* will stand by you.'

'Acknowledge,' Kemp said. 'Stop engines, if you please, Captain.'

'I don't like it,' Theakston said.

'No more do I.'

'I have my ship to consider.'

'Yes, I know. I have the convoy to consider. And my orders. The engines will be rung to stop, Captain.'

Theakston shrugged; he had made his protest. He knew the Commodore was under strain; and orders had to be obeyed. He passed the word to Amory and the telegraphs were pulled over. Soon after the engine sounds had ceased and the telegraphs had reported back that the engines were stopped, Theakston ordered the sound signal to indicate that the way was off his ship: the siren gave four short blasts and the ships astern altered to port and starboard to pass along the sides of the *Hardraw Falls*. In the rear of the convoy HMS *Portree* moved up to take station ahead of the Commodore and act as guardship. The other ships moved on, bulky shapes in the darkness – and what had suddenly become a full-scale snowstorm. They were soon lost to sight from the *Hardraw Falls*. And still no contact from beneath the sea.

iv

Below in the engine-room Weller used words similar to Theak-ston's. 'I don't like it, Chief. Circling like a bloody catherine wheel only not so fast. Too bloody slow in fact.'

'Go fast and you get dizzy.'

'You know what I mean,' Weller said irritably.

'Yes, I know all right. Sitting duck. I'd like to know what's going on. Those buzzes earlier ... something's in the wind, that's for sure.' Sparrow's voice had sounded too loud to be true when the engines had so suddenly been brought to stop and then to slow ahead. 'Maybe this won't last long.'

'Why not ask the bridge, Chief?'

Sparrow laughed. 'You know Theakston. Still, I'll give it a try.' He reached for the voice-pipe, blew down it and put the flexible tube to his ear when the bridge answered.

'Bridge. Captain. What is it?'

'Chief speaking. Wondering what's up, that's all.'

'Nothing to worry about.' Theakston slammed down the cover of the voice-pipe.

'See?' Sparrow said. 'They don't give much away in York-shire. Like Scotland, is Yorkshire. Know what they say, do you?' The chief put on what he imagined was a Yorkshire accent. 'Never do owt for nowt, but if thee do, then do it for thissen.'

On the bridge Theakston was thinking that perhaps he could have taken his chief engineer into his confidence. After all, once the German was embarked his presence would be common enough knowledge. But he had been playing safe in informing only Amory: the Commodore was RNR and although he was as basically of the Merchant Service as was Theakston himself, the RN would have rubbed off on him; and you never knew quite

53

where you stood with the King's men. They had a different outlook and at times they could be as thick as a docker's sandwich, though he didn't think Kemp was that.

Theakston said, 'I think we'd do best to increase to nearer half speed, Commodore.'

Kemp nodded. 'I agree. Signalman ... inform *Portree* I'm increasing to seven knots.'

The signal went out: the destroyer was just about visible, keeping station ahead still, circling with the *Hardraw Falls* as the snow came down. Kemp cursed to himself: the blizzard was making life extremely difficult at just about the worst possible time. It was as he was thinking this that the destroyer's Aldis started flashing again.

'Contact, sir,' Corrigan reported. 'Bearing red four five, an echo, distant one mile and closing.'

A U-boat, or the British submarine?

Almost certainly it must be the latter, though coincidences could occur. Kemp was taking no chances. Action stations had in fact been sounded at the time the *Hardraw Falls* had detached from the convoy, just so that all hands were on the top line and ready. Now Kemp sent Cutler down to warn the guns' crews aft; and at the same time Theakston used the voice-pipe to the engine-room and warned Sparrow that there might be an attack. From then on the men were on a knife-edge above and below as they waited for the unknown, the unpredictable. It became a time for breath holding, for wonderment, on the part of the majority not in the know, that the destroyer wasn't attacking: there was no reverberation from depth-charges going off. Kemp felt a shake in his hands as he peered uselessly through the snow-filled darkness. If he had miscalculated, a torpedo might strike at any moment.

SIX

In the submarine's main control room the lieutenant in command stood by the housed periscope, with von Hagen under guard and ready to be taken up to the conning-tower as soon as the boat surfaced for the transfer. All was quiet, little sound beyond the hum of the motors and clicks from the gyro repeater as the coxswain moved the wheel from time to time. There was a curious feeling in the boat: no one cared much for having a Nazi agent aboard and there would be a strong sense of relief when he'd been disembarked.

The air would be cleaner: there was dirt sticking in large quantities to any Jerry spy and word had gone through the boat that this one was particularly unclean in what he'd been up to in Norway. Not that he looked the sort of bastard the galley wireless said he was. He had a strong face but not a sadistic one; indeed he looked like anyone's father, missed back home and anxious himself to get back to the wife and kids. Tall and thin with a haunted look in his face as if his world had come to an end, which of course it had. Get the sod back to the UK, and after the interrogation he might swing. Or they might keep him till the war was over and then hang him. None of the submarine's ratings knew quite what the law in wartime said about captured spies but there was a general belief that they could be hanged, unless that applied only to traitors, British subjects caught out in passing information to the enemy. Whatever his future might be, the Jerry had been made aware since the pick-up that he wasn't welcome. Loud comments and a fist now and again as the sod had been led from one part of the boat to another, to be taken to the heads and such. Not when an officer was present, because the orders had been very clear, but the officers couldn't be everywhere at once.

The submarine moved ahead for the rendezvous position; a little late. There had been some trouble with the diesels, causing delay, but now they were not far off. The lieutenant in command said as much to von Hagen.

The German smiled. 'You'll be glad to be rid of me.'

'Oh, you've been no trouble.' This was true: von Hagen had been a model prisoner; and well enough aware of his unpopularity not to be arrogant, not to mention the name of his Führer or refer in any way to the Third Reich. He might have been an Englishman: he spoke the language perfectly and had good manners, the manners of an English gentleman. In other circumstances he might have been a good friend: the lieutenant was almost sorry for him, facing at best captivity in the UK . . . it had occurred to the lieutenant to wonder why von Hagen was being put aboard a ship bound for Russia but he'd put the thought behind him. It wasn't his concern. Just a matter of convenience, probably: the outward bound PQ was passing at the right moment, whereas the next homeward convoy out of Russia would have meant too much hanging about.

'Coming up to the position, sir,' the navigator reported. 'Three miles, dead ahead as she goes.'

'Right. Stand by to surface.' As the boat moved ahead and the order was given to blow main tanks the lieutenant took up his position at the periscope, stood back as the great steel shaft surged up from its stowage ready to break through the sea into the wind and snow. He glanced briefly at the German's face: it had a tight, defeated look, even a sadness.

ii

'Submarine on the surface, sir, red eight five – '

'Can you identify?'

'She's making the identification signal now, sir.'

'Thank God,' Kemp said, blowing out his cheeks. 'Make the answer, Corrigan.' He put a hand on Theakston's shoulder. 'I'd like the ladder down now, Captain. And the ship stopped for the transfer.' He watched the bearing through his binoculars, dreading the moment he met von Hagen, or more precisely the moment when he had to follow his orders and put an old friend under threat and worse. The boat was only just visible as she made her approach, visible only from the white curruffle at her stern, just a blur in the foul weather conditions. But within the next couple of minutes she was lying close off the merchant ship's port side, nosing in to bring the fore casing up to the lowered fenders below the dangling jacob's ladder. From the bridge Kemp saw the figures in the conning-tower, saw the fore hatch open and a man emerge followed by two others. The central one was obviously von Hagen, with a rifle at his back, a bayoneted rifle. Snow swirled with the wind, at times obscuring the submarine, but through it Kemp saw the German being propelled along the casing towards the jacob's ladder, saw the rating in the lead reach out to grab for the line dangling from the foot of the ladder and haul it close. As he did so, a seaman aboard the *Hardraw Falls* sent a line snaking down to be caught by a man on the submarine's casing and attached around the waist of the prisoner. When this had been done Kemp heard the shouted, rough command : 'All right now. *Up* you go !'

The German stepped to the jacob's ladder, unaccompanied but with the rifle aimed. The line was hauled taut as he climbed, tended by the man from the deck above : a prisoner could drop in the drink if he preferred the quick end in an icy sea. Alongside Kemp, Theakston commented on the precaution. 'I dare say you'd rather he went,' he said.

Kemp gave a harsh laugh. 'The answer to that is yes. But I suppose it's cowardly of me to want that. Isn't it ?'

'I'd not say so, no. There'll be worse facing him in Russian hands.'

Kemp thought : don't, for God's sake, rub it in ! But Theakston had meant well. As von Hagen reached the deck, hands took him and helped him to find his feet. Leaning over the bridge rail, Kemp called down to the submarine co, 'Thank you, Captain, and well done.'

'Nothing in it, sir.'

'So you say ! Off with you now – and a safe journey home.' Kemp waved a hand, the lieutenant saluted and passed the orders to take the submarine off the side of the *Hardraw Falls*. The boat was soon lost in the snow and the night; Kemp imagined she would probably submerge. The conditions would be a damn sight easier inside the hull than keeping a watch in the conning-tower. He said, 'Well, there we are, Captain. Now let's press on and rejoin the convoy.'

Theakston went into the wheelhouse and passed the order down to the engine-room for full ahead. On the starting platform Sparrow gave a sigh of relief as the shafts began spinning and he felt the screws grip the water. Theakston had said the Commodore wanted the maximum possible speed in order to overtake the convoy. Sparrow was going to give him all he wanted: it wasn't a happy feeling, to be on their own apart from just the one destroyer.

On the bridge Cutler asked, 'Do you want to see the German now, sir?'

'No,' Kemp said. 'I'm remaining on the bridge and I don't want him up here. I'll see him when I go down, Cutler.'

'Very good, sir.'

'As for you – go and get your head down.'

'I'm all right, sir, thank you.'

'Do as you're told, Cutler. I don't want an assistant half doped for lack of sleep.'

iii

'A bloody Jerry,' Petty Officer Napper said in a surly tone, 'and it seems he's being given a *cabin*! What's the idea, might I ask?'

'Commodore's orders is all I know, same as you,' Chief Steward Buckle said. 'Don't agree with 'em myself, but there you are, eh? Treat the bugger proper, the Commodore said. Allocate him a steward, the Old Man followed up with. My arse! He'll have to share Torrence with the Old Man and Kemp and they can make the best they can of it. I suppose he'll be guarded?'

'He will and all. My guns' crews depleted, three 'ands working in watches on the bugger's door.'

'Armed, of course?'

'Of course.'

58

Buckle scratched his head reflectively. 'Well, that's something. Take over the ship else, he could!'

'Stretch of imagination. What d'you think my lads'd be doing, to let that 'appen?' Napper walked away, conscious that he was coming into his own: PO of the Guard – on a wanted spy! A bloody, stinking Hun with the rank of Colonel so he'd been told. One of Hitler's thugs. Or maybe not quite that: he wasn't Gestapo, anyway not one of the ordinary ones. More like an infiltrator into the Resistance and doubtless responsible for a good many deaths and tortures. The way he'd been put aboard, he must be someone of importance . . . Napper preened himself. The Nazi would be good for a number of free drinks in Napper's local when he got back home, so long as he was allowed to talk about it, that was, and most likely in fact he wouldn't. The brass was hot on secrecy and Napper might have to wait for glory till after the war was over. So far he didn't even know the Jerry's name. No one did, except the nobs on the bridge presumably. And it rankled with Napper that according to Mr Cutler the Jerry was to be addressed as 'sir'. Sir, to a Nazi!

'You,' Napper said, emerging up the ladder on to the after superstructure. 'You, Able Seaman Grove.'

'Me, PO?'

'That's what I just said, isn't it? Now, Watch and Quarter Bill. Right?'

'Watch and *what*?'

'You 'eard. Posting of the guard on the Nazi.' Napper felt snappish: perhaps Watch and Quarter Bill was a somewhat grandiose way of referring to the posting of a sentry, but still, Grove had sounded a shade too supercilious. 'You'll take the morning watch on 'is cabin, relieve whatsisname – Park. All right?'

'Yes, PO.'

'An' after that, we'll see.' It was an intricate business, working out watchkeeping rotas, and it took time and thought. You couldn't denude the guns just for a Jerry but on the other hand you couldn't denude an important Nazi agent just for guns, which were pretty useless anyway, decoration mostly, bloody ornaments, though Napper would never have thus denigrated his job this time yesterday, before he'd become gaoler to a high-powered Hun. Napper, as he went down the ladder, was conscious of Grove's long stare behind his back, but he didn't know what Grove was thinking. Later, when he took over guard duty, Grove released his thoughts to Ordinary Seaman Park.

'That Napper.' He told Park about the PO's reference to the Watch and Quarter Bill. 'Anyone'd think he was chief gunner's mate aboard the bloody *Nelson* or such ... working out the watches for fifteen 'undred matloes – port and starboard, red, white and blue, first and second parts thereof, blimey! Action stations, collision stations, fire stations, duties part of ship, duty 'ands of the watch, who falls in when Both Watches is piped, ditto when Both Watches of the *'Ands* is piped. So on and so forth. And God knows how the daft bugger ever made leading 'and, let alone PO.' Grove sniffed. 'He'd make heavy weather of being bosun's mate of a dinghy, would our Napper!'

Having taken over guard duties, Grove bent and peered, or tried to peer, through the slats of the jalousied door. By order of Kemp, the light was to remain on. Grove didn't get much of a view but he reckoned the Nazi was on his bunk and probably sleeping.

iv

When the dawn came up, slowly and with difficulty, to reveal an iron-grey, overcast sky and a restless, leaden sea, the *Hardraw Falls* was snow-covered virtually everywhere from truck to main deck. There were black patches around the funnel casing and the funnel itself stood out and that was all except for the guns, kept clear by the hands on watch. It was a ship in outline only : no visible hatch covers, no anchor cables and no slips or clenches on the fo'c'sle. Even the ladders had their treads under the mantle of white. There was a thick layer on monkey's island, and along the bridge wings Kemp's footsteps led in pits three or four inches deep.

And it was snowing still.

So far no convoy : that was not surprising, though a landsman might think it so when only some thirty-five sea miles had been lost whilst waiting about for the submarine. A ship with only about a knot of speed in hand over and above the speed of the convoy might well take around thirty hours to catch up the tail end. Theakston, who had remained on the bridge all night with Kemp, yawned and rubbed hard at eyes that stung with lack of sleep. His face was blue with the cold: he brushed snow from it with an automaton-like movement of a gloved hand. Blast the war, he thought: in peacetime he had never come this far north. Britain's trade had never been with the Soviets. And now half his mind was in Whitby: so long since he'd had word about Dora. Alive still – or not? But no use thinking, worrying; he must concentrate on the bitter sea, on its potential for danger, on moving towards Russia. He said, zombie-like as Kemp came to rest at his side, 'I reckon we just plug on. . . .'

'H'm?'

'The convoy. Catching up.'

'That's about it.' Kemp peered through the murk, through the whirling snow. He was as cold as charity but, although daylight had come, he was reluctant to go below. A ship's bridge was familiar ground; in every sense of the phrase he knew exactly where he stood. When he went below he would step into an unfamiliar world the moment he confronted von Hagen: a web of broken promises, of bare-faced lies, of deceiving a man who would look upon him as a friend at court, a man he had sailed with so many times. Thus he lingered, postponing what he was under orders to do, and was there when Cutler came up.

'Breakfast, sir.'

'You've had yours?'

'Sure I did, sir.' Cutler hesitated. 'The prisoner . . . he's talked to the sentry. He's asking to see you. Asking by name, sir: Captain Kemp, he said.'

Kemp nodded: so von Hagen knew, or anyway had been struck by the name, which he could have heard one of the ship's crew or the naval party mentioning. The German wouldn't have been able to identify anyone on the bridge in the darkness of the embarkation from the submarine but if he'd picked up the name he would want to know if the Kemp aboard the *Hardraw Falls* and the Captain Kemp he'd known were one and the same. Kemp said, 'All right, Cutler. I'll go down to my cabin. Give me half an hour, then have the prisoner brought in. The escort to remain outside my door.'

In his cabin Kemp washed and shaved and then his steward

61

brought in his breakfast. He ate without appetite, making short work of it, wanting only to get to the coffee and cigarette stage. Precisely half an hour after he had left the bridge, the knock came at his door: Cutler.

'Prisoner present, sir.'

'Thank you, Cutler. Bring him in.' Kemp had stiffened as if expecting a physical blow. He lit another cigarette, with shaking fingers that he couldn't hold still. From the door Cutler jerked his head, saying nothing. Von Hagen came in alone. Cutler said, 'I'll be outside, sir.' Cutler had tact. The door closed behind him.

Von Hagen's eyes had widened with pleasure. 'So it *is* you, Captain Kemp.'

'Yes. A long time. . . .' Kemp held out his hand; the German took it in a strong grip. 'The war brings changes, von Hagen. I'm sorry.'

'So am I. They were pleasant days, the days of peaceful sailing.'

'Yes.' Kemp gestured to a chair and offered his cigarette case and a lighter. The German drew in smoke thankfully as he sat down.

'You asked to see me, von Hagen.'

'To meet an old friend, if you were the same Kemp. That was all. Not to ask favours. I accept that we are enemies now.' The German's look was direct, no shifting away from Kemp's eyes. 'I've lost – that's all.' He paused. 'Have the years, the years of war, treated you well, Captain?'

Kemp shrugged. 'Well enough – I'm still alive and that's something.'

'But not still with the Mediterranean-Australia Line. A Commodore of your naval reserve, I see. You are not captain of the ship?'

Kemp said, 'I'm the Commodore of the convoy, von Hagen.'

'I was not told – I was told nothing. And you are returning from Russia, from Murmansk or Archangel – or should I not ask?' Von Hagen gave a quiet laugh. 'I am, after all, an enemy –'

'Yes. But you may ask . . . and I shall answer.' Kemp found the words coming with difficulty, almost as though he had developed a speech defect. 'The convoy is not returning from Russia, Colonel von Hagen. It is out of Iceland . . . bound for Archangel.'

The German's face had reacted: there was total surprise, almost shock. 'That will be dangerous for me, Commodore. The Russians . . . however, I am, of course, a British prisoner of war. But suppose the ship is searched, what then? British prisoner or not – '

Kemp said steadily, 'The ship will not be searched, that I can guarantee. The Russians are our allies, not our masters, and no search will be permitted.'

Von Hagen relaxed and blew out his breath. 'I'm relieved! The Russians and I don't mix. If I were to be found, well, it would be the end after interrogation by – '

'I realize that – '

'But in British hands . . . it's not to be welcomed, I need hardly say, but at least I know your people behave properly. As I said, Commodore – I've lost, and that's the way it goes.'

'Yes. You're philosophical, von Hagen – very.'

The German smiled. 'I have no option, and I always look on the bright side. I always did, if you remember.'

'I remember.' Kemp did: sometimes von Hagen's business trips had not been as successful as he'd hoped, but he'd never been disturbed. There was always another day, he used to say, always another chance. The same with women: von Hagen had had an eye for them, and he was an attractive man, but sometimes he'd made a wrong choice and ended up with the equivalent – or once the reality – of a slapped face, but that too he had always shrugged off and had come up smiling. He hadn't much to smile about now but was taking it well – because he was bound for British hands, not Russian. No doubt there had always been the possibility of being taken by the Russians; at least he'd been spared that – or so he believed.

Kemp licked at dry lips, searching for the right words, the best way of shattering an illusion. Before he had formulated what he was going to say there was an interruption. His voice-pipe whined and he answered. 'Commodore – '

'Bridge, sir, chief officer speaking. Weather's clearing – '

'Any sign of the convoy?'

'No, sir, but the masthead lookout reports wreckage ahead, fine on the port bow, looks like woodwork in a big patch of oil.'

Kemp said, 'I'll be up, Amory. Better inform *Portree*.' He

turned to von Hagen. 'We'll talk again later, Colonel.' He called for Cutler, and the German was taken back to his cabin under escort. Kemp felt as though he had been reprieved.

SEVEN

Theakston had reached the bridge and all the binoculars were on the wreckage. It was heaving up and down, sliding over the swell, disappearing now and again. There was no snow now and the visibility was fair to good, the sky clearing fast. The cold was worse than ever and each breath was like a knife-thrust in the lungs.

'One of the convoy?' Theakston asked.

'I fear so.'

'You'd think there'd be more.'

'Could be a single straggler, the usual arse-end Charlie,' Kemp said. Arse-end Charlies – like themselves currently – were always at extra risk. You couldn't stop or even slow for just one ship, and you only detached a warship to stand guard if you had a big enough escort, which was not the case this time – the *Hardraw Falls* herself wouldn't have been given a destroyer if it hadn't been for the importance of embarking von Hagen and delivering him to Russia safely.

Three minutes after Kemp had reached the bridge there was another report from the masthead: a boat, some distance beyond the wreckage, a ship's lifeboat and a man waving from it. Theakston didn't wait for orders: he told Amory to alter towards the boat and have men standing by the jacob's ladder.

Kemp demurred. He said, 'We'll leave them to the destroyer, Captain. There's a doctor aboard. Corrigan?'

'Yessir?'

'Ask *Portree* to pick up survivors.'

'Aye, aye, sir.'

'And add that I wish to be informed immediately of any news

of the convoy.' Kemp watched anxiously as the destroyer swept up towards the wreckage. As she slowed her engines the lifeboat was lost to view behind her hull; but within a short time she was once again moving fast and heeling under full port helm to circle back towards the *Hardraw Falls*. As she came up on the Commodore's port beam her loud hailer came on.

There was an amplified shout across the water: 'Commodore ahoy!'

Kemp waved an arm from the bridge wing, and took the megaphone handed him by Cutler. He called back in response. 'How many and where from?'

'Six men in the boat, only two alive, sir. From a freighter, ss *City of Khartoum*. Convoy came under U-boat attack. Two ships known to be lost ... could be more.' There was a pause. 'One U-boat sunk, sir. Our survivors don't know how many there were.'

'We could be steaming right into it.'

'Yes, sir. Any orders?'

'No change,' Kemp said. 'We press on to rejoin the convoy. I take it they're holding their course?'

They were, *Portree*'s captain said. Kemp waved a hand again and turned away. The *Hardraw Falls* would join the battle, if it was still going on when they caught up, with her armament useless against U-boats unless and until one of them was forced to the surface by depth-charge attack from the a/s screen and the destroyers.

Kemp remarked on this to Cutler.

Cutler said, 'You have a dilemma, sir.'

'Have I?' Kemp raised his eyebrows. 'I didn't know I had.'

'Well ... maybe you don't, sir. But it occurred to me ... that is ... we're putting another ship, us, at risk unnecessarily. We have a valuable cargo. And like you've just said, we don't add anything to the fire power.'

'Just a target.'

'In a nutshell, sir – yes.'

'We could just bugger off?'

'Well now, I guess – '

Kemp said evenly, 'It did go through my mind, Cutler, and it went right out again. Of course, you're quite right to bring it up.

But there are two points that come uppermost. The first is that I'm the Commodore. It's my convoy. I have a duty to be there, Cutler.'

'Yes, sir. And the second?'

Kemp gave a mirthless grin. 'It's a hundred to one we'll meet the U-boats in any event, returning to base.'

Cutler nodded. He had half a mind to tell the Commodore that he could deviate, alter course westwards and get the hell out until the returning U-boats had made it south past their position, but he didn't say this. He could guess what Kemp's answer would be, and as for him, he hadn't come over to avoid action. Once again he recalled the words of the RCNVR's theme song: *We came over for the fighting, not the fun. . . .*

That conversation reached the crew of the *Hardraw Falls* via the agency of the seaman on lookout in the port wing of the bridge.

ii

'He's got no right,' Chief Steward Buckle said. 'What bloody use are we anyway, I ask you!'

Buckle had encountered the bosun, who had been checking the fire hydrants along with the second engineer: orders from the bridge, since they might be in need of the fire hoses any time now. Jock Tawney said indifferently, 'I don't reckon that's the point.'

'Oh. What is, then?'

'We're the Commodore's ship, that's what. The Commodore don't scarper from trouble.'

'I don't see why not, Bose.'

'P'raps you don't.' Tawney sniffed; in his view chief stewards thought only of lining their own pockets, which was why they'd gone to sea in the first place, and Buckle saw no profit in this, only danger. The danger was there, all right; but it was always there at sea in wartime, just part of the job and you got on with it. Meanwhile Buckle was getting on with his complaint.

He said, 'The Russians stand to lose a lot of bloody ammo. They won't like that.'

'Let 'em shove it, then.'

'Christ Almighty, Bose, they're the whole reason we're here!'

'More's the pity,' Tawney said, and turned his back. Buckle shrugged; no point in saying any more. Like all seamen, Tawney was thick as a plank. Horny-handed shellbacks, haulers on ropes and tackles, no intelligence but thought they were bloody marvellous just because they *were* seamen . . . Buckle carried on along the alleyway to his cabin, where he had some stores lists to go through. The ship was short on a few provisions, items that couldn't be obtained in enough quantity in UK ports: the war was nothing but shortages. Most likely the Russians would be unable to top up but he would try. Buckle toyed with thoughts of caviar. That should be plentiful, with luck. Probably not much would be eaten aboard and if he could buy in quantity there might be something in it for himself when they got back to home waters, a really good profit from under the noses of the company. If they didn't go and get bloody sunk in the meantime.

Bugger Kemp!

And bugger that Jerry too, Buckle thought. If the brass in Berlin happened to have got word that he'd been nabbed and put aboard the *Hardraw Falls*, well then, obviously they'd be trying especially hard to knock the ship off before he got where he was going and was made to spill a whole lot of beans. . . .

Beans . . . Heinz. Chief Steward Buckle's mind clicked smoothly on to matters within his province. Baked beans were a vital part of the crew's menu and were one of the items he was short of. He didn't know if Russians ate baked beans.

iii

'You there, Corrigan.'

Corrigan looked up: he was sitting at the naval mess table, writing a letter home for posting in Archangel, knowing it would get to his parents no quicker than if he posted it in a UK port on return but wanting to get it off just in case he didn't make it on the homeward run. 'Yes, PO?'

'Letter writing!' Napper clicked his tongue. 'Action alarm might go any time.'

'That's right. Commodore didn't want to have the hands closed up before it was necessary, so – '

'I know that, thank you. Soft-'earted, is Kemp. And bloody right to press on,' Napper said rather surprisingly. He wasn't usually all that keen, Corrigan thought. But now he was leading up to something and it began to emerge. 'Said you was a makee-learn doctor, right? I need an opinion.'

Corrigan nodded, sighed and pushed his writing pad aside. Perhaps it was good practice for after the war. 'What seems to be the trouble?' he asked.

'Dunno. That's for you to say ... I mean, if you'd do me a favour, that is.'

'Of course I will, short of opening you up, PO.'

Napper blenched. 'I never bloody asked – '

'I know, I know. Just my way of saying I'm not on the medical register and it's little I can advise in fact. I'm not supposed to pronounce at all, actually.'

Actually. No doubt about it, Corrigan was officer material. Napper said, 'Exigencies o' war ... exentuating circumstances.'

'All right, PO. Let's have it.'

'I gets a funny feeling,' Napper said, screwing up his face in undiagnosed discomfort.

'Where?'

'All over like.'

'When?'

'When? Never know when it's coming on, do I?'

'When there's a U-boat contact?'

Napper glared. 'None o' your lip, Corrigan. I didn't ask for cheek. And the answer's no ... not specially then.'

'I see. I think you said the doctor aboard *Nottingham* prescribed Black Draught?'

'Yes! 'E did an' all!'

'Very effective stuff, PO.'

'Well, 'e can stuff it, effective or not.'

Corrigan grinned. 'Talking of stuffing it ... there was a well worn joke that used to make the rounds of the medical schools and probably still does. A chap went to his doctor, said he was suffering from constipation ... the doctor prescribed suppositories. A fortnight later, the chap went back and said he'd taken them twice daily as instructed but for all the good they'd done, he might just as well have shoved them up his arse.' He paused; Napper's face was blank. 'You don't get it?'

'Don't sound too likely. To swallow suppositories, they're bloody poisonous, aren't they?'

Corrigan said, 'I expect so, yes, but never mind, it was just a joke.'

'I don't reckon doctors ought to make jokes like that. I'm being serious. There's something wrong. Maybe it's me nerves. Think it could be?'

'I simply don't know. I hadn't got very far in medicine, hadn't even taken my anatomy exams.'

'Taken?'

'Yes, but they're not suppositories, PO.'

iv

The shout came from the masthead lookout: 'Torpedo trail starboard, sir . . . green four five!'

Kemp brought his binoculars up; Cutler beat him to it. 'Got it, sir. Two of them.' He pointed. 'There.'

'Right.' The twin trails, some two cables'-lengths apart, had now come up clear in Kemp's lenses. He called out, 'Steer between them, Captain! Starboard your helm.'

Theakston gave the order: in the wheelhouse the helm went over. Theakston sounded the alarm and Kemp watched closely as the ship's head came round to starboard. The master checked the swing as the bows came to a point midway between the torpedo trails.

'Port ten . . . midships . . . *steady*!'

In the wheelhouse the helmsman met the swing and steadied his course on 046 degrees, saw the thin marks just beneath the surface as they raced towards the ship. Kemp was holding his breath now, staring ahead, staring down the starboard side as the torpedoes closed. One of them passed no more than a dozen yards clear. From the port side, Cutler called out that the second torpedo had also passed: Theakston's judgment had been spot on, but the attack was only just starting, unless the U-boat had no more fish left, the others expended on the convoy ahead, between the *Hardraw Falls* and the North Cape. Kemp found his fists clenched tight: the ship was a bloody great target. The Nazis couldn't miss a second time. But by now *Portree* was flying the attack signal and moving in at high speed, following the pings of her Asdic, water flinging back from her fo'c'sle and the depth-charge racks and throwers ready aft. Aboard the Commodore's ship the close-range weapons were manned in the bridge wings, on monkey's island, and on the after superstructure. Kemp looked around: if only the U-boat could be forced to the surface ... it was time that his gunnery rates were given a chance to show what they could do.

Kemp saw Petty Officer Napper moving along the after well-deck, coming for'ard, an anxious expression on his long, gloomy face. This, unknown to Kemp, was due to the action alarm having cut short Napper's medical consultation. Corrigan had been in the process of giving him some good advice, having got his rotten jokes out of the way, and Hitler had buggered it all up. Corrigan had suggested *inter alia* that Napper should go and see the doctor again, and when Napper had retorted that the quack was about as useful as a whore at a wedding, Corrigan had said he could do worse than put in a request to see a Russian doctor in Archangel. At first Napper had refused absolutely to see a Russian quack, a bloody Communist, but Corrigan, who had had enough of Napper though he didn't let it show, had gone on about the Russians having a lot of advanced knowledge and medical technology and more resources ashore than any ship could have. Napper had been much impressed: Leading Signalman Corrigan was nearly half a doctor, and doctors were important people even if some of them didn't know much, and then there was that very special way in which Corrigan said the word 'actually'. A proper gent, was Corrigan.

Napper's expression of anxiety as he hurried about his gun positions was due to a snag: in order to see a Russian quack, he would have to tell the surgeon commander aboard the *Nottingham*, if ever they made Archangel, that he was too bloody useless to be consulted again. That would take some doing. In the meantime, Napper's stomach was playing him up. He saw a connection with his chest: after all, the two parts were adjacent.

Proceeding for'ard, Napper reached the ladder leading to the midship superstructure just as the *Portree*'s first pattern of depth-charges went up. Napper took the steps fast and arrived on monkey's island panting. Away to starboard the sea was heaving up, boiling water breaking surface in great humps, but no U-boat. Napper checked around the guns.

71

'All right, lads?'

'Yes, PO.'

'Give the buggers hell if they surface,' Napper said, sounding efficient. Then he saw Sub-Lieutenant Cutler coming up the ladder from the bridge.

'Hey there, Napper. Petty Officer Napper.'

'Yessir?'

Cutler reached out and tapped Napper's arm. 'Not so warlike, okay? Remember the orders – no firing except on the order from the bridge, all right?'

'Yes,' Napper said, scowling. Little git. Little *Yankee* git! It was no wonder he didn't feel well. Cutler was enough to give the cat kittens. Cowboys from Texas just didn't fit the sea scene, they were born and bred to be soldiers.

v

There were no more torpedoes: the U-boat was apparently operating singly and there was no way of knowing whether or not it had been part of the attack on the main PQ convoy. But the gunners were going to get their chance even if it wasn't much: *Portree*'s attack, one pattern after another going down with different depth settings on the charges, was effective. The reverberations shattered through the plating of the *Hardraw Falls*, ringing like deep-toned bells in the engine-room and boiler-room, shaking Buckle's office where he was obeying company's orders by gathering up invoices and requisitions and other ship's papers and stuffing them into the big safe with all the cash – aboard the Bricker Dockett ships the chief steward acted also as purser – so that they would go to the bottom rather than float to the possible benefit of the enemy, though Buckle often wondered, why the hell bother? It wouldn't help Hitler much to be in possession of corned beef bills, though possibly it would give away the identity of the supply ports which he might then decide to bomb, but since he bombed them anyway it didn't really seem important.

The job done, Buckle slammed the safe door shut and twirled the combination locks which he'd set to the date of his former mother-in-law's birthday, making the old bag a damn sight more important than she'd ever imagined. Then he went up on deck, circumspectly. Basically anyone was safer on deck than down below, but Buckle didn't want to stop a personal bullet or shell if the U-boat surfaced and attacked by gunfire.

But he wasn't due for that, not yet.

He heard a rising shout along the decks, a shout – almost a baying – of triumph, a real blood-lust, Buckle thought. Not far ahead, a little to starboard of the ship's track, he saw the long, low, black shape, the conning-tower manned by a press of Nazis, officers and ratings, some of whom were spilling over on to the fore casing and running for the gun platform for'ard of the conning-tower. The boat had a list on her as though she'd taken something that had caused some plates to be sprung, and there was smoke drifting up from the conning-tower. But she wasn't done yet and the gun was coming to bear. That U-boat, Buckle thought, she's bloody close, and getting closer.

vi

The U-boat had been forced to the surface fine on the starboard bow of the *Hardraw Falls* and distant little more than six cables – not quite as close in fact as Buckle had estimated. Kemp had brought the guns' crews to readiness to open. Theakston asked, 'Do you want to turn away, Commodore?'

'No point. I'm going to close – and pray! Take her in, please, Captain.'

'You don't mean ram the bugger?'

'I do. A course to ram, as close to the conning-tower as you can make it.'

'But my bows! They may not take the impact.'

'We must chance it. It's our only hope if – ' Kemp broke off, ducking instinctively as he saw the flash from the U-boat. *Portree* was racing in now but seemed unable to bear with her guns since she had the *Hardraw Falls* immediately behind the target. Theakston was forging on now, heading for the U-boat: the two vessels were close. The first shell from the Nazi went over the bridge, the second took the foremast and carried it away in a tangle of wire and shattered wood, some of it falling across the port wing of the bridge and only just missing Cutler. The masthead look-out was thrown clear, coming down in the water off the ship's

73

port beam. Then the *Hardraw Falls* hit, a glancing blow but a heavy one, immediately below the conning-tower, a crunch that sent the U-boat heeling over to starboard, flinging men into the water. The ship gave a lurch as the speed came off suddenly. Everywhere men went sprawling: Petty Officer Napper spun along the after well-deck, legs and arms flying, to fetch up in the scuppers and half-way through a washport: he was jammed there helpless and swearing as, on the order from the bridge, the close-range weapons opened on the Nazis. Chief Steward Buckle was flung back against a bulkhead, only partially cushioned by a sizeable rump. Kemp found himself pressed against the fore rail of the bridge, just for a moment. He looked across at the U-boat: he could see she wasn't going to last – the blow from the *Hardraw Falls* had completed the work begun by the *Portree*'s depth-charge attack. The close-range weapons were proving deadly: the casing was strewn with bodies, some of which had slid into the sea, trailing blood.

'She's going, sir,' Cutler said. The list had increased suddenly.

'Yes. Cease firing, Cutler.'

Cutler passed the word. The order was not immediately obeyed: the crews of the after guns had the bit between their teeth now. The Nazis were in their sights and were going to get it, right up to the end. Cutler took up the Commodore's megaphone and yelled through it.

'Bloody cease firing! Obey the order!' His voice got through and there was quiet as the rattle of the guns stopped.

'Where's Napper, for Jeez' sake?'

A voice came back: 'Jammed, sir.'

'Unjam him, then!'

vii

There was no damage to the bow: Amory had checked round. There had been no chance to retrieve the masthead lookout before the cold killed him. The U-boat had gone down, taking most of her dead with her. Kemp left the bridge feeling dead tired and somewhat sick: the slaughter had been very bloody and there could be no excuse for disobedience of orders, for the continued shooting-up of a defeated enemy who had lost the means to hit back. On the other hand, Kemp could understand only too well the blood-lust that had taken over. In the sea war you didn't often get to close grips with the enemy, you didn't often see the whites of their eyes as it were, but you suffered from them just the same. You suffered via your families, your home under threat from the Luftwaffe, via sons or brothers or fathers who perhaps had bought it in other actions on land or sea or in the air, you suffered via the everlasting days and weeks and months of wondering when you were going to be knocked off by a U-boat or in air or surface attack. When you got the enemy in your gunsights, then you reacted. It was only natural. Even so, disobedience of orders couldn't ever be allowed to go by default. Kemp had some bollocking to do. But there was something else first: von Hagen. That interrupted conversation – Kemp now wanted to get the matter off his chest as soon as possible, though he knew it couldn't be settled in five minutes. There might have to be many sessions, and he must have his mind in order before arrival in Archangel. He told off Cutler to bring the German to his cabin again, and once again to wait outside with the armed escort.

Von Hagen came in. He said, 'One to you, I'm told.'

'Yes. And I'm not gloating, von Hagen.'

'You're not the sort to do that, I know.'

Kemp stared at him as he sat down. 'And you?'

Von Hagen shrugged. 'I doubt if I would gloat but I can't really say. My war hasn't been in the field ... not the battlefield, I mean.'

'But in Norway?'

'I don't believe I follow....'

'The Resistance. When you broke the enclaves, as probably you did from time to time ... and caused men's deaths. Women's too, perhaps. What were your feelings then, von Hagen?'

'I tried not to have them. I did my duty.'

'And hardened your heart.' Kemp pushed himself back in his chair. 'Yes, I understand. Or I think I do.'

Von Hagen shook his head. 'I think this, Captain – it is different for you, for all the British people – '

'In what way?'

Once again von Hagen shrugged. 'Britain is a democracy, with a kindly, gentlemanly King. You are fighters, yes, but you are not fanatics for any cause, like us Germans – '

'I didn't think – before the war – that you were a fanatical Nazi, von Hagen.'

'No. I don't think I am now either. But I am very anti-communist.'

'Yes, I knew that. That's your fanaticism?'

'Yes. A fanaticism in an "anti" sense.'

Kemp got to his feet and went over to the square port, looking out over the bows thrusting into the cold sea. He kept his back turned to the German as he asked, 'Tell me this: what are your views on Hitler?'

'I think that is an unfair question.' There was a rebuke in von Hagen's tone. 'Herr Hitler is my Führer, my Chancellor. It would be unbecoming in me to criticize.'

'Yet I still ask the question.' Kemp swung round and met von Hagen's eyes. 'And I believe – reading between the lines of what you've just said – that in fact you have got criticisms.'

'Have you no criticisms of Mr Churchill?'

'Sometimes, yes. In Britain, we're free to have them. But of course there's no lack of trust, no lack of belief that in basis Churchill's conducting the war properly.'

'And you suggest – am I right – that we in Germany haven't the same belief in Herr Hitler?'

'Yes,' Kemp said. He said it with a touch of defiance. He was out of his depth and he knew it, knew he wasn't putting anything across effectively. What he wanted to say was that trust in Hitler was surely impossible, that no normal person could believe, for instance, that persecution of whole sections of the German community was a good thing, that a leader who was reliably said to act upon his intuition rather than upon considered advice was anything better than a charlatan ... that, and a lot more. The atrocities in the occupied countries, of which von Hagen must know plenty; the waging of the war at sea against women and children – the sinking, early in hostilities, of the *Athenia* crossing the Atlantic with all those children aboard; so very many things that had left a blot on civilization to the horror of intelligent men and women.

Kemp didn't say any of that: he must not antagonize von Hagen too far. But he very much wanted to know the German's thoughts because he needed to make a fresh assessment of an old friend who had been changed by war. If he could perhaps begin to make von Hagen see things differently, get him to question the validity of his loyalty to a mass murderer who was far from sane, if he could get inside the man's mind – then he might probe out something useful, in accordance with his orders but without the need to utter distasteful threats.

It was going to be an uphill task for any convoy Commodore, a plain seaman without political frills.

viii

One of those who was particularly disturbed by the fact of having a Nazi aboard was an able seaman of the ship's crew – Able Seaman Swile, a cockney with a mean face, a closed face with a slit for a mouth. That meanness could have been with him from birth or it could have become superimposed by the events in Swile's life, which had not been an easy one. The family background was not good : his father, who had died when Swile had been two years of age, had been replaced by a stepfather who had detested him and had gone to prison for beating him black and blue and breaking an arm and a leg on different occasions. Swile had mostly played truant from school, had left as soon as he could and drifted into crime of a petty nature – and had begun flirting with the Communist Party. Swile had been in his late teens at the time Mosley's British Union of Fascists had been at their zenith and he'd had many brushes with them. More than brushes : he'd been beaten up more effectively than ever he had been by his stepfather. Clubs had been used on him – clubs and jackboots and sometimes chains and razors. Mosley's thugs had been responsible for getting Swile a long prison sentence for GBH, for Swile had hit back and almost murdered one of the blackshirt boys, and had ended up in Dartmoor. There had been some fascists as well, in the Moor ; and the warders couldn't be everywhere, not all the time, and Swile had been done up more than once, and had hit back, and got his sentence prolonged while the fascists mostly seemed to get away with it.

Swile had a deep and abiding hatred of Nazis, a pathological loathing of all Germans as a result. To have one of them living in

77

cabin luxury aboard the *Hardraw Falls* was not good. Swile went about his work with mutinous mutters, his face more closed up than ever, and a red light in his eye.

EIGHT

'Well, Petty Officer Napper. What precisely happened to you?'
Kemp had sent for Napper to report to his cabin after von Hagen
had been taken below again. Napper stood before the Commodore, at attention with his uniform cap beneath his left arm.

'Got jammed up, sir. Force o' enemy fire, sir.'

'A little more detail, I think.'

'Yessir.' Napper stared over Kemp's head, towards the square
port. 'Got flung acrorss the deck, sir, and landed up in a washport. Nearly went overboard, sir. I ended up with one leg out-
board and the other inboard, sir. If you see what I mean.'

Kemp kept a straight face. 'Like a pair of scissors?'

'You might say so, sir, yes.'

'H'm. Any damage?'

Napper said, 'It's painful, sir, very.'

'Do you need a doctor?'

'I reckon I do, sir, yes.'

Kemp cursed inwardly; he wanted no more delays at sea but
had had to ask the question and now that it had been answered
affirmatively he couldn't deny a man medical attention if it was
obtainable. He said, 'Very well, Napper, I'll make a signal to
Portree. In the meantime, although I realize you were *hors de
combat* . . .' He read the puzzlement in Napper's face and went
on, '. . . jammed in the washport at the time, you still had the responsibility for the close-range weapons. It was a pretty poor
business, Napper – to disobey the cease fire.'

'Yessir. Not my fault, sir.'

Kemp said patiently, 'I've already referred to that. If you'd
been there in person, I'd have punished you by warrant and

you'd have been disrated. As it was, you should have made your presence felt in advance, if you follow me. You'll see that nothing similar ever occurs again.'

'Yessir.'

'If it does, you're for the chop. As it is, I shall speak to all the guns' crews before dusk action stations. In the meantime . . . I understand it was Able Seaman Grove who was in charge aft.'

'Yessir, it was, sir. Grove, 'e's a – '

'Yes, all right, Napper. Bring him to the bridge in ten minutes' time, charged with disobedience of orders whilst in action.'

'Yessir.' Napper remained at attention.

'That's all, Napper.'

'Er. . . .' Napper cleared his throat. 'If I might refer to it again, sir – '

'Yes, the doctor. I have it in mind, Napper. I shall let you know.'

ii

Kemp had gone to town on Grove: disobedience of orders was the worst crime in action, short of deserting your gun. Kemp had quoted the Naval Discipline Act and the Articles of War and Grove had prepared himself for the worst – or not quite the worst, because the Articles of War prescribed death as the ultimate penalty to be exacted and that he didn't expect – and had been vastly astonished to be let off with a caution, which confirmed him in his view that Kemp, notwithstanding all the brass on his sleeves and cap, was a sight more human than bloody Napper. Leaving the Commodore's presence, however, Grove felt a strong sense of grievance that he'd been hauled up at all. Somebody didn't seem to know there was a war on; wasn't it a gunner's job to kill Nazis? Why show them any humanity? Kemp should have let the guns' crews alone. Apart from anything else, the Nazis were better off dead from gunfire than freezing in the hogwash. Grove had an inner certainty that bloody Napper had put in a bad word on his behalf and the Commodore was duty bound to act.

So sod Napper. . . . Making his way aft from the bridge, Grove's face widened in a big grin. He'd got a bollocking from

Kemp all right, but Napper, according to the buzz, had now got bollocked-up bollocks from his fight with the washport. Ever since, the PO had been walking about the decks looking as if he'd had a nasty accident in his pants.

Currently Petty Officer Napper's misfortune was causing concern on the bridge: Kemp had a word with Cutler.

'Bit of a hypochondriac, isn't he, Cutler?'

'You can say that again, sir.'

'I don't want to say it again. I've just said it.'

'Sorry, sir,' Cutler said cheerfully. 'I'm just a goddam Yank. But Petty Officer Napper – you were asking. Always got something the matter, but this time I guess he's real sore where it matters. Or could matter to his old lady.'

Kemp blew out a long breath, irritated that he should have to concern himself and ultimately the convoy with anyone's sex life, which didn't exist at sea. He said, 'Oh, very well, make a signal to *Portree*, then ... ask for their medico to advise by lamp.'

'Yes, sir. He'll want some technical information to go on, won't he?'

'I suppose so. Oh, damn it, Cutler – balls caught in a washport, it's simple enough! If you want to put it in a more medical form, have a word with Corrigan – I understand he was a medical student.'

iii

By now the main body of the PQ convoy was beginning its approach to the North Cape and the bitter weather that would meet the ships as they turned easterly between Spitzbergen and Norway's far north to enter the Barents Sea and then the White Sea for Archangel. Already the decks were icing up and to move about them was little short of suicidal; even the lifelines were strings of ice along which the heavily gloved hands of the seamen slid without hindrance. The fo'c'sle gear was frozen solid, the cables and slips set in ice deposited as the sea and spray froze almost on impact. Before arrival, the crews would be set to chip away the ice in a probably forlorn attempt to beat the weather and free the anchors. Currently only the guns were usable, kept free of ice by their crews working constantly to maintain their defence against anything Hitler might decide to throw at them. There was a curious feeling throughout all the ships, both escort and merchantmen: true, there had already been casualties – two more ships lost, and the Commodore still out of contact which might mean anything ... but the full weight of the enemy appeared to have been held off and that in itself was worrying: the general feeling was that something was being stored up – either that, or Hitler had missed the bus, which wasn't likely. There was also a lack of information from the Operations Room at the Admiralty; that could only mean that the Admiralty was as much in the dark as were the ships at sea. There was normally some indication coming through as to the likely movements of the U-boat packs or the surface vessels, the latter only too eager to attack the convoys eastward of the North Cape when they thought they were safe on the last leg into Murmansk or Archangel. Hitler's naval arm was a long one, as was his air arm.

Rear-Admiral Fellowes was concerned about the Commodore. For the tenth time that early morning he walked into the after part of *Nottingham*'s bridge and scanned the sea astern. It stood empty, bleak; once again there was a hint of snow to come. Fellowes lowered his binoculars and spoke to his Flag Captain. 'The pick-up,' he said. 'Something gone wrong I shouldn't wonder. Or the German was simply late.'

'The *Hardraw Falls* herself – '

'Yes, she could have met trouble, of course. I don't like it.'

'Nothing we can do, sir.'

'No. Just steam on. That's what I don't like ... leaving Kemp to it. Damn it, I can't even slow the convoy! Any day now, Archangel's going to ice up.'

'It was always on the cards we might have to enter Murmansk, sir.'

Fellowes nodded but didn't comment. At the moment the orders were for Archangel and he had to make it in time for the homeward convoy to get out of the port before the ice blocked the entry channel. For some reason the Russians were set on Archangel; and Fellowes saw the German agent as the obvious explanation for that.

'*Portree* calling, sir.' Corrigan read off the lamp flashing from the destroyer's bridge. 'From the surgeon lieutenant, sir: "Please indicate if there is blood in urine."'

'Damn!' Kemp said. 'Cutler, send down for Petty Officer Napper. Or better still, go yourself and ask him.'

Cutler gave a cough and a sideways nod. 'How about Corrigan, sir?'

'Corrigan? Oh – yes. Good idea! Corrigan, you have a medical background. Get your relief up and go and check the details with Petty Officer Napper.'

'Aye, aye, sir.' Corrigan went to the voice-pipe connecting with the naval mess and blew down it. The relief signalman came to the bridge and Corrigan left on his errand of mercy. When he returned he reported that Napper had found no trace of blood.

'Thank you, Corrigan. Make that to *Portree*.'

Corrigan did so; another signal was flashed across within a few minutes: 'Watch and report size of affected part. Medical attention should not be necessary if swelling does not increase.'

'Right,' Kemp said. 'See that Napper is informed of that, Cutler. It'll be up to him to report immediately if – er – '

'If his balls reach balloon size, sir.'

'There's no need to be crude,' Kemp said. The message went down to Petty Officer Napper, who scowled and said the bloody quack should try suffering a similar disability and see how he liked it. There ought to be some sort of treatment to ease the pain, but was the quack going to be bothered? Oh, no! Sit on his arse. ... Napper couldn't do even that comfortably since what the quack so delicately called the affected part was so bloody big he couldn't avoid sitting bang on it, which meant he'd have to stand till doomsday. Muttering to himself, Napper ferreted about in his medical stockpile and found a tube of lanolin ointment.

Lanolin might help. It was worth a try. Napper went along to the heads and annointed the affected part. Afterwards he was horribly greasy but the lanolin seemed to have cooled it down.

'Coming up to the North Cape,' Theakston said, after a look at the chart. 'We should raise it within an hour.'

Kemp nodded. 'Just before dark. Still no convoy.'

'They can't be far ahead.'

'I wish to God,' Kemp said, 'we could break wireless silence! I've got that ice in mind. The convoy might enter Murmansk, and if we haven't caught up, we'll never know.'

'We can make an independent decision from the weather reports, Commodore.'

'Yes. I don't want to deviate – but I may be forced to, of course. I take it your chart's fully corrected for the approaches to Murmansk?'

Theakston answered stiffly. 'You have no need to ask.'

'My apologies, Captain. I was merely going on to say that my own folio's at your disposal if you need it.'

'Thank you. I'll have no need of that.'

Kemp felt severely rebuked. He remained on the bridge until the North Cape was raised on the starboard bow as dusk was setting in and stayed on until after dusk action stations were fallen out. Then he went below: there was work to be done, more talking with von Hagen. On the way down the ladder to the master's deck he encountered Petty Officer Napper checking on the gunners of the watch.

'Well, Napper. How's it going? Still painful?'

'Yes, sir, *very* painful, sir.'

'You have my sympathy. Fortunately it's not lethal.' Kemp went on his way, and Napper scowled at his retreating back in its bridge coat and duffel coat. Not lethal, no! Not to life, anyway. On the other hand you never knew. The body was a very funny thing and its reactions couldn't be predicted. One part rubbed off on another and things could spread, currently in the sense that with swollen bollocks you walked funny, and that could affect the legs, give you lumbago perhaps, upset your spinal cord so you ended up in plaster of paris, and once let that happen and all sorts of things could go wrong through the sheer inertia of being motionless and flat. You could get obese and bugger up the heart, and your liver would go bad and what-all. Constipation would be a natural certainty, a complete gum-up, and that could lead to poisoned intestines and a sour stomach with flatulence and if you were all done up in plaster of paris you couldn't even fart. He'd best have a natter with Corrigan again. . . .

vi

Kemp said, 'We'll be in Soviet waters quite soon now, von Hagen.'

'And then after Archangel, back to England. Will the same ships go back, all of them?'

'Yes. The Russians discharge them somewhat faster than British stevedores. We sail again as soon as the holds are cleared.'

Kemp changed the subject, becoming reminiscent, talking man to man about those Australian voyages of what now seemed centuries ago, another and better life. His orders had to be obeyed: he had to milk the German of as much information as possible before he was removed by the KGB. The only way Kemp could see to do that was to get von Hagen in a reminiscent frame of mind, to talk to him of the England he had known in peacetime, the England he had come to know so well and to like. Something might penetrate, the past might be made to act upon the present and the future. Bound for all he yet knew for imprisonment in Britain, von Hagen might well see no reason not to talk to Kemp so long as he accepted that eventually he was going to be made to talk to Military Intelligence. On the other hand, of course, he might believe that even under intensive interrogation he could retain his secrets for his Führer's sake – or more likely for his own anti-communism.

They talked of persons they had both known and von Hagen talked easily enough, and anecdotally. An old friendship was there still and never mind that they stood now on opposite sides of the fence of war. There was a good deal of do-you-remember, of this and that, of the people who on various voyages had shared the Captain's table. Kemp steered the conversation towards Britain – towards London, where von Hagen had lived in a service flat in Whitehall Court, with big windows looking out over the Embankment and the Thames busy with its strings of laden barges, an expensive and comfortable flat, rather on the large side for a bachelor which von Hagen was then and still remained.

'London,' von Hagen said with an inward smile. 'Yes, they were happy years and I miss them very much to be truthful. English women ... do you know, I found our German *Hausfrauen* heavy going after the English women! Yes, London was a very good place to be in those days.' He paused, eyes now holding a backward look. 'What's it like now, Commodore?'

Kemp shrugged. 'I avoid the place whenever possible. My wife likes to go up for shopping ... it's not my cup of tea. When I'm not being a seaman, I'm a countryman.' He, too, paused and rubbed reflectively at his chin. 'Of course it's terribly changed – it was bound to be. All the bombing. A good many landmarks gone and plenty of debris. And all the casualties ... but you'll know all that for yourself, von Hagen.'

'You hold me responsible.'

'Not you personally – of course not. Unless you were one of the London-domiciled German nationals who were able to be of assistance to your Intelligence services.'

Von Hagen shrugged. 'It would be foolish to deny that I was questioned. Because of friendships and old times I did my best not to be ... too helpful.'

'I'm glad to hear that. I'd like to think you might be helpful now.'

The German's eyes narrowed: he looked watchful, alert. 'Yes?'

'You have many secrets, obviously. Things that could save lives, perhaps.'

'British lives?'

'You enjoyed England once. You liked the people.'

'I think you are asking me to be a traitor, Commodore.'

Kemp gave an involuntary sigh. 'I suppose so. But you're going to be interrogated anyway. I thought perhaps ... if there was anything you'd care to tell me. . . .'

'You would then put in a good word for me?'

'Something like that,' Kemp said. He looked down at his knees: he couldn't face von Hagen, but he went on, 'As an old shipmate, I might be easier to talk to. That's what I thought, anyway.'

There was a smile on von Hagen's face now and he spoke gently. 'My dear chap, you would make a very rotten agent, and a very rotten interrogator!'

'Certainly I would. I have no ambition to be either!'

'No, I would never expect it of you. And you are also very transparent. Another word would be honest.'

'Thank you.'

'And you are out of your depth. You are trying to make me talk, you are trying to deceive and because of that transparent honesty you are failing very badly.'

'Von Hagen, I – '

'You are under orders from someone who does not know you. You are being made use of. Why? Can you tell me that, my old friend Captain Kemp?' When there was no answer from Kemp the German went on, 'There is another point. I am about to enter Russian waters – we have discussed that already, of course. You will hide me, and you will permit no search of the ship by the KGB. You assured me of that. But I see a very plain connection. Please be honest with me. I think our past friendship gives me the right to that.'

Kemp got to his feet and paced the cabin, backwards and forwards, his fists clenching and unclenching. He felt the movement of the ship beneath his feet, saw the sway of the curtain across the square port – now with the deadlight secured behind it to preserve the blackout – listened to the engine sounds and the noise of the forced-draught system, all the familiarities of the sea that had been his life, a clean life lived among predominantly decent men. He felt defiled now, as though he were throwing all the past away. But the country was at war, the country was on the brink of being starved out as a result of the sustained cruelty of the war at sea, of the shattering ferocity of the attacks on the convoys – and he had his orders. Could he have the temerity to set his own feelings, his own self-estimation, against the interest of ordinary people in Britain who were enduring privation and air attack, night after night in so many of the big cities? Which came first?

He turned, and faced von Hagen. He said, 'Very well, I shall be honest. I have orders from Whitehall to get you to talk to me.

You, a top Nazi agent, must know a great deal that would be helpful.'

'Obviously, yes. But the coming interrogation by your Military Intelligence ... or is it not to come?' The German's eyes were hard now. 'I think I see it all. But please put it into words yourself, my old friend.'

Kemp scarcely recognized the sound of his own voice when he said, each word coming out painfully, 'Unless you talk fully to me, I am to hand you over to the Russians on arrival in Archangel.'

NINE

For a while there had been a silence; Kemp wished the sea would open and suck him down. Von Hagen stared at him, his face working, all colour gone from it. He said after almost a minute, 'That would be to sign my death warrant. After torture, that is. The Kremlin has wanted me for a long time.'

'I'm more sorry than I can possibly say.'

'Yes, I believe you. You are a man in a torture of his own at this moment. But tell me something more: how would you know if I told you all I know, how would you know if I was speaking the truth in what I said? Would I not say anything in order to preserve myself against the Russians, against Comrade Stalin?'

'I suppose so.'

Von Hagen laughed. 'You suppose so! And I suppose you do suppose so. What then? What use my speaking?'

'I don't know, von Hagen. I'm simply under orders and I don't even know, precisely, from whom. Whoever it is, he must know his business.'

'Of course. And now shall I tell you what you don't yet know? Shall I tell you what all my experiences of governments and politicians and persons in Intelligence lead to me to assess for certain what will happen in Archangel?'

Kemp nodded.

'You have a British naval presence in Archangel.'

'Yes. A British Naval Liaison Officer.'

'His role is not merely liaison, my friend. He will have an Intelligence officer on his staff, though the fact will be disguised under the cover of some other appointment. This officer will interrogate me before I am handed over to the Russians. He will be an experienced interrogator who will find out, under threat of my hand-over, what you will not have found out. *You* are not being relied upon exclusively, you see.'

Kemp lifted his arms, let them drop again. Out of his depth was a gross understatement. He felt helpless, caught in a trap, a man being used, manipulated by unscrupulous persons. He said heavily, 'I suppose you could be right.'

'I'm certain I am. You may ask, why bother to interrogate me at all when, if I am *not* handed over to the Russians as will be promised in return for my co-operation, I can be brought after all to Britain in the homeward convoy? There is a very simple answer to that . . . isn't there?'

Kemp nodded. There was no need to put it into words: his own orders had already stipulated the hand-over come what may, the broken promise, the cynical disregard of what would happen to von Hagen. And von Hagen knew it all. The German was going on again. 'You yourself told me, you would not permit a search of your ship. But they will know already that I am aboard. You realize this?'

Kemp said, 'That's only supposition.'

'Oh, no! I know my value to the Russians, and it is plain to me now that a deal has been arranged between Whitehall and the Kremlin. You'll not have a chance to hide me away.'

'I shall do my best,' Kemp said simply.

Von Hagen smiled with a touch of sadness, almost of a kind of compassion for a man in torment. 'You will do your best . . . if I talk to you now?'

'Yes,' Kemp answered. 'My best . . . so help me God.'

Von Hagen closed his eyes and held his hands up, parson fashion, the finger-tips together, in front of his face. He could have been in prayer, Kemp thought. There was a lengthy silence in the cabin: a clock ticked loudly from the bulkhead beside the square port, and Kemp could hear the footfalls of the officer of the watch above his head, hear the occasional clatter and rasp of the telemotor steering gear as the quartermaster moved the wheel to keep the *Hardraw Falls* on course. Then at last von Hagen spoke.

He said, 'For me, the war is over – that is what they tell prisoners of war, isn't it? – whichever side takes me I am finished for Germany, and I am split between Britain and Germany. You will believe me, I hope, when I say that I've never worked against the British as such. My experience has been in Norway, against the Resistance. Except when, as I've said, I was obliged to answer certain obvious questions about London and so on . . . I never went further than that.'

'I believe that,' Kemp said, but von Hagen appeared not to listen.

'Now I shall tell you two things, and two things only. I shall tell you out of friendship, because I wish no harm to come to you personally. One of these things is uncertain, the other is very certain.'

Kemp said, 'Go on, von Hagen.'

'The certain one first: there is to be a heavy attack on your convoy after it has passed the North Cape into the Barents Sea, once it is off the Kola Inlet outside Murmansk. I – '

'You knew this, knew it when you came aboard?'

Von Hagen smiled. 'Obviously! I have no concealed radio receiver – '

'But you were surprised to find the convoy was outward bound for Russia. Surprised and – worried.'

Von Hagen nodded. 'Yes. Because I could not believe I was to be taken to Russia. Up to that time, I had made the assumption your convoy was bound for the United Kingdom. When I was told differently, you see – then I knew, that it is *your* convoy that is to be attacked.' He leaned forward, eyes on Kemp's face. 'A battle fleet is lying off to the south of Spitzbergen – I can give you its composition. There are three heavy cruisers and a pocket battleship, with destroyer escorts, and more forces will leave ports in north Norway to cut off any retreat round the North Cape. Also there will be air support from the Norwegian airfields. Those are the certainties.'

'And the uncertainties?'

Von Hagen said, 'It is possible that by now it is known to our High Command that I have been taken. If they wish to get me back – '

'They'll hold off the *Hardraw Falls*? No – stupid of me! They won't know which ship you're in. Or will they, von Hagen?'

'It's possible. There was the U-boat attack, and the U-boat will have reported by w/T whilst surfaced.' It had; Kemp's leading telegraphist had reported a brief transmission. 'Two and two may be put together in Berlin – a ship detached from the convoy, off the Norwegian coast, much closer in than is normal. If, as I said, they know I've been taken – well, the rest is a simple deduction, I think.'

'Perhaps. Is there anything else you want to say?'

Von Hagen shook his head. 'I shall say no more. I shall not burden you, Captain Kemp. I am convinced I am right about your naval staff in Archangel. Let the questioning rest with them. They are not my friends.'

The German got to his feet and held out his hand. With no hesitation, Kemp took it in a firm grip. Then he called for Cutler to remove the prisoner.

ii

Kemp called a conference in his cabin: Captain Theakston and Cutler were present together with the naval telegraphist on the Commodore's staff, Leading Telegraphist Rose.

Kemp told them the apparent facts. He went on, 'The *Admiral Scheer*, with *Regensburg*, *Göttingen* and *Koblenz*. Pretty lethal! The convoy won't stand a chance, except perhaps if the order to scatter is given. The Rear-Admiral may decide to do just that, and then put himself and the escort between the convoy and the attack force. If he has the time. And that's up to me, I fancy.' He took a deep breath. 'I propose to break wireless silence and inform both the escort and the Admiralty.'

Cutler said, 'The Nazis'll pick up the transmission, sir.'

'Yes, they will. So?'

'So they'll move in faster. Before the British Admiralty can redeploy from – '

'That won't matter. According to von Hagen, the attack's imminent in any case. Speed's the watchword now, Cutler, no time even to cypher up a signal – '

'Plain language, sir? Why, that's against – '

'Never mind what it's against, Cutler. Rose?'

'Sir?'

'Make in plain language, from Commodore to Rear-Admiral Commanding the escort repeated Admiralty: "PQ convoy expected to come under heavy attack from Spitzbergen area at any time." Prefix Most Immediate.'

'Aye, aye, sir.' Rose, who had taken down the signal as Kemp had been speaking, left the cabin for the wireless office. Kemp turned to Theakston.

He said, 'As for us, Captain, we're likely to be something of a marked ship – because of von Hagen. We've no idea how much the Nazis know. If they're aware of the facts they may not attack to sink. But they'll try to board and hook off von Hagen.'

'Aye, and *then* sink us,' Theakston said dourly.

iii

Kemp had all officers and senior hands off watch mustered in the saloon. He believed that secrecy would not at this stage be compromised by his taking the ship's crew into his confidence, at any rate so far as possible ; he said nothing of what was intended to happen to the prisoner if he was got as far as Archangel ; but afterwards von Hagen got the blame from the crew. Chief Steward Buckle put it succinctly.

'Best thing if the bugger was dumped overboard.'

'Induced suicide ?' Napper asked sarcastically.

'Why not ? Best way out for him, never mind us ! Bugger'll get the chop anyway, back in UK.'

'Commodore couldn't wear that,' Napper said with a sniff. 'Get himself court martialled, wouldn't he, for neglect o' duty. Come to that – so would I. PO in charge o' escort. . . .'

'And you wouldn't risk *that*, not even for the sake of the ship and all of us.'

Napper said crossly, 'O' course I bloody wouldn't.' He broke off the conversation and went aft with his curious waddling gait : in spite of the lanolin, he was no better. But measurements taken as accurately and carefully as possible had indicated no increase in the swelling. With luck there would be a subsidence by the time he got home again. If ever he did. He didn't fancy taking on what had sounded like the entire German surface fleet, even less so when he couldn't walk straight. But walk straight or walk in a twist, he knew his duty : he went conscientiously on a tour of the close-range weapons, all round the ship in the freezing, perishing cold, slithering on the iced-up decks – you never could get a decent grip with seaboots – feeling round the moving parts of the guns to make sure the ice hadn't got at them, his skin almost sticking to the metal even through his woollen gloves. Peashooters, that was what they were, but they just might stop the jerries boarding. . . .

'Able Seaman Grove – '

'Yes, PO?'

'Wipe that grin orf your face, double quick.'

'Sorry, PO.'

'You'll be fuckin' sorrier if I sees it again.'

Grove kept a straight face until Napper had turned his back and moved on. Napper, in his view, had used an inappropriate adjective for a man in his condition. Grove found himself wondering how crabs did it.

iv

Still ahead of the *Hardraw Falls* Rear-Admiral Fellowes, muffled to the ears on the flagship's bridge, tapped the signal form that had been brought to him at the double. 'Indiscreet – very. Plain language . . . the German Naval Staff – bound to reinforce!'

'It'll make the Admiralty pull its finger out,' the Flag Captain said. He believed Kemp to have been right: out of visual touch with the Flag – what else could he have done? Encyphering would have wasted many vital minutes, decyphering would have wasted more. He repeated his remark about the Admiralty sending in heavy ships.

'Not as fast as the Germans,' Fellowes said.

That was true: if the report from the *Hardraw Falls* was accurate, the German units were very much nearer than any available British ships.

The Flag Captain asked, 'Do you intend to scatter, sir?'

'I don't know. That's pretty extreme.' The Rear-Admiral looked around at the convoy and the shepherding escorts, shadows in the night, the night that from now on would last almost round the clock as they came into the northernmost waters of the convoy route, into the land of the midnight sun in summer, the region where in winter the *aurora borealis* was at its most spectacular, the streaming Northern Lights spreading their colours vividly across the dark sky. The convoy would stand out beautifully beneath those great streaks of light, helpless targets for the German guns. Fellowes did a swift calculation in his head of what the Germans would produce: total gun-power something in the order of six 11-inch plus twenty-four 8-inch, plus secondary armament and anti-aircraft batteries, plus the torpedotubes of the destroyer escort that would be in company with the fleet. Quite a lot, and the convoy covered a lot of water.

Fellowes made up his mind. 'I'm not going to scatter. We're not all that far off Murmansk – and bugger Archangel in the circumstances.' He turned aside and called to the chief yeoman of signals.

'Chief Yeoman . . . make to Captain(D), "You are to detach one destroyer with the A/S corvettes to stand by convoy into Murmansk repeat Murmansk. Heavy German force expected to make contact from Spitzbergen." Message ends. Make to the Vice-Commodore, "convoy will detach to Murmansk repeat Murmansk to avoid expected enemy attack. Executive will follow shortly."' Fellowes paused. 'One more, Chief Yeoman.'

'Aye, aye, sir.'

'To *Neath* . . . and Captain(D) again : "Remaining ships will alter north-eastwards to engage the enemy."'

v

In the Operations Room in the Admiralty bunker beneath Horse Guards Parade there was a high degree of consternation when the message from Commodore Kemp came in. Nothing had been known of any enemy concentration in the waters off Spitzbergen. Heads were due to roll if Kemp's information was correct. In the meantime it had to be accepted that it was.

'We know he picked up von Hagen,' the Duty Captain said. A signal to that effect had been reported from the submarine. His face showing strain, the Duty Captain took up a red telephone and dialled a single digit. The call was answered almost immediately and the Captain made his report. He listened thereafter, saying little. When he put down the phone he got to his feet and went across to the large map that covered most of one wall, with

WRNS officers and ratings standing by with pointers to shift the cardboard silhouettes of the warships in home waters. To his deputy he said, 'Most Immediate to C-in-C Home Fleet from Chief of Naval Staff. "You are to proceed forthwith to give cover to PQ convoy off Kola Inlet and to engage heavy German force believed moving south from Spitzbergen."'

He looked again at the wall map: the 2nd Battle Squadron of the Home Fleet lay currently in Scapa Flow, a depleted force consisting of *Rodney* and the old, slow *Ramillies*; *Rodney* carrying nine 16-inch guns, *Ramillies* eight 15-inch and capable of only twenty-one knots at full stretch, a speed she couldn't hope to maintain for long if, in fact, she could make it at all. Both battleships were only just in from an Atlantic convoy escort, sea worn and with stores to replenish. The stores would have to wait. In Rosyth, also within the command of C-in-C Home Fleet, was the battle-cruiser *Renown* together with the aircraft-carrier *Victorious*. All these heavy units were accompanied by their destroyer escorts; and would leave in company with the 18th Cruiser Squadron consisting of *Sheffield*, *Edinburgh*, *Belfast* and *Newcastle*.

vi

From the bridge of the *Hardraw Falls* Kemp watched, as had Rear-Admiral Fellowes, the play of the Northern Lights as they lit the sky ahead. He felt a sudden shiver of apprehension: there was something about that amazing illumination, something primeval and awe-inspiring.

'"Fearful lights that never beckon, save when kings and heroes die" ... some poet or other wrote that, Cutler.'

'I wouldn't have thought you read poetry, sir?'

Kemp laughed. 'Think it's pansy, do you?'

'Well, sir, no, not quite that.'

'Never mind, anyway. It just came to mind.'

'Because men are going to die?'

'We won't dwell on that, Cutler.'

'No, sir.'

'We'll concentrate on a sharp lookout.'

'Not much we can do if we sight anything, sir.'

'Bugger all,' Kemp said with another laugh. 'Except bugger off!'

Cutler made no response to that: Kemp had already made his intentions known to all hands. They were well round the North Cape by this time and the only viable direction in which to bugger off would be for a Russian port, and the orders were still for Archangel even though Murmansk was handier. The *Hardraw Falls* had no speed to match that of the heavy Nazi units and Cutler believed they were – or would be if sighted – steaming towards oblivion. He felt somehow detached about the prospect: he'd always wanted to go to sea and he'd wanted action, and if in the course of that action he bought it, well, that would be just too bad. No use moaning, and no use trying to avoid the inevitable either. He hoped for just one thing: not yet tested in full action, he hoped he could stand up to it and not let the USA down by showing fear. If he did, there would be those – not many it was true – who wouldn't hesitate to let him know they knew: that Napper for one. Napper didn't like Yanks ... Cutler believed he didn't like action either. There was an expression in the British Navy and it could well be applied to Petty Officer Napper: all wind and piss like the barber's cat.

And what was it like back in Texas tonight?

The rolling hills, the wide-open spaces, the big ranches far from the sea, the ice and the war in Europe ... Tex Cutler's old man ran a ranch, not one of the biggest, but big enough by British standards, and one day Cutler, along with his two brothers, would inherit it. One day – if he lived to see it; he rather hoped he wouldn't give his father the pain of outliving a son, but even with that thought in mind he had no regrets for what might be about to happen. If he had to die, he couldn't die in better company than that of Kemp and Theakston ... he glanced across at Theakston now, standing in the port bridge wing, head sunk beneath the hood of his duffel coat, his body motionless as if frozen to the guardrail, his steaming breath visible in opaque clouds in the glow of the Northern Lights. Theakston and Kemp – they were both like rocks of dependability, each with his own worries probably, personal family anxieties that would not intrude on the duty of either of them.

The night so far was in fact peaceful: but not for much longer, probably. And the shatter came even as Cutler had the thought:

a blue-shaded lamp winked from the bridge of the destroyer escort and Leading Signalman Corrigan reported to the Commodore.

'Surface contact, sir, bearing green four five, distant twelve miles.'

TEN

Tension had mounted throughout the ship: Sub-Lieutenant Cutler was far from being the only one aboard who saw oblivion staring the *Hardraw Falls* in the face. Below in the engine-room Chief Engineer Sparrow stood grim-faced on the starting platform, wondering, amidst his thoughts about being the target for an unknown number of heavy German gun batteries, just how long his engines were going to stand the strain of being pushed to their maximum and beyond. They were not in their first flush of youth by any means, any more than he was himself, and they'd been pushed for too long already in the Commodore's attempts to catch up with the convoy. Before long, something was likely to give. When the bridge passed down the word that there had been a surface contact, Sparrow was in no doubt what Theakston wanted: more speed.

'Not possible,' he said. 'Engines are rattling to pieces as it is.'

'Do your best, Chief,' Theakston said.

Do your best, Sparrow thought, it's the equivalent of the army's 'carry on, sergeant'. He passed the word, just for form's sake, to the second engineer, who shook his head in disbelief that the bridge could expect miracles.

'What's the Old Man think we are, eh?'

Sparrow disregarded the rhetorical question. He said, 'If this is the Jerry heavies, then I reckon they must have missed the main convoy.'

'And found us. If so, it's curtains.' Weller gave the chief one of his calculating looks. The strain of war – of being about to be blown sky-high – would likely tell. Sparrow, seeing that look, knew what it meant. But it was somewhat on the late side now, he reckoned. They'd go aloft to the pearly gates still in the relationship of chief and second engineer. And if they were to make that final trip, then Sparrow wished they would get on with it. The tension engendered by waiting for the big bang and the clouds of boiling steam was acting upon him like they said about a drowning man, all his past life flashing like a cinema screen before his eyes, some good, some bad. Home and the wife and kids, ports all over the world, runs ashore to get boozed up with his friends and then find a woman, white, yellow or black; unfaithfulness had never mattered much then but it did now. He should have been more contained and it was, he thought regretfully, too late now to put in a good word for himself, a sort of apology.

Chief Steward Buckle was feeling much the same: so far in this war he had never been so close to the enemy as to fear the worst, had never been entirely alone on the waters as the *Hardraw Falls* now was, never been the main – the only – target for a strong force who probably believed they were about to make contact with the whole convoy and its escort and would blast away with everything they had the moment the *Hardraw Falls* was sighted. Not much hope now of making a small fortune out of caviar and possibly just as well really since it would have been another shady fiddle to be chalked up against him, and God knew – and might shortly tell – how many fiddles he'd worked in the past, regarding them as chief steward's perks. He wasn't alone, of course: he had once heard a shipmaster say that you could always tell which was the chief steward when the officers and crew went ashore in a home port, out of uniform, because the chief steward would be the only one with a car.

ii

So far there had been no gunfire and there had been no identification either: their destroyer escort had made no further reports, no doubt in the interest of remaining anonymous for as long as possible, though it could be assumed the ship they had picked up on the radar would have picked them up at the same time.

'Playing possum,' Cutler said.

'It seems to be the case, but why, for God's sake?' Kemp stared ahead: the sea was far from fully dark beneath the patterns of light but he could pick up no ship. Whoever it was could not be on a closing course. Was it remaining, as it were, parallel, keeping just outside range, or was it steaming away? For the moment there was uncertainty in the air. Kemp said, 'It could be an arse-end Charlie from the convoy, I suppose.'

After another five minutes *Portree* was seen to be calling up again. Corrigan reported, 'Contact moving north-west now lost, sir.'

'Thank you, Corrigan. Keep the guns' crews closed up, Cutler.' Kemp glanced at Theakston standing by his side. 'This is a mystery, Captain. There's a possible solution ... it could be the Rear-Admiral doing what I thought he might – moving to put himself between the convoy and the German units. *Portree* could have got an echo off one on the extended screen.'

'Sounds likely,' Theakston said.

Kemp turned away and paced the bridge, back into the interminable business of awaiting developments, of trying to foresee the unforeseeable, of attempting to get into other men's minds and act ahead of them. *Would* one of the objectives of the German warships be to get von Hagen back? There was no absolute certainty on that score, and in fact the German naval command would scarcely commit so many heavy ships to that purpose, surely? An all-out attack on the convoy must be presumed to be the first priority. If that was so, should he, Kemp, be in duty bound to stand clear and not force the speed in his attempt to catch up? The *Hardraw Falls* would add nothing to the defence of the convoy, that was for sure. Just another target – and he had that valuable cargo.

Valuable to whom? The answer to that was principally the Russians, and Kemp was determined to do what he could to honour his promise to von Hagen, the promise that he would do his best for him. Even so, he couldn't go against his orders. Von Hagen, it seemed, was an important element in the current game of chess being played between two governments. . . .

Kemp went into the chartroom and looked at the chart spread open on the wide mahogany table with pointers, set squares and parallel rulers laid neatly on top of it. The course for Archangel was marked in pencil from the last fix: near enough six hundred miles to go, but only three hundred and seventy to the entry to the White Sea and safety from German surface attack if not a daring *Luftwaffe* – around thirty hours' steaming. Murmansk lay nearer, some two hundred miles distant – the *Hardraw Falls* could make the port inside some sixteen hours.

But the orders were still for Archangel. No doubt the scene had been set there, all preparations made for an act of betrayal. Or could you ever be said to betray the enemy? Perhaps not.

Kemp left the chartroom, went back into the cold of the open bridge. The wind was keener than ever, and everywhere on deck the ice had tightened its grip. There was no evidence of any other ship. Not yet; but the German force would presumably be sweeping south to engage.

iii

Petty Officer Napper had gone below to the heads and when he emerged he all but bumped into the chief steward. Buckle said, 'Just the man.'

'Eh?'

'Got something for you, if you've got the time.'

'Should be on deck. What is it?'

'Book on medical matters.'

'*Medical?* Yes, I got the time.'

Napper went with Buckle to the latter's office. Buckle produced a volume: *The Ship Captain's Medical Guide.* 'Skipper sent down for it after you got – what you got. Couldn't bloody find it, not then. But it's turned up.'

'Thanks a lot,' Napper said eagerly. The book should prove a mine of information.

'Page 176, testicles,' Buckle said.

Napper flipped through the pages and found the relevant entry and his eyes widened as he read and an expression of indignation spread across his face. Bloody quacks! The doc in the *Portree* – ought to be struck off. The treatment stared Napper in the face: a man with bruised bollocks should be given bed rest and the testicles supported with a pillow. There was even a picture of it, the part all swollen up like a melon, resting on the prescribed pillow.

He should have been put on the sick list, off all duties. As it was, he hadn't even been put on light duty, had just had to carry on. Agitatedly, Napper sucked at a hollow tooth, his face all creased up. It wasn't right, but not much use going to the bridge to complain, not just now anyway, not with the enemy around. Napper, just come from the heads, had carried out a further examination of the affected part. It wasn't any better but it wasn't any worse either, he had to admit that to himself, pillow or no pillow. He went back on deck, still moving awkwardly, and made his way to the bridge for another check on the close-range weapons, making sure the gunners had kept them ice free: in current temperatures they could ice up in seconds, almost. He exaggerated his crab-like gait when he saw the Commodore's eye on him: propaganda wasn't the province of Dr Goebbels alone.

'Petty Officer Napper. . . .'

'Yessir?'

'Contact's been lost for now. But keep the guns at full readiness and the hands alert.'

'Aye, aye, sir.' The corners of Napper's mouth turned down; Kemp hadn't noticed a bloody thing! Napper saw Leading Signalman Corrigan standing by with his Aldis lamp. Talk about useless . . . surely to God even a makee-learn quack ought to know about pillows! It really made a man sick, the way nobody cared. As soon as he got the opportunity he would write a long letter home, unburdening himself on the wife. He always felt better after a good moan.

iv

'Gunfire,' Kemp said, and brought up his binoculars to cover the port quarter. There had been a heavy rumble: big guns in action. Kemp said, 'Only one answer, Cutler.'

'The escort, sir? The main convoy escort?'

Kemp nodded briefly. 'We can't be far off the convoy. The escort's engaging the heavy German ships. Giving the convoy a chance . . . like Kennedy in the *Rawalpindi*, only with more hope of success.'

'Takes guts,' Cutler said.

'It's what they're there for.'

'Sure, but that doesn't – '

'I don't deny the guts, Cutler.'

Kemp's tone had been sharp; the American glanced up at the Commodore's set face and made a diagnosis: Kemp was feeling he wasn't doing what he himself was there for, which was taking charge of the merchant ships in convoy, acting as the rallying point. It wasn't his fault but he was blaming himself. Cutler had an idea Kemp ought to turn away, turn right away around the North Cape and head for Iceland or home waters in order to preserve von Hagen from the Nazis. He could always be negotiated as between the British and the Russians at a more propitious time, a case perhaps of better late than never.

Taking a chance even though he knew what the answer would be, Cutler put the point to the Commodore. Kemp reacted badly.

'I'll do no such thing, Cutler. Bugger von Hagen – my job's to overtake the convoy and get 'em into Archangel! If we're right about the escort's movements, if they've detached to take the German fire, the merchant ships are on their own now.'

'I guess so, sir,' Cutler said, but wondered what difference it would make whether or not the *Hardraw Falls* caught up. Kemp seemed to sense what was in his assistant's mind and said something about the absolute necessity for leadership, of one man to make the decisions and give the orders. Meanwhile the heavy rumbles were continuing, a massive volume of sound that went on and on, menacing, a harbinger of what might be about to come to the *Hardraw Falls*. In every part of the ship men were listening, speculating, wondering what their own chances might be. One shell, if it took the ship anywhere near the holds, would finish off every man aboard as the HE went up in a shattering blast. They felt on the very verge of hell: any man who was blasted overboard instead of being killed outright would freeze within a minute. In the engine-room Sparrow was now straining everything in the interest of maximum speed, just hoping that nothing would give. The gunfire was reverberating even through the engine spaces: it couldn't be all that far off. The moment the Nazis had them in their sights, they would have had it. Sparrow hoped Kemp and Theakston knew what they were doing: he knew all about the German, von Hagen, or anyway as much as the galley wireless had revealed, which Sparrow realized was not likely to be the full story and doubtless inaccurate at that. But the Nazi agent must obviously be of value to the British war effort or they wouldn't have diverted the *Hardraw Falls* to pick him up . . . and come to that, why hadn't that submarine simply carried him on to a UK port? There was something extra in the air and it was to do with von Hagen.

On deck Petty Officer Napper was having similar thoughts, vengefully: if only they could ditch von Hagen, who was acting the perishing Jonah in Napper's view. If it hadn't been for him, they would have been with the convoy; and there was a degree of safety in numbers. At the very least they would have been just one target among many, while as it was they would stand out like a curate in a nudist colony. Napper reckoned that any minute now all the gun-power of the German fleet was going to be deployed against him.

'What d'you reckon, eh?'

Napper whirled about, startled. The bosun had crept up on him unawares. Napper told him what he reckoned. 'Big stuff, not a hope.'

'I don't know so much. If they know that Nazi's aboard us, I don't reckon they'll sink us.'

'Not right off, no – maybe. On the other hand, they might. Just to make bloody certain the Nazi don't give anything away. That's the important thing, to them. Stands to reason, does that.'

'If anything does,' Tawney agreed.

Napper cocked an eye. 'Meaning?'

'Proper shower, they are not much *reason* about them. The Nazis.'

'Efficient, though. Not so many bloody cock-ups as the buggers in Whitehall – or the barrack stanchions sitting on their arses in Pompey.' Napper was still aggrieved, more so than ever in fact, about his draft chit to sea. A former barrack stanchion himself, he was, like the man who suddenly finds religion, completely anti in his views of his erstwhile mates.

v

'Ship, sir, bearing red one eight five. Can't identify yet, sir.'

'Right.' Kemp's binoculars came up on the bearing. All he found was a blur. 'See anything, Cutler?'

'Just an outline, sir, distant.'

A moment later the escorting destroyer was seen to be altering course towards the bearing, heeling over sharply and increasing speed. '*Portree*'s picked it up,' Cutler said.

Kemp nodded. He was about to advise Theakston to turn away and increase the distance when there was a brilliant orange flash from the unidentified vessel and seconds later a rush of air across the bridge indicated the effectiveness of what was presumably German gunfire. Hard on the heels of the firing, a signal lamp was seen to be flashing from the unknown warship.

ELEVEN

'Well?' Kemp was impatient, feeling a surge of blood through his body: he had already made a good guess at what the signal would be.

Corrigan said, 'He's calling *Portree*, sir – '

'Can you read it?'

'Yes, sir.' Corrigan paused. '*Portree*'s being told to heave to.' There was another pause. 'Colonel von Hagen's to be made available, sir.'

'Or we'll be blown out of the water, I suppose!'

'Sort of, sir.' Corrigan added, 'He's giving us five minutes, sir.'

'I see. For now, we ignore the signal.' Kemp brought up his binoculars again: now he could see the outline of the German, a heavy cruiser, no doubt the *Regensburg*, the *Göttingen* or the *Koblenz*. She was coming in fast, but as Kemp watched she slowed. So far there had been no reaction from the *Portree* but a moment later the destroyer began calling the Commodore.

'Asking for orders, sir,' Corrigan reported.

'Make: "Hold off for the time being and maintain speed."' Kemp paced the bridge, watched by Cutler and Captain Theakston. Corrigan, the signal made, waited for further orders. Kemp, he knew, was in a massive dilemma: you didn't surrender without a fight. But there was the German agent, and in that respect the Commodore would obviously have certain orders, though Corrigan didn't know what they might be. They might not, in fact, cover a situation such as this.

And Kemp knew they did not. He had to make his own decision for good or ill. And he had to make it fast, though he doubted if the German cruiser would open fire at the end of the five minutes. They wouldn't want to blast von Hagen out of existence. He would keep them hanging on, uncertain of the British reaction. Kemp turned in his pacing to find himself confronted by the ship's master. Theakston's face was set into formidable lines and he began without preamble.

'I don't know what you propose doing, Commodore, but I know what I intend to do.'

'And that is?'

'Not to be buggered about by any Nazi agent. I'm not concerned what happens to him – '

'Perhaps not, Captain, but I have to be. He has to be got into Archangel.'

'Aye! That's the orders. I have my ship to consider. My ship, my crew, and my cargo. It's a vital cargo. The German has the whip hand, Commodore Kemp. We have to let von Hagen go across – '

'We'll keep them on a string, Captain.' Kemp looked at the luminous dial of his wrist-watch. Three minutes had now passed. The next two minutes seemed to fly away, while the *Hardraw Falls* moved on and Kemp wrestled with his decision. Obviously there could be no hope of engaging the German successfully; *Portree* carried nothing heavier then 4.7-inch guns. But Kemp was in no doubt that Whitehall considered von Hagen of more importance to the conduct of the war than the men or cargo aboard the *Hardraw Falls*. Once again he tried to see into distant, political minds, the brains of the men responsible for the overall strategy. Would it be a better thing, in their view, that von Hagen should die with the rest rather than be returned to Germany?

The answer was a clear yes. The *Hardraw Falls* had to be the sacrifice.

Kemp was about to give his decision when the German began calling again, this time addressing the *Hardraw Falls* direct. Corrigan read off the signal: 'From the German, sir, who's still not giving her signal letters. "You have a passenger who is at once to be put aboard me. You will heave-to". Message ends, sir.'

'Message as before, more or less.'

'Yes, sir.'

Kemp caught Theakston's eye. Theakston said firmly. 'We

must do as he asks. I said before, I don't give nowt for a dirty Nazi spy. I'll not hazard my ship for that.'

'I shall not part with von Hagen, Captain.'

Theakston blew out a long breath of exasperation. 'See sense! Your personal problem would be solved – no broken promise, no dirt done – '

'I can't allow that to weigh. You know that as well as I do. And there's another point, Captain. The moment von Hagen's put aboard the German, we'll be sunk by gunfire. They'll never let your cargo go free.'

Theakston said, 'That need not happen. Von Hagen is your friend, and he ranks high in Germany. He'll not let that happen. You'll have saved him from the Russians, from the KGB.'

'I'm sorry, Captain. I have my orders.'

'And I have my ship,' Theakston said doggedly. That is my responsibility, Commodore Kemp. I, too, am under orders – to reach Archangel with my cargo. *I* command the ship, you don't. In effect you're no more than a passenger.' All Theakston's Yorkshire obstinacy had surfaced now, and he stood four-square on his own bridge. 'If necessary I have the authority to place *passengers* in restraint – as you had in the liners.'

Theakston turned away and went into the wheelhouse. Kemp saw him go to the engine-room telegraph and haul the lever over to stop. He was, strictly, within his rights; and Kemp could appreciate his point of view, would probably in Theakston's place have taken up a similar position. British seamen were at immediate risk now. But von Hagen was a catch; his knowledge, if he could be made to talk – even to the Russians – could possibly shorten the war. Kemp turned away and went down the ladder to his cabin, where he unlocked the safe. When he returned to the bridge he had his revolver in his hand.

ii

The Home Fleet in Scapa and the Firth of Forth had been at immediate notice for steam and no time had been lost in proceeding to sea in accordance with the orders from the Admiralty, on course for the vicinity of the North Cape with paravanes streamed from the bows against possible mines. The battle squadron pushed through wind-blown waters at its best speed, covered by the cruisers and the extended destroyer escort. The distance would be around 1350 miles: some fifty-eight hours' steaming. The estimation was that although they would have no hope of making their arrival in time to save the PQ convoy, they would catch the heavy German units either to the north as they retreated towards Spitzbergen or to the south as they tried to escape back to their bases in occupied Norway – there was no knowing yet what the German choice would be. The Vice-Admiral commanding the battle squadron believed that it would be the latter; the Germans, their work done on the convoy, would wish to scuttle south for shelter as fast as possible. For now the Fleet steamed in two watches, half the armament manned for action, and full alertness throughout on the part of the watchkeepers on the bridges and at the lookout positions as the Fleet came north to leave Iceland on the port quarter, moving into the bitter cold and the great freeze that had gripped the convoy, the gunners' mates, the armourers and the electrical artificers constantly checking for ice in the working parts of the big gun-batteries and secondary armament.

In the Admiralty's Operations Room the counters were moved north, following the dead-reckoning estimation of the Fleet's advance. The position of the PQ convoy and its escort had now, also by dead reckoning, been moved along past the North Cape towards Archangel. The atmosphere was tense, made worse by the presence of the Prime Minister, always an unpredictable and uncomfortable person, his face pugnacious now behind the immense cigar. Beside him was the First Sea Lord, Chief of the Naval Staff.

The cigar was removed and waved in the air.

'What are the chances, First Sea Lord?'

'Slim, sir – of being of any assistance to the convoy. A question of speed. If only we had more of the KG5 class – '

'Yes. I did my best before war came, as I warned everyone it would.' The Prime Minister's face became for a moment cherubic. 'I prodded and prodded and I confess I much enjoyed the discomfiture and indeed the *exasperation* of the prodded, the wretched fellows who put votes before country. I found that Tories could be most remarkably dense, unable to see a day ahead, much less the more distant future. Yes, had they listened, we would have had enough warships.' The cigar was once again thrust back between the full lips. 'The *jackal* of Germany would never have dared to risk a fight with us in the first place if we'd rearmed in time.' For a few moments Churchill glowered towards the wall map, watching the trim figures of the Wrens with their pointers. 'That *Narzi* agent . . . which ship was he transferred to?'

'The *Hardraw Falls*, Prime Minister, an ammunition ship.'

'Ah yes. The Commodore's ship. Commodore Kemp – am I not right?'

'Yes, Prime Minister . . . if you remember, it was because he had known von Hagen that – '

'Yes, yes, I don't need reminding of everything, thank you, Admiral, I'm not in my dotage yet. Now then: what do you suppose Commodore Kemp will do if the convoy encounters the Germans? As to the Narzi agent, I mean.'

'Simply carry on, Prime Minister. What else would he do?'

'That's what I asked you.' The Prime Minister shifted irritably in his chair. 'We must not neglect the possibility that the Narzis know where von Hagen is. In that case – '

'Unlikely, sir.'

'So are many things, but the unlikelihood didn't stop them happening. I hope Commodore Kemp can be relied upon! The safe delivery of von Hagen in Archangel is paramount . . . at this stage of the war we dare not upset that arch villain Comrade Stalin, much as I would enjoy so doing.' Mr Churchill removed his cigar and aimed it like a gun at the Chief of Staff. 'That last remark goes no farther than yourself, First Sea lord.'

'Of course not, Prime Minister.'

iii

Returning to the bridge, Kemp had seen that the destroyer escort had slowed as the way came off the *Hardraw Falls* and was standing off to port, keeping herself between the Commodore's ship and the enemy cruiser. Kemp went into the wheelhouse, where the master was standing beside the engine-room telegraph.

Hearing Kemp's entry, Theakston swung round. He saw Kemp's revolver.

'What's the idea?' he asked.

'A few pot shots of my own,' Kemp answered: he had read in Theakston's face that the master fancied he was about to take over the ship himself by force of arms. The idea had flitted through Kemp's mind but only as an expression of his frustration at Theakston's obstinacy, something he would have liked to do had it been practicable, which it would not. But the fact of Theakston having taken the way off his ship had given Kemp an idea and for what it might be worth he intended to put it into effect. He said, 'The German's stopping too. Any moment now, he'll be lowering a seaboat.'

As he spoke, a searchlight came on aboard the German cruiser and its beam steadied blindingly on the bridge of the *Hardraw Falls* before moving aft. When his vision had been restored Kemp saw in the backglow of the beam that a boat was already being lowered to the cruiser's waterline ready for slipping, a boat with armed seamen aboard.

Theakston asked, 'What do you intend doing?'

'I intend to to take full advantage of a cruiser that's lying stopped – that's all!'

'What the heck – ' Theakston was looking puzzled.

Kemp said, 'That boatload's going to get a reception they're not expecting.' He raised his voice through the wheelhouse door to the open bridge. 'Corrigan!'

'Yes, sir.' Corrigan came across, the lead of his Aldis trailing behind him.

'Call up *Portree*. Tell 'em, do as I do.'

'"Do as I do", sir?'

'Yes. I doubt if that'll convey anything much to the German. And add, "fish".'

Corrigan stared. '"Fish", sir? Just that?'

'Yes. Torpedoes, man, torpedoes!'

Corrigan appeared to tick over. 'Aye, aye, sir,' he said, and doubled away to the bridge wing. Soon after the signal had been made Kemp saw the destroyer using her engines to come up more on the German's beam: *Portree*'s captain had, it seemed, cottoned on nicely. Kemp turned once more to Theakston. He would, he said, open fire on the seaboat as soon as it was within range. To Petty Officer Napper, who had come to the bridge for instructions, he said his own revolver shot was to be considered the order for all the close-range weapons to open, and they would be joined by the guns aboard *Portree*.

'Touch and go, sir,' Napper said, standing bandy-legged like a jockey. There was a stirring in his stomach : if you looked on the bright side, which in fact Napper never did, action was a good cure for constipation. But at the moment all he felt was fear. They could never bring it off, not within range of the Jerry's heavy batteries, 8-inch probably, they'd just go up like a firework, and nowhere safe to hide from it. Kemp, he reckoned, must have gone clean round the bend, like Harpic. . . .

Shaking like a jelly, Napper left the bridge and went round the gun positions, passing the orders in a voice he scarcely recognized as his own. Able Seaman Grove also seemed to find the tone a shade different, sort of high and squeaky like a eunuch, and remarked upon it, cheekily.

'Something not dropped, PO?' Grove, like Napper, believed they'd had it now and giving lip to a petty officer didn't seem dangerous any more. 'Or just dropped off, p'raps.'

'Just shut it, Grove.' Napper went away, all his spirit gone, not bothering to talk about charges of impertinence. He was wondering if he would actually feel anything in the split second during which life might linger after the explosion of the thousands of tons of HE below the hatches fore and aft – terrible agony as the soul parted from the cindered flesh and the powdered bone and wafted away on the upsurge, blown this way and that until it found anchorage on a bloody cloud somewhere. Or did you just snuff it, and pass into total oblivion, not even knowing you were dead or even that you'd ever lived at all? As a small boy Petty Officer Napper had been in the habit of lighting matches beneath garden spiders in their webs, and watching them crisp up and curl into dead husks – that came back very vividly indeed and he saw himself in a few minutes' time like those spiders, and he offered up a prayer that he might be forgiven for what he'd done to them.

Then, as he came for'ard from the after-gun position above the engineers' accommodation, the action started up around him.

As soon as the seaboat came within range of the Oerlikons, Kemp fired the single revolver-shot. He had a moment in which to see, on the fringe of the searchlight beam, the boat's crew check the rhythm of their oars as panic set in. Then the close-range weapons opened, spattering the water around the seaboat and colandering the crew. At the same time *Portree* opened with her main armament and Kemp saw the sudden flare of orange flame on the German's superstructure as some of the shells took her, and the searchlight died.

'Caught nicely with her pants down! If *Portree*'s on the ball with her tin fish – ' Kemp broke off. From the port side of the destroyer there had been a puff of smoke visible beneath the Northern Lights and then a series of splashes that raised enough spray to be seen in Kemp's binoculars. The torpedoes were away and they hadn't far to go. If the torpedo-gunner's mate aboard the *Portree* knew his job those fish could hardly miss on their track towards a ship lying stopped without a hope of getting under way in time, and even if she did move, *Portree* could surely be relied upon to have given the torpedoes a nice spread, one ahead, one astern, two slap bang amidships – something like that. Just a single hit ought to be enough to slow her at the very least, give the *Hardraw Falls* time to make off at full speed and try to dodge the heavy gunfire.

Cutler came up beside the Commodore. 'Looks good, sir.'

'We won't count any chickens, Cutler.'

'No, sir, Commodore.'

Kemp noted the backsliding in the form of address but let it pass. By this time Theakston had his ship under way again, his engines coming up to full and the foam from the bow's thrust already surging aft to join the curfuffle of the screw. Just as Kemp was wondering when the German was going to react, she opened in a thunderous roar with flashes of brilliant light along her decks. There was a whistling sound close overhead and the men on the bridge ducked instinctively. Standing again Kemp saw the destroyer moving fast, twisting and turning, but maintaining a mean course straight for the German cruiser, obviously in an attempt to draw the enemy fire away from the Commodore's ship, all her for'ard guns firing. She steamed through a hail of shells, so far without damage: Kemp fancied the German gunners could have been thrown into confusion by the sudden shift of events.

Then there was a huge explosion: one at least of *Portree*'s torpedoes had hit. The cruiser listed heavily. Kemp saw a great sheet of flame and felt the heat wafting back on the wind, accompanied by a feeling of pressure, of concussion. In the flame he had seen fragmented metal flying up into the sky, and bodies too. Some of the guns were firing yet, pumping away at the destroyer, leaving the *Hardraw Falls* alone for the time being. More of the *Portree*'s shells were finding their marks, and through his binoculars Kemp saw the German's after funnel looking like a sieve. Smoke streamed everywhere, thick and black, beginning to obscure the cruiser's outline. Then the German gunners laid spot on to their target and in a terrible uprush of fire and fury *Portree*'s bridge vanished as though it had never been. Kemp watched in horror as the destroyer's bows started to pay off to starboard: the wheelhouse would have gone up with the bridge, the ship was no longer under command. A fraction of a second later something took the fo'c'sle and both the for'ard guns joined the bridge in a tearing crescendo of sound and leaping flame. Kemp saw men running blindly along the decks, and then very suddenly the end came. There was a shattering explosion from inside the ship – most likely the fore magazine – and the fo'c'sle split away from just before the midship superstructure and vanished beneath the water, to be followed with amazing speed by the rest of the vessel, her stern lifting high until the sea entered her broken hull and took her down.

In a hoarse voice Cutler said, 'There's men in the water. . . .'

'Yes, I know.'

'You're not going to pick them up?'

'No,' Kemp said. He wiped sweat from his face with the back of a gloved hand: it crackled as he did so, starting already to freeze as it left the pores of his skin. Anyone in the water would be dead from the cold already, surely. But Kemp saw Cutler's face, a picture of blame and accusation and a kind of horrified disbelief. They had been into this before and Kemp found no words now to go over it again – the urgent need to keep the vital cargo intact for Russian use, to preserve a ship that would make a trip like this again and again if she were lucky, the need to keep von Hagen alive and out of German hands. To have stopped engines now would not have been merely to put all that at risk: it would have been a stupid act of recklessness. There was little point in trying to rescue men only to have them blown to strips of bloody flesh the moment the German landed a shell anywhere near the ammunition-filled holds of the *Hardraw Falls*.

Kemp turnd away and went towards the wheelhouse. Theakston had the engine-room telegraph at full. Catching Kemp's eye he said, 'Getting the hell out?'

'Right – we are! Put her on a zig-zag course, Captain. The German's in difficulties, but she'll still try to get us.'

'Aye, no doubt she will.'

Abruptly Kemp said, 'Those men – in the water. God damn this bloody war!'

'Aye,' Theakston said again. 'But remember this – you had no alternative. Not unless you were a lunatic.' He stared ahead through the wheelhouse screen, into the half-darkness beneath the Northern Lights still streaming across the sky. 'We who go to sea – ' He broke off as once again the sound of gunfire cut through the night. 'There she goes again, Commodore.'

'Can you squeeze out any more speed?'

Theakston gave a harsh laugh. 'My chief engineer knows what's going on. He'll need no prodding. He has what you might call a vested interest.'

'Of course. I'm sorry.' Kemp moved out again into the bridge wing, into the bitter cold, the cold that entered the body like a knife-thrust. More wind had come up, a bitter east wind from Novaya Zemlya, and there was, Kemp believed, a hint of more snow to come. If it came on the wings of that bitter wind, it would be a real blizzard through which the ships would steam blind. Meanwhile the German was firing again but erratically: Kemp believed the gunnery control system had been thrown out, that the cruiser was in gunlayer's firing. And Theakston's zig-zag course was helping too.

Kemp looked astern at the cruiser. She was now stopped and there was a curious glow that seemed to be coming from behind her plates: she appeared to be on the point of blowing up. But then, as Kemp stared through his binoculars, the *Hardraw Falls* swung on the port leg of the zig-zag and a final shot from the doomed cruiser found its target. There was a blast from for'ard, hot air that swept up and back over the bridge, and the ship's way checked suddenly, throwing men off balance. Kemp staggered, almost fell, and was caught by Cutler.

'Hit on the bow, sir!'

Kemp heard Theakston's voice, passing the orders to the chief officer to sound round, calling the engine-room on the voice-pipe. The *Hardraw Falls* moved on, a little down now by the head. Kemp prayed that the damage might be small; and gave thanks that the shell hadn't struck near the cargo holds.

v

Petty Officer Napper had gone for a burton once again, skidding on his backside along the after well-deck, but this time suffering no damage. He had a furtive feel to assure himself of this, delving beneath his duffel coat and into his waistband. He had just finished doing this when, looking aft towards the Nazi cruiser, he had a full and perfect view of what happened next. The glow that Kemp had seen from the bridge increased suddenly to extreme brilliance, almost white heat, just for a moment, a split second, and then the cruiser blew up, just like that. The whole sky and the sea for miles around lit like day and an enormous volume of sound crashed across the water and she was gone in flying metal fragments and bits of bodies that could be seen while the flame lasted, arms spread like dolls flung into the air by some wilful child, then nothing but a pall of smoke to mark where the warship had been.

'Bloody hell,' Napper said aloud. He was badly shaken up: you didn't see sights like that in Pompey barracks and in the last war Napper hadn't seen any action either, joining only at the tail end. His legs felt like a blancmange, and he hung on to a lifeline for support. Poor sods ... but of course they were only Jerries who had been trying to do something similar to himself. Napper steadied: serve the buggers right, it did. And the *Hardraw Falls* might be safe, anyway for now – so long as the damage from that shell hadn't been too great, that was. Napper shook again and muttered to himself: if they had to abandon and drift

117

about the Barents Sea in an open boat it could be just as fatal as being blown up – and a bloody sight more lingering. And – Napper strongly suspected – all because of that there Nazi agent.

TWELVE

Chief Officer Amory came to the bridge to report to the master.

'Bows opened up, sir, bosun's store and forepeak gone, but the collision bulkhead's holding.'

'You're shoring up, I take it, Mr Amory?'

'Yes, sir. As I said, the bulkhead's holding but I can't say for how long. It'll be a question of speed and weather now.'

'Aye.' Theakston had already reduced speed to half; he and Kemp were both reluctant to reduce further but the collision bulkhead itself would have to be the deciding factor. 'I'll come down for'ard, Mr Amory, and take a look for myself. Are there any casualties?'

'There are, I'm afraid, sir. Two men who went down to the messroom without orders.' Amory gave the names. 'The bodies were wedged behind a bulkhead that had curled itself around them. And the bosun....'

'Tawney? Dead, d'you mean?'

Amory nodded. 'He went down to look at the damage and missed his footing – the broken plates had iced up already. One of the hands saw him go, nothing he could have done about it.' Amory saw the reaction in Theakston's face: the Old Man and Tawney had sailed together for many years, transferring together, at the request of each, to the various ships of the Bricker Dockett Line. Each had an enormous respect for the other and in the eyes of Captain Theakston, Tawney would have no replacement as bosun – this, Amory knew. And currently, with the ship in trouble, Jock Tawney and the two other seamen were going to be very badly missed. Amory said, 'We shall be short-handed now, sir. I was wondering if the Navy could assist. The PO, Napper – '

'To take Tawney's place? That'll be the day!' Theakston had already summed Napper up, but he shrugged and approached Kemp with Amory's request.

'Of course,' Kemp said. 'The ship comes before the guns now.' He turned to Cutler. 'Sub, send down to Napper. He's to give the chief officer any assistance needed – leave one gunnery rate to report to the bridge and man one of the Oerlikons until further orders. And the guard to remain on von Hagen's quarters, of course.'

'Aye, aye, sir.' Cutler turned away and went at the double down the starboard ladder. Kemp, hunched into his bridge coat and duffel coat, with the hood of the latter pulled over his uniform cap, stared down towards the shattered fo'c'sle. In the loom of light from the streamers in the sky he could pick out the jag of the lower bow plating, blown out at almost ninety degrees from the hull, although the deck plating of the fo'c'sle, together with the anchors and slips and the cables themselves, was intact. The collision bulkhead, set abaft the stem at the regulation five per cent of the ship's length, would have a colossal weight of water to hold if much speed was maintained. That bulkhead had specially thickened plating to withstand free water, and extra-strong stiffeners, but the thrust of water from the ship's headway into wind and sea was a different kettle of fish and Theakston, when he had made his inspection, might want to reduce still further. Kemp did sums in his head: there would be a considerable delay in his arrival at Archangel and now he would have no hope whatsoever of catching up the convoy. He must proceed alone and unescorted through the Barents Sea and chance the attention of the heavy German ships coming down from the north to run into the inadequate guns of the escort under Rear-Admiral Fellowes. In the meantime there was nothing that he, personally, could do. Such was the lot of the Commodore of any convoy for much of the time. Just wait and hope and curb an abounding impatience. Inaction chafed at Kemp: it always had. But it was one of the limitations and frustrations of command at sea and along with the loneliness had to be accepted without complaint. Always the Captain was the loneliest man in the ship: in the RN the Captain lived alone and entered the friendliness of the wardroom only by invitation. In cargo ships as opposed to the liners, the master normally took his meals at the head of the table in the officers' saloon, but he was expected to leave them in peace afterwards and return to his own quarters and his own company. No one liked the master breathing down his neck.

Kemp brooded, his head sunk now on his arms crossed on the teak rail of the bridge. The loss of the *Portree* so suddenly had shaken him; the inability to pick up survivors was a sword-thrust. Neither event was Kemp's first experience of war by a long chalk but somehow this had been more personal: he had made the decision to reject the German demands and however correct and inevitable that decision had been he couldn't escape the knowledge that his order had led to the deaths of an entire ship's company. Fathers, husbands, sons – around one hundred and sixty of them, gone down beneath the freezing cold of the Barents Sea, leaving grief and despair to strike hard in many parts of the British Isles. Kemp thought of his own two sons, both of them at sea with the RN ... at any moment he too could be hit by bad news, he and Mary, the result of some other responsible senior officer's decision.

Kemp turned as he heard a step on the ladder: Theakston was coming back to the bridge. 'Well, Captain?'

'Not so good. The bulkhead's showing signs of strain. You know the principles, of course. The bulkheads bring total rigidity to their sections, making them unduly strong. The local excess must be distributed by the brackets to the stringers, shell plating and so on – '

'And the collision bulkhead more so – yes.'

Theakston said, 'My chief engineer and carpenter have had a look. They're not happy. Something's been set out of true by the impact of the explosion, you see.'

'The shoring beams'll help?'

Theakston nodded. 'Yes, to some extent. But not to be relied on if – '

'You want to reduce speed, is that it?'

'Yes. We have to, if we're to have any real hope. There's no alternative. Indeed I'd go further: in my opinion we should make sternway at least until Amory has the beams in position and chocked down. That way, we'll take all the strain off.'

'Damn slow progress!'

'Aye, it will be. But there's nowt else ... and it's better than foundering.'

Kemp lifted his hands and let them fall again. 'Your ship, Captain. You have the right to save her.'

'Aye, and the duty too. I shall proceed astern. I shall review the position when Mr Amory reports the beams in place.' Theakston moved into the wheelhouse and gave his orders. The ship's head swung as the quartermaster brought her round on to a reciprocal of her course, and she rolled heavily as she came across the waves, then steadied as the swing was met by opposite helm and the engine-room telegraph was put to half astern. Theakston moved out once again to the wing, looking aft to see the water swirl for'ard as the sternway came on.

Kemp said, 'As I remarked – slow progress. How about putting her on full, Captain?'

'There'll be a deal of yaw.'

'I know it's not easy to keep on course astern. But there happens to be a need now.' Kemp's voice was sharper than he had intended.

'Oh, aye,' Theakston said. 'There's no call for anger.' He waited for a moment; Kemp, restraining his temper, said nothing. Theakston gave him a long stare and then marched away, back to the wheelhouse. Kemp heard the ring of the telegraph, followed by the repetition from below, and then the *Hardraw Falls* began to shudder to the full stern-thrust of her engines. Kemp let out a long breath: Yorkshiremen, he told himself firmly, had sterling virtues. . . .

ii

Amory had the hands hard at it, his own crew and the naval ratings. The shoring beams had been brought out and mostly set in place against the collision bulkhead, all ready to be wedged down with the chocks and blows of the carpenter's sledgehammer. Amory was in an impatient mood: Petty Officer Napper was as much use as a flea at a bullfight and managed to get constantly under everyone's feet at the wrong moment.

'Never set up shoring beams before, have you?' Amory asked.

'No, sir, I haven't,' Napper answered in an aggrieved tone that suggested that RN ships never got themselves into a situation where they needed to shore up, an attitude that infuriated Amory by its sheer nonsense. Napper was all thumbs and a loud voice, but fortunately the junior ratings had him weighed off and weren't taking too much notice of him, following the chief officer's orders instead. Napper didn't like that, and was fizzing like a fuse. He went on, 'Anyway, we do things different in the Andrew, see.' He added in a pained voice, 'That apart, sir, I've me injury. It don't help.'

'I don't suppose it does,' Amory said unsympathetically. 'Perhaps you'd rather go away and nurse it better.' He turned his back on Napper and lent a hand himself in the hefting of the final shoring beam into its place against the collision bulkhead, noting as he did so a small trickle of water forming a pool at the bottom of the bulkhead: not very serious so far but it might mean they wouldn't be able to resume moving with headway. Even if the bulkhead was only very slightly sprung Theakston couldn't risk bringing heavy pressure to bear. And then God alone knew how long it would take them to reach Archangel.

iii

Napper's ears had burned red: *nurse it better!* Who did Mr bloody Amory think he was? Regarding the chief officer's words as a dismissal, Napper took himself off in a huff, glad enough to get to hell away from the collision bulkhead, the vicinity of which was a potentially dangerous place. If the bulkhead should go suddenly, it would be all up with the hands nearby – they'd be engulfed, not just by water but by flung beams and breaking timber as well. Napper climbed ladders aft of the collision bulkhead and emerged from the starboard door beneath the fo'c'sle, coming into the fore well-deck and leaving the wreckage of the seaman's quarters behind him. He spared a fleeting thought for the deck-hands, now with most of their gear gone for a burton and their living quarters with it. From now on they would have to doss down where they could; it wouldn't be comfortable in the alleyways and storerooms. Napper moved on. They had daylight in the sky now, dim and murky, and he saw Commodore Kemp looking down from the bridge, and at once he smartened his bearing so as to look as though he was going about his duties, and marched left-right-left while keeping a hand on the lifelines until he disappeared from view into the midship superstructure feeling like a moving icicle, even his lips cracking with frozen spittle. It came to him suddenly that he'd been talking to himself all the way up from the depths of the ship, first sign of madness, or in his case just a furious reaction to what Amory had said. Not that he hadn't enough to drive him crazy, what with Able Seaman Grove's cheek, and the perishing cold, and the bloody awful danger of being half disabled in the Barents Sea of all places, and the fact that he should have been sitting comfy in Pompey barracks drinking a cup of char while the matloes carried out part-of-ship duties around the parade and blocks.

On his way to the chief steward's office for another look at *The Ship Captain's Medical Guide* Napper passed the foot of the ladder leading up to the officers' accommodation and became aware that his name was being called.

He halted and looked up: the armed seaman who was supposed to be guarding the Nazi's cabin was at the head of the ladder. 'PO?'

'Yer. What are you doing, deserting your place of duty, lad? Bloody Jerry could break out, couldn't he? And then what, I'd like to know!'

'Sorry, PO. It's the prisoner.'

'What about him?'

'Says he's ill.'

'Ha! Ill, is he?' Napper lifted his cap and scratched at his thinning hair. 'What's he got?' he asked hoarsely, his own interest in medical matters coming to the fore.

'I dunno, just ill.'

'Hang on.' Napper climbed the ladder and accompanied the sentry back to von Hagen's cabin door. He thumped on it. 'Petty Officer o' the Guard here,' he said in a loud voice. 'What's the trouble, eh?'

There was no answer. Once again Napper scratched at his head, pondering. What was the Jerry playing at? Could be dead for all Napper knew, or could be dying, and if he was allowed to die then somebody would be sure to blame Napper for losing a valuable source of information. On the other hand, Napper was buggered if he was going to open up the cabin door, notwithstanding the sentry's rifle and bayonet. Nazis were slippery customers and up to all manner of tricks, like monkeys. 'Hang on,' Napper said once more, and went fast for the bridge to report to the Commodore.

Kemp asked, 'How genuine do you think this is?'

'No idea, sir. The prisoner, 'e didn't utter after I got there, sir.'

Kemp looked at Cutler. He said, 'Something I didn't think about but should have. Agents ... they're said to be supplied with lethal tablets, keep 'em in their mouths or something ready to swallow.'

'I doubt if it's that, sir. He'd have taken it back in Norway, when he was nabbed. Or aboard the submarine.'

Kemp grunted. 'Yes, perhaps.'

Napper said, 'If it had been that, sir, he wouldn't have said he was ill.'

'That's right,' Cutler agreed. 'They act fast. Instantaneously.'

Kemp said, 'We'll have to investigate. I'll go down myself. You'll stand by with the sentry, Napper.'

'Yessir.'

Kemp went along the ladder, followed by Cutler and Napper. He approached the cabin door and knocked on it. 'Kemp here. What's the trouble, von Hagen?'

Again there was no response; Kemp banged again, with no result. He stood back, and nodded at the sentry. 'Right,' he said. 'Aim for the doorway. I'm going to open up. Hand me the key. If there's any trouble, shoot – but not to kill him. Just to disable.'

'Aye, aye, sir.' The sentry passed the key to Kemp, who put it in the lock and turned it. As he did so he felt pressure on the door and started to call a warning to the others. Before the words were out of his mouth the door came open with a crash, sending Kemp flat on his back as von Hagen emerged like a bullet, fists flailing. The sentry fired and missed, just before he too was bowled over, and the bullet singed past the German into the cabin. A fist connected with Napper's jaw and he lurched back against a bulkhead as von Hagen ran along the alleyway for the door at the end, the door to the open deck running alongside the officers' cabins. Kemp was up and in pursuit as fast as he could make it; he and the sentry went through the door to find von Hagen climbing the guardrail. Below, the cold sea rose and fell as the ship rolled. Kemp reached the guardrail, calling out to von Hagen, got a grip on the German as he jumped and was himself lifted to the rail. Before he could let go his grip, he had lost his balance and was plummeting with von Hagen towards the sea's freezing cold. The sentry reached the rail and reacted fast.

'Man overboard starboard!' He yelled the words up towards the bridge and at the same time grabbed a lifebuoy from its stowage on the rail and threw it, with its securing line running out behind it, towards the heads visible in the water close by the ship's side.

As the lifebuoy took the water, the sound of aircraft engines was heard coming in from the direction of the Kola Inlet.

THIRTEEN

Theakston was leaning out over the water from the bridge wing, his face angry. 'Damned idiot! Why didn't he let the German go, for God's sake?' He had stopped engines and was about to order a boat to be lowered from the falls when the sound of the aircraft engines came and he left the open bridge and doubled into the wheelhouse to press the action alarm. Strident din echoed through the ship. For'ard at the collision bulkhead Amory ordered the naval gunnery rates to their close-range weapons, remained himself with half a dozen of the crew to tend the beams. Any fresh strain coming on the bulkhead could mean total disaster unless men were handy for instant response, not that they would be able to do a lot if the shoring beams themselves should crumple.

On the deck outside the officers' accommodation, Petty Officer Napper was in a state of dither: should he lend a hand with rescuing the Commodore or should he get to his action station pronto? 'Christ,' he said to no one in particular, 'this bloody would go and happen!'

It was Cutler who solved his problem. 'Bugger off, Napper, and get shooting – I've got the line and the fish is on the hook.' He'd seen Kemp reach out and grasp the lifebuoy, pull it in to his body so that he could take a turn of the line itself around his waist. Kemp's other hand was fast on von Hagen's collar. So far, so good, Cutler thought. They could both be hauled aboard just as long as Kemp's frozen fingers could retain his grip on the German. If they couldn't – too bad; at least Kemp had the line fast, and now a heavier line was going down to him. It was a question of speed, of getting them out from the water and into the warm. The Commodore was no longer young and the submersion could be enough to finish him off. As Cutler hauled in, assisted by the sentry, there was a rattle of gunfire above his head and bullets spattered the gray-painted bulkhead behind him.

ii

'Fighters,' Theakston said as he ducked down behind the bridge screen. A line of bullet holes dotted the deck planks and panes of glass shattered in the wheelhouse. From monkey's island above, the Bofors and Lewis guns cracked out, a sustained return of fire towards the belly of a German fighter, which missed its mark. Petty Officer Napper, feeling dangerously exposed so high up in the ship, his stomach loosening fast, saw the bigger shapes of JU 88 bombers : the Nazis had evidently been carrying out an attack on the Russian military and naval installations in the Kola Inlet, probably concentrating on Murmansk where, for all Napper knew, a homeward convoy could be assembling. Deciding that the ship's master might like to know his prognostications, Napper made a dive for the vertical ladder down to the bridge as two more fighters came in from the south. And just in time, he reckoned a moment later as the fighters came in again and cannon fire swept monkey's island and there was a scream of agony from one of the gunnery rates. Another second's delay and he would have caught that lot up. Napper had felt his bravery seeping away with every knot made, this trip. . . .

He approached Captain Theakston in the lull that followed. Theakston said, 'No bombing. I wonder if they've been warned about the German aboard us.'

'Maybe, sir. Maybe it's just that they've already dropped their load on Murmansk. If that's the case – '

'We can consider ourselves lucky ! They may not bother overmuch with us, if they're bound back to base.'

'Well, sir, I dunno.' Napper wiped the back of his glove across his face. He wanted to keep Theakston talking ; if he remained with him, the wheelhouse was handy to dodge into when the next attack came. 'They'll be bound south for Norway, see. That means they deviated out, special like, when they picked us up.'

128

'We shall have to see,' Theakston said. He turned as Cutler came up the ladder, his duffel coat stiff with frozen seawater. 'Well, lad?'

'Both aboard, sir.' Cutler was breathing heavily. 'Being stripped and given brandy by the chief steward. Blankets, hot-water bottles. I don't think they're too bad, considering. Commodore wanted to come to the bridge.' Cutler grinned. 'Afraid I took your name in vain, sir. Said you'd have him removed by force – your personal order.'

Theakston gave a thin smile, about the first time Cutler had seen his face relax. 'He took it?'

'Like a lamb.'

'That doesn't speak too well for how he's feeling, does it?'

Cutler said, 'As a matter of fact, he did try to come up. But his legs gave away. I still don't think he's too bad, sir, all the same.'

Theakston nodded; he wished Kemp well but was not displeased to have his own bridge to himself for as long as it took Kemp to recover. Cutler looked at Napper, hovering by the wheelhouse door. 'Everything under control?' he asked.

'Yessir. Casualties on monkey's island, but – '

'And you, Petty Officer Napper?'

Napper stared and felt uncomfortable. 'Me, sir?'

'Yes, you. What precisely are you doing?'

Napper said, 'Advising the Captain, sir. About the aircraft, sir. I said like, they've been giving Murmansk a pasting – ' He broke off as two more fighters came in, keeping low, appearing suddenly from the murk to rake the decks once again. The noise was deafening as everything opened on them: their cannon fire ricocheted from bulkheads and stanchions, peppered the funnel and the funnel casings, slammed into the griped-in lifeboats at the falls, and left pock-marks along the length of the boat deck. From above the engineers' accommodation aft the close-range crews pumped out bullets, firing almost vertically as the aircraft roared across, lying back in the straps to increase the angle as far as possible, but the fighters passed on unhit, vanishing as suddenly as they had appeared.

'They'll be back,' Cutler said edgily. Air attack was a bloody business and, Cutler thought, no one ever got used to it. Probably it grew worse the longer you were subjected to it. It brought him a feeling of total helplessness: ack-ack fire, he believed, was no more than a gesture, to shoot down aircraft was easier said than done unless you were part of a big fleet with a huge flak umbrella. They came in suddenly, at high speed, raked you or bombed you, and were gone before you could lay or train with any effect. But as it turned out, they didn't come back this time. When more aircraft sounds were heard they were from the north; and it was Napper who identified them first.

'Ours, sir . . . Fleet Air Arm! Seafires, sir!'

Seafires, the naval version of the Spitfire, were fast and furious. No wonder the Nazis hadn't lingered. Cutler, looking up through his binoculars, said, 'Carrier from the Home Fleet. Thank God!' A cheer went up raggedly from the decks as the Seafires were recognized and as one of them detached from the squadron to circle the *Hardraw Falls* a lamp was seen to be winking from it. Leading Signalman Corrigan read off the message and reported to Cutler. 'Signal, sir: "Message intercepted from Murmansk indicates heavy damage to port installations. Fairway blocked by sunken vessels awaiting QP convoy homeward. Do not attempt to enter." Message ends, sir.'

Theakston lifted an eyebrow: 'That pilot's making assumptions, I reckon, all about nowt. We're still bound for Archangel far as I know.'

'He's seen our damage, sir,' Cutler said. 'He thinks we'll alter – ' He broke off. 'Signalling again, Corrigan.'

'Yes, sir. "Do you require assistance."'

Cutler looked interrogatively at Theakston, who said, 'That's for the Commodore, lad. Best ask him.'

'I'll go down,' Cutler said. He slid down the ladder, the palms of his gloved hands sliding on the rails thick with ice. He knocked at Kemp's door and went in on the heels of the knock. Kemp, blue in the face and shivering, managed to give him a grin.

'All right, sir?'

'Oh, I'll survive, never fear! What's the state of things, Sub?'

Cutler reported. He added, 'Seafires from the Home Fleet, sir. Ask, do we require assistance.'

At first Kemp made no comment, giving an oblique response. 'Those Seafires . . . any indication of contact between the Home Fleet and the Germans?'

'No, sir – '

'Ask them, then. Keep me informed – then I'll make a final decision about assistance. I'll probably enter Murmansk and to hell with the orders about von Hagen.'

Cutler shook his head. 'No hope of that, sir.' He reported the blocked fairway as a result of heavy attack. 'It'll have to be Archangel, sir. If anywhere at all.'

'You sound defeatist,' Kemp said sharply. 'Don't. Now – up top and contact the Seafires.'

Cutler went back to the bridge at the rush. Corrigan passed the Commodore's message: the answer came back that up to the time the Seafires had been flown off from their parent carrier there had been no contact but the C-in-C was steaming to stand between the PQ convoy and the threat from the north. Cutler sent an acknowledgment and went down again to report to the Commodore.

Kemp said, 'I'm going to take a chance that C-in-C Home Fleet'll reinforce the escort – or order 'em to rejoin the convoy if they've moved north to engage the enemy as we guessed they might. And now the Home Fleet's here, it's only prudent to accept the offer of assistance. Make a signal to the aircraft, Cutler – my thanks and I'd appreciate a destroyer or corvette to stand by me. All right?'

'Yes, sir, Commodore.' Cutler returned to the bridge at the double and the message was passed. A few minutes later the Seafire banked and turned away. The gunners were fallen out from action stations and reduced to two watches once again. Petty Officer Napper went round the gun positions and saw to the removal of two bodies from monkey's island. Going aft he found Able Seaman Grove flinging his arms about his body, his teeth chattering.

'Got away with it again, did you?' Napper asked in a surly tone.

Grove grinned, cheeky as ever, Napper thought. 'That's a nicely expressed sentiment from a bloke's PO, I *don't* think.'

'Get stuffed,' Napper said.

iii

The cold seemed to increase, although it hadn't seemed possible that it could worsen. The temperature stood at nearly fifty degrees below freezing. The *Hardraw Falls* made desperately slow progress in her sternway motion; the collision bulkhead, watched constantly by Amory and the ship's acting bosun and the carpenter, was holding yet and the seepage hadn't got any worse, though this was probably due to the lack of water pressure even though some water was splashing up against the bulkhead as a bitter east wind drove against the metal. By nightfall Kemp was back on the bridge, his sea-soaked bridge coat and duffel coat dried out in the galley. He still looked a little pinched about the mouth but otherwise, he insisted, was fit enough, and he didn't like being confined to his cabin. Von Hagen, according to the chief steward, was also recovering but was in a state of serious depression. Kemp said he would talk to the German agent in the morning: he preferred to let him stew for the time being. If the depressive state worsened, he might be made to be more forthcoming: Kemp still had in mind his orders to extract any information that was going.

At a little before midnight the snow started again, coming down heavily and at times almost horizontally, borne along that piercing east wind that felt as though it was coming direct from the Siberian wastes. Emerging from the comparative warmth of the ship's interior into the driving snow was sheer torture. Cutler, staying on the bridge with the Commodore, was concerned for Kemp. In his view, Kemp didn't look at all fit. Cutler came out with it straight, said he ought to go below. There was nothing he could do by remaining in an exposed position: with the shattered glass of the screens, there was no protection even in the wheelhouse although temporary canvas dodgers had been secured across the lower halves.

'I'm all right, Cutler.'

'You won't be by the morning, sir.'

Kemp said, 'Do you know something, Cutler? I served my time, my apprenticeship, in sail. I just caught up the tail end of the windjammer era. Four years, a little more by the time I had my second mate's ticket, then three more for first mate and master. I was on the South American and Australian run ... around Cape Horn for Chilean ports – Puerrto Montt, Valparaiso, Iquique, and then across to Sydney, Melbourne, Adelaide, Fremantle. Cape Horn, the Australian Bight – the Horn especially, of course – the Barents Sea has nothing on them.'

'You were younger then, sir.'

Kemp laughed. 'Kindly don't remind me! You're right, of course, but we were given a toughness that lasted. I'll remain on the bridge, Cutler. Don't forget that damaged bow. And don't forget that in this muck, we're going to be hard to find.'

'You mean the ship detached from the escort to stand by us, sir?'

'Exactly. I want to be handy. There's no need for you to stay. You've done your share, Cutler. Go below and get some sleep – and that's an order.'

After Cutler had left the bridge Kemp wedged himself into a corner of the bridge wing and sunk his head down on to his arms crossed on the guardrail, the hood of his duffel coat pulled down over his ears. He faced aft, in the direction of the ship's stern-way, into the appalling drive of the heavy snow. The night was very dark now, no sight of the Northern Lights, with only the faint loom that was always present over the world's oceans to allow a faint glimpse of the snowflakes. The ship was covered now, its outline vanishing more positively than in the earlier blizzard. Kemp's thoughts, once aroused by his brief conversation with Cutler, went back to those early days at sea.

Happy times, however hard – good comradeship and the world at his feet as the wind blew a sixteen-year-old youth in his old windjammer away from Liverpool town on a thirty-thousand-mile round journey. A motley enough crew at times, but all of them knowing that each depended on the other for his life in the many dangerous situations that could and did arise. Kemp recalled the desperate battering into the teeth of the westerlies off the pitch of the Horn – Cape Stiff, as the old shellbacks had known it – the attempts to find a shift of that never-ending wind that would carry them round towards the South Pacific. On many a voyage a ship had taken up to six long weeks of cold and hunger to beat round, with all hands and the cook aloft on the swaying footropes to take in sail or adjust the trim, frozen hands grabbing at frozen canvas whipping in the gale and sometimes throwing men off the yards to land on deck with broken backs or go sheer into the icy water with no hope of rescue. One hand for the ship and one for yourself had been the watchword, but with some of the more bullying mates right behind you, you didn't take that too literally: the discipline was iron hard, even at times sadistic, and if you didn't survive, you didn't and that was that. No questions asked afterwards, no letters of complaint to Members of Parliament. 'Lost overboard' was the notation in the log, and that was enough.

Why had he ever gone to sea? Why had he endured the hardships, the food that consisted of such messes as burgoo, cracker hash, sea pie, weevily biscuits, corned dog and so on, why had he settled for no pay as an apprentice and the gradual advancement to what was then a master's niggardly twelve pounds a month?

He grinned to himself: it had been bred into him by his old grandmother ... her father had been a master in sail and so had Kemp's grandfather, her husband; their memories had been idolized and kept alive in the young Kemp's home, and he had listened to many yarns of the old times and had become imbued with a perhaps over-romanticized view of the seafaring life, a life of adventure far removed from the humdrum business of the shore. Seamen were a race apart, with a different set of values of honesty and fair dealing, men working together for the good of each and for the ship; ships had been prideful things to sailors and to Kemp's grandmother. He had found the reality not quite the same as the dream but even so there was still some of the romance left, some of it in the form of the shantymen and the nostalgic songs sung with the fiddler on the capstan as a ship put out to sea for a voyage that could last two years before they sighted a home port again. Stirring times for a young man, experiences that had left behind them that enduring physical hardness of which he had just spoken to Cutler. But Cutler would probably never really understand, even though he clearly liked the sea himself, even though his own country of America had also had a long sea tradition of hard men and hard-driven ships, bucko mates in plenty and grim masters who pounded the down-easters along the trade routes of the world, ruling their kingdoms with the fist and the belaying-pin, and the cruel punishments of being mastheaded for long periods in bitter weather or in blazing tropic sun.

Kemp gave a sudden deep-seated shiver: the immersion hadn't in fact done him any good and never mind the hardness of sail. As Cutler had hinted, he was growing old – at any rate in

Cutler's eyes. In his own view, the early fifties didn't make anyone an old man. Kemp shook himself free of the snow that covered him, and beat his arms around his body. Old be buggered!

iv

The *Hardraw Falls*, missing bosun Tawney, was by now short of officers as well: a watch had to be kept at the collision bulkhead as well as on the bridge, which meant the Captain had to take a turn on his own. The bridge watch was being split between Theakston and the second officer, while Amory and the third officer shared the duty for'ard, protected from the weather but as bitterly cold, or almost, as the bridge. There was a deadness, a particular kind of coldness, about being enclosed in metal that you couldn't touch with an unprotected fingertip unless you wanted the flesh to freeze to what was touched and remain there until it was torn bloodily away. Amory, taking the middle watch, the twelve to four known at sea as the graveyard watch, walked up and down with difficulty, dodging past the great beams that shored up the collision bulkhead, for'ard of Number One hold with its lethal cargo of high explosive, trying to keep his circulation going. For want of anything better to think about as he kept an eye lifting for trouble, Amory, like Kemp, found his mind going back into the past, fruitlessly and painfully. The bomb that had killed Felicity had changed Amory a good deal and he had little left in life except a consuming hatred for the Nazis. The killing of Nazis was his interest now; he wanted to live so that he could go on contributing what he could to the defeat of Hitler's pestilential doctrines, so that he could have the final satisfaction of seeing the Allied armies entering Berlin, even though he would see it only on the newsreels in his local cinema – that, and the surrender of the German Navy, the last striking of their detested, flaunted ensign.

Vengeful?

Amory gave a hard, humourless laugh. Of course it was, and why not? He'd had the prospect of a whole life to live with Felicity; now all he had to go home to was a crusty and widowed father, pensioned off, too old now even for the police War Reserve, and not liking it, and taking it out on his neighbours as an air-raid warden. On leave, Amory had heard him at it: *'Put that light out . . . don't you know there's a war on . . . who the hell d'you think you are?'* He'd also heard the remarks, sotto voce when he was recognized, in the local pub, about the old bastard who thought he was still a police super.

Not much of a life, on leave. Might just as well stay aboard the ship, really. Better, in fact: Amory was a vigorous man with normal wants. The girls were more co-operative in the seaports than at home with their little respectabilities and what would the neighbours think. Amory meant girls – not prostitutes. He'd been at sea quite long enough to see the results of risks taken in extremity. For the same reason he was always careful not to drink too much: tight, you lost your discrimination and the urge grew stronger even if the ability tended to lessen at the crucial moment. . . .

Up and down, up and down, half stumbling with sheer tiredness, frozen right through, the very marrow in the bones feeling it. The ship heaving, groaning, weird and disquieting noises from distorted frames. Could they ever reach Archangel, arse first, at little more than four knots?

Just watch the bulkhead, that was the thing. Forget the past, don't worry about the future – just watch the bulkhead for the smallest sign of further strain. Amory knew that if anything happened it was likely to happen suddenly and he wouldn't have much time to clear the compartment.

v

Dawn came, weak and straggly, no sun but still the everlasting blizzard. It was no more than a faint lifting of the dark, you couldn't really call it a dawn. Kemp had at last given in and gone below when Theakston had come up at 0400 hours to take over the bridge from the second officer. Once on his bunk, he had dropped off to sleep almost fully dressed – weariness had overcome him by the time he'd got his outer clothing and seaboots off. At 0800 his steward, Torrence, looked in, shook his head at the inert figure and went out again, closing the door gently behind him. Moving along the alleyway he met Cutler. 'Good morning, sir,' he said briskly. 'Not that it is.'

'Morning, Torrence. How's the Commodore?'

'Sleeping, sir, flat out and snoring. I was going to bring 'is breakfast but I thought, well, why disturb 'im, sir, let 'im rest.' Torrence flicked at a speck on his white jacket. 'Did you want 'im, like?'

Cutler shook his head. 'No. But he wanted to see the prisoner . . . leave him for now, though. Keep a watch now and again, all right? And let me know when he's awake.'

'I'll watch over 'im like a mother, sir,' Torrence said cheerfully. Cutler was glad of the happy tone; there had been too many long faces around the last few days. Not surprising since there was nothing to be cheerful about, but depressing.

Even more depressing was the snow, which was cutting them off from all contact with the outside world; he felt they were like a blind man trying to walk across Dartmoor. They moved in a world of their own with no knowing if the promised destroyer or corvette from the escort would ever reach them.

Cutler went back to the bridge, refreshed after what passed in wartime for a full night's sleep. He had just reached the wheel-house when there was a buzz from the wireless room and Theakston, who was handing over the watch once again to the second officer, answered it. He swung round on Cutler.

'Signal from the Admiralty,' he said. 'In cypher. Prefixed Most Immediate.'

FOURTEEN

Cutler brought out his naval decyphering tables and broke down the signal into plain language. Then, need for sleep or not, he knew he had to call the Commodore.

Kemp came awake at once, the attribute of a seaman, the ability to clear the mind fast.

'What is it, Cutler?'

'Signal from the Admiralty, sir.' Cutler held out the naval message form and Kemp read fast, his forehead creased into a frown.

'God damn and blast,' he said. 'What do the buggers expect of us?'

'Miracles, sir?'

'It bloody well looks like it!' Kemp swung his legs off the bunk and stood up. He swayed a little and reached out to steady himself on the bunk board, reading the signal again as if he hadn't taken it in fully the first time. It read: 'Moscow anxious about delay. Vital repeat vital that passenger reaches Archangel within seventy-two hours of time of origin of this signal. Met reports now indicate freeze likely at any time.'

Kemp said, 'So we take orders from the Kremlin now.'

'Seems so, sir.' Cutler paused. 'Why not have breakfast, then –'

'Oh, balls to breakfast, Cutler. I told you I was tough. We didn't often have *breakfast* in the windjammers in the old days!'

Cutler grinned. 'The days when ships were wood, and men were made of iron?'

Kemp stopped in the act of pulling on his monkey-jacket and stared at his assistant. 'Where the hell did *you* hear that?'

'Read it somewhere, sir.'

'You surprise me, Cutler. But never mind. I'll be on the bridge directly. I'll take a look at the chart on the way.'

'Aye, aye, sir – '

'And my compliments to the Captain . . . tell him what's in the signal and say I'll be asking for the impossible – more speed.'

'Yes, sir.' Cutler left the cabin and went back to the bridge. Theakston had in fact gone below. After a word with the second officer Cutler used the voice-pipe to the master's quarters and gave him the news. There was a curse but Theakston was back on the bridge before Kemp had entered the chartroom.

Theakston said, 'I can't get any more out of her, lad, and that's flat.'

'Perhaps a knot or two, sir?'

'Just you say that to my chief engineer! Engines don't like going astern for too long. Or too fast. She has to be nursed. And there's another point, isn't there?'

'What's that, sir?'

'The visibility. Just look at it, eh?'

Cutler nodded: the snow was thickening and the visibility was down to something like two cables, coming down farther in patches as an extra swirl of snow was driven into their faces. 'Bad,' he said. 'But I doubt if there's much shipping around.'

'Oh, no! Only maybe a homeward convoy coming the other way.' Theakston lifted his binoculars and stared into the white blanket ahead; then lowered them again. It wasn't worth the effort of lifting, the glasses brought up only a thicker blank. He said no more; a couple of minutes later Kemp emerged from the chartroom and approached Theakston.

'Good morning, Captain. You'll have heard about the signal . . . I've just looked at the last dead reckoning position on the chart. We have around four hundred miles to go. Say a hundred hours' steaming . . . it's too much, in the light of that signal.'

'There's nowt to be done about it, Commodore.' Theakston's tone was stubborn; Kemp had expected no less. He pressed, but tactfully. The ship was Theakston's responsibility, he reminded himself for the hundredth time since leaving the Firth of Lorne. Theakston, however, did come under the overall orders of the Trade Division of the Admiralty as he did himself, and if necessary, with reluctance, Kemp would make the point forcefully.

Theakston said, 'She'll not take more speed ... just maybe another knot,' he added grudgingly as he saw the set of Kemp's jaw.

'I shall need more than that, Captain. I'm sorry, but there it is. We have the Kremlin at our throats, if that's not too dramatic a phrase – '

'I give nowt for the Kremlin.'

Kemp laughed. 'I don't give much myself. But I do have my orders. And there's the ice – we haven't all that long. The signal says it's vital – you know the contents.'

'Aye, I do. Why is it so vital?'

'I don't know. I'm just the Commodore.'

'You should maybe find out from the prisoner.'

'That,' Kemp said, 'is what I propose to do – to try to, anyway. But in the meantime we can't afford to fall behind the progress of the freeze off Archangel. I have to assume the Admiralty knows its own business.'

Theakston's face was aggressive. 'I said, there's nowt – '

'Yes, I know. I'm going for'ard, Captain – '

'What for?'

Kemp said, 'To look at the collision bulkhead.' He didn't wait for any explosion from Theakston; he turned away and went down the starboard ladder to the well-deck, into the fo'c'sle accommodation and down again to where Amory was once again at his station abaft the bulkhead, watching the shoring beams.

ii

The word had spread quickly that something extra was in the wind along with the blinding snow, that fresh orders had reached the Commodore. No one knew what it was, but all were certain it wasn't good news: it never was, in wartime. Chief Steward Buckle nabbed Petty Officer Napper as the latter went crab-wise past his office.

'Mr Napper – '

'Yer?'

'No better, eh?'

'Worse.'

'Well, well. Never mind, it'll clear up soon, bound to.' Buckle lowered his voice. 'Heard the buzz, I s'pose?'

'Yer. What about it? You heard something too?'

'Not me – Torrence, Captain's steward. Flapping ears. He says it's to do with the Russians. Well, of course, I know we're bound for Russia, so I reckon there may not be anything special in it, but then again, you never bloody well know, do you?'

'Not often, no. Brassbound buggers don't give much away to the lower deck, not usually.' Napper sucked at his teeth, glad to have someone of about his own status to moan to: and it wasn't often he got called mister, and he was flattered and grateful. 'Want to know what I reckon? It's that there Nazi, my prisoner.' Napper liked the sound of 'my prisoner' and said it again. 'If 'e wasn't my responsibility, I reckon I'd do 'im in and settle it. Another thing – I reckon Stalin comes into it somewhere.'

'Stalin, eh? How?'

Napper shrugged. 'I dunno. Just does. I don't like it, not at all I don't. I reckon we'll never be allowed to leave bloody Archangel ever again.'

'Go on!'

Napper wagged a finger. 'You just see. That Stalin and 'is secret police, OGPU, isn't it? I dunno the ins and outs like. But we're carrying a load o' dynamite and I don't mean the flipping cargo either. That there von whatsit, Hagen ... and Stalin, 'e won't be letting us off the hook once we're in 'is grasp. You mark my words, Mr Buckle. We're *political* now. Bloody *political*. You know what that means.'

Buckle didn't, but he nodded sagely. 'Dirty,' he said. 'Dirty bastards the lot of them, politicians.'

'Out for their own ends like, all the time. . . .'

It wasn't only Torrence who had flapping ears. So the word spread. The *Hardraw Falls* was to be seized by the Russians the moment she entered Archangel. But in the meantime there were other and more immediate worries. Napper was still talking to the chief steward when the ship gave a lurch and her roll increased sharply. There seemed to be a shift of wind at the same time, a curious silence on one side and a battering of waves on the other, and a sudden heightening of the creaks and groans that had started soon after the bow had been blown apart.

'Christ above,' Napper said in an alarmed tone, 'they're turn-

141

ing the bloody ship around! And I don't reckon it's back the way we came either!'

Kemp was well aware of the enormous risk: but there was an emergency and in his view the risk was justifiable in the new circumstances. Amory had reported the collision bulkhead holding up; it should be capable of taking the strain so long as it didn't go on for too long and so long as no attempt was made to go beyond half speed. Theakston had been aghast at Kemp's suggestion, but Kemp had been firm, as obstinate as Theakston himself, and in the end had quoted the Trade Division's authority. Theakston had said he wanted it entered in the ship's official log that he, as master, had objected strenuously but had been overruled by the Commodore. He wanted it entered also that in his view the ship would be in immediate danger of foundering with all hands.

'I shall take full responsibility,' Kemp said.

'Aye, and that's to go in the log as well.'

'It will. It's very proper of you to insist, Captain – '

'Thank you for nowt!' Theakston snapped. 'I know my job as master.'

Kemp hadn't liked it; he understood Theakston's point of view very well, and would have had a similar reaction himself if his command had been interfered with. But that signal had had every possible ring of urgency; and reading between the lines Kemp believed that the delivery of von Hagen had become more important than the *Hardraw Falls* herself or her cargo, however vital that might be, and was, to the Russian war effort and the repulse of Hitler's hordes. On the other hand, to lose the ship would be to lose von Hagen as well, a prospect that would scarcely command itself to the Admiralty or the Russians. So it was to be a calculated risk, everything depending now on the collision bulkhead and its ability to withstand the pressures of wind, snow and the Barents Sea.

When the ship made the turn, with Theakston clicking his tongue at every shudder, Kemp went below to talk to von Hagen. As on the previous occasions, he spoke to the German alone, with the armed sentry standing by outside and backed up by Petty Officer Napper. Von Hagen, Kemp thought, looked a sick man: the immersion was still having its effect, and the Nazi's face was drawn and full of stress. He lay on his side on the bunk, fingers plucking.

Kemp asked, 'How are you feeling now, von Hagen?'

'Not good. But not all that bad.'

'I'm glad to hear that. It was a damn stupid thing to do – going overboard.'

Von Hagen laughed, a sad and bitter sound. 'And that, if I may say so, Captain Kemp, is a damn stupid thing to say! Isn't the Barents Sea better than Siberia – or any other kind of lingering death the Russians might inflict on me?'

Kemp shrugged. 'You have a point, I don't deny. But – '

'But you are going to do your best for me. You said that. I may not be handed over – you said.' The eyes gleamed in sardonic humour. 'Do you still say that?'

'I gave no promises of success. Only of trying . . . and that I shall do. I gave you my word on that.'

'Yes. I'm sorry.'

'But I still ask your help. I want to know many things, von Hagen.' Kemp had sat in the chair close to the bunk; now he leaned forward and spoke insistently. 'I want any information – you know this already – that you have in your head. Tell me that, and you will have a better chance. Oh, I know you believe a British Intelligence officer will board us, but you can't be sure of that, not wholly sure. And there's another and more specific thing I want to know.'

'And that is?'

Kemp said, 'What your personal importance is. I believe there's something beyond your acquired knowledge that makes it so vital that you be handed over to the Russians. Why should Britain agree to part with you? What's behind all this, von Hagen?'

'Call it the dirt of inter-governmental intrigue.'

'Yes. I know all that. But what's the reason?'

'It wouldn't help you, old friend! You would still have your duty to do . . . and if possible your promise to keep, your promise to try to help.'

'It's not a question of possibility or otherwise. That promise stands. But I'd like to be forearmed with the full story, the whys and wherefores. And I don't see that you would lose anything by telling me.'

Von Hagen shook his head and blew out his breath in something like despair. 'What makes you think I know?'

'Because you are an agent, and a top one as I understand it.'

'It makes no difference. In Germany, in the Third Reich, there are many secrets and they are strictly kept. There are so many right hands that don't know what the left ones are up to. In any case it is not my people, not the Government, who are handing me over, is it?'

'No. But I thought that with your special knowledge – '

'Yes, yes, I understand.'

'And I believe you do know, von Hagen.'

'Then you must continue to believe that. I cannot enlighten you. For the sake of an old friendship, I ask you not to press any further.' There was the glimmer of a smile. 'Like your former Prime Minister Stanley Baldwin on a certain occasion, my lips are sealed!'

iv

'I'm driven to the conclusion,' Kemp said to Cutler later, 'that the reason's personally discreditable to von Hagen and he doesn't want to talk about it.'

'Such as, maybe, he's operated inside Russia?'

'Possibly committed atrocities there.'

'Pure revenge on the part of the Russians, sir?'

Kemp nodded. 'One can't blame them. But I'm not sure I like being used as an agent of revenge. Especially as I've known the man so well.'

'Some years ago now, sir.'

Kemp raised his eyebrows. 'What the hell difference does that make?'

'Sorry, sir. But in fact there *is* a difference. Just the fact we've gone to war since then.'

'Don't try to teach me about loyalty, Cutler.'

'No, sir.' Cutler gave a cough and went off at a tangent. 'There's something you may have noticed. I certainly have.'

'What?'

'The crew, sir. Funny atmosphere. It's spread to the naval party too.'

'I hadn't noticed, no. Can you expand, Cutler?'

Cutler screwed up his face. 'Hard to pinpoint it, but there's a wary look and everyone's on edge over something – '

'Over von Hagen for my money! That's natural, if the galley wireless has painted word pictures about the man.'

'Sure, but I think it goes deeper. It's not the danger to the ship either. Or I don't think so. It's ... oh, I guess I really don't know, sir ... something about the voyage itself maybe....'

'That's not very explicit, is it?' Kemp looked hard at the young sub-lieutenant's face: clearly Cutler was anxious and was disinclined to let the matter go by default. Kemp believed there was nothing in it; Cutler hadn't the sea experience to understand the gloom that so often affected a ship and her crew. On the liner run to Australia a miasma of ridiculous depression usually settled over the crew once they had left Fremantle homeward bound for the London River and Tilbury. It was a feeling that they simply couldn't wait to see the white cliffs of Dover again and another long voyage done. They called it an attack of the Channels. It was pretty well universal.

Cutler said, 'With your permission, sir, I'll have a word with Petty Officer Napper.'

'I wouldn't if I were you. All you'll get is a classified list of symptoms. But if you really want to, don't mind me!

v

'I dunno, sir.'

'Oh, come off it, Napper. *Petty Officer* Napper. I thought Navy senior rates kept a finger on the pulse.'

'Well, yes, sir, they does, that's true.' Petty Officer Napper, who believed that it could have been his conversation with Buckle that had started the buzz about dangers waiting in Archangel on its rounds, was trying to be non-committal. 'I remember once, sir, when I was in the old *Emperor of India*, the commander – '

'Okay. Project your mind into the here and now, all right?'

Daft little bugger, Napper thought angrily, still wet behind the ears was Cutler. In an aggrieved tone he said, 'The hands is worried, that I've noticed, yes. They don't like going into Russian waters, sir. No more do I.'

'For God's sake . . . they aren't cannibals!'

'Not far off, sir. Not far off.'

'Oh, boloney –'

'Tisn't, sir! I've 'eard yarns, seen it in the papers, spitting babies on bayonets and frying the poor little sods like eggs –'

'That was the Nazis.'

'Oh.'

'Or said to be. And I don't know about the frying, that's a new one. Back to the point, Petty Officer Napper: what's the mood?'

'They're pissed off, sir.'

'That all? They'll get over it.'

Napper was just about to say, but had decided not to in case he got any backlash, that the mood was nasty and deteriorating, when there was a sudden booming sound from for'ard and the *Hardraw Falls* checked her way through the water as the engines shuddered to full astern.

FIFTEEN

Theakston reacted fast: the moment he heard that hollow booming sound he had personally wrenched the telegraph over to emergency full astern. In the engine-room Chief Engineer Sparrow, cursing the way his engines were being mistreated, responded as fast. Quickly the strain came off the shored-up collision bulkhead for'ard. Theakston shouted across the wheelhouse at Kemp.

'Just what I feared likely!' He had spoken to Kemp's retreating back: the Commodore was on his way down the ladder, making for the site of the damage. On the way he was joined by Cutler and Napper, the latter white around the gills and moving with obvious reluctance to put himself behind the bulkhead where the danger lay.

Kemp reached the fo'c'sle door and went down the ladder into the compartment abaft the collision bulkhead. There was total confusion: he found Amory and the hands standing in around three feet of water, with more welling up from the starboard lower corner of the bulkhead, where one of the shoring beams lay snapped in two and half submerged, broken right away from the metal that it should have been sustaining. There was blood on the water, and Kemp saw two men supporting another of the hands, holding the head above the level of the water. The man was dead: the head was stove in and brain matter was oozing through the hair.

Sickened, Kemp looked away. 'What happened?' He asked Amory. 'A gradual weakening, or – '

'I reckon it was more than that,' Amory said. 'I can't say for sure, but there could have been floating ice, broken pack ice. We're likely to get plenty of that from now on.'

Kemp nodded; from the bridge no floating ice had yet been seen, but with the snow still driving down so thickly it could have been obscured from sight as it drifted past. And a big wave could perhaps have smashed a sizeable block of it against the already weakened bulkhead. A quick visual examination had already shown up a number of sheared rivets. Kemp asked, 'Any hope of controlling it, Amory? How about the pumps?' He could hear the pumps in motion but was not surprised when Amory said they were being overtaken by the water pouring through. Even since Kemp had arrived on the scene, the level had deepened by a matter of three inches or so. He saw nothing that could be done for the moment: already, under Theakston's orders, the *Hardraw Falls* was swinging round across the sea, back once again to a sternwise progress. Once she was round and steadied, Amory said, he would wait till the pumps had overcome the reduced inflow and then he would try to encase the lifted section of the bulkhead in the seaman's last hope, a cement box – the construction of a wooden framework around the damage and pouring in of enough general dunnage mixed with sand and cement to seal it off.

Kemp waited until the ship was turned and all the weight was once again off the bulkhead. As the water level came down, he returned to the bridge and put Theakston in the picture.

'One man lost, I'm sorry to say, Captain.'

Theakston said nothing but his look was formidable. Kemp moved away from him: he didn't want a barney over the man's death, for which he felt responsible. Had he not gone against Theakston's advice . . . but that was in the past and he had only responded to what he had seen as his duty to reach Archangel as fast as possible. In war, men died. That was axiomatic. But it didn't lift the lead weight from the Commodore's mind.

ii

The death made its presence felt throughout the ship. The man who had died was not in fact a particularly popular member of the crew; he had become known as something of a scrimshanker. But his death, the crunch of that shoring beam, had changed all that and he had become a symbol, a focal point of the mounting unease that had permeated the fo'c'sle hands. To die in action was one thing, to die because a stuffed-shirt commodore thought he knew better than the Old Man was quite another. It had been an unnecessary death and there might well be more, since there was still a party standing by the collision bulkhead and, according to the acting bosun, would remain there even after the cement box had been set up. Anything might happen at any moment, and most of the seamen would at one time or another find themselves taking a turn at bulkhead watch.

'And balls to that for a lark,' one of them said – the closed-face Londoner with a nasty twist to his mouth, Able Seaman Swile.

'Nothing we can do about it, mate. . . .'

'I dunno so much. We can make representations, can't we?'

'Fat lot of good!'

'Worth a go. Not to Amory or the Old Man. The bloody Navy, what was responsible in the first place.' Swile didn't say any more just then, he kept his own counsel until a propitious moment. He had his sights set on Petty Officer Napper, who had spent the voyage looking as disgruntled as a caught herring, the more so since his sad encounter with the metal rim of the washport. Napper had just the sort of fed-up look that said he might be a willing co-operator.

Swile's moment came when Napper was seen coming down a ladder and making for the naval ratings' messroom. Swile buttonholed him outside the door.

'Can I have a word, mister?'

Mister again; Napper nodded and managed a smile. 'Yer. What can I do for you?'

'Matter of me mate. The one what got it at the collision bulkhead.'

'Oh, ah? Mate of yours, was he, eh? Sorry about that, son.'

'So are we all. We don't want no more.' There was truculence in Swile's tone and Napper stiffened slightly, scenting trouble in a biggish way. 'That Commodore, he don't know what he's doing, went against the Old Man's advice . . . so we heard.'

'Who's we?' Napper asked cautiously, moving closer to the door of the messroom.

'Me and me mates.'

'You representing them, like?'

'Yes. Round Robin.'

'Round Robin, eh? Round Robin my arse! In the Andrew we call it mutiny – '

'We're not bloody Navy, mister.'

'Maybe not. I am. And you're under the Commodore's discipline and he's a rocky – RNR. A decent bloke too.' Napper might be chokker with this trip, but he resented criticism of Kemp and the Navy. 'Know something, do you? If two or more persons sign a request form – that's to say, if the request isn't made by one man as an individual – then we calls it mutiny. A mutinous gathering, see? Even though only on paper.'

Swile sneered. 'Load of crap is that.'

'Laid down in King's Regulations, crap or not.'

Swile lifted a bunched fist and waved it at Napper's nose. 'You just pass on what I said. It's not just you bloody Navy lot. It's that Nazi. All this is because he's aboard. You can't deny that. No one can. We don't want our lives put at risk for a fucking Nazi.'

'Well,' Napper said hastily. 'I see your point, of course, but don't you bloody involve me.' He dodged the threatening fist and managed to open the messroom door and slide to safety. Once inside he sank down on the bench running alongside the mess table and blinked in agitation. He found his hands were shaking. Mutiny was very, very nasty and although Napper didn't know quite how it worked out aboard a merchant ship he did know he had to shift the buck very quickly indeed, and that meant having another word with Cutler and being rather more forthcoming than last time. Cutler had seemed already to have a suspicion so he would have a ready ear.

After allowing the disaffected seaman time to bugger off, Napper climbed to the bridge. Arrived there, he sensed an atmosphere: ructions between Kemp and Theakston? Not his business. He approached Cutler and saluted through the driving snow.

'Mr Cutler, sir?'

'What is it, Petty Officer Napper?'

'What we was talking about earlier sir. What you asked me about – '

'Right! Go on, I'm listening.'

Napper reported the conversation with the crew member. Cutler asked, 'He approached you, did he?'

'Yessir.'

'What for?'

Napper stared. 'I just said, sir. Round Robin ... from the ship's crew like – '

'Yes. But what precisely was he asking?'

There was a longish pause, then Napper said, 'I – I dunno, sir.'

'He must have asked something.'

'Yessir. But – '

'He didn't say and you didn't ask. I'd have expected better than that of a PO. Wouldn't you?'

'Yessir. No, sir.' Napper, flustered now, felt his face going red beneath the layers of wool that almost obscured it. Bloody little ponce, young enough to be his son, talking to him like that. He'd been daft not to have approached the Commodore: the ship wasn't RN and Kemp, he wasn't the pusser sort who'd turn his back on a rating who addressed him direct rather than through proper service channels.

'Well?'

In a surly tone Napper said, 'He spoke of the prisoner, that's all I know, sir. Point is, the crew's upset about that bloke being lost for'ard. They don't think it should have happened.'

'What's that got to do with the prisoner?'

'I dunno, sir.'

'H'm.' Silence; the *Hardraw Falls* moved slowly backwards towards her Russian landfall, nearer and nearer to the nastiness, as Napper saw it, of Comrade Stalin's iron fist. You couldn't blame the crew for being uneasy. Napper was uneasy too, for all sorts of reasons – the Nazi himself, the damage to the ship and the resulting danger, the likelihood of further German attack, and his own personal problem which in the end might mean an enforced visit to a Russian quack after all. Cutler ended the silence abruptly. 'All right, PO. Ears to the ground and report as necessary. Do a little discreet probing, and in the meantime I'll have a word with the Commodore and Captain Theakston. What was the man's name?'

Oh, bugger, Napper thought. He said woodenly, 'I dunno, sir.'

'Jeez!'

Theakston said, 'It sounds like Swile. Able seaman. A bolshie sort.'

'Dangerous?' Kemp asked.

Theakston nodded. 'Aye, he could be. This sort of thing's always potentially dangerous – but I don't need to tell you.' He gave one of his rare smiles. 'You'll have to forgive me, Commodore. Your RN cap badge keeps on making me forget you're one of us basically. The grey-funnel lads look at things differently.'

'I know what you mean,' Kemp said. In the RN discipline was maintained, at any rate in the gate-and-gaiters world of the capital ships, under the overall threat of the Naval Discipline Act and King's Regulations; merchant shipmasters had no such sanction to back them up beyond a bad discharge at the end of the voyage. Discipline had to be maintained by the sheer force of personality of the master and his officers, maintained over a crew that was much more individualist than any warship's company.

Theakston broke into Kemp's thoughts. 'They see a Jonah. That's obvious.'

'Yes. Von Hagen – equally obviously.'

'I'd watch it if I were you, Commodore.'

'In what way?'

'Why, the Nazi. There could be trouble.'

'You don't mean they might try to get him?'

Theakston nodded. 'That's exactly what I mean.'

Kemp gave an incredulous laugh. 'That'd be madness, sheer insanity! They wouldn't have a hope in hell – '

'I don't know so much. A concerted attack, a rush of men against your sentry. Would you open fire, Commodore, if that happened? Somehow I don't think you would.'

Kemp said, 'We'll cross that bridge if we come to it. I don't believe we will, not for a moment. What would be the point, anyway?'

Theakston shrugged. 'Aroused passions don't always worry about a point, do they? I could quote many an instance . . . if Swile stirs them up to it, I'd not call it impossible by a long chalk.

Of course, I agree with what you said just now – madness. It would be. We'd not get much of a reception in Archangel, not from the British, not from the Russians. But I never underestimate the destructive power of Jonahs, Commodore – ' He broke off. 'I'm teaching my grandmother again!'

'Grandmother,' Kemp repeated in a curious tone, and Theakston gave him an enquiring look. 'I happen to have a grandmother.'

'Still alive, d'you mean?'

'Yes. Old, of course, very old. Seafaring background – my grandfather and great-grandfather were both square-rigged masters.'

'Uh-huh?'

Kemp said, 'She believed in Jonahs, too. She'd heard so many stories. So have I – from her. Many times. She's got repetitive in her old age.' Kemp's thoughts, by a natural mental process, had gone back across the lonely, bitter sea to the cottage in Meopham. In the last conversation he'd had with Mary, on the phone back in Oban, she had hinted that his grandmother wasn't too good, feeling the cold ... He brought himself back to the present, sharply. 'Very well, Captain. I'll have my ratings alerted.'

iv

Swile had done a lot of talking around the ship, having worked himself up into an inflamed state of mind. His words had penetrated and all hands were thinking hard thoughts about the Nazi agent. Swile had hinted, no more so far, that the ship would be better off without him. He was received with jeers: sure, the ship would be better off without a Jerry aboard, but what could be done about it? Why worry anyway? There wasn't far to go now to Archangel, and the rumour said the Nazi was to be handed over to the Russians.

'Bloody likely I don't think,' Swile said, thumping a fist down on the mess table. His face was blue with the cold: he'd just come in from a turn at the collision bulkhead, surrounded by all that frozen metal and a slop of water from time to time that froze immediately it had entered and turned the compartment into a skating rink. There was a bruise on Swile's cheek where, as the result of a skid, he had impacted against one of the shoring beams. 'Buzzes ... they're not always right, we all know that. Put around deliberate, half the time. Stands to reason, they're not going to hand a Nazi spy over to the Russians – he'll be wanted in UK.'

'So what? Where do we come in?'

'We don't want the sod aboard all the way home, that's what. For one thing – look, he's a kind of bloody magnet, right? The Jerries'll want him back. We know that – there was that Jerry cruiser. That won't be the only try, will it? Homeward bound, they'll be waiting for us, the whole bloody German fleet will!'

Swile spent the greater part of his off-watch hours that afternoon in persuasion, elaborating on the threat posed by the Nazi's presence aboard. Hook the German away, he said – surprise the Naval sentry, that wouldn't be difficult – then he remembered he'd spoken of the German to that Napper. Well, he could cover that, stop any extra guard by having another word with Napper and disperse any anxieties. He went on: hook von Hagen out of the cabin. But not just yet. They would wait till the ship was almost into Archangel and the attention of the Commodore and his assistant was on the business of safe entry through the ice, then they would attack.

And then what?

Hide the Nazi away, Swile said. Hide him and then at the right moment produce him, but produce him into Russian custody. With Russian port officials, and probably the secret police, aboard they couldn't go wrong. Kemp wouldn't have a chance. The Russians would be grateful and the *Hardraw Falls* would be free of its Jonah. And by the time they joined a homeward convoy, von Hagen's delivery would be bound to have become known to the Nazis and there would be no special attention paid to the ship. So what about it?

Nothing about it was the general verdict: Swile had gone round the bend. Where could you hide a bloke so he wouldn't be found? You wouldn't have a hope. It wasn't as though he could be nabbed and hustled away unnoticed. There would have to be a fight to get him out of naval custody.

'Just you wait,' Swile said.

The cement box had been constructed and Amory reported that the collision bulkhead could take more strain. They were able to move a little faster. But Theakston was adamant that his ship would not be turned back again. They must make the best way they could astern. By this time the *Hardraw Falls* was only about some eighty miles from the entry to the White Sea – say, thirteen hours' steaming at their new speed – with another two hundred and forty miles to Archangel itself through enclosed waters. There had been no further enemy attacks and Kemp believed they were safe now in that regard.

'Fingers crossed, though,' he said.

'Aye. The snow's thinning. We're going to be visible again if there's anything around.' Theakston lifted his binoculars and examined what there was of a horizon. There wasn't much but it was tending to extend as the snowfall lessened. He looked down at his decks: the ship was a moving snowdrift, with the stuff piled everywhere, thickly, half-way up the after end of the central island superstructure and against the fo'c'sle, with the windlass kept as clear as possible and in working order so that the anchors could be used if necessary as they made the final port approach. As well as the snow, there was ice in plenty, so much topweight of it that the ship was a little below her marks. The wind was still bitter, painfully so to exposed flesh. Inside his thick gloves, Theakston's fingers were numb, no feeling in them at all other than a dull pain like toothache. His feet were the same: Russian convoys, he thought, you can keep them ... as so often on this trip he thought again about his wife. No news, nothing at all, the lot of any seaman in wartime, and it was no use hoping for any on arrival at Archangel either. The PQ convoy itself was carrying the mail and no more would come through until the next sailing from a UK port. They would all have to wait for that. The ship was likely to be in Archangel for the whole of the winter now: the collision bulkhead and the torn bows would have to be repaired and at any moment the ice would close the port and that would be that.

Theakston had spoken of this to Kemp. Kemp said it would be

a pound to a penny the *Hardraw Falls* would be left with a care and maintenance party while the rest of the crew and the naval contingent were entrained for Murmansk to take passage in the next homeward convoy.

'And von Hagen?' Theakston had asked.

Kemp said heavily, 'What happens to him depends on our naval liaison staff in Archangel. I don't seen any hope for him.'

'Anything more from Napper?'

'He seems to think it's died down.'

'Von Hagen'd be better off left to my crew! Better than the Russians.'

'Perhaps. But that's not a philosophy we can afford to indulge in, Captain.'

Theakston, recalling that conversation now, thought again about his sick wife: he couldn't afford to spend the winter iced up in Archangel with Dora on her own and missing him, but the ship had to have an officer left in charge. Maybe Amory . . . Amory had no home ties. But, of course, that wouldn't be Theakston's decision. Once his owners had been informed of the situation, orders would come through and he just had to wait. Kemp would be all right: they wouldn't leave a convoy Commodore kicking his heels in a Russian port.

Throughout the ship, as the end of the outward run loomed, others were having similar thoughts of news and home. Cutler wondered if he might pick up those slender threads with Roz. There could be a chance; if there wasn't, well, there would be other girls looking for a good time in the midst of war, chasing that good time avidly, in fact, in case it was the last they ever had.

Petty Officer Napper was wondering how long the swelling was going to last: he didn't want to go home with *that*, though it would be nice to have the comforts and the wife's attention to his many ills. He was wondering, too, if he would be able to re-stock his cure-all kit in Archangel. Or even if it would be wise: the coms could have some weird ideas on medicine for all he knew, they were a primitive lot and probably unhygienic with it. But he was getting short of aperients, and that was important. The Russians must have something in that line, even if it was only old-fashioned stuff like Gregory powder, or liquorice powder, or Epsom salts or such . . . Napper's wife swore by Epsom salts but

Napper himself found them not strong enough unless you took a triple dose and that was painful to say the least, talk about griping pains in the stomach! Once, Napper hadn't been for a fortnight, during which he had taken everything he could think of but with a nil result, and then at last he'd taken an enormous dose of Epsom salts that acted as a catalyst, making the last fourteen days' aperients explode together in one God Almighty go.

Napper was thinking about this when he stepped gingerly out on to the open deck. The ice was hell and very dangerous but could be negotiated so long as you kept a tight grip on the lifelines, and exercise was necessary to help keep things working internally. Moving along the starboard side of the after well-deck, past the cargo hatches invisible under the lying snow, he saw that the visibility had increased a good deal and the snow was coming down thinly and half-heartedly although still propelled against his body by that terrible east wind, a wind that had never agreed with him and always made him feel more out of sorts than was his norm.

Then, dimly through the overcast that was still with the ship, he saw the loom of a vessel away off the starboard bow. He gave a yell towards the bridge just as Cutler had reported to the Commodore. A moment later there was the flash of a signal lamp from the unknown ship.

On the bridge, Leading Signalman Corrigan reported the challenge. 'One of ours, sir!'

'Make the reply,' Kemp said.

Corrigan sent out the answer to the challenge and then reported, 'She's made her pendant number, sir. *Neath*, sir.'

One of the cruiser escorts. 'A little late,' Kemp said unsteadily, but there was enormous relief in his voice.

'She asks, do you require assistance, sir.'

For form's sake Kemp lifted and eye at Theakston, who gave a shrug. Kemp said, 'Make: "Thank you but do not require assistance currently. Glad to have you standing by should I need a tow."'

After Kemp's signal had been acknowledged, and the lean lines of the cruiser had become fully visible, more signalling came across. The convoy had been diverted into Murmansk and the battleships and cruisers of the Home Fleet had engaged the

157

German heavy ships; there had been losses on both sides but the German force had broken off the action and steamed away to the south, shadowed by a cruiser squadron. The remainder of the PQ escort had entered Murmansk with the main body of the convoy.

Kemp said, 'All's well that ends well, if you'll forgive the cliché.'

'It's not ended yet,' Theakston said.

'You mean von Hagen?'

'Aye! And him apart, there's nowt so daft as complacency.'

Kemp felt reprimanded, and was to have cause to remember Theakston's words.

SIXTEEN

Theakston brought down his glasses. He said, 'Cape Kanin, dead ahead. And dead on my ETA. I'll be altering course when we're off Kiya. Plenty of time yet.'

Kemp nodded, studying the seas ahead. The visibility was a lot better now; the snow had stopped altogether a few hours before, and for a while before that there had been nothing more than occasional flurries. The wind remained, as did the biting cold. There had been more drifting ice through which the stern of the *Hardraw Falls* had pushed at her painfully slow speed. All in all, Kemp thought the PQ had been the most worrying, the most frustrating convoy he had ever been with. The slow progress had been agonizing and the presence aboard of von Hagen seemed to have distorted everything away from the normal run of convoys. Not long after his conversation with Theakston, Petty Officer Napper had made another report, somewhat ostentatiously showing how dedicated he was to his duty.

'That there Swile, sir.'

'Yes?'

'Acting furtive, sir.'

'In what way?'

'Just furtive like, sir. Talking to the others out of the corner of his mouth . . . looking around first.'

'But without noticing you?'

'Yessir. Kept meself hidden, sir. Or anyway, looking as though I was doing something else and not aware of him.'

'Very cloak-and-dagger,' Kemp said, tongue in check.

'Beg pardon, sir?'

'Never mind, Napper. Carry on the good work, that's all.

Have you any definite ideas yet, any clue as to what Swile might be preparing to do?'

'No, sir, not yet, sir.'

'Very well.' Kemp made a dismissive gesture; Napper saluted and left the bridge. He would have liked to do some closer eaves-dropping on Swile, but so far hadn't found a way of achieving this. Swile clammed up whenever he caught a sight of the naval ratings and short of disguising himself as a ventilation shaft there was no way Napper could get up close at the right moment. Being honest, Napper didn't see what Swile could possibly do; it was too late in the voyage, for one thing, they were coming right slap into enclosed Russian waters now, would soon have the communist land mass right around them, which was a terrifying thought in itself and never mind Swile and von Hagen. It was giving Napper the shivers: Stalin, the Man of Steel, was a real bully boy and by all accounts Russia was a joyless place at the best of times, all snow and ice and east wind and hunched-looking foodless peasants dressed in old sacks and such and fur hats – he'd seen shots on the newsreels in the Apollo cinema in Albert Road in Southsea, the posh part of Pompey, though Albert Road itself wasn't posh – but a sight posher than bloody Russia had looked like! Napper would heave a sigh of genuine relief when he was west of the North Cape again and heading south. The Russians could keep the *Hardraw Falls* so long as they parted with Petty Officer Napper . . . which in worrying fact they just might not. You never knew with dictators, they were so filled with a sense of their own import-ance that they thought they could get away with anything and possession being nine parts of the law so to speak, Stalin might go and impound all hands once they were in his net with the hammer and sickle being brandished over them.

Bloody communists!

Napper had always voted Conservative: there was no muck-ing about with the Conservatives, they understood class dif-ferences and were a bolster to Napper's position as a petty officer, above the common herd of seaman. With the coms, all were equal, so Napper understood. Why, they even called their admirals Flagmen, just as though they were stokers or supply assistants! Napper recalled the programme for the fleet review back in 1937, for the coronation of King George VI . . . the USS had sent along the old 23,000-ton battleship *Marat*, with a daft-looking bent-back fore funnel that was said to keep the fumes away from the bridge and foretop – anyway, she had carried an admiral, Flagman Ivanov.

For all Napper knew, Flagman Ivanov could be lurking in Archangel ... maybe this Ivanov could even have come to the Pompey review as a spy and knew that Napper voted Conservative and never mind the sanctified secrecy of the ballot box.

Napper's jaws worked like those of an old-age pensioner without teeth. He was getting himself into a panic and that would never do – he was talking bollocks to himself, of course he was. Nevertheless, the awful feeling of doom persisted as the *Hardraw Falls* crept on arse backwards, as he put it, and came inshore of Cape Kanin, pushing into the White Sea and more ice that cracked and banged and scraped along her sides, making her sound like a drum gone wrong. By this time Napper had a full view of actual Russia for the first time in his life, only a fragment of it, of course, but quite enough.

Slowly, the ship slid on into the White Sea: twelve thousand tons of high explosive, a Nazi agent, a crew showing signs of a cack-handed mutiny, and the continuation of Napper's own personal problem that was defying his reduced stock of lanolin.

ii

'Ship approaching from ahead!'

The shout came down from the lookout in the crow's nest. Kemp called back, 'Can you identify?'

'Looks like an ice-breaker, sir.'

Theakston said, 'Clearing a channel. We're going to need it by the look of things.' By this time they were acting as their own ice-breaker, not very effectively since all they had to push with was the stern. To go through ice you needed not only a nice sharp bow but a heavily reinforced one at that, such as the proper ice-breaker would have. The *Neath*, however, had moved ahead of the *Hardraw Falls* and was doing her best to clear some sort of fairway. Both Theakston and Kemp knew they were only just going to beat the big freeze, the total ice-up of the port – beat it inwards, that was. If there had been a normal turnround they would have beaten it outwards too, most likely, but the damaged bow had put paid to that prospect.

'Ice-breaker signalling, sir,' Corrigan reported some minutes later. 'From British Naval Liaison Officer Archangel to Commodore: "Intend to board. I shall approach your starboard side."'

'So BNLO's come out in person,' Kemp murmured. 'I wish us both luck!' To Corrigan he said 'Acknowledge.'

'Aye, aye, sir.'

Cutler, standing in the bridge wing with the Commodore, said, 'This is where it starts, sir. Von Hagen.'

'Yes. The interrogation, I imagine, while we go on for Archangel.'

'And the hand-over. . . .'

Kemp nodded, his face set into hard lines, deep clefts from the corners of his mouth. The dirt had come home to roost, or was about to. It went right against all his principles but, despite his promise to von Hagen, he saw no way out. Perhaps he had been wrong to make that promise, wrong to lift the man's hopes, but the promise had been only to try his best, nothing more, and he could still do that whatever the abysmal chances of success. In any case, von Hagen was an enemy with, apparently, a record of dirt on his own account. Kemp said. 'When they come alongside, Cutler, go down and meet BNLO. He's to be taken to my cabin and he's not to contact von Hagen in the meantime.'

'Very good, sir.' Cutler gave one of his American-style salutes and left the bridge. The Russian vessel was not so far off now. Theakston had passed orders for a ladder to be put over on the starboard side, from the fore well-deck, and Cutler went down to stand by with Amory and four seamen of the ship's crew, among them Able Seaman Swile. By now the *Hardraw Falls* had stopped engines so as to make it easier for BNLO to jump for the ladder and climb aboard, and was drifting slowly through the ice under what was left of her sternway.

There was a crunching sound as the ice-breaker moved closer and great broken floes of ice surged up between the two hulls. From the bridge Kemp saw BNLO as he took him to be – an officer wearing the gold oak-leaved cap of a commander or captain. 'He's come with plenty of company,' he remarked to Theakston. There was an unidentifiable muffled figure and three seamen of the British Navy, armed with rifles and bayonets, plus another rating, obviously a signalman since he was carrying a battery-fed Aldis lamp and two hand flags for sending semaphore. Also waiting their turn to leap for the dangling rope ladder were two uniformed Russians who had the look of the OGPU, and a civilian in a vast fur hat, pulled down low over a dead white face with a slit for a mouth.

'I don't like the look of that bugger,' Kemp said as he looked down from the bridge. Unkindly, he had a hope that the man would miss the ladder and plunge into the cracking ice. But none of them did that; they came over the side behind BNLO and stood in a group in the well-deck as the ice-breaker moved away. Kemp saw Cutler salute BNLO and have a few words with him before turning for'ard and leading the way up the ladder to the central island and on up to the master's deck. The fur-coated Russian, Kemp noted, was having a good look around as he climbed and for an instant their eyes met. The Russian's, Kemp thought, were like those of a fish, cold and yet liquid.

A couple of minutes later Cutler came to the bridge.

'In your cabin, sir. Captain Brigger – BNLO, with a Lieutenant Phipps of the RNVR. And a Russian by the name of I. K. Tarasov.'

'H'm. What's his function, Cutler?'

'He's a colonel, sir. That's all BNLO said when he made the introductions. I guess he's probably secret police. He kind of looks that way.'

'So I noticed. All right, Cutler, I'll go down.'

Theakston asked, 'All clear to move on in, Commodore?'

'Yes, please. I'd be obliged if you'd let me know immediately if I'm wanted on the bridge, Captain. Never mind BNLO or I. K. Tarasov.'

'Right you are,' Theakston said.

Cutler asked, 'Do you want me with you, sir?'

'No, thank you, Cutler. If I do need you, I'll shout up the voice-pipe.' Feeling oddly and unusually nervous, Kemp clattered down the ladder to the master's deck and went into the alleyway. He glanced at the armed sentry on von Hagen's door and then went into his own cabin, outside which the British naval ratings and the uniformed Russians waited in a silent group, making way for the Commodore as he came up.

In Kemp's cabin, Captain Brigger and Colonel Tarasov were standing waiting with Lieutenant Phipps, now seen to have the

163

Special Branch green cloth between the gold rings of his rank. Kemp shook hands and said, 'I'd like to know to whom I'm speaking, Captain Brigger. Colonel Tarasov's function, I refer to.'

Brigger said, 'He's a special envoy, Commodore.'

'From?'

There was a nervous tic in BNLO's face, a twitch of a beetling eyebrow accompanied by a contraction of the puffy flesh below the right eye. He said, 'From the Kremlin. From Marshal Stalin, personally.'

Kemp nodded. 'Yes, I see.' He faced the Russian. 'Do you speak English, Colonel Tarasov?'

'I speak good English, yes.'

'That makes it easier, then.'

'You do not speak Russian.' It was more a statement than a question. Kemp said regretfully he had no Russian; Colonel Tarasov looked down his nose with something of a sneer: the English, his expression seemed to say, were uneducated.

'Please sit down, gentlemen. Er ... you'd like a drink, I expect?'

'Thank you, vodka,' Tarasov said.

'No vodka, I'm afraid. Gin?'

'Ah, gin. Very well, gin.' Tarasov made a face. BNLO and Phipps opted for gin-and-bitters. Kemp pressed his bell and Torrence entered the cabin with a clean cloth over his arm. He took the Commodore's order, which included whisky, and left the cabin with his usual brisk air, wishing he could linger outside the door after he'd served the drinks, but with such a mob around that wasn't possible, which was a pity. On the other hand, it was sometimes possible to overhear conversations in his pantry which wasn't all that far from Kemp's cabin. There were interconnecting pipes and ducts that could carry sound, and even though there was interference from the hum of the forced draught system Torrence's ears were sharp with much practice.

In the cabin BNLO started the ball rolling, glancing at his wrist watch as he did so. He had the look of a harassed man and one who had a good deal of work to do. 'You'll know why we're here, of course,' he said.

'Yes.' Kemp wasn't going to give him any help, was going to be non-committal, anyway at the start.

'You've had no trouble?'

BNLO obviously meant, trouble with von Hagen. Kemp said, 'No, no trouble.' He saw no reason to make anything of the abortive suicide attempt. The episode had been noted in the ship's log and his own log as Commodore of the convoy and in his view it had nothing to do with BNLO

'That's good,' BNLO said a little lamely. Kemp made a guess that Captain Brigger was as much out of his depth as he was himself: both of them were seamen, not diplomats or Intelligence agents. That would be the province of Lieutenant Phipps of the Navy's Special Branch – another guess and an obvious one now confirmed as correct by BNLO, who said, 'Phipps here – he has some questions to put. To von Hagen.'

Tarasov said, 'In my presence.'

'We've been into that,' Brigger said, twitching.

'I am adamant. I have taken note of what you said, Captain Brigger, and I am adamant.'

Brigger showed a line of yellowish teeth, briefly. He said, 'Like Stalin.'

'What was that?'

'Nothing – I'm sorry. Marshal Stalin is a strong man like you, Colonel Tarasov – '

'Yes.'

Kemp said, 'Would someone explain, please?'

'Yes – I'm sorry, Commodore. Colonel Tarasov wished – '

'Wishes.' Tarasov's narrow, peaked face was shoved forward.

'Wishes to be present when Phipps – er – talks to von Hagen. However, that's not in accord with my own orders from the Admiralty, as I have explained. But Colonel Tarasov is – er – '

'Adamant?' Kemp asked with the makings of a grin.

'Yes.'

'That's easily settled,' Kemp said. 'For now, von Hagen's in my charge. I'm responsible, and I shall not permit Colonel Tarasov to interview von Hagen at this juncture. I am adamant too.' He turned to Lieutenant Phipps. 'He's all yours. You may go to his cabin, alone.'

There was a tap at the door and Torrence came in with the tray of drinks and glasses.

'A little local difficulty I'd call it,' Torrence reported a few min
utes later to Chief Steward Buckle, whose mind was once again
on caviar for the black market. Torrence had contrived to linger a
little outside the cabin door, appearing to tap on it but not allow
ing his knuckles to make contact until he'd heard some of the
natter. 'There's this Russki bloke, nasty little sod ... wants to
talk to the Jerry. Kemp, 'e won't have it. Got all hoity-toity about
it and raised 'is voice like. Now one of our blokes that come
aboard, RNVR officer, 'e's in the Jerry's cabin alone with him.'
Torrence paused. 'Course, that von Hagen's an old mate of
Kemp's, we know that.'

'Can't fall out with the Russians when you're in Russia, eh?'

Torrence scratched his head reflectively. 'Oh, I dunno. They
can't interfere with a British ship. International Law.'

'In time of war?'

'Dunno. I expect so, Chief.'

'You didn't hear any more?'

Torrence shook his head. 'No. Did me best, but no luck. Acou
stics went off as you might say. Shame, that.'

Buckle went back to his calculations, trying to balance the
likely price of caviar in Archangel against what the market back
in UK would bear. Trouble was, the bloody Russians would
guess what he had in mind and would up the price to reduce his
profit margin.

Swile said, 'Came down from Buckle ... the buzz. Makes nasty
hearing.'

'What was it, then?'

'Kemp. He's getting von Hagen in on the Old Pals' Act, see.
And I've bin doing a lot of thinking. Putting two and two
together. Those Russians that come aboard with the Navy ...
reckon they've come for the Nazi and Kemp's not letting him go
in case he's in for a lousy time, which of course he is if the Russ
ians get hold of him. And you know what that means: like I said
all along, the bugger comes with us, all the way to UK – right

Swile lit a fag and blew a trail of smoke. He was not blind to the obvious fact that the *Hardraw Falls* would be in Archangel for a full due; but, like Kemp, he believed that most of the crew would go home in another ship leaving ice-free Murmansk, and go home with von Hagen. So his anxieties remained.

'Don't see what anyone can do about it.'

'I'll be thinking,' Swile said. 'If the Nazi can be got out of that cabin, I reckon that's all we need do. The Russians'll do the rest. After all, we're in Russian waters, eh?' He left the fo'c'sle mess and went out to the fore well-deck. The *Hardraw Falls* was proceeding inwards through the channel cleared by the *Neath* and the ice-breaker, which had moved ahead of the British cruiser. Swile had gathered from one of the quartermasters that it was a long haul into Archangel itself, anyway at their current dead slow speed and moving astern. There should be time. Swile brooded: that Nazi had really got on his wick. He wanted to see him suffer and he knew the Russians would make him do that. Swile brooded on the past and what Mosley's thugs had done to him in London's East End in those prewar days, brooded on the years he'd spent in prison and the lessons he'd learned whilst inside, lessons not in going straight but in ways of getting even and causing damage to persons in the process. He'd had some tough companions in HM prisons, some tough enemies too, but he'd survived by the strength that had been in his own body and still was.

He looked towards the Russian coastline. The place was iron hard, grey dismal, oppressive – just the place for a Nazi to ponder on past misdeeds in the short time that would be left to him. Swile looked up at the bridge, saw Theakston looking aft from the wing, using his binoculars. That Cutler was with him. No sign of Kemp – he'd still be below, putting in his oar on the Nazi's behalf. Swile flung his arms about his body: he'd never known such cold. The crunch of the ice as the ship pushed her stern against it had a sound of doom and foreboding and ahead of the two British ships the Russian ice-breaker appeared to have slowed a little as if waiting for the *Hardraw Falls* to catch up.

SEVENTEEN

Lieutenant Phipps was a patient man; he'd learned patience in the corridors of the Foreign Office, the long career corridors that led to power. A prewar diplomat, Phipps had been specially commissioned into the RNVR without having to go through the often lengthy process of being commissioned from the lower deck. Phipps was a valuable man and since entering the Navy had added to his attainments a formidable ability to interrogate. He was a linguist and spoke both German and Russian amongst other languages. And he had an ability to make people trust him. He had a youthful face that belied his maturity and he looked honest: he had a happy smile, which currently he was using on von Hagen.

'Just a few words,' he said. 'You must see there's no reason why you shouldn't talk to me in the absence of Colonel Tarasov.'

'Before I'm handed over to him.'

'Well – yes. I admit that's the idea. Under certain circumstances, that is.' Phipps paused and held out his cigarette case. Von Hagen took one and Phipps leaned forward, flicking a light. 'I think you understand me, don't you, Colonel von Hagen?'

Von Hagen nodded. 'Oh yes. If I talk, I'll not be handed over. Commodore Kemp has already told me that.'

'Yes, of course. You and he – you knew each other before the war.'

'Yes, indeed we did.' There was an inward look in the German's eyes. 'They were good times. . . .'

'But you haven't told Commodore Kemp anything, have you?'

168

'No.'

Phipps smiled. 'He's not a good interrogator, is he? Not his line. But it's mine.'

'You mean – '

'I mean only that I'm in a position to help. I'm not suggesting . . . anything crude. That can be left to the Russians, if you get that far. All I'm suggesting is that you take advantage of a kind of salvation. Not too strong a word, Colonel von Hagen. In Britain you'll be treated properly, and after the war you'll go back to Germany. If the Russians have custody of you – '

'Yes, yes, I know very well, you have no need to elaborate, Lieutenant Phipps.'

'Quite. Then perhaps you'll – '

'No.' The German shook his head.

'But surely – '

'No. If you ask the reason, it's this: I don't believe your promises. I believe that even if I talked to you, I would still be handed over to the Russians. I believe this because I know my own value to them, and also, and over-ridingly, because it is the Russians whose waters we are in and who have the whip hand.'

'Oh no. I assure you – '

Von Hagen made a dismissive gesture. 'Your assurances . . . no! You will tell me that pressures would be put on the Kremlin by Whitehall, that Winston Churchill himself would erupt like a volcano over his cigar, that the course of the war would be interrupted in the interest of my salvation. All that would be words only. Matters would not happen that way. I am not a fool, Lieutenant Phipps.'

'I never suggested you were, though I had hoped . . . however, there's something else.' Phipps looked away for a moment. 'You never married, Colonel.'

'No.'

'But there was someone in London, before the war called you away.'

Von Hagen's face went white and he jerked a little, but he said nothing.

'Marie-Anne de Tourville. A Frenchwoman.' Phipps stubbed out his cigarette half smoked. He lit another and blew smoke towards von Hagen. 'She's still there. Completely unmolested, but under surveillance.'

'Why under surveillance? She was never a Nazi sympathizer, that was separate from my activities, she knew nothing – '

'We know that, Colonel. She's clean.'

'Then – '

Phipps smiled. 'She can be brought in on suspicion. We can do that at any time. We can always find charges.'

'Trumped-up, of course.'

'Of course. If you think that's dirty, have a good look at your own hands and Herr Hitler's, Colonel. Even the British can be beastly, you know, if pushed. We – '

'This, then, is the threat?'

Phipps said, 'Yes, I'm afraid so. I honestly don't like it, but there it is, I'm under orders from a certain department of state – '

'The monster Churchill?'

'Not the monster Churchill, and I'm surprised at you of all people falling for propaganda. Mr Churchill knows nothing of this – there are many things he has to be kept in ignorance of.' Phipps looked at his wrist-watch as if assessing how much longer he had before I.K.Tarasov began creating. 'If you don't answer the questions I shall put, then a message will go to London once we have reached Archangel. Mamselle de Tourville will be arrested on certain charges. She will be imprisoned without trial, held under Regulation 18b. She won't be comfortable, Colonel.' Phipps brought out a handkerchief and blew his nose. 'Matters could become, well, fairly extreme.'

ii

Kemp sat on in his cabin with Captain Brigger and I.K.Tarasov, the latter obviously furious at having been baulked – quite why, Kemp didn't really know: Tarasov's time was presumably to come unless he, Kemp, could find a way of keeping von Hagen aboard. The prospect of that looked so dim as to be invisible although Brigger could be an ally. But he would have no more effect than Kemp, probably – and of course he was under orders from the Admiralty even though he wouldn't be liking them any more than Kemp. Kemp and Brigger meanwhile chatted of this and that, of prewar days largely, innocuous stuff, reminiscences of ships that had gone already in the war, men whom both had known, naval officers with whom Kemp had served when doing his RNR time annually aboard a ship of the fleet. I. K. Tarasov listened, no doubt hoping to pick up an indiscretion. His face, Kemp thought, was like that of a rat: the fur collar and the fur hat, still on his head, gave him the appearance in fact of a rat peering out of a ball of oakum. . . .

The *Hardraw Falls* moved on.

Tarasov spoke. 'Your Lieutenant Phipps, Captain. He is taking a long time.'

'Yes, isn't he?' BNLO said in a pleasant tone. Tarasov's thin mouth clamped shut like a trap. He got to his feet, brushed impatiently past Kemp, and glared out from the square port at the barren sea and the desolate land sliding past in the distance. Maybe, Kemp thought, he was wondering if that terrible land was going to be so welcoming when he had to report that the British had interrogated von Hagen without his own presence, that he had been unable to shift the British Commodore. . . . All at once Kemp was seized with a hatred of the land he was approaching, a deep loathing of its totalitarianism, as bad as that of Adolf Hitler with his tantrums in Berchtesgaden or wherever. If I. K. Tarasov was typical of Stalin's secret police, which no doubt he was, then it would be a sordid act to hand over von Hagen, to deliver him into the hands of barbarism.

There was a tap at the door.

'Come in,' Kemp said. Tarasov turned round. One of the armed British naval ratings stood in the doorway. He addressed Brigger.

'Lieutenant Phipps, sir. He'd like a word. Just with you, sir.'

Brigger got to his feet, lifting an eyebrow at Kemp. 'All right, Commodore?'

Kemp nodded. 'Of course.' BNLO left the cabin. Tarasov went back to his study of land and sea.

iii

'Any luck, Phipps?'

'Yes, sir. In the end.'

'You used the woman angle, did you?'

'I did. I went the whole hog. As far as the death penalty.'

171

'On a charge of which she's wholly innocent.'

'Yes – '

'You're a hard customer, Phipps.'

'We have to be, sir. We're all bastards now, thanks to Hitler.'

'What did he tell you, Phipps?'

Phipps said, 'There are German agents operating inside Russia – that's not news to us, of course, and in a general sense it won't be news to Tarasov either. The point is, these are specially infiltrated agents and von Hagen has the names and whereabouts – and the orders. The orders are simple, very straightforward. The agents are inside Russia to carry out an assassination.' Phipps paused for effect. 'Guess who?'

BNLO's mouth tightened. 'Not – ?'

'Yes. Stalin. Stalin himself.'

'So that's why he has to be handed over!'

'It's vital to them,' Phipps said. 'If Stalin's knocked off, that gives Hitler his chance against a Russia *in extremis* – the Kremlin couldn't hope to hide it, not with all the hierarchy jockeying for position, in-fighting for the succession.'

'But why should the British government – how could the Kremlin have known – '

Phipps interrupted. 'My guess would be that the Kremlin has picked up a little but not enough. They don't know who, how or when. Von Hagen does. The Kremlin presumably knows he knows, hence the pressure on our war cabinet to cough him up.'

'Yes, I see.' The two officers were out on the open deck, in the bitter cold that currently they scarcely felt. BNLO walked up and down, with quick, rather nervous steps, with Phipps keeping step beside him. 'Has von Hagen given you the details, the full facts – names and so on?'

'Yes, he has.'

Brigger said, 'I don't see why he caved in on your threat about the woman – or rather, I don't see why he should believe you when you said she'd be left alone if he talked.'

'That's easy, sir. He knows she's not involved in anything, just as we do. We really haven't use at all for her other than as a lever. There'd be absolutely no point in *not* letting her go once he'd talked – he knows that.' Phipps added, 'We were just going to be – er – '

'Complete and utter shits,' BNLO said, 'if he *hadn't* talked!'

'Yes, I'm afraid so. But now we haven't got to be. Not in regard to the woman.'

'And von Hagen? Surely we can pass his information to Tarasov ourselves?'

Phipps shook his head. 'There's no change in his position, sir. The orders were very precise: he's to be handed over in Archangel, whether or not he's talked to us. I know it's nasty, but it's war. The Russians want do some pumping of their own.'

'But – ' Brigger broke off suddenly as one of the ship's crew came up the ladder from the after well-deck, moving at the double, eyes staring in what appeared to be terror. He flung past Brigger shouting out something about a bomb, and went on past the master's alleyway to the bridge ladder, still shouting. The shouts penetrated Kemp's cabin, where Tarasov came away from the port like lightning, pushed his way out of the cabin, and yelled an order in Russian at the uniformed security police waiting outside. As Kemp came out from the cabin behind him, making for the bridge, he saw Tarasov and his armed bully boys approaching the sentry on von Hagen's cabin. Kemp, when he reached the bridge, saw that the man who had shouted was Swile and that caused him to smell a biggish rat. Seeing the Commodore's approach, Theakston called to him.

'Report of ticking alongside Number One hold, Commodore. If the report's right we may not have long to abandon – '

'Unless we find the object,' Kemp said. There was something in his tone that made Theakston look at him sharply and with a look of puzzlement. 'I'd be obliged if you'd leave this to me,' Kemp went on. Before quitting his cabin he had brought his revolver from the safe. Now he showed it, ostentatiously. 'All right, Swile. We're going on a bomb hunt, you and I.'

iv

It was no more than a hunch and Kemp was very aware of the risks as he went below to the tween-deck and the hatch leading to Number One hold with its cargo of high explosive. They could all vanish in one split second of fire and fury, all of them, Theakston and the bridge staff, the engine-room complement, BNLO, the Russians, von Hagen ... but Kemp felt pretty sure inside himself. Bombs didn't appear all that suddenly after so long at sea from the Firth of Lorne, although it could perhaps be possible for a device to be so timed that it didn't start its tick until it was ready to detonate – but had there been no delays it would presumably not have gone off until some while after the Archangel arrival when it could have activated itself in a ship emptied of its cargo, not such a useful thing to do.

'Now,' Kemp said. 'Where is it, Swile?'

Swile put on a puzzled look. 'Dunno, sir. Seems to have stopped.'

'Yes, it does, doesn't it? You're an exceptionally brave man, Swile.'

Swile made an indistinct sound and looked warily back at Kemp. Kemp said pleasantly, 'You don't look at all scared, Swile. Not like a man who's about to be blown sky high.'

'That's cos it's stopped bloody ticking, innit?'

'Pull the other one, Swile. I didn't come down with the last shower! This has something to do with the German agent – right? I've had reports – '

'That bastard!' Swile said – almost screamed. His face was contorted with hate. 'Well, it worked, didn't it? I looked into the alleyway as we come past – the Jerry had been hooked out by the Russians – '

'Yes.' Kemp, too, had noted the fact. It had worked only too well, but even if it hadn't Kemp saw no way of keeping von Hagen aboard now. Dirt would have its course. 'All right, Swile. This will be gone into later. For now, get out of my sight – fast!'

Swile scuttled away. Kemp's face was savage as he climbed to the well-deck and went on up to the bridge. On the way he went into the master's alleyway and found Petty Officer Napper in red-faced argument with I. K. Tarasov.

'You'd no right,' Napper was saying. 'I'm in charge o' the prisoner – '

'Shut up.'

Napper bristled. 'Don't you speak to me like that, bloody civvy – '

'*Russian* civvy. You are in Russian waters.'

'Makes no difference! This is a British ship and you'd no right. Why, I – '

I.K.Tarasov went up close to Napper and stared at him with his fish-cold eyes. 'I am Colonel Tarasov. I am of the OGPU. I am powerful, and you are rude. If I lift my little finger – '

'Sorry, sir, I didn't know you was an officer, sir, I thought you was a civvy.'

'Yes. So now you will do as you are told by me, and shut up. Yes?'

'Yessir!' Napper said, and saluted. Kemp went on towards the bridge. Napper had been so agitated that he hadn't seen the Commodore, and Kemp saw no point in interfering – there was nothing to interfere about, the whole thing was a *fait accompli* now, and he felt weary to death with the voyage and the intrigue. He had almost to drag himself up the ladder to the bridge. There had been so little sleep, so much anxiety, so many things continually on his mind. He found Cutler on the bridge, standing beside Theakston. Theakston was looking grimmer than Kemp had yet seen him, his face stiff as he glanced round at the Commodore's approach.

He said, 'It's all over.'

'Almost, yes.'

'I don't mean the voyage, Commodore. Brigger brought a signal from the Ministry of War Transport. It's only just been sent up.' Theakston's voice faltered for a moment and suddenly Kemp understood.

'Your wife, Captain?'

'Dead,' Theakston said. 'Three days ago ... while we were flogging along the Kola Inlet. So many bloody miles away ... not that it would have made any difference.'

Kemp found no words to say. He laid a hand on Theakston's shoulder and squeezed. His heart seemed like a ball of lead. Theakston's voyage had been no easier than his own, and now landfall had brought its bombshell. It had always been Kemp's own fear that something would happen to Mary while he was away at sea. Theakston turned away and went into the wheelhouse. Kemp remained where he was, with Cutler.

'That's rotten,' Cutler said.

'Yes.' Kemp pushed it to the back of his mind: it had to be just one of those things and the *Hardraw Falls* was not far off the final stretch into Archangel. 'What's up with that ice-breaker, Cutler?'

Cutler brought up his binoculars. 'Stopped, sir.' A moment later the Russian began signalling and Corrigan read it off.

'Well?' Kemp asked.

'Stuck, sir. Stuck in the ice.'

Theakston had heard. He passed the order to stop engines. Already, ahead of them, the cruiser escort was turning under full helm, beating it out before she stuck fast for the winter, her signal lamp busy as she moved past.

Corrigan reported, '*Neath* to Commodore, sir: "I will wait outside the ice boundary."'

'Acknowledge. Add: "Much obliged but don't bother."'

'Aye, aye, sir.'

Cutler said, 'I guess he expects us to move out, sir – not to enter, but –'

'Yes. But I think he's over hopeful, Cutler. The damage – and the question of fuel. There may be a tanker in Murmansk, I suppose.'

'If we could do it –'

'If we could do it, Cutler, we could keep von Hagen and have the additional bonus of I. K. Tarasov. But that's being over hopeful too. In any case, there'd be a Russian warship waiting for us off the Kola Inlet.' Then Kemp added, 'But I don't think we're going to make it out anyway. Look down there.' He gestured down the ship's side, and then astern. There were great chunks of broken ice tumbling in the wake of the departing cruiser and even as Kemp and Cutler watched the chunks froze into a solid, rocky mess, while similar things happened along the sides of the *Hardraw Falls*. A moment later the ship crunched to a full stop.

v

'Just our bloody luck!' Napper said some motionless hours later. 'God knows when we'll get back to UK now.' He glowered down at the solid freeze, which linked them all with Archangel still many miles ahead. 'I wonder if the buggers'll send a quack out if Kemp asks for one?' He was speaking to Able Seaman Grove, past impertinences forgotten in his hour of anguish. He was standing with his legs apart: it eased the ache a little, pressure was not a good thing, and when he moved it was still crab fashion.

Grove said, 'Dunno, PO. If they do they'll likely take you to hospital, I shouldn't wonder.'

'No! In bloody *Russia*?'

'Grove grinned. 'Where else?'

'They're not getting me off of this ship! This ship's England as far as I'm concerned.' Petty Officer Napper gave a sound like a bleat and went below where he could no longer see Russia. If you tried, if you didn't look, you might fool yourself in the end and of course with any luck they mightn't have long to hang about, but his knackers could hardly wait till they made contact with civilization again. Before BNLO had gone ashore, or anyway gone down to the ice to embark aboard what looked like a horse-drawn sleigh, he'd assembled the crew and the naval party and told them he would make arrangements, or hoped he could, for such hands as could be spared to be transferred across the ice to Archangel and the train for Murmansk and a homeward convoy, but it might take time since they would have a low priority.... Napper prayed that BNLO's efforts would be successful. In Napper's view the shore party had looked a right lot of Charlies setting off behind a horse, and the OGPU man had looked furious, in just the mood to tear strips off the local weathermen who'd been caught out by the advance of the ice. With Tarasov had gone the German spy and bad luck to him. Napper had been on deck when the party had left and he fancied he would never forget the look in Kemp's face as von Hagen went over the side. Odd, that; such a hoo-ha over a rotten Nazi, just as though he'd been the Commodore's brother or something....

Napper rooted about in his medical stores and went off into a loud moan. One more squeeze and that would be the end of the lanolin.

Convoy Homeward

ONE

It was a brilliant dawn, the best time of any eastern day before the sun had had a chance to scorch away the freshness and bring lethargy in its train. From the bridge of the Commodore's ship, the former liner *Aurelian Star*, John Mason Kemp looked at the awesome colouring of the sky as the sun began to show its tip from somewhere over Burma, somewhere over the embattled troops of the Fourteenth Army, General Slim's 'forgotten army' sweltering in swamp and jungle as they fought the hordes of the Japanese emperor. Not for the first time in this seemingly endless war, Kemp gave thanks that he had made his career at sea. The sea was clean, at least until the bombs or shells turned it into a hideous hell of screaming, torn bodies and often enough – should a deep-laden tanker be hit – a murderous, burning carpet of spilled fuel oil.

But that colouring: crimson, green, orange, yellow, streaking like fingers across the lightening sky, touching the blue of the sea and turning it to gold as the convoy, behind the warship escort, moved out of Colombo for Simonstown and then the long haul up the South Atlantic and North Atlantic for the sanctuary of the Firth of Clyde.

Scottish waters, the great anchorage of the Tail o' the Bank between Greenock and the Gareloch.

Kemp turned as he heard a cough behind him. His assistant, Sub-Lieutenant Finnegan of the RCNVR – Finnegan, a citizen of the USA who had got into the war in advance of his countrymen by joining up in Canada back in 1939 and not too many questions asked.

1

'What is it, Finnegan?'

Finnegan tore off one of his curious American salutes. 'Reporting a moan from Petty Officer Ramm, sir.'

'Already?'

'Already, sir. Four of his guns'-crews, they've got the gut rot.'

Kemp grunted. Convoy Commodores had many worries, from sickness to air attack, from defaulters to bombardment by heavy ships, from bad weather to torpedoes from the ever-ready U-boat packs into which the convoy would steam once they came towards home waters. 'Hangovers from last night ashore, Finnegan?'

'Just simple Colombo tummy, I guess, sir.'

'They'll have to get on with it,' Kemp said. 'We're not going to enter the danger zone for twenty-four hours at the least. But keep me informed.'

Another salute. 'Yes, sir, Commodore.' Kemp forbore to comment; he had been totally unable to break his assistant of his habit of addressing him by, as it were, two titles at once. It was an irritation but one Kemp had learned to live with. In every other way young Finnegan was first class, and had brought an American keenness and freshness of outlook to the onerous task of shepherding the great convoys across the world's oceans, those vital convoys that had endlessly carried troops and food and the hardware of war from Canada, the USA, Australia and South Africa to the Mediterranean and the Far East, and into the Arctic Circle past the North Cape for the replenishment of the Russian armies repelling Hitler from his wintry march on Moscow.

Finnegan was lingering, staring like Kemp at the sky as the sun's rays extended to bring the first hint of the day's coming heat. He was screwing up his eyes and there seemed to be a pensive look, Kemp thought, beyond the effort to protect his eyesight.

'A penny for 'em, Finnegan.'

Finnegan nodded. 'You know something, sir?'

'Not what's in that American mind of yours, Finnegan.'

'No. Well, I guess I'll tell you, sir, Commodore. Me, I just can't wait to see the Clyde again.'

'Not the Ambrose Light . . . or Nantucket Bay . . . or the hot spots of New York?'

'Well, them too I guess. But the Clyde. It's got something, you know that?'

Kemp nodded. 'I know that, Finnegan. It's been home from so many wartime convoys. I think everyone who's ever been to sea feels something special about the Clyde. And not just the Scots.'

'I guess that's probably right, sir.' Finnegan paused. 'I've just been listening to a guy singing on the radio.'

'Ah?'

'About sailing up the Clyde.'

'I know it. Sing it, Finnegan.'

Finnegan stared. 'Me, sir?'

'Yes, you, sir.' Kemp's face was dead-pan.

'Right here on the bridge, sir?'

'Yes, right here on the bridge.'

'Well, I'll be . . . do I take that as an order, sir, Commodore?'

'Yes, Finnegan. And sing it with a Scottish accent.'

Looking as though he believed the Commodore to have gone suddenly round the bend, Finnegan obeyed orders. He obeyed them to the best of his ability.

'We're sailing up the Clyde,' he sang, 'Sailing up the Clyde . . . Sailing home tae Scotland and ma ain firrreside . . . an' a lump comes in ma throat, an' a tearrr Ah canny hide, for we're sailing hame tae Glasgie where the auld folks bide. . . .'

From the corner of his eye Kemp saw the *Aurelian Star*'s master approaching from the starboard wing of the bridge. Kemp, grinning, said, 'That was in your honour, Captain. I hope you found it nostalgic.'

Captain Maconochie, a large, jovial man whose home was in Ayr on the Firth of Clyde laughed and said, 'Music-hall Scots. Was it Will Fyffe, or Harry Lauder? Anyway – the effort was appreciated. But it's a long haul yet to the Mull of Kintyre. I hope to God we make it intact.'

Kemp said, 'Amen to that, Captain.'

A long haul by the exigencies of the wartime tracks to the Mull of Kintyre and the great seagull-whitened rock of Ailsa Craig at the entry to the Firth of Clyde it certainly was. Some fourteen thousand sea miles of hostile waters to be left behind them by the time they reached journey's end. The convoy was to proceed largely empty as far as Kilindini in East Africa; at Kilindini the

Aurelian Star would embark a battalion of the King's East Africa Rifles, a native regiment with British officers bound for the UK for training before being drafted for service in the Second Front against Germany, a concept not yet formalized but which by this stage of the war was on everybody's lips as an inevitable follow up to the thrust of the Desert Rats through Italy. At Simonstown the convoy would be joined by two vessels carrying explosives and a formation of Australians and New Zealanders would be embarked aboard the three former liners, while the fifteen cargo vessels would load mixed cargoes urgently needed in the UK. Also at Simonstown a tanker carrying sixteen thousand tons of crude oil for the refineries at Grangemouth and Milford Haven would come beneath the umbrella of the escort. From Colombo to the Cape the cover would consist of the old R-class battleship *Resolution*, the escort aircraft carrier *Rameses*, the cruisers *Lincolnshire* – wearing the flag of cs23, the Rear-Admiral Commanding 23rd Cruiser Squadron – *Swansea*, *Bodmin*, *Marazion*, *Lydford* and *Okehampton*. The destroyer escort, the anti-submarine screen, would be provided by the 32nd Destroyer Flotilla. *Resolution*, on temporary detachment from the British Far Eastern Fleet and wearing the flag of the Commander-in-Chief, Admiral Sir Geoffrey Layton, would leave the convoy at Simonstown.

A large convoy; and a vital one for Britain.

This had been stressed at the sailing conference the day before departure. 'You'll not have an easy passage, gentlemen,' the Naval Control Service Officer had said. 'It's known that U-boats are operating in the southern half of the Indian Ocean, and there's this surface raider at large in the South Atlantic – the *Stuttgart*.' He addressed Kemp: 'You'll know all about surface raiders, Commodore.'

Kemp nodded. The NCS officer continued. There was going to be an unceasing need for full alertness on the part of the watch keepers and lookouts; the destroyers of the A/S screen would need continual use of asdics to inhibit submarine attack; they would share the duties of 'eyes of the fleet' with the aircraft from the carrier. Kemp had heard it all, or something like it, countless times before since back in the autumn of 1939 he had brought the Mediterranean-Australia Lines' *Ardara* into Tilbury from Sydney via Colombo and the Suez canal, to be informed by the chairman of the Line that his peacetime days as a shipmaster were over for the duration of the war. He had as an officer of the Royal Naval Reserve been called into naval service to act as commodore of convoys. Now, he found his mind going back to the convoy he had only recently brought out from the UK to Trincomalee. A difficult passage, what with air attack in the Med, the fact of having girls of the WRNS aboard, the cholera that had struck the troop convoy after leaving Port Said, and then, after passing through the Strait of Bab el Mandeb – known to seafarers as the Gates of Hell – the attack in filthy weather by the German surface raider, the *Admiral Richter*. The Commodore's ship, the liner *Orlando*, had been sunk, damaged as much by being broached-to by the sheer force of the typhoon as from the effect of the German guns. Kemp, along with many other survivors, had spent some days in an open lifeboat.

And there had been the OC Troops, Brigadier Pumphrey-Hatton, who had cracked under pressure after making life as difficult as possible for the troops under his command. Also for the Convoy Commodore.

And Pumphrey-Hatton was now bound back for the Clyde. He was to be a passenger aboard the Commodore's ship. Kemp foresaw any amount of trouble.

When on sailing day the convoy had moved out of the port, Kemp, from the bridge of the *Aurelian Star*, saw the slim figure standing in the sternsheets of a launch, touched by the early sun's rays. First Officer Jean Forrest, lately in charge of the WRNS draft . . . Kemp had not expected her to see him off, though he had half hoped she might. Now she was where she had no business to be: aboard a harbour launch belonging to the King's Harbour Master. She was following him out; but not too far. Kemp gave her a wave, resisted the temptation to blow a kiss across the water. She returned the wave and then the launch turned away, back into the port. Kemp brought up his binoculars, watched until the launch was out of sight. His hands shook a little as he lowered the binoculars to dangle at the end of their codline stay. Jean Forrest . . . they'd been through a lot together in the outward convoy and he would miss her badly on the long haul to the Firth of Clyde. He had almost made a fool of himself, not that she had been any slip of a girl infatuated by a man old enough to be her father – Jean Forrest was a little on the wrong

5

side of forty. But it was not to be. A master mariner with a solid career behind him and a good few years to go yet, a commodore RNR in charge of a number of merchant ships in convoy, a happily married man: he had no business thinking in terms of infidelity.

He had a home in the village of Meopham in Kent, until the war so handy for the captain of an incoming liner to the London River. A happy home, and Mary now struggling with war conditions, the shortages of everything, the blackout, the air raids, the worries about a husband and two sons at sea in wartime, always half expecting the telegram from the Admiralty.

Resolutely Kemp turned his back on Colombo. There was work to be done, a war still to be fought.

Petty Officer Ramm, gunner's mate on the Commodore's staff and thereby very important in his own eyes, sucked at a hollow tooth and glared across the sea at the huge bulk of the *Resolution* as the battleship with its admiral's flag – a red St George's Cross on a white ground – took station ahead of the two columns of merchant ships, disposed abeam to starboard. Aboard the battlewagon his status as gunner's mate in charge of one of the big fifteen-inch gun-turrets would have been assured and respected. Here, he looked like being dog'sbody. The *Aurelian Star* carried DEMS ratings – standing for Defensively Equipped Merchant Ships. And there was another PO, also a gunner's mate in charge of the DEMS party, Petty Officer Biggar. PO Biggar had refused to concede an inch to Petty Officer Ramm, who had already mentally renamed him Petty Officer Bugger.

'A matter o' seniority, chum,' Biggar had said. 'Stands to reason, don't it, eh?'

Ramm, who resented being called chum on first acquaintance, said, 'That's all very well. But me, I'm on the staff, see?'

Biggar stared rudely. 'So what? Still comes down to seniority. got me rate in –'

'Yes, all right, all right, you've already told me that –'

'And my draft chit from Guz says I'm in charge o' the guns.'

Ramm had walked away in disgust. Guz meant that Biggar was a Devonport rating. Ramm was Pompey; and Pompey was in all things superior to Guz. And for bloody Biggar to talk about guns! Peashooters more like. Aboard the *Orlando* Ramm had had a six-inch gun. Obsolete certainly, and liable to blow up when fired

6

but a sight more gun-like than three-inch and two-pounders which, apart from such articles as Oerlikons, was all the *Aurelian Star* was equipped with.

The most dignified thing to do, Ramm decided, was to ignore PO Biggar as though he didn't exist. Easier said than done; and Ramm was delighted when, just after sailing, Biggar reported sick with gut rot. Immediately, Ramm had taken over. Almost as soon as he had done so, three more of the DEMS ratings turned green and were sent off to the sick bay.

All too soon, the day took on its heat. The convoy steamed over a glassy sea beneath spread awnings that would be quickly frapped if action stations were sounded. The water was of deepest blue, turquoise, cut now by the white wakes of the ships as the screws churned the water into tumbling foam and the stems cut their swathes to stream aft down either side. In his cabin, Brigadier Pumphrey-Hatton fiddled with his electric fan. There was something wrong with it; it wouldn't turn and twist as it should but remained stuck obstinately in one position, which wasn't the right position to bring comfort to Brigadier Pumphrey-Hatton, who was sweating like a pig. He had been on a search for flies, the flies that he was convinced had brought the scourge of cholera to the outward-bound convoy in the Red Sea. He could find no flies but he was convinced they lurked somewhere.

He rang for his steward. The summons was not answered. Growing angrier by the minute, he rang again. Confound these seafaring people – no discipline, not like the army where everyone jumped to it instantly or else.

He went out on deck. It was almost as hot as his cabin. True, there was a little wind made by the ship's own progress through the water but it was a *hot* wind and brought out his dormant prickly heat so that he was obliged to scratch furiously.

Some things had to be brought to the attention of the ship's master. Or that of the Commodore of the convoy.

Pumphrey-Hatton made for the bridge ladder. His dark, lean face was set into angry lines. Kemp, who happened to be at the head of the starboard ladder, saw the brigadier's approach and thought: here it comes. Already.

He said, 'Good morning, Brigadier.'

'Morning. I have a complaint to make.'

7

Kemp sighed inwardly. 'Flies?' he asked.

'I've searched for flies. I've found none – so far, that is. My complaint's to do with my electric fan. It's not working as it should. I find that inexcusable – damned inefficiency if you ask me. And the blasted steward doesn't answer my bell.'

It was not Kemp's business. He glanced towards Captain Maconochie. Maconochie was checking his station, taking bearings on the flagship. Kemp wouldn't interrupt. He said shortly, 'A matter for –'

'Fiddlesticks! Kindly don't fob me off, Kemp. What do you propose to do about it, may I ask?'

Again Kemp sighed inwardly. There was no point in provoking anything. Pumphrey-Hatton was in a poor state mentally and needed kid-glove treatment. He said, 'I'll report it to Captain Maconochie. A message will be sent to the chief steward. That's all I can do, Brigadier. It's not my ship.'

Pumphrey-Hatton was trembling now. He said harshly, 'That's all you people ever say. Always passing the buck. When I commanded a brigade . . . things were very different, I assure you. It was the same with those blasted flies, even in my gin if you remember though I don't suppose for a moment you do, you were never a help, never blasted well listened.'

'I'm sorry if you felt like that, Brigadier.'

'It's a little late to be sorry now. I've no doubt you put in a word against me to that blasted medico in Trincomalee –'

'I –'

'Oh, don't bother to deny it and kindly don't argue with me, I'm not fit.'

Pumphrey-Hatton, who had remained clinging to the rails at the foot of the ladder, turned away and stalked aft, his angular body having a suddenly frail look about it. Kemp couldn't help feeling immensely sorry: it was not pleasant to be relieved of one's command in the middle of the war, to have to hand over an infantry brigade to the senior colonel until such time as another brigadier could be appointed. Kemp had been told privately (which he was aware he should not have been) of the result of the medical board: Pumphrey-Hatton had little wrong with him physically apart from the after-effects of the cholera and had in fact made a remarkable recovery considering his sojourn in the open boat in the Arabian Sea; but he was in no mental state to continue in any command capacity. The military medics in the convoy, and the *Orlando*'s own doctor, had reported Pumphrey-Hatton's over-riding concern with flies, for one thing, also his lunatic behaviour in ordering the confinement below decks of the troops in the appalling heat of Port Said, the Suez canal, and the Red Sea, all in the interest of what he had believed to be secrecy. Kemp wondered now what his future would be, what the War Office would do with him after arrival and disembarkation in the Clyde. A desk job in Whitehall, probably; he couldn't do much harm pushing paper around. A sad end for an officer who had been a fighting soldier in the First World War when as a subaltern he had seen his battalion of the Duke of Cornwall's Light Infantry wiped out around him at the Marne. . . .

Kemp turned away himself and joined Captain Maconochie at the binnacle. Maconochie, his ship now in station on the flagship, handed over to his Officer of the Watch and glanced at Kemp's somewhat set face.

'Difficulties?' he asked.

'A fan that doesn't work properly. And a steward who doesn't answer bells.' Kemp hesitated. 'Look, Captain, I don't want to be a pain in the neck and I certainly don't mean to interfere, but –'

'That's all right.' Maconochie laid a hand on Kemp's shoulder. 'I've heard a lot about your late OC Troops. I dare say you and I have similar thoughts. I'll send down at once to my chief steward. We'll do what we can to make things as easy as possible for him.'

Kemp was about to express appreciation when there was a report from Yeoman of Signals Lambert taking the signal watch. 'Flag calling up, sir.'

Kemp saw the signal lamp flashing from the *Resolution*'s flag deck. Yeoman Lambert's lamp clacked out the acknowledge-ment. Lambert took down the message on his signal pad, then reported to Kemp.

'From the Flag to Commodore, sir. Captain (D) reports single contact bearing red zero two five distant four miles. Message ends, sir.'

'Thank you, Yeoman. Repeat to all merchant ships in convoy.'

'Aye, aye, sir.'

Kemp caught Maconochie's eyes. 'The buggers are quick off the mark. This, I did not expect.'

'Nor me. Do we scatter?'

9

Kemp shook his head. 'Not at this stage, Captain. We hope the destroyers can deal with a single contact. But we'll take prudent precautions.' He turned to Sub-Lieutenant Finnegan. 'Close up guns'-crews, sub.'

'Yes, sir, Commodore.' Finnegan saluted and ran for the wheelhouse and the Tannoy. As he went, Kemp passed orders for the zig-zag to be started. The danger area had indeed come sooner than expected.

TWO

'If they're going to get us at all,' Petty Officer Ramm observed to his gunlayer, Leading Seaman Purkiss, 'they may just as bloody well get us 'ere, nice an' close to bloody Colombo. I've done my time floating around in a lifeboat.' He fished out a packet of Players cigarettes and lit up without offering the pack to Purkiss. Ramm, Purkiss thought sourly, was a man who watched his pennies: he needed them for his philanderings ashore. Purkiss, who had joined the Commodore's staff at Colombo as a casualty replacement, was a time-expired Royal Fleet Reservist like Ramm himself, and also like Ramm was of the Portsmouth Port Division. He'd come across Ramm back in the thirties, in RNB, when Ramm had been number two to the Parade Chief Gunner's Mate and a right bastard with it. Ramm had been known as Ramm by Name and Ramm by Nature and Purkiss doubted if time had dimmed his desires to any great extent.

'Zig-zagging,' Ramm said suddenly, as the *Aurelian Star*'s gun deck lurched a little to starboard. 'Increasing speed, too.' Aft, the water was churning like a mill-race, and the wake was widening as the ship turned to the zig-zag pattern. In the van the destroyers of the A/S screen were moving ahead and a little to port at their maximum speed of around 35 knots. Ramm and Purkiss watched and waited for the first of the depth charges to rip open the flat blue Indian Ocean water. Ramm began to look restive; he wasn't specially worried about a solitary U-boat, not with all the armour floating around him, but personal inaction could look bad from the bridge and he didn't want that young Yank balling him out. All subbies, in Ramm's view, were bloody

11

useless, wet behind the ears and full of bull with it, British as well as American.

He looked around for something to make his presence felt: in no time at all he found it. The panacea for all fault-finding gunners' mates: rust on the barrel of the three-inch alongside which he and Purkiss were standing. Just a pinpoint.

'Look at that,' he said in a tone of shock.

'What, PO?'

'Rust, that's what.'

'Can't see any rust.' Purkiss peered around.

'Need glasses, you do. Like a ploughed field. Get it removed pronto, all right?'

'I still can't see it, PO.'

Ramm jabbed with a finger. In so doing, he caused the rust to disappear. 'There. Blind as a bat, you are, Leading Seaman Purkiss. Should 'ave spotted it before me. Mind, it's PO Biggar's fault, that I *don't* deny, but it's your job too and if you can't do your job you're not fit to 'old your rate as a killick. Get the 'ands onto it. I'm not going into action with me guns looking like a derelict plough in a farmer's barn.'

Looking surly, Leading Seaman Purkiss detailed a hand from the gun's-crew to dig out the cleaning materials from the ready use ammunition locker. From the bridge, where he had reported back after checking that all guns'-crews had been closed up in obedience to the orders, Finnegan looked down in wonder. There were some things about the British Navy that he would never understand. It was true the limeys had a reputation for spit-and-polish, true that they were almost main deck awash with bullshit, but to see a petty officer busting his guts about cleaning a gun when within the next few minutes the ship could take a tin fish in her innards was quite something. Maybe it said a lot, but Finnegan didn't know quite what.

In addition to the zig-zag, which would now be maintained, Kemp had swung the merchant ships away from the bearing indicated by Captain (D) via the Flag and had steadied them on their original course five miles to the west of the U-boat's position. By this manoeuvre he had brought the great bulk of the *Resolution* between the convoy and the enemy while the destroyers closed in. The cruisers, under the orders of CS23, had shifted with the convoy and were guarding the flanks. From all the ships a sharp lookout was being maintained, binoculars constantly sweeping on all bearings: there might well be another U-boat, or more than one, on the starboard side, not yet picked up by the asdics.

It ended in anti-climax. Yeoman of Signals Lambert reported the next signal: 'Lost contact, sir.'

Kemp nodded. 'I fancied that might happen. She's gone deep. Stopped diesels as well. She'd probably been on the surface just before dawn, recharging batteries, and picked us up as we came out. For my money she'll let us get well ahead, then keep just out of range of the asdics.'

'Tail us, sir?' Finnegan asked.

'That's what I'm suggesting, sub. And I think the Flag has had a similar thought.' There was an exchange of light signals between the Flag and Captain (D) on the heels of which the flotilla leader began signalling himself to his destroyers. A moment later two of them began swinging heavily to port, then steadied to come up astern of the convoy to act as rearguard. Captain (D) with the remainder of the flotilla raced ahead to resume station while the cruisers remained on the flanks. Astern of the convoy, immediately ahead of the guarding destroyers, the escort carrier *Rameses* came on with her aircraft – Barracudas of the Fleet Air Arm, ranged ready for take-off on her flight deck.

Kemp left the open bridge and strode into the wheelhouse. He switched on the Tannoy. 'This is the Commodore speaking to all hands.' He paused. 'Well, it's begun. Something of a damp squib you may think. Don't be fooled. That U-boat won't go away. From now on out, we have to be ready – for her and any other U-boats that may be around. That is all.'

Kemp returned to the bridge. He swept his binoculars all around the convoy, all over the smooth, peaceful-looking Indian Ocean. The peaceful look was a mirage; it could all change within moments. A thought passed through Kemp's mind: the naval flag that was flown in peacetime when submarines were exercising in company with surface ships was a two-coloured one, blue over red. Danger under the Blue, they called it. For Danger, in wartime, read Death.

Twenty minutes later, seeing no virtue in keeping men at

13

action stations too long, Kemp passed the word for the guns'-crews to fall out.

The Captain's message had gone down to the chief steward, Mr Chatfield. Chatfield was an experienced chief steward; he'd seen and suffered all sorts, particularly when he'd been a dining-room steward in the liners many years before. Passengers came in all shapes and sizes, mentally as well as physically. Many of them were nice enough; many chucked their weight around and treated stewards as dirt. Haughty: they had a special inflexion in their voices when addressing stewards, like addressing shop assistants – you could hear the change, like a car changing gear, when they turned to their table companions. That had riled Chatfield, though he'd never let it show through his professional urbanity. End-of-voyage tips were important; a steward's rate of pay was poor enough. And passengers could be generous if you didn't get their backs up and did a bit of arse-crawling, much as doing that went against the grain of a self-respecting man. A few years of that before becoming head waiter (which meant even more arse-crawling) had turned Chatfield bolshie. Not exactly a communist, but certainly very red. When later, as assistant second steward, he had observed practices in the galleys that would have sent the directors of the Line into apoplectic fits, he had turned a blind eye – a red eye. Spitting in the soup destined for the first class, gobbing after a lot of hacking and hawking. The rubbing of chicken legs into hairy armpits running with galley sweat before they were delivered to the commis waiters. That and other things were passed over.

But that was in the past. As chief steward with a position to keep up after changing Lines, Chatfield had himself changed. Like many a politician, in fact. But he still didn't go much on nobs and he still didn't like that special voice. And another thing: Chatfield had had a mate aboard the ill-fated *Orlando* and this mate, who had been a survivor, had told him a lot about Brigadier Pumphrey-Hatton.

'Fans,' he said to his second steward when the message from the bridge reached his office, 'is engine-room. When will the deck department ever learn? Not answering bells – that's you. Chase up the steward on 'Is Nibs' cabin, all right? But let me know pronto if there's any trouble from Pumphrey-Hatton. I'm not

14

having my lads turned into bloody army batmen, on duty twenty-four hours a day every day.'

The message dealt with, Chief Steward Chatfield sat back and read for the tenth time a letter from home that had come aboard with the last mail before leaving Colombo. The letter was not from his own home, oh no, it was from that scourge of husbands serving overseas, the Well-Meaning Busybody. There had been Carryings On in Southamptom, where Chatfield lived. Men had been seen coming and going; and in spite of petrol rationing there had been a Morris Eight parked outside Chatfield's house. Not once but on numerous occasions, and where was the petrol coming from was what the writer wished to know. Unpatriotic was that; the letter was about patriotism, or so it made out. But obviously what was being got at was Roxanne's virtue. Innuendoes – very nasty! Untrue, of course – Roxanne was devoted to him, he knew that because she had said so, and Chief Steward Chatfield knew he was a fine figure of a man, very little excess stomach for a man of fifty-four, a man in his sexual prime and one who brought home the bacon – like all chief stewards, Chatfield was by no means poor. In one of the liners of his former company, the chief steward, on return to their home port, used to be met by a fur-coated wife driving a car, and had once or twice given a lift to the Captain, who would otherwise have had to walk or pay for a taxi.

Roxanne wouldn't risk all that; she knew which side her bread was buttered, all right.

There was, of course, another angle: Roxanne was only twenty-six. Also, the war had meant that Chatfield was away from home for very long stretches. So in that respect, well . . . it was a worry, he had to admit that. Roxanne was very attractive, very seductive, and he'd picked her up in the first place, in the pub where she'd worked as a barmaid. People who'd been picked up once could perhaps be picked up again. Some nasty-minded, war-dodging salesman most likely, with a flattering tongue. Chief Steward Chatfield had never liked salesmen ever since his first wife, later crushed by a Southdown bus when visiting her old ma in Pompey, had been sold a very expensive lounge suite on the never-never, a suite that had collapsed under Chatfield's weight when he returned home and the firm had refused to honour the guarantee and had indeed been bloody rude about it.

15

If there was any truth, it had to be a salesman because salesmen had the opportunities. Chatfield ripped the letter up and dropped the pieces into his waste-paper basket. Of course it was all vicious lies, simple jealousy about the Morris Eight. But, admitting tacitly the Morris Eight, there had to be a reason for its presence. Hadn't there? Chatfield would have liked to write a stinging answer to that letter, if only to find out more, but he couldn't, because there was no address given. Nag, nag, nag – his Roxanne with a furniture salesman and a hell of a long way to the Clyde, and then the train south.

Kemp was still on the bridge when a wireless message was received in the radio room and was brought to the Commodore by the telegraphist rating on his staff.

'From NOIC Kilindini, sir.'

Kemp nodded, and read the transcript from the naval code. The message was brief, informing him that the convoy would embark two unexpected groups of people at Kilindini for transport to the UK: one, fifty-six British civilians, men, women and children, families caught in East Africa by the war and wanting to return home. This had been the first opportunity of accommodating them. Two, there would be embarked one hundred and fifty Germans, prisoners-of-war taken when an enemy cruiser had been sunk off the port some three weeks earlier. Kemp was instructed to allocate these persons among the ships of the convoy as expedient.

He passed the transcript to Captain Maconochie.

Maconochie said, 'We have spare capacity ourselves, Commodore. Some at any rate.'

'How many?'

Maconochie shrugged. 'We can take the families. Some of the Germans too. If we have to.'

'You don't sound keen, Captain.' Kemp grinned. He wasn't keen himself. Prisoners-of-war would not be popular aboard. He said, 'If you'd get precise figures from your Purser, then I'll signal the other masters and see what they can take.'

Within the next fifteen minutes Chief Steward Chatfield, on orders from the purser, had gone through his berthing lists with his second steward. He reported to the bridge that, taking into account the troops to be embarked both at Kilindini and at the

16

Cape, the *Aurelian Star* could take the families plus fifty of the Germans. Not a soul more. While the Commodore made signals by light around the convoy asking for berthing figures, the word spread through the ship that POWs were to be embarked for the prison camps in the UK. Petty Officer Ramm had much to say on the subject later on in the small caboosh allocated as petty officers' mess – there were just the three POs, himself and Yeoman of Signals Lambert on the Commodore's staff and PO Biggar of the DEMS contingent. Lambert, relieved from the bridge by his number two, was smoking a fag along with a cup of tea almost black in colour and syrupy with sugar.

'Huns,' Ramm said angrily. 'Buggers what 'ave bin shooting at our lads.' Too many escorts and merchant ships had been sunk by raiders in the Indian Ocean over the months of war. 'They'd best steer clear of *me*, that's for sure.' He added, 'That young Featherstonehaugh, what calls 'is bleeding self Festonhaugh. In for a commission, 'e is. WC candidate.' To the lower deck, the Commission and Warrant candidates, properly known as CWs, were known as WCs. 'On Number Two gun.'

'What about him, GI?'

' 'Is dad. Blown up aboard the old *Barham* in the Med. Blown to little pieces probably. Commander(E) 'e were, down in the engine-room when a bloody bomb went down the funnel. What's 'e going to think, eh?'

'Same as anyone with any sense,' Lambert said mildly. 'As POWs, they're out of it, facing God knows how many years of being shut away somewhere where it's not nice. No use blaming 'em for what bloody Adolf made 'em do.' He drank tea noisily. 'Me, I won't let it worry me.'

'Your dad didn't get killed by the sods, Yeo. Anyway,' Ramm added with a smirk, 'you still got other worries, I s'pose. Get any mail in Colombo, did you?'

'No, I didn't. Would you believe it, eh? Not a thing all the way from the Clyde.'

'Maybe she's still chocker,' Ramm said, smirking again. 'Teach you not to be bloody careless another time.'

Lambert made no reponse; it was a very personal matter and no business of Ramm's to go on and on about it and never mind that he, Lambert, had sought consolation in sharing his worries with Ramm in the first place. That had been a mistake: Ramm, a

17

salacious man, had merely thought it funny. To Lambert it was very far from funny. During his leave immediately prior to rejoining Commodore Kemp for the long eastbound convoy, a french letter had popped out of his top pocket when he'd brought out his pen. Explanations had been useless. Lambert had bought the object years ago, before the war, when as a young signalman in a cruiser on the China station he had been advised by an older shipmate that matelots should always take precautions. Just In Case, Like. You Never Knew, his mentor had said, poking him in the ribs with a heavy hand. Situations could arise, and then what? Nasty diseases was what. Or even, if the woman concerned was not a Chinese prozzie but a respectable young girl who'd let a matelot go too far, children. Bastards, like. Lambert had taken this good advice but had never used the french letter, which had in fact perished. It had remained a virgin packet, if you could use the word virgin, to the day his wife had found it. By the time he had been given the advice, Lambert had already been a married man, the wedding having taken place just a week before his draft to China. He had never had any intention of being unfaithful, certainly not with a Hong Kong or Wei-hai-Wei prostitute. When he had explained this, fervently, to his wife, she had not unreasonably asked him why, if such was the case, he had equipped himself with the offending object?

There had been no really convincing answer to this. Lambert had mumbled the words of his shipmate: Just In Case. You Never Knew. This had made things worse. By the time he had left Pompey by train for Greenock and the Tail o' the Bank Doris was still nagging. Currently, Lambert had no idea how the land lay. But there was one thing he did know, at any rate about Ramm, because Ramm had come out with an anxiety of his own. Ramm's worry centred around a barmaid in the Golden Fleece in Pompey who had discovered not only that Ramm was married but Ramm's address as well. Ramm's anxiety could be summarized in the words of the traditional wardroom toast always drunk after dinner on Saturday nights at sea: 'Our wives and sweethearts – may they never meet.'

Ramm, Lambert thought, was a bloody hypocrite, his pot being slightly blacker than Lambert's kettle.

Others aboard the *Aurelian Star* were concerned about the

18

Germans. Several of the crew had lost fathers, sons or brothers in this war, not all at sea – there was the army and the RAF, and there had been the ferocity of the air raids at home in which in many cases wives or mothers or sisters had also died or been horribly wounded.

The ship's Chief Officer, Andrew Dartnell, spoke of this to Maconochie. 'Bad blood, sir,' he said. 'There could be trouble.' At sea, you didn't come into much physical, personal contact with Germans. They just attacked from a distance. 'When they're here in the flesh –'

'I don't think you need worry, Mr Dartnell. There'll be a perfectly adequate military escort.'

'They'll have to be allowed on deck for exercise, sir. The Geneva Convention –'

'Yes, that must be observed, of course. There'll be a conference with NOIC and the army people on arrival in Kilindini. Just start planning for it, and any difficulties'll be sorted out then.'

Dartnell had to be content with that. He had his own conference with the junior deck officers and with the bosun, the ship's master-at-arms, the chief steward and the carpenter, the latter likely to be required to carry out structural alterations on deck or below. Meanwhile Kemp had his own reservations about the Germans and to a large extent agreed with Dartnell's ideas. Also, he'd already been informed about Featherstonehaugh and his loss – throughout his seafaring life Kemp had made a particular point of knowing the details so far as he could – the worries, the hopes and ambitions – of all the men under his command. Featherstonehaugh had been very deeply upset about his father's death in action and when Kemp had spoken to him in private, man to man, he had sounded bitter. Kemp hadn't been surprised; but he hoped the bitterness would pass. Now, the advent of Germans aboard would be exacerbating. Kemp considered young Featherstonehaugh – he was little more than nineteen years of age – promising material and in due course hoped to forward his recommendation for a commission as sub-lieutenant RNVR to the Admiralty. Featherstonehaugh was in the position of not being able to put a foot wrong if he wished, as of course he did, for that recommendation to go through. He would need to watch himself when it came to the German POW presence. If Featherstonehaugh had a fault it was a tendency to impetuousness and an over-eagerness. If he became over-eager on his dead father's behalf, as it were, there would be trouble. Kemp decided to have a word with Petty Officer Ramm.

In the meantime he had reports to write up: reports on the departure of the convoy from Colombo, on the contact with the U-boat, and on the preparations for the reception of civilians and POWs at Kilindini.

'I'll be in my cabin,' he said to the Officer of the Watch, 'chasing bumph. I'll be up inside thirty seconds when I'm needed.' He went below, clattering down the starboard ladder to the Captain's spare cabin beneath the wheelhouse, which had been placed at his disposal. Kemp detested paper-work, tended to put off the task whenever possible. Today he sighed and temporized: first, he would start a letter to Mary his wife, for landing with the mail at Kilindini. At Colombo, just before leaving with the convoy, Kemp had had depressing news in a cable sent by Mary via the good offices of the chairman of Mediterranean-Australia Lines and addressed to him c/o the naval base. The cable had brought the news that his grandmother, who lived with them in Meopham, had died. She had gone peacefully whilst asleep. Kemp, who had so often reflected that he must be the only Master Mariner in his fifties to have a grandmother still alive, would miss her. On the early death of his mother, Granny Marsden had brought him up as her own son, and later when she had become unable to cope on her own, the Kemps had given her a home. At ninety-two she'd had a good innings and was probably better off where she had now gone. On getting the news John Kemp had gone down on his knees in the privacy of his room and had offered a prayer for her to the God in whom he very strongly believed. He had always thought Granny was wonderful. But it had been, of course, Mary who had borne the brunt of a very old lady's whims and fancies, a very old lady's constant demands on her time amidst the wartime worries and privations, Mary who had mostly answered the call of the walking-stick constantly banged on the floor of Granny's bedroom after she had become bedbound, Mary who had patiently listened time and again to often-repeated, rambling stories from the long gone past, stories about how little Johnny had been a naughty boy and so on.

Sighing again, Kemp unscrewed his fountain pen and began the letter by thanking Mary for all she had done for so long. He made a guess that she might even miss that walking-stick; at least Granny had been company in a house otherwise empty except when either he or one or other of the boys had been home on leave. Now Mary would listen alone to the bombings as Goering's *Luftwaffe* loosed off its remaining bomb-loads before streaking home across the Channel for the airfields in Occupied France.

THREE

Ashore in a hotel in Mombasa, not far from the port area of Kilindini, the families for UK had assembled to await the arrival of the convoy and the long, dangerous voyage home. They were a fairly typical representation of British Colonials, Britons who had come out over the years before the outbreak of war, in a number of cases shortly after the end of the First World War, to make their fortunes in the ownership of coffee or tea plantations or merely to enjoy a better way of life than had become possible in England where servants were often unreliable or less hard-working than once they had been or were simply less and less easy to find. Income Tax, too, had a lot to do with their seeking a new life. Now they were going back, for a whole variety of reasons. The younger menfolk to join up and fight for the country their parents had left, the older ones either because the war had put an end to profit or because they, like the sons and daughters, felt they should rally round in Britain's hour of need.

Old Colonel Holmes and his wife were going because they were old enough to know that death was not far away and they preferred to die in their native land. Colonel Holmes, formerly of the Royal Berkshire Regiment, had had himself seconded years before the war to the King's East African Rifles where the chances of promotion were better; in the British regiments of the line, it was a case of waiting for dead men's shoes and if men didn't die you could remain a captain until into your forties.

Colonel Holmes reached out a hand as thin as paper and rested it on his wife's knee. He said gruffly, 'It's a wrench, of course, Mildred. I realize that. So many years.'

22

'Yes.'

'Still, the regiment's being embarked with us. There'll be things to talk about.'

'There's nobody left, Stephen.'

'Nobody that we served with, my dear. But there have been friends.'

'Yes, Stephen.'

'So we shall be in good company.'

Mildred Holmes nodded but didn't comment further. It would never come from her lips that the present officers of the regiment looked upon her husband as a fuddy-duddy, a relic of the past, a dug-out who appeared at guest nights in the mess, was politely talked to for as short a time as possible and then disregarded. Stephen had never seen that for himself; he had continued to believe as the years went by that his stories of garrison life before 1914, of the Flanders trenches, and of gay days in the twenties were well received and of interest to a totally different generation. Year after year after their retirement she had tried to dissuade him from accepting the polite invitations but his reply had always been the same: 'Oh, nonsense, my dear. They'd be disappointed.' This had invariably been followed by a gentle laugh. 'I'm a tradition, don't you know.'

A traditional bore: even as the thought came to her Mildred was distressed at her own disloyalty. Now there would be no more guest nights, no more dinner-jackets and evening gowns. In England they would be nobodies at last: an ancient colonel and his wife in a private hotel in Cheltenham, which was to be their destination. Destination, she thought, and final resting place. That was, if the Germans didn't get them first. Mildred half wished they would. They had little money beyond her husband's minuscule army pension, and the five guineas a week for the two of them in the Cheltenham hotel would absorb virtually all of that. But Stephen was determined to go home so that was that. He had been born in the North Riding of Yorkshire and had gone to public school at Sedbergh. Until Sandhurst, he had never been out of Yorkshire and now he wanted to see it again. They would have found a hotel up there if Mildred hadn't for once been adamant and made it plain that after Kenya she would be unable to stand the northern climate, the long winters, the snow that regularly blocked the roads for weeks on end.

Colonel Holmes gave a wheezy cough and fingered his close-clipped white moustache. 'I had words with Oliphant just after breakfast.' Captain Oliphant was the Naval Officer in Charge of the port. 'Very helpful. Told me we'll be going aboard the Commodore's ship. I regard that as an honour, don't you know. Told me the name of the Commodore, too.'

'Really?' Mildred wasn't particularly interested.

'Kemp,' Holmes said, as though she was expected to know the name. There was no response. 'Don't you remember?'

She shook her head. 'Kemp,' he said again. 'The time we went home via Colombo. British India to Colombo. Then the *Ardara*, Mediterranean-Australia Lines. Surely you remember, Mildred?'

'Well, of course I –'

Holmes shifted irritably in his basket-work lounge chair. 'We were at his table in the saloon. *Kemp*. Staff Captain, he was then. You *must* remember, my dear.'

Mildred's face seemed to vanish in fresh wrinkles. 'Yes, I think –'

'Very good chap – Kemp. Took to him immensely. First-class feller and a fine seaman. RNR, don't you know – that accounts for him having a naval appointment.'

'Yes, I see. Do you think he'll remember us, Stephen?'

'Oh, I should think so. Even –'

'Liner captains must meet a very large number of people,' she said warningly. Stephen could be in for a snub and she wouldn't care to see that; besides, the Commodore of a convoy would presumably be a very busy man.

'I had many yarns with him, my dear. Many. He was in the last war. I remember we talked about that.'

Mildred reached into a motheaten bag beside her chair and brought out some knitting. Something for a baby. The Holmeses had no children of their own, thus no grandchildren, but there was a great-niece of whom Mildred was fond and this great-niece had a baby of six weeks. Mildred was very anxious to see her; the little scrap, a boy, would make a long sea voyage worthwhile.

Kemp said, 'I wonder who they've got for us, Finnegan.' He lowered his glasses. The *Aurelian Star* was making her approach to Kilindini now. She and two more former passenger liners would enter the port to embark the native troops, the POWs and

24

the families, while the remainder of the convoy stood off with the naval escort. Kemp added, 'The civilians, I'm referring to.'

'A bunch of expatriates, sir. Empire builders, I guess.'

'You sound disparaging, Finnegan.'

'Maybe I do, sir, Commodore. The British Empire, it's kind of a sore point, back in the USA.'

Kemp grunted. 'Don't let it show, then. They may be touchy, and they're packing up a whole segment of their lives.' He paused. 'Not that I don't know what you mean, or what I think you mean, sub. They can be a difficult bunch, used to chivvying natives around, plenty of servants, that sort of thing. Stiff-necked very largely.' Kemp's liner experience had all been on the Australia run, and passengers going to Australia had on the whole been of a different sort from those going to, say, India. They had mostly been going out on business trips, or conversely returning from visits to families who had emigrated and had become absorbed into the Australian way of life and outlook. As for the Australians themselves, they were a very free-and-easy bunch and had no time for the snobbery that they associated with the English. Most voyages had been good fun, with a good social life for the ships' officers when off duty. The India-bound ships were very different. Kemp had had a number of friends in the P & O and B. I. Lines, and he'd heard enough about the sahibs and mem'-sahibs, the colonels and their ladies, the gentlemen of the India Office and the civil servants going to and from Bombay to make him glad he'd chosen the Australia run on which to build his career. The British Colonial families he was about to embark could have at least a touch of India about them. Also, he was apprehensive about carrying children to sea in wartime. The German U-boat captains, even supposing they knew, would not hold back on account of children. Kemp reflected that on the heels of the outbreak of war back in 1939, the *Athenia*, carrying predominantly women and children seeking safety in the USA, had been attacked and sunk.

Captain Maconochie conned his ship in, his engines reducing to slow as the liner neared the berth, where numbers of native dockers stood ready to act as berthing parties and take the ropes and wires from for'ard and aft. Below, Chief Steward Chatfield was engaged with the Purser, John Scott. The full details of the families, the breakdown of sexes and the number of children, had

25

not reached the ship until, half an hour earlier, the nominal lists had been put aboard from the pilot boat. The lists showed a predominance of women: eighteen men, twenty-five women, thirteen children, six male, seven female, ages ranging from four to eleven.

Chatfield said, 'The women without husbands, sir, they'll have to share.'

'Yes. How many without husbands, Mr Chatfield?'

'Nine I make it, sir. The younger gentlemen appear to be mostly single.' Chatfield tapped a pencil against his teeth. 'All those excess women travelling single, sir. A bit of a problem. If you see what I mean.'

Scott looked up, grinning. 'We've all travelled with excess women, Mr Chatfield.'

'Yes, we have. But in peace. Not war. There's a difference.'

'What difference? Oh, all right, don't bother to explain. War loosens morals, though there's never been any noticeable tightness even in peacetime. I imagine it's not the troops you're worried about?'

'Not the Kilindini lot, sir, no, being as they're black.' Chief Steward Chatfield, bolshie as he might have been where self-important passengers were concerned, knew the status of persons with black faces. 'The ladies is white, sir. There won't be any hanky-panky there, stands to reason. After the Cape, it might be different, of course. All them Australians and New Zealanders.'

'Well, we'll cross that bridge when we come to it, Mr Chatfield. For now, the women without husbands go into two four-berth cabins.'

'Which leaves one, sir.'

'Damn, so it does. Put the lady in a double berth for now, and we'll take another look after Simonstown.'

Chief Steward Chatfield went down to his own office. His second steward was there, going through his overtime lists. Chatfield passed him the berthing plan for the Kilindini embarkation. 'I see trouble,' he said.

'Women?'

'What else, eh?'

The second steward gave his own version of what Purser Scott had said: 'Perennial problem, Chief. No good looking for trouble till it strikes.'

26

'Well, maybe not, but I dunno . . . a lot depends on who gets the berth in the double cabin. There's going to be nine men on their tod, missing it.' Chatfield went across to his desk and sat down heavily, wiping sweat from his face. 'I heard a good one from the chef this morning. Want to hear it?'

'Go on?'

'When royalty has a baby, they fire a twenty-one gun salute. When a nun has a baby, only a dirty old canon gets fired.'

The second steward's face was deadpan. 'One of the single women a nun, then, is she?'

Chatfield made a swiping motion towards his assistant. 'Trouble with you, Charlie, is you've no bloody sense of humour.'

Brigadier Pumphrey-Hatton was on deck a little later as the troop embarkation began. He looked down critically as the native soldiers of the King's East African Rifles were marched by companies onto the jetty. They were smart enough, he thought, marching as he had marched with the DCLI to the light infantry and riflemen's step of 130 to the minute. As ever, the tall ones looked stiffly uncomfortable – it was hard on a tall man, and some of the natives were very tall. The companies were halted and turned into line and reported by the sergeants, who were black, to the Regimental Sergeant-Major, who was white. The RSM reported to the Colonel, who was also white of course. Pumphrey-Hatton feared that one day after the war was over and everything had gone to pot – just look at some of the appallingly common temporary officers that had been foisted onto good regiments already – at some future date officers might be black. Pumphrey-Hatton shuddered at the very thought. Black men in the mess when His Majesty's health was drunk, black lips around glasses that might next be used by white ones. It would be the end of the world for such as he.

Pumphrey-Hatton lifted a hand to his uniform cap, a hand that shook badly, and eased the leather band on his head: it was giving him a headache and he didn't feel at all well after a sleepless night during which he had got up to pursue what he had believed to be a fly, one bearing disease. He had not found it, and had rung for his steward. A nightwatchman had answered and had clattered in heavy boots about the cabin, without success. The man had been polite enough but had seemed to treat Pumphrey-Hatton as though he were not a brigadier who had been OC Troops aboard a transport but as a child who had had a bad dream. Pumphrey-Hatton was still thinking angrily about this when he spotted something. A movement in the ranks of riflemen, a black man picking his nose. Pumphrey-Hatton saw red, a sudden blinding light of fury at everything in sight.

'That man,' he roared out in his parade-ground voice. 'Number Four, front rank, B Company. Hand to his blasted nose. Stop it instantly!' As he finished shouting there was a dead silence all around. The RSM looked startled but quickly recovered his composure. The Colonel looked up at the liner's deck, opened his mouth, shut it again when he saw the red tabs. But he looked extremely angry. Into the silence Pumphrey-Hatton was heard to say something about blasted black beetles then, as though suddenly becoming aware of an unforgiveable *faux pas*, he put his hands over his face for a moment, recovered himself, and marched stiffly below and out of sight.

'Not my affair or yours,' Kemp said to Maconochie. 'We leave this to the military. It was damned embarrassing,' he added. 'He'd never have done it if he'd been in his right mind. It's all very unfortunate and it could lead to a lot of friction if he ever gives a repeat performance. But I say again – it's not our affair. We can't interfere.'

'You could, if necessary. As Commodore –'

'I have a responsibility to maintain the peace – if necessary, as you said. But only if it's represented to me by the Colonel of the rifles, who'll be OC Troops as far as the Cape.'

'The brigadier permitting,' Maconochie said with a grin. Kemp nodded; the remark had been tongue-in-cheek but there was a serious side to it. Pumphrey-Hatton was just the sort to pull rank and make things awkward, notwithstanding the fact that he was on the sick list for home. As to the Colonel, now seeing his troops aboard, all Kemp knew about him was that his name was Carter and that, from Kemp's brief sight of him from the bridge, he looked a reasonable sort, young for his rank and thus – or so Kemp hoped – not verging on blimpishness like Pumphrey-Hatton. With luck, Colonel Carter would have come up against senior officers like Pumphrey-Hatton before now, and would know how to deal with them. Tactfully.

For a while longer Kemp and Maconochie watched the native troops streaming up the embarkation gangway to the gunport door, then went below to meet the various port officials and deal with yet more bumph, the inevitable accompaniment to any ship's arrival in any of the world's ports.

One of the visitors from the shore was the Naval Officer in Charge, Captain Oliphant, wearing on the shoulder-straps of his white uniform the four straight gold stripes and curl of a captain RN. After a formal conversation with the ship's Master and the Convoy Commodore he offered a silver cigarette-case to Kemp and Maconochie and accepted a light from Kemp. Blowing smoke he asked, 'How is your memory for things past, Commodore? Or should I say, persons from the past?'

'Fair,' Kemp said. 'Who have you in mind?'

'The name's Holmes. Colonel Holmes.'

Kemp shook his head slowly. 'Can't say I recall anyone of that name.'

'Another clue, then: *Ardara*, Colombo home . . . several years ago.'

Again Kemp shook his head. 'I'm sorry, Captain. The penny fails to drop.'

'Well, do have a good think – and don't let on you don't remember him. He's embarking here with his wife, for UK. He's a decent old stick. They both are. Pretty far gone in years, and the old lady's apprehensive about the voyage. I told them I'd put in a word.'

Kemp said, 'I'll look out for them. But they'll have to accept that this is no peacetime liner. No question of being necessarily allocated the Captain's table in the saloon, that sort of thing.'

'Oh, I'm sure they'll realize that.' Oliphant added, 'It was at your table – Staff Captain's table – in the saloon that they met you. See if that aids the remembering process, Commodore.'

Kemp would do his best. But there had been so many Staff Captain's and Captain's tables over so many years, outward and homeward bound, so many dozens of faces of which only a very few were really memorable. What was much more on Kemp's mind was the content of a w/T signal from the Admiralty passed to him by Oliphant when he had come down from the bridge. This signal was addressed to Commander-in-Chief, Far Eastern Fleet, repeated NOIC Kilindini and Commodore Convoy sw03. It indicated that survivors from a merchant vessel sunk by gunfire confirmed the presence of the German raider *Stuttgart* two hundred miles east of the port of Durban in Natal.

Not so far off the track of the south-bound convoy.

Petty Officer Ramm's face was sour as the decks of the *Aurelian Star* filled with the native troops, now being chivvied by their corporals and sergeants, none of whom seemed able to find their way below. There was a lot of eyeball rolling and a lot of unintelligible chatter.

'Don't know if they're on their arse or their elbow,' Ramm said to no one in particular. He was responded to by the ship's bosun, a grizzled seaman who had done time in sail, in the old windjammers that had battled their way through the everlasting storms off Cape Horn, from Liverpool to Australia the long way, the hard way.

'Not surprising, is it? Never been aboard a ship before, and they don't know what to expect, none of 'em.'

Ramm sniffed. 'Puke their guts up, soon as we put our nose into the 'oggin outside, that's what I reckon. *And* run amok if we meet a Jerry.'

Bosun Barnes disagreed. 'They're soldiers, never mind if they've got black skins, mate. Me, I've known blacks before. We had 'em from time to time in the windjammers –'

'Well, bully for you,' Ramm said sarcastically. 'Any use, were they?'

'When they'd learned their trade, mate, they made bloody good seamen, and strong with it. Talk about muscle. A lot of 'em came from Sierra Leone – Kroos. Fishermen, used to boats from the start, they were.' Barnes paused and rolled a cigarette with a flick of his fingers. 'Mind, there was always the odd black sheep that got shanghai-ed aboard in places like Iquique or Valparaiso, you can't –'

'Black sheep, eh? That a joke, bose?'

Barnes gave him a hard look. 'Not meant to be, no. I reckon you got black on the brain, Mister Ramm. Prejudice, that is. Know that bloke Kipling, what wrote poems? "For all 'is dirty 'ide, 'e was white, clear white inside, when 'e went to tend the wounded under fire." Gunga Din, that was. North-West Frontier of India.'

'My, my,' Ramm said, eyebrows lifted. 'Walking bloody encyclopaedia, you are, mate.' He stepped backwards suddenly as some of the natives came past and he almost got a kitbag in his gut. 'Watch it, you lot,' he said in a harsh voice, and gave the offending kitbag a shove. The native stumbled and fell heavily against the guardrail of a hatch down which a steel ladder led into the bowels of the ship. He let go of the kitbag in trying to right himself, and the bag went down the hatch, making a lot of noise in its descent. The soldier seemed distraught; there was fear in the rolling eyeballs. Ramm laughed coarsely.

'Be on a charge, you will,' he said. 'Up before the Colonel an' all, just you see.'

The transports, the embarkation completed, moved off the pierhead and re-joined the rest of the convoy and the warship escort. The ships formed up again in their allotted stations and when Kemp had reported by flag to the *Resolution* there was immediate activity on the flagship's signal bridge, her chief yeoman of signals personally using the all-round masthead lamp to send the general message to all ships from the Commander-in-Chief informing them of the Admiralty's wireless signal. On the admiral's bridge of the flagship, Sir Geoffrey Layton, a short, very thick-set officer, had conferred with his Flag Captain, the Fleet Gunnery Officer, the Fleet Signal Officer and the Master of the Fleet, a specialist navigating officer.

'Not much change,' he'd said. 'We knew the raider was out, though we didn't expect him here. I'm not unduly worried. But I shall bear in mind that we may have to alter nearer to the coast and farther from the bugger's track.' He moved up and down on the balls of his feet, like a policeman in a shop doorway, resting from his beat. 'I'm not running from a fight, gentlemen. I trust you know me better than that. But my first responsibility is the safety of the troops and the convoy as a whole. In the meantime, we're ready for anything that may happen, and if we fall in with the *Stuttgart* my fifteen-inch batteries will blow the bugger out of the water. Understood, Fleet Gunnery Officer?'

'Understood, sir.'

'Good!' The Admiral rubbed his hands together and grinned, a somewhat impish grin. 'It's getting dark, Flag Captain. I suggest a further signal to all ships: *good night, sleep tight, mind the bedbugs don't bite*. I'll be in my sea cabin if I'm wanted.' He turned away and was saluted down the ladder.

31

When Kemp was informed of the last signal from the Flag, he said, 'For bedbugs read U-boats.'

The convoy steamed on into the gathering night, all ports and deadlights clamped down hard, no lights showing anywhere except right aft where the shaded blue stern-lights enabled the convoy to maintain station. But there was plenty of light all around, too much light for the safety and the peace of mind of any convoy commodore or any shipmaster in time of war: as the night wore on the stars shone out like beacons, glittering with an intensity that made them look so close that a hand could reach them. Thousand upon thousand of them covering the arch of heaven, and with them the moon, hanging low and large, a lantern to silhouette the ships and bring them to the immediate attention of any U-boat's captain, watching through his periscope beneath the flat calm of the Indian Ocean's surface.

Half asleep in the stifling heat of the seamen's messdeck deep down in the ship, Ordinary Seaman Featherstonehaugh sweated like a pig into his pyjamas and listened to the irregular snore coming from the wide open mouth of Able Seaman Sissons who, like himself, had been drafted to the Commodore's staff back in Colombo to replace casualties caused to the guns'-crews aboard the ill-fated *Orlando* when under attack in the Arabian Sea. Able Seaman Sissons was a three-badgeman – three good conduct chevrons on the left sleeve, gained, as it was popularly said, for thirteen years' undetected crime – and was thus by tradition known as Stripey. Stripey, an RFR man recalled for service in 1939, was well on the wrong side of forty and, like virtually all lower deck men, was accustomed to sleep either in the bare buff or in his vest and pants. Featherstonehaugh's pyjamas had been the cause of a good deal of mirth on the part of Stripey Sissons, who thought them pansy and had said so. Real men, he said, wouldn't be found dead in such. Only officers wore them, and officers were pigs. Saying this, Stripey had addressed Featherstonehaugh by his name, as spelled.

Featherstonehaugh had at once put both feet in it. 'Festonhaugh, actually. That's how it's pronounced. And my father's – my father was an officer.'

'Was 'e – actually? Was. Got disrated, did 'e?'

The young OD had flushed at that. 'He was Commander(E) in the *Barham*.'

32

'Oh. Lorst, was 'e?' Sissons changed his tone.

'Yes.'

'Sorry, lad.' Stripey put a hand on his shoulder. 'Didn't mean no offence. But do I take it you're one of them wcs?'

'If you like to put it that way, yes.'

'I do like. So don't get uppity with me, lad o' your age. And if I want to call you – whatever your bleedin' name is, in full, well, that's what I shall do. An' for Gawd's sake chuck them bleedin' pyjamas in the 'oggin.'

Featherstonehaugh had not done so. Back in his training establishment and in RNB Portsmouth most of the others in the new entries' mess had also worn pyjamas, having only recently left their civilian status behind them. Now, in the Indian Ocean night punctuated by Stripey Sissons' snores, he came fully awake. He listened to the steady beat of the engines, the slight swish of the sea against the ship's plates, and he thought of the Mediterranean and of the horrific end of the old battleship *Barham*. The *Barham* had gone up, like the battle-cruiser *Hood*, in a split second, there one minute, gone the next, in a shattering explosion, a sheet of flame and clouds of thick, heavy smoke, the guts blown out of her. He thought of what the end must have been like for his father, caught on the starting-platform below in the engine-room, caught in the fires, the escaping steam under immense pressure that could strip the flesh from a human body in seconds, the total dark as the ring main went, the tangle of steel ladders that would have been twisted into unrecognizable shapes, the inrush of water from gaping plates that would douse the fires but drown anyone still left alive.

To think of his father in that context was shattering; but the image kept recurring, and with it the memories of past days in their home in Southsea, memories of his father coming back from foreign commissions – two years with the Mediterranean Fleet, three years China-side in the light cruiser squadron – opening up wooden chests to bring out presents for the family, exotic things to Paul Featherstonehaugh as a child, things of jade and pressed Chinese silk, ornate daggers from North Africa, opium pipes . . . and over-ridingly of his father himself, smiling, happy to be home again, making them once more into a complete family unit until, inevitably, his leave was over and another ship was waiting to snatch him away. Paul had determined to follow his father into

33

the Navy, either as an engineer or executive officer; but his maths had not been up to the standard required and he had failed to get a naval cadetship. But by this time the war had started and on his eighteenth birthday he had volunteered for the Navy as a hostilities-only ordinary seaman. Shortly after joining HMS *Royal Arthur*, the 'stone frigate' that had in pre-war days been Butlin's holiday camp, Skegness, he had been recommended by his Divisional Officer as suitable for training for a commission. His father had known that before his appointment to the *Barham*.

Paul Featherstonehaugh knew by now that the path of the CW rating was not an easy one. To attain a commission you had to stand out, to know your job better than your contemporaries, and to keep your nose clean. The fact that your father was an officer and you spoke the King's English and had been to a certain kind of school was a help in getting the first recommendation, but after that it was up to you.

Stripey Sissons' snores continued but despite them sleep came as the past images faded. He was woken again by the torch beams of the ship's master-at-arms making night rounds, then again drifted off to sleep. His next awakening came when the urgent sound of the action alarm broke the peace.

FOUR

The first alarm had come from the *Aurelian Star* herself, a report to the bridge by telephone from the masthead lookout. The senior second officer, Officer of the Watch, immediately called the Captain.

'Masthead lookout, sir, reports a feather of spray two points on the port bow. I've not picked it up myself yet.'

'I'll be right up,' Maconochie said. 'Call the Commodore at once.'

Maconochie was on the bridge inside thirty seconds, his uniform jacket over his pyjamas. Bringing up his binoculars he scanned the area around the given bearing. He found nothing. As Kemp joined him he called the masthead lookout.

'Captain here. And you sure of your report, Jones?'

'Dead sure, sir, but I've lost it again.'

'Right.' Maconochie swung round on the Commodore. 'Evidently no contact by the asdic screen. Could be imagination.'

'Or could be that she'd been lying low and had only just come to periscope depth. We'll go to action stations just in case, Captain.' Kemp added, 'We'd better report by lamp to the Flag – shaded lamp. If there's a U-boat there, we'll obviously have been seen already so nothing's lost.' The signalman of the watch was already at his side with his signal pad; Kemp passed the message for the Flag; even as the signalman was passing it, a blue lamp was seen flashing from Captain(D) in the flotilla leader. This was read off by Yeoman of Signals Lambert as he reached the bridge.

'Contact bearing red four five, sir, distant ten cables. Am attacking.'

'Thank you, Yeoman. Finnegan?'

'Sir?'

'Inform the guns'-crews. Use the Tannoy.'

Finnegan went into the wheelhouse at the double. Kemp, watching through his binoculars, saw the destroyers altering course to port and increasing speed. They were clearly visible in the moonlight; and the kerfuffle of their streaming wakes stood out in bright green phosphorescence as they hurtled towards the given bearing. As the reports came in from Petty Officer Ramm that the guns'-crews were closed up at action stations and had swung onto the bearing, the series of splashes on the convoy's port flank indicated that already the destroyer screen was attacking with depth charges from the chutes and throwers; and shortly after that the ocean seemed to rip apart as the charges exploded, great spouts of water flinging up astern of the racing destroyers. The hull of the *Aurelian Star* shuddered to the shock waves; and below decks cork insulation showered down from the deckhead of Brigadier Pumphrey-Hatton's cabin. Having slept through the stridency of the alarm rattlers, he had been woken by the racket from the depth charges and had sat up in his bunk with a jerk.

He fumbled around for the bunk-side light, cursing as at first he couldn't find it, then seized the cork life-jacket from the hook on the cabin door. The ship vibrated to more underwater explosions; and a moment later both the three-inch guns went into action overhead. Pumphrey-Hatton pulled on his khaki drill, felt around for his shoes, struggled into the life-jacket and left his cabin. In the alleyway outside, the recently embarked families, men, women and children, seemed largely to be in a state of panic. Boat drill had been held as required by Ministry of War Transport regulations as soon as the *Aurelian Star* had cleared away from Kilindini and all passengers, the military contingent included, had been fully instructed by the ship's officers. But now there was a strong degree of uncertainty in the air. Pumphrey-Hatton compressed his lips, showing anger and frustration. He pushed at an elderly man who was shepherding an old woman, presumably his wife, towards the companion-way at the end of the alley.

'Kindly get out of my way,' he snapped.

Colonel Holmes looked round. 'Really, I – '

'Kindly don't argue with me. I happen to be Brigadier Pumphrey-Hatton.' He pushed again and Holmes stumbled aside, protesting at a lack of manners. Pumphrey-Hatton continued to thrust his way through, calling out loudly that he was trying to reach the bridge. When he reached the companion-way and climbed it to the deck above he was virtually submerged by the press of native troops. He began shouting for a sergeant, but there was no NCO to be seen. There were more sharp cracks as the three-inch guns continued firing; and as Pumphrey-Hatton struggled in a sea of black men sweating with terror of the unknown, there was a whistling sound followed by a rush of air close overhead as a shell from a U-boat scored a near miss on the *Aurelian Star*.

'Commodore, sir – Flag reports more contacts on the starboard beam.'

Kemp nodded and ran across to the starboard wing of the bridge. To port, the original contact had come to the surface, forced up by the depth charges. One up to the convoy; but the German was not quite finished yet. Her fo'c'sle-mounted gun was in action, as was the machine-gun mounted on her conning-tower, and her fire seemed to be directed towards the Commodore's ship. Kemp was relieved when Maconochie, from the port wing, called out that two of the destroyers were closing the U-boat and, a moment later, reported that a direct hit had been scored on her conning-tower, and she was already beginning to settle low in the water.

As more depth charges exploded to starboard Brigadier Pumphrey-Hatton, his uniform awry, was seen coming up the starboard ladder to the bridge. Eyes blazing, he approached the Commodore.

'Now look here, Kemp –'

'Not now, Brigadier. Please leave the bridge. Unless,' Kemp added, just in case, 'you have something relevant to report?'

'You're damn right I have! Those native troops, blasted well indisciplined, never seen such a shower. I was almost trampled under foot. And there's another thing. My bedside light. Very badly positioned. You have to *grope* for it. In an emergency –'

'The point is noted, Brigadier. Now leave the bridge, if you please –'

'I *don't* please,' Pumphrey-Hatton interrupted in a shrill tone. 'I have come to state a complaint and I shall not leave until –'

'The ship, the convoy, is in action, Brigadier Pumphrey-Hatton. I am ordering you to leave the bridge. If you don't do so immediately I shall have you placed in arrest and then confined to your cabin once the attack's over. I trust you understand.'

Pumphrey-Hatton gaped. Kemp's face was set, icy. He would carry out his threat. Pumphrey-Hatton waved a fist in his face. He said hoarsely, 'I intend to break you for this, Kemp. Be very sure of that. My God, you'll be sorry for what you've just said.' He turned away and went down the ladder, every inch of him bristling.

Kemp was joined by Maconochie. 'I heard that, Commodore. Does he carry any weight?'

'If he does,' Kemp answered evenly, 'I can take the strain.' A moment later there was a loud explosion on the starboard bow, followed by a brilliant sheet of flame from one of the cruisers of the escort. The first explosion was followed by others, smaller ones, and the cruiser's quarterdeck was seen to be on fire. Her after turrets stood out in the flames, one of them wrenched from its position, the guns twisted and broken.

'*Bodmin*, sir,' Lambert reported.

Kemp lifted his binoculars. He could see bodies draped across mushroom ventilators and lying below the turrets as the flames spread. There was a signal being flashed to the Flag from the cruiser's bridge. Lambert was able to read it off. He reported to Kemp. 'Am able to steer and maintain way.'

'Maybe he is,' Kemp said grimly. 'But if that fire reaches the magazines . . .' He had no need to say more; imagination completed the thought. The shell-handling rooms, deep down in the ship, were approached by way of steel-lined shafts topped by heavy hatches which, when the clamps were put on, were fully watertight. In action, the shell-handling parties were sent down these shafts and the hatches were clamped down after them, leaving no escape. There might come a moment when the cruiser's captain would see the urgent need, if the fires encroached, to flood the magazines and shell-handling rooms. When such an emergency struck there was seldom time to open up the hatches and bring out the seamen of the shell-handling parties. The valves would be opened by remote control and the men would drown, forced up on the deepening water until they met the unyielding steel of the clamped-down hatches, openable only from above.

As Kemp faced these thoughts, there were more explosions and the cruiser seemed to glow throughout her length as her plates grew red-hot from the fires that had now made their way below. Then the inevitable final explosion came, a great blast of noise and flame, and the ship disintegrated, became nothing more than flying chunks of metal outlined in the blaze, metal and bodies together, raining down on the Indian Ocean. As the *Bodmin* died, the destroyers continued their attack. Two more U-boats were forced by the depth charges to the surface and were then despatched by gunfire. An eerie peace, a calm, descended. Fifteen minutes later a laconic report came from the *Resolution*: lost contact. The convoy, minus the *Bodmin*, steamed on for the Cape. Fifteen more minutes and the order came from the Flag to secure from action stations. At the after three-inch Petty Officer Ramm removed his steel helmet and wiped at his forehead. The hard rubber band of the tin hat always gave him a nasty headache when worn for what he considered too long.

He spoke to Featherstonehaugh. 'First taste of action, lad? Didn't do so badly, I'll say that. Bet you was shit scared, though, eh?'

'No, PO, I –'

'Don't tell bloody lies! *I* was. Reckon you never get really used to it, wondering if your name's going to be on the next projy. Though sometimes you think to yourself, maybe that'd be the best bloody way out of it.' He gave a guffaw.

Featherstonehaugh asked, 'Out of what, PO?'

'Never mind that, you're too young and bloody innocent to appreciate it.' The barmaid at the Golden Fleece was still much on Ramm's mind. If she made an approach to Ramm's old woman, well, the old woman in action was a sight worse than anything Adolf Hitler could chuck at a matelot. He'd sooner face the enemy any day of the week.

As ever when a ship went down in wartime, there was, afterwards, a man's conscience to plague him. It was in fact very unlikely that many of the *Bodmin*'s company would have survived that final explosion that had ripped the cruiser apart. But there might have been a handful. This was the Indian Ocean, not – for instance – the Denmark Strait where the mighty *Hood* had gone down, leaving only three survivors out of a ship's company of some sixteen hundred men. There had in fact been some who had been thrown clear but all except for those three had perished quickly in the icy waters. The three had been picked up by the destroyer escort in the nick of time before death came. Here, south of Kilindini, that would not have happened. On the other hand, there would be the sharks, scenting blood. But in any case you didn't hazard a vital convoy by stopping to pick up possible survivors – not in a situation where other U-boats could be closing in, as yet beyond the range of the asdics, or a surface raider might be lurking. You didn't turn a convoy into a sitting duck, a perfect target for attack. This was true; but it was a facet of the war that all hands detested, however inevitable it might be. This was far from the first time Kemp had been faced with such a situation; but he had never grown inured to it. He suffered each time. With two sons at sea, there was a personal angle to it in addition to his own sense of inadequacy to help: would another ship one day steam away from a sinking and leave one or other of the boys to drown?

He became aware of Finnegan at his side as he stood there on the bridge, not going below again to resume his sleep. Already dawn was not far off; soon the brilliance of the stars would start to fade as the eastern sky lightened, and the guns' crews would be at routine dawn Action Stations. He said, 'It's a rotten business, sub.'

'Yes, sir, Commodore. Nothing you can do about it, though. What it comes to is . . . it's up to the Flag.'

Kemp sighed. 'Admirals have a hell of a lot of gold braid. They also have a hell of a responsibility. They earn their privileges.'

'Yes, sir, I guess they do.' Finnegan had, very briefly, met the Commander-in-Chief at a reception held in Colombo before the convoy had left. Kemp and his assistant had been invited along with Captain Maconochie whose ship would wear the Commodore's broad pennant, and the commanding officers of the escort. Admiral Layton had taken pains to talk to Finnegan, to congratulate him on being almost the first citizen of the USA to join the war. The Admiral had seemed immensely human, with a kindly twinkle in his eye, although he had a reputation for being a strict disciplinarian. Sir Geoffrey Layton had altered Finnegan's view of British admirals, whom he'd imagined would be a remarkably stuffy bunch of self-important shellbacks who wouldn't dream of speaking on friendly terms with a mere sub-lieutenant of the RCNVR. There was nothing stuffy about Admiral Layton. He had asked a lot about America; he had great admiration for President Roosevelt, and was appreciative of the immensity of America's war effort which was largely due to Roosevelt himself. And he had seen to it that Finnegan's glass was topped up with gin while they had been talking.

Finnegan knew that the Admiral would be feeling as bad as Kemp about steaming away from the *Bodmin*.

The Commodore did not attend meals in the saloon: the Captain's table remained the Captain's table. Kemp had had enough of that during his years as Master with the Mediterranean-Australia Lines, where he had had to suffer many bores along with more congenial voyagers. But he did not forget the recommendation of NOIC Kilindini that he should spare some of his time for old Colonel Holmes and his lady wife: During the forenoon of the day after the U-boat attack he sent Finnegan down with an invitation to the Holmeses. He would be delighted if they would come to his cabin for a pre-luncheon drink.

They would indeed be delighted; but only the Colonel would come. He asked for his wife to be excused; she was feeling a little off-colour.

At eight bells in the forenoon watch Kemp left the bridge and waited in his cabin for Colonel Holmes. He arrived very formally dressed in a white sharkskin suit with a stiff white collar and his regimental tie, the Berkshires, to which parent regiment he had mentally reverted on retirement. To Kemp, who quite failed to recognize him, he looked thin and papery. He apologized again for his wife's absence. 'The racket, you know, Captain. The gunfire and all that. Not used to it. We've lived a pretty quiet life since I retired.' He gave a somewhat croaky laugh. 'Quiet! Certainly no heavy gunfire. Or depth charges.'

Kemp smiled. 'I imagine not, Colonel. It would have been upsetting, naturally.'

'Yes.' Holmes, who had not yet made any reference to their

41

previous, peacetime meeting, took a glass of gin-and-bitters from a salver held out by Kemp's steward. 'Thank you, steward,' he said.

'It's a pleasure, sir.' The steward handed his salver to Kemp: Kemp's glass contained only orange squash, something he more or less detested but he seldom drank alcohol at sea in wartime and never in company with passengers. When the steward had returned to his pantry Holmes said, 'As a matter of fact . . . there was something else that upset my wife. Not that I'm making any formal complaint, nothing of that sort. It's not really important. But it was upsetting.' Holmes took a sip of his gin and swallowed. A large adam's-apple rippled in a scrawny throat. Then he asked, 'Who is this Brigadier Pumphrey something?'

'Pumphrey-Hatton. He –'

'Ah, yes, that sounds like what the feller said. I remembered the Pumphrey part. By association, really. When we were serving with the Berkshires in Colchester . . . my wife had a cat named Pumphrey. Tabby.'

'Really?' Kemp sat forward in what he hoped was an attitude of interest.

'Yes. Now, who is this officer? Do I take it he's oc Troops?'

Kemp felt he had to go carefully, act with due caution when speaking of Pumphrey-Hatton. He said, 'Not oc Troops, Colonel. He's a passenger, the same as you.'

'That's odd. He appeared to be wearing a uniform. And he doesn't strike one as retired. What's up with him, Commodore?'

'In what respect do you mean?'

'Feller's a boor,' Holmes said briefly. 'Damned rude to me and my wife.' He explained about the shove in the back from Pumphrey-Hatton and the way in which the brigadier had spoken and had forced his way through the passengers. 'Quite unnecessary,' he said. 'Is he going to the Cape?'

'No,' Kemp said. 'All the way to the Clyde.'

'Home? Do you know why?'

Kemp shook his head: it was not his business to reveal anything about Pumphrey-Hatton's recent past. 'I really can't say, Colonel –'

'Or won't? As the Commodore of the convoy, you're surely . . . well, I won't press. It's not my pigeon, of course. But the feller didn't strike me as normal somehow.'

Kemp thought it time to alter the course of the conversation. He said, 'I understand we've sailed together before, Colonel. I have to confess I didn't remember you at first.'

'Yes, I was coming to that – our previous voyage together.' Holmes waved a thin hand. 'It's natural enough not to recall . . . so many faces, don't you know, in between. And I dare say I've grown older.'

Kemp murmured some polite disclaimer of age. After that the old man did most of the talking. Did Kemp remember . . . various names from that long forgotten Staff Captain's table were trotted out and remarked upon. When that was exhausted Holmes turned to other aspects of his life, mainly military. Many names were mentioned, people whom Kemp was not remotely likely to have met. Good old Bill Palmer of the gunners: when stationed in Victoria Barracks in Southsea, good old Bill, who was a real character apparently, had by some subterfuge managed to switch off all the lights at a Kimbell's dinner dance and had then hurled rolls of toilet paper across the dark dance floor, with hilarious results when he switched the lights on again. Did Kemp know Kimbell's? No. It was the fashionable place to go to, in Osborne Road. Good old Bill was followed by Arse-end Portlock of the KOSB, so called because he was always late on parade and had to be covered for by his company sergeant-major. General Montgomery, whom Holmes remembered as a subaltern in the Warwicks, right back in the First World War . . . Holmes couldn't recall just where he'd met Monty, and he cudgelled his brains for a while before deciding that it didn't really matter. He mentioned a few other names and then went back to good old Bill and Arse-end Portlock, both of whom had retired some years before the war and had been recalled to the colours to act as Railway Transport Officers, good old Bill at Crewe and Arse-end Portlock at Paddington, where he had been killed by a bomb in an air raid. Late again: Holmes said he'd been slow to reach the air-raid shelter. He'd been, after all, pretty elderly, though younger than Holmes himself.

Somehow, Kemp was unable to tie up the old man with people such as good old Bill with his toilet-paper japes, and Arse-end Portlock. But he reflected that everyone had been different in their salad days, himself included.

Colonel Holmes' visit was terminated by the luncheon bugle:

43

war or no war, the *Aurelian Star* maintained at least some of the niceties of a first-class peacetime liner.

In the saloon, Holmes was joined by his wife. 'Charming feller, Kemp,' he said as he sat down in the chair withdrawn for him by the saloon waiter. 'Just as I remember him. Sad to say, he didn't remember me, but that's understandable, as I told him. Pity you couldn't have come along, my dear. Anyway – it's nice to see you better.'

'I'm afraid I shan't eat anything, Stephen.'

'Oh, dear.' He looked at her with concern. 'Think you ought to see the ship's doctor? Or perhaps Kennedy would stretch a point.' Major Kennedy was the MO of the native battalion. 'I can have a word, Mildred, if –'

'No, no.' She shook her head vigorously. 'I really don't want to bother anyone, Stephen.' She changed the tack of the conversation somewhat quickly. 'What did you and Commodore Kemp talk about?'

'Oh, this and that.' Holmes waved a hand. 'Reminiscences, don't you know.'

'Yours?' There was an affectionate amusement in her eyes.

'Well – yes. Largely. Kemp was never a particularly talkative man as I remember. Not a man for small talk.'

'You told him about Captain Portlock I dare say.'

'Oh, yes. He was very amused. Or was it the story about good old Bill . . .'

There were no further attacks; a sense of peacetime began to descend on the liner as with the accompanying ships she continued on her way south for the Cape. The zig-zag was being maintained despite the absence of any submarine contact: no chances were being taken. Kemp kept his personal staff and his guns'-crews at a high pitch of efficiency. Ramm was constantly, as it seemed to the gunnery ratings, exercising the three-inch crews, largely under the surveillance of Sub-Lieutenant Finnegan which Ramm didn't go much on and said so to Leading Seaman Purkiss.

'Gets on me wick,' he said. 'What's 'e know about gunnery, compared to a Whale Island gunner's mate. Eh?'

'He's an officer,' Purkiss said, tongue-in-check. 'Got to know best, hasn't he?'

Ramm's breath hissed between his teeth. 'You,' he said. '*Feather*stonehaugh.'

'Yes, PO?'

' 'Ow long before you aspire to the bleedin' wardroom, lad?'

Featherstonehaugh shrugged. 'I don't know, PO. It depends on more recommendations, and on –'

'All right, lad. Reckon you know more about gunnery than I do, do you?'

'No, PO –'

'Dead right you bloody don't,' Ramm said grimly. 'So just learn while you can, eh? Before bloody 'Itler says it's too late, like. Shift round, take Leading Seaman Purkiss' place on the gun. We'll see how you make out.'

As gun-drill recommenced, Finnegan was seen once again making his way aft. As Ramm began shouting orders to bring the three-inch to bear on imaginary targets, Finnegan kept a special eye on Ordinary Seaman Featherstonehaugh as per orders from the Commodore. Watching, Finnegan reflected that the limeys made heavy weather for themselves even over their own names. Not only their own names but trade names too. Even Dooars whisky: the limes called it Dyouars . . .

That afternoon the wireless office received a WT signal from the Admiralty, a Top Secret classification addressed to the Flag repeated Commodore. The signal being in cypher and not plain naval code, it was decyphered by Sub-Lieutenant Finnegan. He handed the plain language version to Kemp in the latter's cabin.

Kemp read: the surface raider *Stuttgart* was no longer in the Indian Ocean. Intelligence reports indicated that she had rounded the Cape of Good Hope, having kept well to the south, and was now believed to be back in the South Atlantic.

Kemp tapped the message form. 'This could mean she's waiting until we've embarked the main troop draft at Simonstown. A more worthwhile kill, sub.'

'Yes, sir. And I reckon there could be another angle to it.'

Kemp looked up. 'Well?'

'*Resolution*, sir. She's due to leave us at Simonstown. With her escort. It's likely the Heinies know that, wouldn't you say?'

Kemp nodded. 'It's possible. Damn spies everywhere, and big mouths not taking in the message of the posters. You know – Be

Like Dad, Keep Mum.' Kemp got to his feet. 'I'm showing this to Captain Maconochie. I'll be with him on the bridge. My compliments to oc Troops . . . I'd be grateful if he'd join us right away.'

When the three senior officers conferred within the next few minutes, Kemp put forward his assistant's guess. Colonel Carter, oc Troops as far as Simonstown, concurred but made the point that the reduced convoy escort was bound to be reinforced with another battleship.

Kemp was not so sure. The briefing at Colombo had made no mention of a replacement for the *Resolution*. There was in any case a shortage of heavy-gun ships and many of those that might be available – might being the operative word – were old and slow like the *Resolution* herself and their presence would slow the convoy when eventually it moved into the principal operating area of the U-boat packs – the North Atlantic. He added, 'It was known from the start that *Resolution* would be leaving us –'

'But surely this makes a difference, Commodore? The fact of the *Stuttgart* going back around – ?'

Kemp gave a hard laugh. 'It ought to. Perhaps it will. It'll be on the minds of the staff in the Operations Room at the Admiralty. But staff minds are unpredictable, and a lot depends on what other uses they have for the heavy ships. Don't forget, there's been a lot of talk about a second front in Europe. I have it in mind, and so will the staff, that the battlewagons are going to be needed to bombard the coasts, soften up for the landing craft to disembark the troops.'

'So what you're saying is this: the convoy could be left without proper protection, set at risk in the interest of something bigger?'

Kemp said, 'I'm not saying that, Colonel. All the same . . . it's happened before. All we can do is – wait and see. You can be dead sure Admiral Layton will make urgent representations to the Admiralty just as soon as we reach Simonstown. Until then, he can't break wireless silence.'

Three days later the convoy and escort reduced speed for entry to the base at Simonstown. Shortly after the ships had secured at the berths, Brigadier Pumphrey-Hatton, who had lain low ever since the contretemps with Kemp on the bridge, was observed making his way ashore.

FIVE

'Gibraltar,' Pumphrey-Hatton said reminiscently. 'Eight years ago. Or was it nine – one's lost count of peacetime years, I find. It all coalesces. I see you have flies here too,' he added, sweeping a hand across his face. 'Damn brutes! It was they that brought the cholera, back there in the Red Sea.'

Pumphrey-Hatton was seated in the office of a rear-admiral, who held the appointment of Senior British Naval Officer, Simonstown. Pumphrey-Hatton, then a major, and Rear-Admiral Thomas, then a commander, had met in Gibraltar when Pumphrey-Hatton had been stationed in Buena Vista barracks with the foreign service battalion of the DCLI; Thomas had been Executive Officer of the battleship *Queen Elizabeth*, flagship of the Mediterranean Fleet. They were both men of a largely similar outlook and they had got along together when they had met at the various social occasions that had been part and parcel of naval and military life in peacetime. There had been drinks at the NOP, the Naval Officers' Pavilion, swimming at Rosia, parties at Government House, functions at the Royal Gibraltar Yacht Club and so on. There had been expeditions across the guarded frontier into Spain. Now, Pumphrey-Hatton spoke of some of this.

'Lamorna,' he said. 'No blasted flies. You'll remember, of course.'

'I do indeed.' Lamorna was the name of a guest house where many service families had stayed when out from home on a visit to their husbands – mainly naval wives since the army families mostly had quarters in the garrison. Commander Thomas' wife

47

and children had stayed there on two or three occasions when the flagship had been in the port; and Pumphrey-Hatton and his wife had dined with the Thomases. Pumphrey-Hatton remembered what he had privately called 'the Thomas woman' as a somewhat faded beauty who spent much of her time talking about horses and had a voice and a laugh to match.

Now, he enquired after her.

'Oh, she's very well . . . when I last heard, that is. Sent her off to a sister in the country when the war came. Plenty of riding, that sort of thing.'

'Yes, quite. There's another fly.' Pumphrey-Hatton swatted again.

The rear-admiral raised an eyebrow. 'Flies really bother you?'

'Yes, they damn well do.' Pumphrey-Hatton spoke viciously.

'Don't let them, then. They don't bother me, so long as they keep out of the gin.' The rear-admiral gave a hearty laugh.

'That's just it – they damn well don't! I had them in my gin in the Red Sea, you know. Really damnable – I've had the devil of a time I don't mind telling you. What with the cholera and the sinking. Of course, you'll have heard I'm being invalided home.'

'Yes. I'm very sorry – rotten luck, that.'

'And all because of flies. Largely, anyway. And other things that are just as bad. Confounded inefficiency. And *damned* impudence!'

'I'm sorry, my dear chap. I agree things aren't what they were in peacetime, but . . .' He glanced at a clock on the wall to his right: he was verging on an appointment with a member of the South African government. He continued with what he had been about to say. 'We have to make the best of things as they are. It' been good to meet you again, old boy. We had some wonderful times in Gib. If there's anything –'

'I've not finished yet,' Pumphrey-Hatton said. He brought out an envelope and handed it across to Rear-Admiral Thomas. 'In there is a report, compiled by myself, on the conduct of the Convoy Commodore. Kemp's his name as I dare say you're aware. Confounded inefficiency is rampant, *absolutely rampant* in that man's ship. Not just the flies. Other things. Electric fan that don't work, stewards who fail to answer bells. And personal rudery to boot. The man had the blasted cheek to order me off his bridge – and then threatened me with arrest! It's all in

48

there. I'm asking you to read it and then forward it to the Admiralty.'

At Simonstown, the mail came aboard. Kemp read five letters from his wife. The death and funeral of his aged grandmother was gone into; the Chairman of the Mediterranean-Australia Lines had attended the funeral out of respect for Kemp who had been one of his senior captains. There were also letters, one each, from his sons at sea on naval service and unable to write much about their lives on account of the censorship; but both were in good spirits and, so far anyway, safe and well.

Yeoman of Signals Lambert also had a letter from his wife. Just the one, and a little restrained in tone: reading between the lines Lambert believed the episode of the french letter had not been entirely set aside. The letter seemed to contain a rueful sniff, a sort of self-pity that didn't exactly help a man thousands of miles away across the sea.

For Chief Steward Chatfield there was a long letter, heavily scented, from Roxanne in Southampton. It was very loving and there was no mention of a salesman but she did say she was having as good a time as was possible in wartime and without him by her side. A friend (what sort of friend?) had managed to get her a bottle of gin, rare as nectar these days, and each supper time she gave herself a teensy-weensy one and drank to hubby's safety at sea. She hoped – and he could almost hear the coy giggle – that he wasn't going after all those uninhibited popsies out east, the word 'east' being heavily scratched out and 'where you are' substituted.

There were other letters for Chatfield: a reminder that the rates hadn't been paid; a bill for a wireless repair; an invitation from Dr Barnardo's to make a donation. These had all been forwarded by Roxanne. There was one that had not been: one from the anonymous busybody. The Morris Eight had been seen again, many times. Its driver had been seen: a man of around thirty, maybe a little less, who should have been in uniform but wasn't. He was handsome if you liked that sort – rather slick with Brylcremed dark hair and padded shoulders – and he hadn't looked short of a bob or two, or of petrol either come to that.

As before, Chatfield ripped the letter up angrily. He turned his attention to his stores list. There was quite a bit to come aboard in

Simonstown, including booze for the passengers and ship's officers. Chatfield also had his own personal stock to consider: he was very partial to van der Humm, the very excellent brandy that they produced at the Cape.

Petty Officer Ramm's wife had also written. So had the blonde bombshell from the Golden Fleece. Ramm opened each letter to the rapid thump of his heart, but all was well so far. And never the twain must meet . . .

During the afternoon Kemp made his formal call on SBNO – Rear-Admiral Thomas. After his morning appointment, Thomas had read Pumphrey-Hatton's lengthy report. It was a diatribe of complaint, an extension of what the brigadier had already reported verbally: flies, fans, stewards and rudery, right back beyond Colombo where the current convoy had originated, back to the Red Sea, the Suez Canal, and the Mediterranean. It seemed to substantiate what Thomas had gleaned about Pumphrey-Hatton's mental state. Nevertheless, it was a report officially delivered from a senior military officer who until disaster had struck had been OC Troops aboard the Commodore's ship.

After Kemp had made his formal report, also for transmission to the Admiralty, of the conduct of the convoy from Colombo to the Cape, the rear-admiral mentioned Pumphrey-Hatton.

'How,' he asked abruptly, 'do you get on with Brigadier Pumphrey-Hatton?'

'In what respect do you mean, sir? Socially – or in the course of duty?'

'Let's say both, Kemp.'

'I'd say he's fairly typical of a certain sort of army officer.'

Thomas gave a short laugh. 'And what's that supposed to mean?'

Kemp said, 'I rather think you get the meaning – don't you?'

'Perhaps. Not all beer and skittles. Of course, there's no question of duty for Pumphrey-Hatton now. I find it all rather sad. He's a prickly character.' Thomas got to his feet and took a few turns up and down the room. He seemed about to say something further but thought better of it. He returned to his desk and sat down. 'Question of your escort,' he said. 'There'll be the usual sailing conference with NCSO but I thought a word first . . . you'll know you're losing *Resolution* and her destroyers, of course.'

Kemp nodded.

'Admiral Layton will leave Simonstown after refuelling. And I dare say you've noticed there's no other battleship in the port.'

Kemp said, 'Yes, I had noticed that.'

'With some misgivings, I suspect?'

'Yes, sir, you could say that.'

'Well, we can't produce battlewagons out of thin air. Layton's destroyers will be replaced and there'll be one additional cruiser, a heavy one – *Vindictive*. Ten thousand tons. She's been down here boiler-cleaning. *And*,' Thomas added with a grin, 'replenishing her wardroom wine stocks. She's normally based at Freetown in Sierra Leone and that's where she's bound. She'll detach at the latitude of the Rokel River.'

'And be replaced?'

'No, I'm afraid not, Kemp –'

'But that German raider, the *Stuttgart* –'

'Yes, we know all about the *Stuttgart*. Except, that is, her current exact position and course. But you've not been forgotten. The Admiralty's well enough aware of the risks. C-in-C Home Fleet has been ordered to detach a battleship from Scapa and steam her south to rendezvous with the convoy. We don't yet know where the rendezvous will be nor which ship C-in-C will detach, but it seems likely it'll be the *Duke of York*. And that's all I can tell you for now, Kemp.' He paused. 'By the way, your report didn't have much to say about those POWs. I take it you've had no trouble?'

'None at all, sir.' Kemp hesitated. 'Nothing beyond a few long faces amongst the merchant crew. And my own staff . . . nothing that can't be contained, of course.'

The rear-admiral nodded thoughtfully and after a pause said, 'You have a CW rating aboard. Featherstonehaugh.'

'Yes, I have –'

'How's he making out?'

'I've only had him since Colombo, sir. But I've no complaint to make. He does his job, according to my assistant and the gunner's mate.'

'Keep an eye on him, Kemp. I knew his father – commander(E) in the *Barham*. Lost, of course. I met the boy on a couple of occasions before the war. Seemed the right type. No favouritism, of course – but keep an eye open whenever you can, Kemp.'

51

Kemp promised to do so. But if that eye detected any shortcomings, it would not be the Nelsonic blind eye. Too many men's lives depended in war and peace at sea on the efficiency and personal qualities of those set in authority over them for high-ranking connections to over-ride any defects.

After Kemp had left his office, Rear-Admiral Thomas read again through the report prepared by Brigadier Pumphrey-Hatton. It was, in his own unuttered phraseology, a load of bullshit. Flies and faulty fans might be irritants but personal comfort had no place in a formal report from a brigadier. Thomas had more than a suspicion that Pumphrey-Hatton wouldn't bat an eyelid at flies and airless heat along the troop-decks. And any commander at sea had the unassailable right to chuck anyone off his bridge if he felt so inclined. The threat of arrest was perhaps, but only perhaps, going a little far. But from what he had just seen of Kemp, Thomas was inclined to believe that his judgement was unlikely to have been at fault. In other words, Pumphrey-Hatton had asked for it. Thomas had played with the idea of telling Kemp about that list of complaints but, since it had been delivered in confidence, he had felt his hands, or his tongue, to be tied. Which he very much regretted. Pumphrey-Hatton and he had got along together in those pre-war days. Pumphrey-Hatton had been a keen soldier and dedicated to his regiment. A harsh disciplinarian, or so it had been said, but there was nothing wrong in that. Something of a nit-picker, but then so were many regimental officers with little to occupy their time on foreign service. Thomas recalled that his wife hadn't really liked him. Too starchy, she'd said, and no interest in horses. Now, sitting brooding in his Simonstown office, Thomas believed that that ill-natured report, when received eventually at the War Office via the Admiralty, might prove to be the final nail in Pumphrey-Hatton's military coffin.

Leading Seaman Purkiss, right-hand man of Petty Officer Ramm, had gone ashore just as soon as libertymen had been piped. He had gone ashore with two objectives: to get drunk, and to find a popsie, black, coloured or white didn't matter all that much. By the time Commodore Kemp was on his way back, in a taxi, to the *Aurelian Star*, Purkiss was well on his way to achieving his first objective, having consumed several pints of beer, six gins, and a couple of large Van der Humms. There was, however, still some spare capacity, and it was while that capacity was waiting to be filled that Leading Seaman Purkiss left the bar where he had been seated on a high stool and made his way to the gents to empty tanks, a precautionary move on his part.

On emerging he bumped into a uniformed figure. Swaying, he blocked the way, uttering a belch of fumes.

'Get out of my way,' Brigadier Pumphrey-Hatton said.

Purkiss lurched and almost fell against the brigadier. 'An' 'oo says so?'

'I'm Brigadier Pumphrey-Hatton.'

'I don't give a fish's tit if you're Pontius bloody Pilate, mate –'

'You're stinking drunk, man, and a disgusting sight. If you don't get out of my way immediately, I shall call the Military Police and have you arrested. *Move!*'

Purkiss remained where he was. He was seeing two if not three Pumphrey-Hattons now. 'Look, mate –'

'Don't call me mate!' Pumphrey-Hatton said in a voice that was becoming frenzied. 'I shall charge you with lack of respect in addressing an officer and I warn you –'

'Bollocks,' Leading Seaman Purkiss said loudly, and as another person loomed up behind the brigadier he shoved a fist forward into Pumphrey-Hatton's face. Pumphrey-Hatton stepped sharply back, at the same time flinging out an arm. Losing his balance, he not only cannoned into the person behind but managed to strike this person a blow in the face with his outflung hand. The newcomer happened to be Petty Officer Biggar of the *Aurelian Star*'s DEMS contingent. Biggar lost his footing and fell flat, with Pumphrey-Hatton coming down on top of him. As the two struggled to their feet, Biggar became aware of the identity of the rating who had caused the fracas.

'You, eh. Just bloody look at what you done now, you bleedin' object. Striking an officer. Thus causing the officer to strike a rating. Me. Court Martial charges both. What a fuckin' awful potmess, begging your pardon, sir.'

He saluted. Pumphrey-Hatton stared, his face working with a number of emotions. Then tears began streaming down his face and suddenly he pushed past Biggar and vanished along the passage. Petty Officer Biggar pulled out a handkerchief and wiped at his face. 'What I'd call embarrassing,' he said. 'Poor sod's likely had a hard war. You didn't ought to 'ave done what you did, Leading Seaman Purkiss, putting me in a bloody pickle an' all. I reckon we keep mum, hope 'e don't recognize either of us. An' don't you do any more drinking, Leading Seaman Purkiss, an' that's an order, right?'

'Right,' Purkiss said in a slurred voice. 'Got other things to do now anyway.'

'Oh, yes? Such as?'

Purkiss gave a leering laugh. 'One guess, PO.'

'Bollocks. In your state? You'll never make it, boyo.'

Early the following morning, the Commodore of the convoy along with the masters and chief officers of the merchant ships and the Commanding Officers and navigators of the escorts attended the briefing by the Naval Control Service Officer. There was no fresh information so far as Kemp was concerned: what the rear-admiral had already told him was still virtually the extent of current intelligence. The whereabouts, in any precise sense, of the *Stuttgart* was still not known. The raider apart, there would be the usual hazards of any ocean convoy: the hunting packs of U-boats as the ships came towards the latitude of Freetown, where the *Vindictive* would detach into the Rokel River. The one fresh piece of information available was that the Home Fleet battleship would make a rendezvous three hundred miles to the north of where the *Vindictive* would detach. Also it was confirmed that the battleship would be HMS *Duke of York*, wearing the flag of the Vice-Admiral Commanding, 1st Battle Squadron, together with her own destroyer screen and two light cruisers, *Caradoc* and *Cardiff*. As Kemp returned from the conference with Sub-Lieutenant Finnegan and Captain Maconochie, there was movement in the port: HMS *Resolution* was moving out with her escort, the Admiral's flag fluttering from the masthead in a strong southerly breeze. With her went her escort: as Maconochie remarked, it left them fairly naked.

'Like the mistress of the Alsatian,' Finnegan said with a straight face.

'I beg your pardon, Finnegan?'

'A filthy story, sir. Told me by a guy in a bar –'

'I don't think we want to hear it, Finnegan.'

Finnegan waved a hand. 'Just as you like, sir.'

The taxi deposited them at the gangway of the *Aurelian Star*; as they climbed Kemp saw the *Vindictive* moving across the harbour towards the fuelling berth. Her boiler-cleaning completed, the cruiser was entering the final stages of her preparation for sea. Big and well-armoured, one of the last of the heavy cruisers, she was a reassuring sight. But she was no battleship.

The returning officers were saluted aboard by the Chief Officer and the quartermaster at the upper platform of the accommodation ladder. Captain Maconochie took his Chief Officer aside.

'Prepare for sea, Mr Dartnell. We leave at 2200 tonight.'

'Aye, aye, sir.'

'And a message to the Chief Engineer. My compliments – and I'd like him to come to my day cabin.' With the Commodore, he climbed the ladders to his accommodation below the bridge. In the space allocated as seamen's messdeck for the RN ratings, Leading Seaman Purkiss was nursing a head that still clanged like a bell at the slightest sound. He had little recollection of what he'd done in the later stages of the day before, no recollection at all of having been brought back aboard by the naval patrol and more or less poured into his bunk. He had been apprised of this by Petty Officer Biggar early in the 'morning after'; charges, PO Biggar said, pended. Purkiss knew that he stood to lose his rate as leading seaman but Kemp might be lenient and merely put him under stoppage of leave for a while, which wouldn't be any hardship once they'd gone to sea. His worry was Brigadier Pumphrey-Hatton. If *he* pressed charges, then this current voyage would end for Purkiss in the Naval Detention Quarters in RNB Pompey. Ninety days was the least you could expect for striking an officer. Another thing that bothered him was a very personal matter: he had not the remotest idea as to what kind of woman if any he had eventually landed up with. He might have got himself a dose, and what would his wife say to that? Edith was the jealous sort and weepy with it. Also, her old man, an ex-chief gunner's mate, was still alive and active and had once been the heavyweight champion of the Navy.

Purkiss had consulted PO Biggar, whose advice was to see the quack and set his mind at rest. Or not, as the case might be. But Biggar had also offered consolation. 'Like I said back in that bar. A pound to a penny you 'ad the droops. Not that I know where you went after, but I reckon you're safe enough. Anyway, you were so bleedin' pissed not even a prozzie would have taken you on. Not beyond taking your cash off you.'

At 2130 special sea dutymen were piped throughout the warship escorts, the cable and side parties were closed up, and the ships that had been at anchor shortened-in and prepared to weigh, while those at the berths alongside cast off wires and ropes fore and aft, retaining the springs until the word came from the various navigating bridges to let go all.

Kemp was at Maconochie's side as the final order was passed. Below on the starting platform, Chief Engineer French stood by as on the bridge the handles of the telegraphs were pulled over, the repeaters below calling for slow ahead both engines. As the order came the great shafts began turning to bring the former liner off the wall for the long haul to the Firth of Clyde, the really dangerous part of the voyage beginning. On the troop-decks above the engine-room the Australians and New Zealanders, who had been embarked late that afternoon, were still settling in and sorting themselves out for the last long leg before they joined in whatever awaited them thousands of miles from home.

In his cabin Chief Steward Chatfield grew maudlin on Van der Humm and thought about Roxanne and the hypothetical bloody salesman. At this stage there was really no point at all in writing, since he would be in touch by telephone from Greenock long before any letter could arrive. He began to rehearse that telephone call: he would be all nonchalance, simply asking in an innocent voice if Roxanne had gone and spent all the money that went by monthy allotment from his pay to her bank account in Southampton.

'Whatever makes you think,' she would reply, 'that I gone and done that?'

'Oh, nothing really,' he would go on to say. 'But I s'pose you'll be meeting me at the Central station . . . with that Morris Eight you just got with my spondulicks?'

That would put the fox among the chickens, all right; especially if the bloody salesman happened to be there when he rang.

Chatfield felt the sea movement as the *Aurelian Star* came out from the lee of the breakwater, felt the lurch as she met the ocean swell and more than a little of a seaway. Roll on the Clyde, he thought, the Tail o' the Bank and a touch of vengeance. He drank more Van der Humm. Spanking, that was what was called for. Women liked the firm approach. Put her across his knee, and wham. After that, well, she'd come to heel, and the salesman, who was likely enough married and wouldn't want his old woman to get to hear, would scarper into his bloody Morris Eight and vanish . . .

There was quite a weight of wind outside the port as the merchantmen and warships turned to starboard to come past the Cape, the actual Cape of Good Hope itself.

'The Cape of Storms,' Kemp said.

'What was that, sir?'

'History, Finnegan. Vasco da Gama called it the Cape of Storms when he discovered it. It's pretty appropriate tonight – or it will be in an hour or so. The wind's freshening fast from southerly.'

'You can say that again, sir, Commodore.'

Kemp sighed. 'Two Americanisms in one sentence, Finnegan, is a bit much. I've no desire to say it again. However, I gather it's registered, right?'

'Right, sir –'

'So gather your wits, young man, and check that Petty Officer Ramm has taken due precautions with the ship's armament.'

'Or Petty Officer Biggar, sir?'

'I said Ramm, and I meant Ramm. He can sort out the niceties with Biggar.' Kemp lifted his binoculars around the assembly of ships, no more than blacker bulks in the night's darkness, showing only the usual shaded blue stern-lights. Dimly he could see the bow-waves of the vessels on either beam, could see the bones in the teeth – as the saying went – of the destroyers as they raced ahead to take up their stations to act as anti-submarine screen. Already the water was heaving over the bows of the *Aurelian Star*, and spray was flying over the fore cargo hatches to reach the bridge, where canvas dodgers had been rigged. It was going to be a dirty night, with the wind slap on the port beam, making the ship roll badly. Kemp spared a thought for the troops crammed in along the troop-decks: never mind that they'd already made the voyage from their Australian port of embarkation, they still wouldn't really have their sea-legs, not in many cases.

Below, Finnegan made contact with Petty Officer Ramm.

57

Ramm, surly at being chased, went in search of PO Biggar. Well away to the north, and standing handily to the west of the northbound shipping lanes, the *Stuttgart* received word by wireless that Convoy SW03 had left the Simonstown base and was steaming for the Firth of Clyde with no escorting battleship.

SIX

The German prisoners-of-war, under guard of sentries found by the King's East African Rifles, were mainly a surly bunch, not liking their lot and not liking the fact of being under native control, an unseemly thing for pure-bred Aryans, members of the master race, sailors of their Führer. But, up to the present anyway, they were behaving themselves. Sergeant Jeremiah Muhoho of the Rifles, who with Sergeants Mgala and Tapapa took his watch as NCO of the guard, was a diligent man who took his duties very seriously and would stand no nonsense. None of the Germans would risk a tongue-lashing from a native. But beneath the surface there was a stir of hatred for the British, for the newly embarked Australians and New Zealanders, and for the natives themselves who had taken King George's shilling against the might of Adolf Hitler and the German Empire that the Führer had stated would last a thousand years.

OC Troops – Colonel Harrison of the Australian Army who had now replaced Colonel Carter – was aware of the feeling as he made rounds of the troop-decks and POW accommodation on the first day after leaving Simonstown. He remarked on it to his adjutant: Captain Mulvaney agreed, pushing his bush hat to the back of his ginger hair and wiping sweat from his face.

'Right you are, Colonel. They want to hit back at the poms. Can't say I blame 'em and that's fair dinkum. You met that pommie brigadier?'

'I have. Point taken, Mulvaney. But don't forget this: pommie brigadiers are going to be a fact of life once we hit the Clyde –'

'Take me back to bloody Wagga Wagga.' Captain Mulvaney

59

blew out a long-suffering breath. 'Why did I ever join up?'

'Because you had to,' Harrison said with a grin. 'Why did I, come to that? Anyway – those Krauts, they aren't allowed to have hate feelings, not to let it show anyway. Same applies to you.'

Mulvaney said, 'And that's an order. Right, Colonel?'

'Dead right, Captain. So watch it. Meantime, I'm going to have a word with the Commodore.' Harrison paused. 'For a pom, he's a good bloke.' Leading the way out from the POW accommodation, low down in the ship, Colonel Harrison returned a smart salute from the native NCO. 'What's your name, son?'

Standing rigid at attention, Sergeant Muhoho answered. 'Muhoho, sah! Jeremiah Muhoho, sergeant, sah, the King's East African Rifles.'

'Uh-huh. At ease, Sergeant. Well now, son, I'm relying on you and your mates to keep that bloody bunch under full control. I note you speak English. Some English anyway. How much?'

'Plenty good English, sah! Very good speaker, learning from British officers, sah, all white.'

'Well, good on yer, bloke.' Colonel Harrison fished in a capacious pocket of his khaki-drill tunic and produced a packet of cigarettes. 'Take a fag, bloke. Go on, they won't bloody bite.'

'Sah! I do not smoke, sah.'

'Oh, well, that's your loss. Not that some people don't call 'em coffin nails.' Colonel Harrison laid a hand on Sergeant Muhoho's shoulder and grinned in his shining face. 'Don't look so bloody shit scared, bloke. Like the fags – I don't bite.'

'Sah!' To Sergeant Muhoho's immense relief, the Colonel moved away, undoing the buttons of his tunic and giving a loud belch before sticking a cigarette in his mouth. The Australians were a very curious species, Sergeant Muhoho thought in perplexity, very different from the officers of the King's East African Rifles and as if from a different form of life from the very old officer, Colonel Holmes. Never in all his life had an officer addressed Sergeant Muhoho as 'bloke'. He wasn't sure that he liked it, in front of the rank-and-file, the riflemen. He was, after all, entitled by long and faithful service to be addressed as Sergeant.

Colonel Harrison climbed to the bridge. As OC Troops, he was permitted so to do. He was greeted by both Maconochie and

Kemp. Waving his right arm in a kind of salute to the Convoy Commodore he started right in, no small talk about Colonel Harrison when he was being official.

'Those Germans, Commodore. Pretty rat-faced bunch if you ask me. And a shade too bloody quiet. If you get me.'

'Still waters?' Kemp suggested.

'Eh?'

'Still waters that run deep.'

'Oh, right, I get you. Sums it up. They're fermenting. Or that's what I think. Waiting their chance. Thought I'd mention it.'

Kemp said, 'They're well guarded, Colonel, and all the regulations regarding the conveyance of prisoners-of-war have been complied with and their officer – a *kapitan-leutnant* named Stoph – has been informed of them.' Kemp, who had been given the bumph at Kilindini, ran through it even though Harrison probably knew it all. 'No cutlery such as could be used as weapons allowed, no pepper that could be thrown into the eyes –'

'Sure thing. Done me homework too.'

'Good. Well, whatever chance they're waiting for, they'll not get it. I repeat, that guard's strong.'

'So let's hope you're right, Commodore. They're a tough bunch . . . and what worries me is this bloody raider that's loose around here. If the shooting starts, they c'd be well placed to make any God's amount of trouble. With the ship's crew at action stations. If you get me.'

'Yes, I do. But the native battalion won't be part of action stations –'

'You mean they stay guarding the POW contingent?'

Kemp nodded. 'That's the idea, yes. They'll guard the Germans with their lives. The native troops . . . they're among the loyalest of all the regiments. But don't let me teach my grandmother,' Kemp added with a smile. 'You know the army. I don't.'

'Just a simple sailorman?' Harrison returned the grin.

Kemp laughed. 'You could say that, Colonel. But don't you worry about the Germans. I don't.'

Colonel Harrison reached forward and dug Kemp in the chest with a thick, nicotine-stained forefinger. 'Maybe you should.' Kemp, who disliked being dug in the chest, moved back a fraction. Harrison went on, 'On a point of protocol, Commodore. One thing wasn't made too bloody clear back in Sydney. To be fair, they may not have known about the POW element, not then. But whose are they? Yours or mine? Eh?'

Kemp said, 'In the first instance, they're Captain Maconochie's as Master of the ship. In a sense they're his passengers. I'm merely the Convoy Commodore. In no sense do I command the ship. But to the extent that I have a responsibility for the convoy as a whole, the POWs are mine.'

'Because they're seamen, not pongoes?'

'Not exactly that. Because they're part of the convoy.'

'But in a sense, they're part of the troop draft. Even if they're seamen. Now, that'd make them mine. Eh?'

'There's another angle,' Kemp said, and said it firmly. 'In any passenger ship – currently, any troopship, the responsibility is the Master's. That includes the troops, I have to say – except in regard to internal matters of military organization and discipline, of course.' He was unable to resist adding, 'If you get me.'

There was a glint of something like anger in Harrison's eye. He said, 'Get you, eh? Does anyone outside Britain ever get a pommie? Answer: no, they bloody don't. What you said . . . it sounds like a load of gobbledegook if you don't mind my saying so.'

Kemp's response was a laugh; he intended to keep the peace, not wishing for any repeats of the Pumphrey-Hatton situation. He said, 'I know all about the shortcomings of pommies, Colonel. I spent the peace on the Australian run – Mediterranean-Australia Line. I've spent more time down under than I have at home.'

'Well, I'm blowed! Know Sydney well, do you?'

'Like the back of my hand. And Melbourne and Fremantle. And the outback to a lesser extent.'

'My oath! Well, Commodore, reckon that makes us mates. Why let a bunch of lousy Germans come between us, eh?'

'Why indeed?'

A possible disagreement had been neatly averted. But Kemp was well aware that there could be some truth in what the Australian had said about the Germans taking advantage of any attack. A word with Colonel Carter might not come amiss. And frankly Kemp was not entirely sure of whose initial responsibility the POWs might be. He had not been given a clear answer in Kilindini, nor when he had raised it at the Cape. If all poms used gobbledegook, then officialdom and the top brass used it three times over. Not that it was worth losing any sleep over; when the chips were really down, they were all literally in the same boat. And enemy seamen though they were, the Germans would be accorded the lifeboats or rafts, if it ever came to abandoning, as surely as anyone else aboard after the women and children of the returning British families.

Brigadier Pumphrey-Hatton, the red tabs of the staff adorning the open collar of his khaki-drill tunic, walked the promenade deck as the sun went down, keeping to leeward to avoid the wind and spray and muttering to himself as he paced back and forth. He was still seething about the fracas that had taken place back at the Cape. He had no idea who the drunken man was; nor had he recognized Petty Officer Biggar. The men could have come from any one of the many warships in the port of Simonstown. After the occurrence he had made no report ashore; neither had he done so on his return aboard the *Aurelian Star*. He was aware that he had not come very well out of the encounter; a weeping brigadier was something to be concealed. But he brooded: the whole world as he'd known it was going downhill, heading straight for hell and the devil. There was no respect any more, no discipline in a pre-war sense. Of course, Pumphrey-Hatton knew quite well why that was: the influx of civilians, persons with no concept of service life. Counter-jumpers, clerks, artisans, labourers . . . bolshies all of them very likely. It took years to make a soldier from scratch, and the younger they joined the better. Drummer boys and so on, brought up from a tender age to obey their officers and NCOs instantly and without question. And some of the people with temporary commissions were of course utterly impossible, not fit to enter any officers' mess. It had become a disgraceful state of affairs when men virtually straight from civil life, with no public school and Sandhurst behind them, were put in charge of troops. That alone had led to the decline in discipline: it was a fact that the men had no respect for them and the rest followed from that.

It was cold on deck now. Pumphrey-Hatton entered the shelter of the B deck lounge. As he did so, he saw that the old man,

Colonel Holmes, was getting to his feet and trying to catch his eye. Holmes called out, 'A nightcap, Brigadier. If you'd care to join us my wife and I would be delighted.'

Pumphrey-Hatton gave a nod. He'd spoken on a few occasions to the Holmeses, who had decided to forget the incident of the shove in the back. He'd found the old man a bore but at least he was a gentleman and had been a soldier, so they spoke the same language. He thanked the old man and sat down beside the wife, who smiled at him. 'We always indulge ourselves in a nightcap,' she said.

'Very civilized, Mrs Holmes.'

'A long-standing custom,' Holmes said. 'In East Africa, don't you know –'

'Yes, yes.' Pumphrey-Hatton's tone was brisk: he wanted no more monologues. He said, when asked, that he would like brandy. Not Van der Humm: a genuine brandy, from France. The lounge steward was already waiting with a tray. The order was given: both the Holmeses asked for whisky. Whilst awaiting the drinks, they chatted desultorily. Mrs Holmes was worried about the sea passage. There had been rumours about a German surface raider being at large.

'Do you know if that is correct, Brigadier?'

'Can't discuss that,' Pumphrey-Hatton said briskly.

The old lady seemed disconcerted at the abruptness, but she said, 'No, of course not, I'm so sorry. Careless talk – I really shouldn't have.'

'Better not,' Pumphrey-Hatton said. 'Get in the habit – when you reach UK you'll find you need to be very careful. England isn't East Africa, you know.'

'Yes. Such a pity. We shall miss the life. We had some very good days, such very *happy* days.' Mrs Holmes was growing a shade maudlin; she brought a wispy handkerchief from her handbag and wiped at her eyes. The old colonel became gruff.

'Yes, yes indeed, my dear.' He raised the glass that had just been brought by the lounge steward and looked across at Pumphrey-Hatton. 'Your good health, Brigadier.'

'Good health,' Pumphrey-Hatton said automatically, reflecting that a temporary officer would almost certainly have said 'cheers'. As he drank, a gust of wind came into the lounge. A door had opened to admit a man in naval uniform, a rating, wh–

after a look around headed for the ship's Chief Officer who was sitting with Colonel Carter of the rifle regiment. Some sort of report was obviously being made; the Chief Officer excused himself and made his way towards the door to the open deck, followed by Petty Officer Biggar.

Pumphrey-Hatton stared at the PO. Biggar stared back briefly, seemed to blink a little, looked away, then recovered his poise and moved on. Blood coursed through Pumphrey-Hatton's head and his face became flushed. At his side Colonel Holmes was going on talking. 'I said, Brigadier, that the Germans –'

'Never mind the Germans, man, or what you were saying about them.' Pumphrey-Hatton jerked to his feet, leaving his brandy mostly untouched. 'I wish you goodnight.' He went at a jerky walk across the lounge, leaving by the door opposite that taken by Biggar.

'Well, I'm damned,' Holmes said in some agitation. 'What on earth did I do to bring that on?'

'I don't believe it was anything you said, Stephen. It was when he saw that naval man.'

'But surely –'

'Who was the man, do you know, Stephen?'

'Oh . . . the PO in charge of the DEMS people, I believe. Don't know his name.'

'I think,' Mildred Holmes said in a quiet voice, 'that Brigadier Pumphrey-Hatton knows him. I wonder . . .'

'What do you wonder?'

'Nothing, really. Nothing that I can lay a finger on. But it was really rather curious.'

'Nothing to do with us, Mildred.'

'No, of course not. But I do dislike bad manners, Stephen.'

'Well, yes, so do I. The staff always did think a lot of themselves though, and tended to be brusque – even rude.' Holmes sighed. 'They're all so damned *young* these days compared with what they were before the war. Insolent puppy was what we'd have called the feller once.'

Later that night, when the guns'-crews were relieved by the oncoming watch at eight bells, Petty Officer Biggar approached Petty Officer Ramm, oozing unctuous intent not to prod his nose into a fellow PO's territory. 'Mind if I 'ave a word with one o' your party, eh?'

'Fill your boots,' Ramm said off-handedly, then added on a note of suspicion, 'What about, then?'

'Not official, this isn't. We 'appened to meet ashore, an' I got a message for him after he'd gone on his way like. Your leading 'and it was, Purkiss.'

Ramm wasn't particularly interested in anything but getting turned into his bunk. Petty Officer Biggar drew Purkiss aside and muttered into his ear, 'Best watch it, Purkiss.'

'Watch what?' Leading Seaman Purkiss was sorting out his anti-flash gear, the gloves and face protection that were required when the guns opened fire.

'Pumphrey-Hatton. He recognized me, that's what. No doubt about it at all.' Biggar elaborated on the exchange of looks. 'He may make something of it now he knows, or again he may not. Both ways there's reasons, see. An' just you remember, you 'it him. Struck an officer.'

'He hasn't recognized me yet, PO.'

'Maybe not. But now 'e'll be poking his nose around the ship, won't 'e?'

'What am I supposed to do about it, then, eh?'

'The obvious: keep your 'ead down, all the bloody way to the Clyde. Request permission to grow a beard p'raps – something like that. Basically, you just keep out of 'is way.'

'What about you, PO?'

Biggar shrugged. 'I'm not worried. I didn't strike him, did I? 'E struck me . . . in a manner o' speaking. Sort of lashed out blind. So 'e won't want that to come out, not if 'e's got any sense 'e won't. But I don't want it to come out neither, and for why you might ask? Reason's obvious. As a PO I should 'ave shoved you in the rattle, 'ad you up before the Commodore one-one-two. Which I didn't. Which makes me an accessory after the bleedin' fact or whatever it is them legal johnnies call it. See?'

Leading Seaman Purkiss gave a long sniff and then, blocking one nostril, expelled air through the other one, leaning over the ship's side as he did so. He said, 'I don't reckon you can keep out of the way of anybody, not aboard a ship you can't.'

Petty Officer Biggar made his way for'ard, checking right round the guns, surface and ack-ack. He had come to an accommodation with Ramm: they shared the duties of gunner's mate and that satisfied both of them. More or less; PO Biggar still thought of himself as being in overall charge.

SEVEN

When the noon sight was taken next day, the second officer fixed the ship's position in longitude 33°40′ south, latitude 10° east. They had made good some 540 sea miles from the Simonstown departure and were steaming on a north-westerly course that would take them clear of the coast of South West Africa towards, eventually, the Cape Verde Islands off French West Africa, a long way ahead yet. Many miles of ocean, and many hours of tension for the civilian passengers, the homeward-bound families. Tension and in many cases boredom: there was little to do but worry about the surface raider and later the U-boat packs. There was plenty of drinking time for those who were most at home propped on a bar stool.

One of these was Gregory Hench. Hench had owned a coffee plantation back in Kenya, not a very successful one, the lack of success having been mostly due to a lazy disposition and a liking for whisky. At thirty-nine he was returning home a failure: the plantation had gone bankrupt and he had just about raked up the fare for UK plus enough to keep his thirst at bay. In point of fact he had no need to pay over the bar: he signed chits. He would probably not have enough to cover them at the end of the voyage, but saw no need to cross that bridge for some while yet. In any case, you couldn't get blood out of a stone. He'd made that point to the bankruptcy court. He'd had few assets beyond the run-down plantation and he'd had a number of debts. It had not been until after the proceedings that he'd cabled his old mother for the fare home plus expenses. Longing, as she'd said, to see him again, the cash had been instantly forthcoming. The fact that she couldn't afford to part with it without sacrifices was just too bad. What were parents for?

Hench pushed his empty glass across the bar. 'Same,' he said.

'A large one, sir?'

'That's what I said. Same.'

'Coming up, sir.' The bar steward, a cheerful-looking Scot who had been with the Line since the middle thirties, studied Hench in the mirror behind his optics. He saw a man with a florid face, a disagreeable expression, a man as thin as a rake whose fingers shook as he fumbled with a propelling pencil and a book of wine chits. Steward MacInnes was pretty adept at summing up his customers. He foresaw trouble with Mr Hench, who would be truculent when drunk, really drunk – he'd not been exactly drunk since embarking at Kilindini, just very well oiled, but give him a few more days and he might go over what appeared to be his set limit. Four large whiskies at the lunchtime session, six large whiskies at the evening session, two large brandies after dinner. MacInnes had already made a mental note to have a word with Chief Steward Chatfield about the future: MacInnes reckoned Mr Hench might well default on his booze chits. He didn't give the impression of being well lined; his khaki shirt and shorts had seen better days and his shoes were scuffed and his hair too long and ragged, as though he economized on the barber.

'There we are, sir.' The glass was pushed across. The response was a grunt; never a thank-you from Mr Hench.

Hench took a gulp from the glass and set it down again. His fingers seemed a shade less shaky: MacInnes had noted that the shake tended to subside after the second large whisky. As the steward polished glasses with the cloth that he always carried over his arm he saw another passenger joining Mr Hench at the bar. Miss Gloria Northway, aged at a guess thirty-five. She too had a good intake – gin in her case. She also had a predatory look, one well known to Steward MacInnes. Women at sea – single women or women travelling without their husbands, it came mostly to the same thing – were different from women ashore. Different in that they really let their hair down as though it didn't matter a tinker's cuss. Aboard a ship they were divorced from shoreside life, no one ashore need ever know what they'd been up to at sea, and they lived in a sort of safe cocoon within which they could behave as maybe they'd always wanted to behave but hadn't dared to. Grinning to himself as Mr Hench looked around at the newcomer and made welcoming noises, a grunt of a different sort from that used to stewards, MacInnes wished Miss Northway luck with Mr Hench but didn't reckon she would achieve much. A pound to a penny Mr Hench suffered from distiller's droop.

'Morning, Gloria.'

'Is it?' Her voice was hoarse.

'Hangover?'

'Bloody awful. As per usual. Steward?'

'Yes, madam?'

'Hair of the dog. Fast before I die. And have one yourself.'

'Thank you, madam. I'll take a pale ale.' MacInnes, knowing the particular dog, mixed gin and grapefruit in a long glass with a straw. Gloria Northway sucked avidly and said something about the bottom of a parrot's cage.

'I've a good mind to go on the wagon,' she said, still hoarse, 'but I don't suppose I will. Too painful. Got a cigarette, have you, Gregory?'

Hench produced his cigarette-case. Silver, salvaged from the wreck. He flicked a lighter and Miss Northway blew smoke towards MacInnes. Stale breath accompanied it. With a long finger-nail she removed a fragment of breakfast from a tooth and deposited it in an ashtray. She said suddenly, 'Sod the war.'

Hench looked surprised. 'Why, in particular? I mean – just like that, out of nowhere so to speak?'

'Oh, I don't know.' She shifted about on her stool; her breasts wobbled, more or less tantalizingly. 'Just sod it, that's all. All the shortages, and the dangers, and everyone here today and gone tomorrow, you know what I mean.'

Hench nodded but didn't comment.

'Take you and me. Waifs of the war.'

'Yes.'

'Funny we never met in Kenya.'

'You said you'd been in –'

'Nyasaland, right, so I did. And was. Anyway, we've met now and that's something good come out of the war. Coffee, didn't you say?'

'Yes,' Hench said.

'Coffee's good and safe. I just drifted and I don't mind

admitting it, Gregory, I don't mind at all. I suppose you could say I was a bit of a bum, actually.'

Kept woman was more like it, Hench thought, but he said, 'Oh, no, surely . . . you shouldn't say that –'

'I do say it.' She reached out a little unsteadily and laid a hand on his arm. 'Someone like you is good for little me,' she said.

'Think so?'

'Damn right I do.' She belched, put a hand to her mouth and said, 'Pardon me, so sorry. Where was I?'

'I'm good for you. May one ask why?'

She waved her cigarette in the air. 'Morale. I'm not proud, I've had a few rejections. Could be I drink too much, but so what?'

Hench grinned. 'Have another,' he said, noting that her glass was already nearly empty.

'Don't mind if I do.' Miss Northway drained the glass and pushed it across towards MacInnes. 'That's what I meant,' she said to Hench. 'You don't criticize.'

He shrugged. 'Live and let live.'

'And so say I . . . dear Gregory. Oh God – my head.'

She would very probably be willing. Hench was willing, at any rate in spirit; any port in a storm and Gloria Northway wouldn't expect to be – what was the word – wooed. No need for extended preliminaries. But there was a snag, an overwhelming one. Hench, who had never married, had had sundry brief affairs over the years, mostly with the wives of fellow planters until they found out he was no use in bed, however strong and urgent the desire. With deadly accuracy, Steward MacInnes had put his finger on it. Desire, heightened by the treacherous effects of whisky, was always frustrated by its own bolsterer and Gregory Hench had come to dread the moment when a woman showed signs of being ready.

Once again he pushed his glass across and recommended Miss Northway to take a couple of aspirins.

Below in his cabin, Bridadier Pumphrey-Hatton found that once again his electric fan was not turning properly. He muttered furiously to himself, then, with hands that shook badly, he took hold of the fan, jerked it hard so that the flex parted, and cast it down on the deck by his bunk. The moment he had done so, he regretted it. There would now have to be explanations to his steward and he was damned if he was going to explain himself to anyone of that sort. He slumped into the hard, upright chair that was all he had to sit on, and put his head in his hands. The business at the Cape was much on his mind, having seen that petty officer. He should be taking action over that, should be making a formal report to the Commodore, or Captain Maconochie if the man turned out to be one of the DEMS party. Ratings should never be allowed to get away with crimes . . . but if he made a report far too much would come out. In the meantime the man was no doubt sniggering away behind his back, knowing that he had him by the short hairs.

'Cypher, sir.'

Kemp turned, lowering his binoculars. The report came from the leading telegraphist on his staff. The leading telegraphist said, 'From Flag Officer West Africa, sir. Freetown, sir.'

'Thank you, Phillips.' Kemp took the cypher, passed it to Finnegan who had come across from the starboard wing of the bridge. 'Over to you, Finnegan. Break it down straight away – the prefix is urgent.'

'Okay, sir –'

'Not okay, Finnegan. Dammit, you've been long enough with the British Navy!'

'Sorry, sir.' Finnegan grinned. 'For okay, substitute aye, aye, sir –'

'Oh, just get on with it,' Kemp said irritably. Americans were irrepressible, though God alone knew how Britain would have survived without them. Kemp, pacing the bridge in deep thought, pondered on the likely purport of the signal, which was in fact addressed to the senior officer of the escort, CS23, the prefix indicating that it was repeated to the Convoy Commodore. In naval signalling procedure, this meant that any action required would be taken by the naval escort commander; the Commodore was merely being informed. But to Kemp, the urgent prefix meant that it was a report of enemy activity somewhere in the vicinity of the convoy's north-westerly course.

He had a word with Maconochie. 'There may be an alteration signalled from the escort. He may move us farther west.'

Maconochie nodded. 'That's about the only option. Are you expecting word of the raider?'

'It could be, yes. Or submarine packs farther south than was

72

thought likely back at the Cape. Let's take a preliminary look at the chart, Captain.'

They went into the chart room just abaft the bridge. The chart of the area was laid out on the polished mahogany table, a pair of dividers and parallel rulers laid upon it, and the ship's position at the last fix noted by a small pencilled cross inside a circle. Kemp scanned the area; the South Atlantic was vast, but both Kemp and Maconochie knew from long experience that in war there was little enough of the needles-in-haystacks element. A determined enemy had ways of making contact however immense the area of operations. Long-distance radar, intelligence passed from the German Admiralty in Berlin, intelligence passed by a great network of operators – spies was the better word – throughout the world; and intelligent guesswork and anticipation by the enemy captains to fill any gaps. Kemp, as he waited for Finnegan to report back to the bridge with the broken-down, plain language version of the signal, found his mind going back to the days of peace when the great liners kept to their regular schedules without any need to deviate, any need to cover their tracks, any need to wonder what intelligence agents were reporting behind their backs. All the way – in his case – from the locks at Tilbury, all the way to Sydney via the ports of call – Gibraltar, Port Said, the Suez Canal, Aden, Colombo, the long stretch across the Indian Ocean to Gage Roads at Fremantle, round stormy Cape Leeuwin and across the Great Australian Bight and the Southern Ocean to Adelaide and Melbourne, through the Bass Strait and round Cape Howe for Sydney Heads and the berth at Woolloomooloo or Circular Quay or under the harbour bridge to Pyrmont. All that way like clockwork, the whole voyage worked out minutely months before so that the Line could publish its passenger schedules well in advance. Long before you dropped the mud-pilot at the Downs, you knew the precise moment you would, four weeks ahead, pass into Sydney's Port Jackson harbour.

They had been fabulous days in many ways, and Kemp doubted if after the war was over they would ever be quite the same again even if there were any liners left. For years now, the pilots and crews of, for instance, Imperial Airways had been predicting the end of the ocean liner. Speed was to be the watchword of the future, the great god of speed and never mind the comfort and atmosphere of a liner. Attentive stewards, excellent and varied meals in the saloons – mess dress at night for the ship's officers, dinner jackets and evening dresses obligatory for first-class passengers, a bugle blown warningly for dinner and all that went with all of that. So many ports with excursions laid on for those that wanted them . . . and the glamour of the sea itself, the low-slung stars in the night skies of the Mediterranean, myriads of them like glowing lanterns, a sight never seen beneath British skies; the moon sending its beams over the violet waters of the Indian Ocean, and then the contrast, after Cape Leeuwin, of the grey, heaving seas – often majestically spectacular – of the Bight.

Kemp had never grown tired of the sea's variety, of the satisfaction of bringing his command into each port with miles of safe steaming behind him. He thought now, in the *Aurelian Star's* chart room, of many years ago and his very first sight of the great Rock of Gibraltar, the bastion that now guarded the Mediterranean from entry by Adolf Hitler's warships. Turning between Algeciras on the Spanish coast and Europa Point at the southern extremity of Gibraltar he had seen with awe the immensity of the Rock, green and brown looming into the sky above the white buildings of the town behind the breakwater guarding the naval port, looming huge and impressive as though to block out the very sky. The winking lights of the port and town as the scented dusk descended, the sound of bugles and Royal Marine bands as the battleships and cruisers of the Mediterranean Fleet struck their colours for Sunset. Or in the daytime the evocative sounds of the fifes and drums, or when a Scots regiment was in garrison the pipes and drums, from the parade grounds of South Barracks, or Buena Vista Barracks, or Red Sands fringed with palms, pepper trees and eucalyptus. They were the sounds to stir the heart, the sounds of Empire and a long history of valour and sacrifice.

But such thoughts were best put behind him for the duration of the war. Kemp straightened and returned to the bridge, leaving Maconochie to confer with his second officer, one of whose responsibilities was the navigation of the ship.

There was a blustery wind coming up from southerly, taking the ship on her port quarter and causing her to roll somewhat heavily as her course took her across the wind and a rising sea.

The men on the troop-decks would be having an uncomfortable time. Kemp hunched himself into a corner of the starboard bridge-wing and used his binoculars to scan the horizons all around. Still peaceful, and the convoy was maintaining its formation well, no need for chasing by signal from the Commodore or from the escort, which was often the case when unwieldy cargo vessels fell behind their station or surged ahead of it to lie dangerously close astern of their next ahead. Convoys could become a nightmare: each ship was an individual with her own characteristics of handling, very different from, say, a cruiser squadron each member of which had similar power and helm-answering habits, even though it was true enough that no two ships of the same class handled precisely the same. Merchant ships came in all shapes and sizes, the average convoy containing some deep-laden, some in ballast, some big, some smaller – tankers, dry-cargo ships, transports, some liable, simply because of the unending sea-time that the merchantmen were putting in now, to sudden and unpredictable engine-room breakdowns, usually at impossibly awkward moments.

No picnic; and it looked as if it would go on for ever, world without end.

'Mind if I join you, eh?'

Pumphrey-Hatton looked up from some notes he was making. He was sitting in the B deck lounge with a gin-and-bitters, and jotting down items for the rough draft of a list of complaints that he proposed submitting to the War Office when he reached London. Unless you made notes, you forgot. You forgot even important things, oddly enough, though certainly you couldn't forget the damn flies. Fortunately the flies had by now been left behind, but there was still the electric fan and the attitudes of various people, and various lapses in efficiency . . .

Looking up, he saw the Australian colonel. Harrison, now OC Troops.

'I'm rather busy. Surely you can see.'

Harrison wasn't in the least disconcerted. Australians, Pumphrey-Hatton thought, probably never were; they were much too brash. Harrison grinned and said, 'Sorry about that. Just wanted to ask your advice, that's all. But if you're writing your bloody memoirs, or your love letters, why, I reckon –'

'You are damned impertinent, Colonel Harrison.' Pumphrey-Hatton half rose from his chair. 'I would expect –'

'Sorry again, mate. Just take it easy, eh? Reckon I didn't intend any disrespect, nothing like that. Only you're experienced in things I'm still green at and I don't mind admitting it.'

Pumphrey-Hatton made a sound like, 'Hah.'

'Me first go at OC Troops. I need to get the oil.'

'Oil?'

'The dinkum oil. You know? The . . . gen. The bloody know-how. Don't want to go and make a duck's arse of it.' Colonel Harrison turned to a hovering lounge steward. 'A refill for the brig,' he said, 'and then there's me, eh? Got a Foster's, have you? Swan beer, eh?'

'I think we can manage, sir.'

'Good on you, bloke. Let's have 'em.' Harrison sat down, pulling up a chair close to Pumphrey-Hatton, who looked furiously angry and was in fact quite speechless at the fellow's effrontery. And the appalling modes of expression, of terminology – duck's arse, bloody love letters, dinkum oil, the brig, mate, and take it easy! It was utterly grotesque that such a person should be found wearing the crown and two stars of a full colonel even in a colonial army. Trembling as if with a high fever, Brigadier Pumphrey-Hatton hoisted himself to his feet, spilling his gin-and-bitters as he did so. He stuttered incoherently with sheer fury, unable at that moment to express himself. Muttering, he moved away, out of the lounge, while Harrison mopped the spilled gin off his uniform trousers. Pumphrey-Hatton heard the shout just as he reached the door.

'Clumsy bloody bastard! Bloody pommie snob.'

That, too, would go in the report for the War Office. The man was obviously totally unfit for the position of OC Troops. A moment later, Pumphrey-Hatton faced another upset. Moving with his jerky walk aft along B deck, he came face to face with Petty Officer Biggar, proceeding for'ard from aft. Stiff-faced, Biggar saluted and moved past.

'You, there. That petty officer.'

Biggar turned. 'Yes, sir?'

'Name.'

Biggar licked at his lips. 'Biggar, sir. PO, Royal Fleet Reserve.'

'That will be noted. You may carry on.'

Biggar remained where he was. 'Sir, I –'

'That will do. You may carry on. Is it necessary for me to repeat my orders?'

'No, sir. I'm sorry, sir, but I –'

Pumphrey-Hatton lifted a foot and stamped it on the deck. 'Hold your tongue and do as you're told!'

Petty Officer Biggar's face flushed. As a petty officer, the equivalent of a sergeant, he was not accustomed to be bawled out publicly – bawled *at* publicly – nor to be told to hold his tongue. He had a bloody good mind, he told himself, to make an issue of it and report to that Mr Finnegan for transmission to the Commodore. As Pumphrey-Hatton marched away aft, Petty Officer Biggar continued angrily but thoughtfully for'ard. It needed reflection – that it did. There were many angles to it, and he had to consider Leading Seaman Purkiss.

Sub-Lieutenant Finnegan reported back to the bridge with the plain language version of the Admiralty signal.

Kemp and Maconochie read it together. The estimated position of the *Stuttgart* was indicated: Kemp and Captain Maconochie, with Finnegan, went back into the chart room and laid off this position on the chart.

Maconochie said, 'Her superior speed's taken her a long way nor'-nor'-west.'

'But she's on a closing course. More or less. A little north in fact.'

'So as to cross our track?' Finnegan suggested.

Kemp nodded. 'Looks like it, sub.' He glanced again at the signal. 'No information as to whether or not it's suspected that the *Stuttgart* knows our position currently. But we can certainly assume she knows we've left the Cape – and what our present course will be.'

'So what do we do?' Maconochie asked.

'Mastery inactivity for the moment, Captain,' Kemp said with a grin. 'We wait for orders from cs23. If his signal officer's as quick off the mark as young Finnegan, we'll know any moment now.' He added, 'And to forestall what I think you're going to ask, Captain, we announce nothing to the troops and other passengers about the raider. Not yet, that is.'

EIGHT

The reaction came quickly from the senior officer of the escort, in a signal made by lamp addressed to the Convoy Commodore and repeated to all ships. *Convoy will alter ten degrees to port on the executive and will steer 320 degrees until further orders. Ships to maintain second degree of readiness continuously from now.*

Kemp nodded at Yeoman Lambert. 'Thank you, Yeoman. Acknowledge.'

'Aye, aye, sir.' As Lambert went back to his signalling projector, the alter-course signal was hoisted from cs23's flag deck to her fore upper yard, being held at the dip. When all ships had made their acknowledgements, the signal was hoisted close-up to indicate the executive order for the turn to port. Kemp nodded at Maconochie, who passed the orders to his Officer of the Watch. The ships came round, and for a while the convoy was in some disarray as each vessel altered its speed either up or down to resume the original formation. Across the bows of the Commodore's ship came a big freighter – dangerously close in Kemp's view. Maconochie reacted fast.

Moving at the double to the wheelhouse he shouted the orders. *'Emergency full astern, wheel hard-a-starboard!'*

Kemp held his breath, hands gripping the bridge guardrail until the knuckles showed white. If two big ships should hit . . . but Maconochie's instant reaction had saved them from that, if only just. As the stern pull of the engines took effect and the *Aurelian Star*'s head began to pay off, the freighter slid past to safety with what looked like only inches to spare.

When the next order reached the engine-room by the

78

telegraphs, the order to resume normal speed, the Chief Engineer let out a long breath and wiped a fistful of cotton-waste across his forehead. A moment later the Captain came on the sound-powered telephone from the bridge. 'A near miss, Chief. All's well now, thanks to your engines.'

Chief Engineer French grinned into the mouthpiece. 'We try to give satisfaction, sir.'

'I know you do, Chief. What's more – you succeed.'

French clipped the telephone back on its holder. He was lucky in the Old Man. With some masters, it was a case of running warfare. Many deck officers regarded what they called the black gang as beneath their notice, nasty foulers of God's good fresh air with the smoke that they sometimes made, especially when more oil fuel was fed to the furnaces when the call came for extra speed. Not Maconochie: he recognized that in the last resort it was the engines that got the ship home. As from the starting platform John French surveyed his noisy, pulsating kingdom, watched his engine-room ratings moving about the great spinning shafts with their long-necked oil-cans, he thought of home and of homecomings. Thirty-three years at sea, Chief of the *Aurelian Star* since the outbreak of war, he'd had more homecomings than he could remember. As many departures too, leaving home life and his family behind while he set out on the world's oceans, living a bachelor existence for months on end until his next leave, seldom more than a fortnight before the next departure.

A hell of a life for a married man.

Daft, really.

Absolutely potty. That was his wife's term for it. Monica hated those departures that came like the clockwork that regulated the Line's sailings. But John French had seen no alternative. When he'd married he'd been senior third engineer, which meant many years in the Line's service, too many years to throw away in an attempt to find a job ashore where he'd have had to start all over again, at the bottom. He'd left the bottom behind a long while ago, signing as a junior engineer, little more in truth than an oiler or greaser, with a tramp shipping company running out of Cardiff. There was a world of difference between a junior engineer in a tramp line, and senior third in a liner. So he'd stayed at sea, because of that and because, despite the absences, he liked

79

the sea and its variety, its challenges when something went wrong and he was able to put it right.

But Monica, now. When the war had come she had been devastated. She lived a nightmare all the time he was away, always fearing the worst, always dreading the telegram that would come without warning from the Line or maybe from the Admiralty. She'd had a cousin who'd been an engine-room artificer in the RN. He'd been aboard an aircraft-carrier that had been hit by a torpedo and had then taken an eight-inch projy from a German cruiser, slap in her starboard engine-room. The cousin had in fact survived, but only by a miracle, and survival hadn't been worth while. He was now confined to one of those contraptions made of basket-work, bed-length, on four wheels, paralysed from the neck down, couldn't do anything for himself and a pittance of a pension from the Admiralty. John French had been at sea when the cousin had been brought to the Royal Naval Hospital, Haslar; and he hadn't been there to stop Monica hearing all about it when she visited her cousin.

She knew the horrors now. The scalding, escaping steam, the raging fires as the oil fuel spilled, the oil fuel that covered men's bodies, spewed into their mouths and nostrils, the twisting of the network of steel ladders that led from the deck of the engine-room to the air-lock at the top, the only way out from hell. She heard about the burns suffered by the cousin before he had managed to reach the air-lock, only to lose his grip and fall from the upper platform, back down into hell, to break his back on one of the shafts before being hauled to safety by a heroic stoker petty officer.

Since then, she'd been a bag of nerves. Not surprising, of course; but that had reacted badly on their two children. They had become tearaways as a result of too much protective mothering that had never let them out on their own. Taken and fetched to and from school, inquisitions every time they were asked home by a school friend, every movement to be accounted for in detail, that sort of thing. They'd rebelled and that wasn't surprising either. With dad away at sea, there was no one to appeal to. The family home was in Southampton, and both sets of grandparents were in Sunderland, right up north and too far to visit in wartime, travel being not all that easy.

And now they'd both fallen foul of the police. A long and rather hysterical letter had reached John French in Simonstown: Alan and Billy had been caught shoplifting in Woolworth's. The case was pending.

A worry he could do without as the troop convoy steamed for home.

Sighing, John French wiped his hands on a fresh bunch of cotton-waste and told his senior second engineer that he would be in his cabin if wanted. He had, he said, reports to write. What he really wanted to do was to read Monica's letter again.

'We seem to have altered course,' Colonel Holmes remarked to his wife. He had noted that the sun was in a slightly different position relative to the ship.

'It's probably after that scare,' Mildred said. 'When that ship –'

'No, no, it's not that. The whole convoy's altered.'

She looked up at him. 'Why's that?'

'I don't know, my dear.'

'There's obviously a reason.'

'Yes. But I don't know what it is.'

'You could always ask the Captain, couldn't you?'

'I suppose I –' Holmes broke off, feeling irritated by his wife's non-perception of their status as passengers, nosey ones they would be considered. 'One can't bother busy people with questions they probably don't want asked. We'll be told in due course.'

'Yes, but when?'

'When the Captain considers it necessary. Not before.' The old soldier believed the convoy's alteration to have more than a little to do with the lurking enemy, but he wasn't going to say so to Mildred, there being no point in worrying her too soon. Hearing footsteps on the deck behind him, he turned his head then turned it back again. In a low voice he said, 'There's that damn cad Hench. And that appalling woman.'

'Which –'

'Don't look now,' Holmes hissed urgently, but there was no avoiding an encounter when Hench stopped by the rail and leaned over alongside Mrs Holmes.

'Something going on, Colonel,' he said, speaking across Holmes's wife. She moved back a little; the smell of stale whisky was strong.

'Yes,' Holmes said briefly. 'We seem to have altered course, but not by very much.'

'I didn't mean that, though I expect it's connected. I meant all the signalling. Flags, and flashing lights. See it, did you?'

'Yes, I did –'

'Something's up,' Hench said. He sounded nervous. 'As I was saying to Gloria –'

'Gloria?'

'Miss Northway. You've not met?'

'Not formally,' Holmes said.

'I'll rectify that.' Gregory Hench made the introductions. 'Gloria Northway . . . Colonel and Mrs Holmes.'

'How d'you do?' Holmes said perfunctorily.

'Fine, thanks, and you?'

There was really no answer to that, and neither of the old couple gave one. Miss Northway went on to say, anyway, she was pleased to meet them. She hoped to God they would all reach the UK safely but now she was worried because Gregory had said the flags and lamps and so on meant that the escorting warships had had word about an enemy attack. Everybody knew there were hundreds and hundreds of U-boats at sea and what did Colonel Holmes think?

'For a start, Miss Northway, I doubt the hundreds and hundreds. In the South Atlantic, anyway. Hitler has other fish to fry. Not just our convoy.'

'Well, maybe, but it's terribly scary. I'll bet your wife's having kittens right now.'

Holmes glared. 'I beg your pardon?'

Hench said, 'She meant Mrs Holmes must be worried, Colonel –'

'I gathered that, thank you, Hench. Naturally my wife is anxious. But we are a military family, which perhaps Miss Northway doesn't understand. Doesn't understand the significance of the fact of coming from a military family.' He looked Gloria Northway directly in the eye. 'Stiff upper lip, you know. All that sort of thing. Face up to the enemy. It's a British characteristic. I have every confidence that we shall reach the Clyde in safety.' He turned away and stared out to sea.

'Weird old couple,' Miss Northway murmured as Hench, taking her arm, drew her away from the Holmeses. 'Stiff upper lip, my *God*! What next?'

'Colonial forces,' Hench said. 'Bred in the bone. Used to kicking the natives around. They're sort of . . . cocooned from reality. Flies in amber.'

'Stiff upper lips don't stop torpedoes,' Miss Northway said. 'Or do they, in the minds of ossified old fuddy-duddies like those two?' She added, 'The old girl never opened her mouth. I reckon she has to wait for orders . . .'

The word had gone from the Chief Officer via the bosun to all hands of the troopship's deck department that extra vigilance would be required from all watchkeepers, the lookouts especially; Chief Engineer French was warned that within the next few hours there might be a need for sudden alterations of speed and that extra revolutions might be wanted at short notice. He in turn passed orders for the remaining boiler to be flashed up in readiness. Finnegan spoke to the two petty officers: the guns'-crews would now be working in two watches, which meant that extra guns would be manned at all times.

'Meaning the Nazis are around, sir?'

Finnegan nodded. 'We've had a report that the *Stuttgart* is not all that far off. That's for the information of the guns'-crews only. The Commodore doesn't want the civilian passengers alarmed, get it?'

Ramm said, 'Got it, sir. We keep mum. What about them other Jerries? The POWs?'

'That's another reason the Commodore doesn't want any loose talk.' Finnegan added, 'If it seems inevitable that we're going to fall in with the raider, an announcement will be broadcast from the bridge, okay?'

Finnegan moved away, making back for the bridge. He found the Commodore deep in conference with OC Troops and Colonel Carter of the rifles. The subject under discussion was the one that had been raised by Petty Officer Ramm: the POW contingent, under guard below the troop decks. Kemp was concerned as to the possibilities of a breakout if and when the German raider was encountered. Harrison didn't believe there would be any trouble. The Germans were, he said – and Carter agreed – under strong enough guard to ensure that they would remain firmly below in action.

'Unless they have to be brought up,' Kemp pointed out.

'You mean if we have to abandon?'

'Yes. In fact I'd prefer not to leave them below once action starts. There's always a chance it'll be too late as things develop. I don't like to take that chance. So what I'm suggesting is this: the Germans should be brought up under escort and held in, let's say, the B deck lounge, which of course will have been cleared of all passengers, the civilians. They'll be in the firing line as it were, but so will we all be, and it's better than being confined below if anything happens suddenly. Which is a fair enough prognosis, I think.'

'Reckon you c'd be right at that, Commodore,' Harrison said. 'But I'd call it not all that *likely*. Because I don't reckon that Nazi raider's going to attack a convoy with a strong cruiser escort. Isn't it a fact that the surface raiders concentrate on the less well-escorted convoys?'

'Yes and no,' Kemp said. 'Don't forget, we're a prize target. Troop convoys always are. There would be a lot of prestige and a lot of celebration in Berlin after a successful attack on a troop convoy.' He paused. 'Normally, I agree, I'd not expect an attack by a single surface raider even on a troop convoy.'

'So what's different this time?' the Australian colonel asked.

Kemp spoke quietly. 'The Admiralty signal indicated something extra. There's known to be two U-boat packs operating off Freetown – off the Rokel River. They don't know the strength of these packs, but going on general intelligence knowledge of the German submarine command, they could be of six boats each. Now, if those packs are operating – and this isn't known for sure either – if they're operating with the *Stuttgart*, that puts a very different complexion on what might be going to happen.'

Harrison nodded thoughtfully. 'Reckon you'll get any further intelligence, do you, Commodore?'

Kemp shrugged. 'That's in the lap of the gods. If I do, you can be sure I'll pass it on, Colonel. In the meantime – and I'm confident I don't really need to say this – not a word to anyone outside your own trooping staff. I don't want to cause any worry to the civilians over something that may never happen.'

Again Harrison nodded. 'What do you reckon yourself?' he asked.

Kemp said, 'I think we're going to have a fight on our hands. And just as soon as I'm able to make a positive appreciation, everyone will be fully informed.'

*

84

'Off your arse, *Featherstone*haugh.'

Featherstonehaugh jumped to his feet as though stung by a wasp; he had been sitting on a fairlead alongside his gun, daydreaming. 'Sorry, PO.'

'You'll be sorrier,' Petty Officer Ramm said, and went on to diagnose what the OD had been doing. 'Dreaming oh my darling love of thee. Dreaming of thee. Right?'

'Just thinking, PO.'

'Oh, yes! You're not supposed to bloody think. Got it? Here to do a job, you are. In case you don't know, there's a war on.'

'I know that, PO.'

'Eh? Now and again I doubts it.' Ramm ticked over. 'Sorry, lad. Your dad. Don't take all I say too much to 'eart. That said, remember the ship needs all the eyes it's got. To spot bloody Adolf that is. Got a fag, have you?'

Featherstonehaugh produced a packet of Players. Ramm took one and flicked a lighter for himself and Featherstonehaugh. He blew a cloud of smoke and wondered how the armed services would ever manage if the brass hadn't insisted on a constant supply of cigarettes being made available to the troops and seamen. Life itself depended on a quick draw, it took the tension out of things and all sensible officers turned a blind eye to smoking on watch other than at night when the flick of a lighter or even the glow of a cigarette-end could be seen through a periscope. The fag in his mouth, Ramm went on with his job, which currently was to inspect the guns, make sure that all was shipshape and that all moving parts were greased and ready. Not that the *Aurelian Star*'s armament would be any use against the *Stuttgart*: the Nazi cruiser was a big job, around 11,000 tons with a main armament to match – eight 8-inch guns in twin turrets, a secondary armament of six 5.9s plus ack-ack and six torpedo-tubes, all of which she could carry around the oceans at some 27 knots.

But of course they had the escort.

With any luck, the Nazi wouldn't risk it.

The POW contingent had in fact been brought on deck daily for the exercise period laid down by the Geneva Convention for the treatment of their ilk. They were herded from their accommodation by a company of the African riflemen, and another company stood by on the boat deck as extra security, all the natives carrying rifles with bayonets fixed.

On the day of the early-morning receipt of the Admiralty's signal the regimental sergeant-major of the Australian trooping staff watched as the German naval ratings emerged on deck. RSM Treddle was a formidable-looking man, tall, hefty and imposing in his bush hat and khaki-drill shirt and shorts, bunches of hair visible at the open neck of the shirt and the Royal Arms that denoted his rank as a Warrant Officer 1 prominent and shiny on the leather strap that secured it to a thick, hairy wrist.

'Look almost human, eh?' he remarked to Harrison's adjutant.

Captain Mulvaney nodded. 'Some do. Some don't. Scraggy, some of the bastards.'

RSM Treddle went on watching. He observed that the native troops were treating the Germans with caution, very trigger-happy he reckoned, but at the same time seeming almost apologetic in their roles as guards on white men, as though they sensed the anger of the prisoners at being herded by men with black skins. RSM Treddle remarked on this to Captain Mulvaney.

'Reckon they know about Hitler's ideas, do you?'

'What particular ideas?'

'Race. The pure-bred Aryan idea. All others being inferior.'

Mulvaney gave a coarse laugh. 'I doubt it. Reckon they don't have enough bloody English for that, Sar'nt-Major. But I reckon I get what you're driving at: the blacks expect trouble. But I doubt that too. The Jerries won't start anything aboard a ship crammed with troops.'

'Tempers,' RSM Treddle said, 'can erupt, Captain Mulvaney. Sudden incidents deliberately inspired, eh? Look at that bloke over there – see him? The tall bloke at the back end of the deck. By the rail.'

Mulvaney looked. The tall German, by his dress a petty officer, was getting up on the rail and looking forward towards the bridge. As the two Australians watched the German gave a Nazi salute, arm extended, hand palm down. They heard his shout: '*Heil, Hitler!*' A number of other Germans followed suit, and there was a general stir from the prisoners.

Mulvaney met the RSM's eye. 'Not really our patch,' Mulvaney said. 'Not really. But let's get in there just the same, eh?'

'Right with you, Captain,' Treddle said.

They moved aft, RSM Treddle in the lead. As they reached the native escort, the riflemen parted to let them through. They pressed on through the bunched prisoners. The man who had given the Nazi salute watched their approach, smiling, still in his position on the rail.

RSM Treddle halted in front of him. 'You,' he said.

'Yes, Sergeant-Major?'

'So you speak English, eh?'

'Yes.'

'Well, good on yer, then. Pull your ears back and we'll see if you understand Australian too.' RSM Treddle took a deep breath that visibly increased his chest measurement. Staring the German in the eye he said, 'You're aboard a pommie ship and you bloody respect the fact, right? For a start, you'll not mention the name of fucking Hitler, never again. We don't want to bloody hear about that little bastard. And if you give the Nazi salute in my presence again, I'll wrench your fucking arm from its fucking socket with my own fucking hands. Got that, have you?'

As he finished, he moved closer, flexing his muscles. The German flinched away, lost his balance on the guardrail, and fell straight down to the after well deck, a long drop. Breathing hard RSM Treddle said, 'I hope he's bust his fucking neck.'

'For your sake, Sar'nt-Major,' Mulvaney said, 'let's hope he bloody hasn't.'

They each drew their revolvers and began the move back through the prisoners. They made it in safety; but the mood of the Germans was obvious enough.

Major Kennedy, the medical officer of the native regiment, was quickly at the scene. A moment later he was joined by the ship's surgeon, Dr Grant. An examination was made: it didn't take long. Their eyes met over the broken body: there was no need for speech. Death from a broken neck was all too obvious.

It was now a matter for higher authority: in the first instance Colonel Carter commanding the riflemen, the official guard on the POWs. And then OC Troops. And an unwelcome worry for the Commodore. Whoever was ultimately responsible for the safe conduct of the prisoners to the UK, the authorities in London were not going to be happy with any breach of the Geneva rules.

*

There would be an enquiry. In the meantime RSM Treddle went about his duties, supervising others doing theirs. Each day, after the POWs had been taken back to their quarters below, there were parades of the Australian and New Zealand contingent. Parades for the inspection of arms and equipment, parades for physical training, parades for this, that and the other, anything to keep the troops on their toes and as fighting fit as possible. When inactive for too long, men grew soft. It was RSM Treddle's mission in army life to stop them getting soft and he was pretty good at it, inventing all manner of things to keep them on the hop. Also being there in person to make sure the sergeants and corporals kept them at it. It was no use giving orders and then not see them carried out.

This morning Treddle was pre-occupied following upon a preliminary interview with OC Troops. Colonel Harrison had turned the air blue in the privacy of his stateroom and Treddle was still smarting. He'd held nothing back; and he knew he hadn't laid a finger on the man. If the Nazi wanted to move away from him, that was his own choice and his own bloody fault, Treddle had said. Harrison had more or less agreed but had said the matter could obviously not end there. There would be shoals of reports to be written to all sorts of authorities, Harrison said, and RSM Treddle had been a bloody nuisance, while Captain Mulvaney was initially at fault in suggesting a move into the ranks of the prisoners. It was, Harrison said, a bloody fuck-up he could well do without. Treddle would hear more about it shortly.

It was in the middle of one of his parades and around half an hour before Captain's Rounds of the troop decks that RSM Treddle was bidden to the bridge. This order was almost immediately negatived. In the short interval that had elapsed between the two messages, the Commodore had had a report from the senior officer of the escort, made by light and repeated from the leader of the anti-submarine screen: the Asdics had picked up two echoes. U-boats were in the vicinity.

NINE

'Action stations, if you please, Captain.' Kemp found this one of the unwelcome irritations of being the Convoy Commodore; he was not in command of his own ship and it was the Captain's responsibility to handle her and pass the orders. A moment later the action alarm sounded throughout the ship. By Kemp's order passed earlier, the B deck lounge was cleared for the reception of the German prisoners. Gregory Hench was sitting on a bar stool when Steward MacInnes began lowering the metal cage over the bar in protection of his stocks and to indicate that no more drinks would be served until orders came from the Purser.

'Just one more,' Hench said, holding the descending cage up by thrusting his hand through, the hand holding a glass.

'Sorry, sir.'

'Come on, man. Be a sport.'

'Sorry, sir,' MacInnes said again. 'Orders, sir.'

'Whose orders?'

MacInnes stared him in the eye. Hench was already a little tiddly. 'Captain's. You heard the alarm, sir. Ship's at action stations. You'd best get –'

'Bugger that,' Hench said in a harsh tone. He made as if to force the cage up, turned with a start as he felt a hand on his shoulder. He faced Purser Scott, three gold rings on his shoulder-straps. white cloth between. 'Leave the bar, Mr Hench.'

MacInnes completed the lowering of the cage. Hench said in a hectoring voice, 'So they don't teach you manners, Purser, in this Line. I happen to be a fare-paying passenger, not some uniformed bod in a military draft.'

'Everyone aboard is under orders, Mr Hench, you included. Leave the bar immediately or I shall send for the master-at-arms to escort you out.'

Slowly, Hench slid off the stool. His voice slurring a little now, he said, 'Don't think I won't be reporting this to the Line in London. Because I shall.'

He moved away towards the open deck. MacInnes said, 'We get all sorts, sir.'

Scott nodded. Any complaint to the Line's head office would get the reception it deserved. A few minutes later the German prisoners began streaming in under guard of the rifles and bayonets. Going below, Purser Scott saw Gregory Hench going along an alleyway, his own cabin alleyway. With him was Miss Northway. What a time to choose, John Scott thought, if that was what was intended. On the other hand, it could be a pleasant way to die.

Finnegan had asked if the Commodore intended to scatter the convoy. Kemp's answer was no. The ships were better off keeping within the guns and depth charges of the warship escort. If they should encounter the surface raider, then would come the time to scatter.

The reports were coming in now: all watertight compartments sealed, fire mains ready, fire hoses run out. All the military draft and civilian passengers mustered at their boat stations, Hench and Miss Northway included. Their station happened to be under the orders of one of Scott's assistant pursers and when Scott checked round he saw Hench and Gloria Northway struggling with their cork lifejackets. He grinned to himself: he'd obviously been wrong, maybe they'd just been going below for the lifejackets.

At the guns, the crews were ready for action. Petty Officer Ramm spat on his hands and observed that he hoped they'd spot a Jerry, forced to the surface by the depth charges.

'Sink the bugger by gunfire,' he said with advance satisfaction.

'Probably a false alarm,' Leading Seaman Purkiss said.

'Trust you to spoil the fun, Purkiss. Not that I'd mind all that much, not being keen to get bloody sunk if they get us first like.'

'Which they probably will. If they're there.'

'Defeatist talk, Leading Seaman Purkiss, so can it.'

'Whatever you say, PO.'

Ramm moved to the ship's side and stared out over the water. By this time there had been a good deal of signalling between the destroyers of the A/S screen and the senior officer, and between the senior officer and the Commodore. Already the destroyers had moved ahead at full speed, creating big bow waves and wakes that streamed astern to mingle with the kerfuffle kicked up by the churning screws. The cruisers of the escort were maintaining a close screen on the merchantmen, steaming at convoy speed on the port and starboard beams. As Ramm watched, the great humps of water began spouting into the air as the depth charges from the racks and throwers began exploding at their set depths beneath the sea.

'Contact's real enough,' Ramm said, and moved back to his gun. 'Stand by, you lot, you never know. I reckon –'

He was interrupted by Featherstonehaugh. 'Something moving, PO!'

'Where, lad?'

Featherstonehaugh pointed away on the starboard bow. 'Just astern of the *Vindictive* –'

'God almighty, lad, that's not a something, it's a bloody tin fish!' Before he had finished speaking Petty Officer Ramm had grabbed the sound-powered telephone to the bridge. 'Torpedo bearing green one five,' he reported. He had just replaced the hand-set on its hook when there was a heavy explosion from the starboard beam, a merchant vessel that had strayed outwards from her station and was, or had been, moving on steadily astern of the *Vindictive*.

Now she was virtually gone.

'It's the ammo ship,' Ramm said in a shaking voice. 'Poor sods. There won't be any survivors from that lot.' A moment later the debris from the massive explosion began dropping in the water all around, some of it landing on the decks of the *Aurelian Star*. Blazing pieces of woodwork, white-hot metal fragments, parts of dismembered bodies blown through the air with tremendous force. Ramm ordered the gun's-crew to get below the shelter deck. Leading Seaman Purkiss, Ramm noted, was there already.

On the bridge, Captain Maconochie had lost no time when the report had come in from Petty Officer Ramm. He had ordered thirty degrees of starboard wheel, following the proper procedure so as to present as small a target for the oncoming torpedo as was possible: bows-on. Steadying his course when the torpedo's track was still a little on the starboard bow, he waited, watching narrowly as the menace sped towards his ship. Kemp stood by the rail in the starboard wing, found himself clutching the rail like a vice. Then came the shattering explosion as the big ammunition ship blew sky-high and the debris began to fall. Kemp's and Maconochie's whole attention remained on the approaching torpedo, evidently one of two – maybe more – that had been fired. Kemp blew out a long breath of relief when the tin fish passed down the troopship's starboard side. He found his whole body soaked with sweat.

'Well done, Captain,' he called. 'Very nicely timed.'

Maconochie was also wiping away sweat from face and neck. 'We had better luck than those poor beggars,' he said, waving an arm to starboard. There was drifting debris, and flames shooting up from what was left of the ammunition ship. Some ten thousand tons of munitions had gone up, lost to the Allied war effort, but it was the fate of the men, the human factor, that was on all minds. Husbands, sons, fathers. So many families ashore whose lives would be in ruins.

'Bugger this war,' Kemp said. His voice was filled with anger. Then he stiffened. Incredulously he said, 'Did you hear that, Maconochie? *Cheering*! From the B deck lounge.' His face was unbelieving. 'Finnegan, restrain me from going below with a revolver!'

Finnegan said, 'I feel the same way as you do, sir. So I guess we restrain each other, okay?'

There was another thought in both their minds: at any moment they might go the same way as the ammunition carrier. If that happened, there wouldn't be much help given to the Germans.

The Commodore's ship under port wheel moved back to her course and carried on. The detonations of the depth charges continued, one after the other. Kemp remarked that it seemed likely there was a whole pack of U-boats attacking.

'Jumping the gun, sir?'

'What gun, Finnegan?'

'Not waiting for the *Stuttgart*. One of the theories was that the *Stuttgart* would attack together with the U-boats.'

'Correct, Finnegan. But they're always full of theories, shore-side.'

'Guess that's right, sir, Commodore. But this one was yours. The conference with OC Troops –'

'All right, Finnegan, I've never pretended to be an oracle. But just bear in mind that there may be, probably will be, other packs around.' Kemp swung his binoculars, scanning the assembly of ships ploughing doggedly along beneath a clear blue sky with enough breeze to ruffle the sea's surface and make the spotting of periscopes difficult. He said, 'Whoever picked up that first torpedo was a live wire. We failed to spot it from the bridge.'

'Guess we did, sir.'

'When this is over, find out who it was.'

'I'll sure do that thing, sir.'

'Just aye, aye, sir is quite enough, Finnegan. Three words instead of . . . how many was it?'

Finnegan counted on his fingers. 'Six, sir.'

Kemp grunted. 'Verbal diarrhoea, Finnegan.'

'Why, I guess you could be right at that, sir, Commodore –'

'Shut up, Finnegan.'

The convoy steamed on. Inside the next two minutes there was the whine of the sound-powered telephone from the lookout at the foremasthead. Finnegan answered and reported to the Commodore. 'U-boat surfacing, red four five, sir!'

Kemp swung round. A long black bow was starting to emerge, to be followed by the conning tower breaking through the water. 'Damaged by the depth charges,' Kemp said. 'But she can still be dangerous. Warn the guns'-crews, Finnegan.'

Finnegan ran to pass the word fore and aft. The U-boat was on a clear bearing from the *Aurelian Star's* decks and was within gun range of both the three-inch. Two destroyers were moving towards her but were still some way off. As Finnegan reported the Commodore's message passed, a stream of machine-gun fire arced towards the *Aurelian Star*, and there was a puff of smoke from a gun mounted just for'ard of the conning tower.

Kemp said, 'Open fire, Finnegan.'

'Open fire!' Ramm roared out. The gun went into immediate action, as did the for'ard gun under Petty Officer Biggar. There were sharp cracks and a shudder ran through the ship; down below cork insulation was brought down in showers from the deck-heads immediately beneath the gun-mountings. A rapid fire was kept up. The first shots from both guns went over the target. The next shells fell short.

'Straddled,' Ramm shouted in high excitement. 'We'll get the bastard with the next.'

They didn't; there was another shortfall. But after that they had the range more closely and a shell took the upward-canted bow of the U-boat. There was an explosion, and the bow slewed to port. Two more that were near misses; and then there was a further explosion, this time slap on the conning tower. There was a burst of smoke and flame. Ramm had the impression that the conning tower and its adjacent gun had ceased to exist. On the heels of the strike another shell took the base of what had been the conning tower, ripping away the plating of the pressure hull.

The order came from the bridge to cease firing. As the guns fell silent there was a further tongue of flame from the gap left by the shattered conning tower and this was followed by a burst of pressurized steam just before the U-boat settled in the water and then, her broken bow lifting to point upwards like a finger, slid back beneath the sea.

'Let the bloody Nazis cheer that one,' Ramm said with a great deal of satisfaction. 'One up to us, eh? Well done, lads.'

Purkiss said sourly, 'Bet you a day's pay PO Biggar'll claim it as his.'

'Put a sock in it, Leading Seaman Purkiss. Biggar can claim what he bloody likes. I see *our* shell 'it.'

'Ha, ha,' Purkiss said, but he said it *sotto voce*, very much so.

The guns'-crews were kept closed up; the action was not over yet. Ahead of the convoy another U-boat was brought to the surface and despatched by gunfire from the *Vindictive*. One of the cruiser escorts, HMS *Okehampton*, was taken by a torpedo on her starboard bow. Her Captain reported damage and casualties but indicated that he could proceed at slow speed while makeshift repairs were carried out. The cruiser was given orders from the senior officer to detach from the convoy once the U-boat attack was over and to enter Freetown. In the meantime a destroyer would be detached from the A/S screen to stand by her to the Rokel River. On urgent representations being made by the Commodore, the senior officer indicated that he would break wireless silence, the position of the convoy being already known to the Germans now, and request back-up from Rear-Admiral West Africa in Freetown.

When the asdics of the escort reported lost contact Kemp said, 'Either there were just the two, or the rest took fright. We'll keep the ship at first degree of readiness for a while longer, if you please, Captain. The Germans don't usually get cold feet. There could be a boat lying deep with engines stopped.'

Kemp went round the upper decks, having a word here and there with the troops and the civilian passengers, doing his best to allay fears. The blowing up of the ammunition ship had had its effect on morale in a number of cases. Old Mrs Holmes was shaking and pale, and her husband was doing his best with her. There was a good deal of stiff-upper-lip about Colonel Holmes. War was war and had to be faced up to. And he was certain they were all in good hands. The Navy would never let them down.

Kemp agreed heartily with this, though he doubted if the crew of the ammunition carrier would take quite the same view.

Moving aft, Kemp spoke to Ramm and his gun's-crew.

'Very well done, all of you,' he said. 'We don't know if it was this gun or Petty Officer Biggar's that got the U-boat, but –'

'This one, sir, for certain sure. I see the projy 'it like, sir.'

Kemp concealed a grin. 'I've no doubt Petty Officer Biggar saw his do the same thing. Let's say it's honours even. The result's the same and you all contributed. Which of you was it who saw the torpedo track?'

Ramm said, 'It were Ordinary Seaman Featherstonehaugh, sir.'

Kemp reached out and shook the OD's hand. 'Splendid,' he said. 'I'm proud of you. It's not too much to say you may have saved the ship.' He would have liked to add that he would be putting in a word to the right quarter, but he refrained. The young man was in for a commission and there must be no suggestion of anything that might be construed by his messmates as favouritism, or any apparent leaning over backwards to commend an ordinary seaman destined for the wardroom. Kemp was well enough aware of jealousies along the lower deck and indeed he could understand them. Often he had reflected that it must be galling for, say, any PO such as Ramm or Biggar, men of long sea experience in the fleet, fine seamen all of them, to see a youngster virtually only just out of school vault over their heads to the wavy gold stripe of a sub-lieutenant RNVR. He had occasionally overheard the comments: 'Bin in the Andrew 'alf a dog-watch and just look at 'im.' That he, Kemp, could understand the feelings was not to disparage the RNVR – far from it. The green sub-lieutenants learned from experience and became as reliable as anyone else, and quickly too. Moving on again, Kemp grinned inwardly at another thought: the green sub-lieutenants not infrequently equipped themselves with two officers' cap badges and kept them alternately in glasses of salt water to make them look as though they had faced years of bad weather . . . and reflected also that he had done the same thing himself years before when he had first joined the Mediterranean-Australia Lines as a junior fourth officer.

Going back for'ard Kemp met Brigadier Pumphrey-Hatton at the foot of the starboard bridge ladder. Pumphrey-Hatton said, 'A word in your ear, Kemp.'

Kemp waited. The brigadier went on, 'That RSM. You'll know what I'm getting at. Of course, the feller's the responsibility of his own OC Troops, I know that. But as Commodore you may come into the picture. Or Maconochie might, as Master. I just wanted to have my say. I'm not inexperienced when it comes to men, you know.'

'Of course not, I appreciate that. I'll be glad to have your views, Brigadier.'

Pumphrey-Hatton looked at him sharply. 'Do you mean that, Kemp?'

'I do.'

'Very well then, here they are. Try to get that Australian colonel to play it down. Regimental Sergeant-Majors are the back-bone of any army. Damn fine fellows, with a damn hard job to do. Follow?'

Kemp nodded. 'Yes, I do. The Navy's never had quite the equivalent. We have warrant officers, but they don't entirely equate. Nevertheless –'

'Nevertheless, what the fellow did was wrong. Dead wrong – know that. If you look at it that way – as death caused to a prisoner-of-war. Personally, I do not. The RSM never laid a hand on the man. And the RSM's reaction was perfectly understand

96

able, don't you see, a natural response to the giving of the Nazi salute. Don't tell me you'd not have done the same.'

Kemp said, 'That's possible.' He laughed. 'Oh, I'd have had the initial urge, I expect, but I'd like to think I'd have exercised more self-control.'

'Ah, but you're not an Australian. I've fought with the Australians – the Australian Division at Tobruk, under Morshead. Their discipline wasn't that of the British infantrymen, but, by God, they achieved results.' Pumphrey-Hatton paused. 'I'm just asking you to put in a word if you get the chance. Not that it's any business of mine. Except that I'm a soldier too.'

He turned and walked stiffly away. Kemp remained for a moment at the foot of the ladder, staring after him. Pumphrey-Hatton hadn't seemed the sort to intercede on behalf of anyone not of commissioned rank . . . or had he? Kemp recalled the events of his previous convoy, the outward convoy from the Clyde to Trincomalee when Pumphrey-Hatton had been OC Troops. The Regimental Sergeant-Major of the trooping staff, Mr Pollock late of the Border Regiment, had fallen victim to the cholera that had raged throughout the Commodore's ship and other vessels of the convoy and escort. Kemp had heard via the galley wireless that Pumphrey-Hatton, visiting his RSM's sickbed, had found two of the ship's crew, one a man who had been a sailmaker in the days of the old square-riggers, already measuring the dying man for the canvas shroud in which he would shortly be slid overboard. Pumphrey-Hatton had been outraged and had booted the pair of them out of the cabin in no uncertain fashion. And when Mr Pollock had died, it had been Pumphrey-Hatton who had insisted that the regimental depot at Carlisle Castle be informed and urged to do all they could for Pollock's family.

Pumphrey-Hatton was a long-serving officer. He'd soldiered through the peace between the wars. He had, no doubt, a fierce pride in the British Army and in its regimental system where all the members of the regiment formed a family, very much along feudal lines – the squire, the parson, and, below the salt as it were, the villagers. But a source of great strength and pride and, by and large, fairly benevolently conducted. Kemp guessed that what got under Pumphrey-Hatton's skin were the civilians turned soldiers, men who hadn't at all the same outlook, and in many cases were villagers transported to the Hall.

Kemp climbed the ladder to the bridge. There were other matters that he had learned about, sketchily, from the galley wireless: trouble ashore at the Cape, involving Pumphrey-Hatton and two of the *Aurelian Star*'s naval party. Pumphrey-Hatton had never said anything about that and although Kemp was very curious to know he didn't intend to get involved with any galley wireless or tales told out of school.

Reaching the bridge, he saw signalling from the senior officer's flag deck, an Aldis lamp trained on the *Aurelian Star*'s bridge.

Yeoman Lambert reported, 'Commodore from cs23, sir. Enemy drawn off, am resuming cruising stations.'

'Thank you, Yeoman. Captain, I suggest we follow suit.'

Captain Maconochie passed the word by Tannoy throughout the ship. On the starting platform below in the engine-room, Chief Engineer French eased his cap on his head, wiped his forehead with the inevitable ball of cotton-waste, and gave silent thanks to God that he'd survived another U-boat attack and would live to face the next, and the next, and the next . . . there was never any enduring let-up in this war, only when you were on leave at home in UK and even then the buggers got at you with their perishing *Luftwaffe*, night after night of air raids that got a weary man and his wife out of conjugal bliss and sent them down into the shelters to listen to the crump of bombs, the ringing of bells from the fire appliances as the incendiaries rained down along with the high explosive, police whistles, the crying of young children, and then, when you emerged, the terrible sights of the smashed and gutted buildings, all the rubble and the bodies, and more cries, this time the pathetic cries of people buried beneath the fallen masonry, the results of Adolf Hitler's night's work.

In the B deck lounge, Steward MacInnes re-opened his bar.

'So what about it, Greg?' Gloria Northway asked.

'Yes . . .'

'What d'you mean, yes?'

'I mean yes.' Hench shifted uncomfortably.

'But.'

'But?' Hench stared, rather glassy-eyed.

'Yes, but. There's always a "but" in your voice. You don't really want to, do you?' She looked at him accusingly. 'Well, go on, do you?'

'Of course I want to, Gloria. Only . . . well, the way I see it . . . to take advantage of – of the sea surroundings and all that, if you follow, the build-up of tropical seas, and the moon . . .' He waved a hand around, vaguely. 'Phoney romance,' he said. 'You'd come to regret it. When we reach UK, you see.'

'Bollocks.'

Hench was a little startled. 'What?'

'You heard. You're just being stupid, Greg, really stupid. Taking advantage my bottom, I've been taken advantage of too many times to bother and I don't mind admitting it. I *like* being taken advantage of. I thrive on it, as a matter of fact. So don't worry about me, I'll not follow you crying my eyes out all the way from the Clyde to wherever it is you're going. Worthing, isn't it, your dear old mum?'

'Yes.'

'Well, then.' She sighed impatiently. 'Look, Gregory Hench, if you don't come up to scratch there's others aboard who will, get me?'

'Oh.'

'I'm not that bad looking.'

'No, no –'

'So watch it.'

He didn't answer right away. When he spoke it was to say, 'How about a drink, Gloria?'

'Oh, for God's sake. Past master at evading the issue you are. Get me a long gin-and-grapefruit if you must, but lay off the booze yourself.'

As ever on a long convoy, there was a necessity for the escort and merchant ships to take on fuel. Bunkers taken at the Cape would lower them as far as the Azores, but the Azores under the Portuguese flag were strictly neutral. Fuel would therefore be taken at Ascension Island, where two deep-laden naval tankers of the Royal Fleet Auxiliaries would be in readiness to discharge into the tanks of the convoy as they lay off the port.

Ascension Island was now two days ahead, and the re-fuelling would take place before *Vindictive* and the damaged *Okehampton*

99

with her single destroyer escort detached for the Rokel River and Freetown.

Maconochie discussed the operation with Kemp and his own Chief Officer and Chief Engineer.

'Not as easy as going alongside for fuel,' he said. 'We'll need all the fenders we can muster when the RFA ship comes alongside. They're big ships to handle, very deep draught of course. Do you see any problems from your point of view, Chief?'

French shrugged. 'So long as it's oil fuel, the intake's all the same to me. The rigging of gantries to take the pipelines, that's the deck, but my lads'll be there to see to the connecting up. No, don't expect any problems.'

Maconochie nodded, and turned to Kemp. 'The A/s screen'll lie off to act as guardships, I understand?'

Kemp said, 'That's the ticket. They'll fuel singly after the rest of us have bunkered.' He added, 'It'll be a long job, of course, and the sooner it's done and we're away again the better I'll like it. We're going to be pretty well exposed, never mind the destroyers. And pretty damn immobile, not to say helpless – sitting ducks in fact.'

Kemp had fought the issue back at the Cape, wishing to enter Freetown for bunkers, but the brass had brushed his protest aside. U-boats, they had said – and this was true – tended to lurk outside the Rokel River. But plenty of convoys, Kemp had pointed out, had put into Freetown before now. The response to that, also true, had been that Kemp's was a big convoy to fuel from barges, which was all Freetown had to offer by way of facilities. That would take time, and because of the urgency of the troops' arrival in UK speed was of the essence. No notice was taken of Kemp's strong representations against what would amount to fuelling at sea, a technique that was bound to be developed in the future but which was currently in its infancy. Kemp knew that the Masters of the RFA were experienced in manoeuvring their heavy ships in confined waters, such as when going alongside the battleships and cruisers and aircraft-carriers of the Mediterranean Fleet, in the Grand Harbour of Malta. It was not easy to handle a 12,000-tonner in such constriction. But in carrying out the operation outside a port, with the ships to be fuelled lying, perhaps, in an ocean swell and heaving about on open waters . . . Kemp's imagination told him very many things adverse things, that could happen. Using that imagination, as he had done on and off ever since leaving Simonstown, he saw a time when the Admiralty might devise a system of extended gantries that would carry the fuel-oil pipelines across, say, a cable's-length of sea, joining the tanker and the receiving ship at a fairly safe distance apart so that the risk of sides being scraped and damaged would be minimal. It might even be possible, given that safe distance, to carry out bunkering whilst under way. And Kemp wished fervently that he was not faced with the prospect, as he was, of heaving-to outside Ascension Island.

Sighing, he said, 'I suppose they know what they're doing. I refer to those who control our destinies. One of the senior bods at Simonstown gave me the impression of having just disembarked from the Ark. I'd not be surprised if the last time he took bunkers it was coal. And I'm not to be quoted on that, gentlemen.'

With unease in the Commodore's heart, the troop convoy steamed on.

TEN

There had been discussion about the body of the German POW: following the medical examination, the corpse had been placed in the ship's cold store. The discussion, between OC Troops, the two doctors, Captain Maconochie and Kemp, had been to decide what to do with the body finally. Carry it on for disembarkation at the Tail o' the Bank, or have a sea committal?

Maconochie was all for a sea committal. Seamen, he said and Kemp was in full agreement, didn't like corpses aboard ships. Not even in peacetime. They were largely a superstitious bunch and corpses brought bad luck. OC Troops disagreed.

'Evidence,' he said. 'Can't destroy evidence, right? I'm answerable to Canberra, maybe to your War Office. Because of the Geneva Convention, treatment of POWs. How do I come out of it, reporting a dead Nazi already disposed of?'

'I don't believe it's any skin off your nose, Colonel,' Kemp said. 'The facts are known, no one's attempted a cover-up, and the doctors have established the cause of death. The Geneva Convention's all very well, but we're here, at sea, with a body that could cause a lot of bad feeling among the seamen. Further, I think that from the POW viewpoint it would be better disposed of. I'm sure the incident is rankling along the German accommodation and it could fester. We certainly don't want that. What we want is a clean ending. Agree, Captain?'

Maconochie nodded. 'Very much so. I see absolutely no point in keeping that body aboard and I think the disposal should be done soonest possible.' He added, 'The weather's fair for burial now. As we make our northing later on, it very likely won't be.'

'That's your view,' Colonel Harrison said.

'It's the sensible one,' Kemp said sharply. 'With all due respect, Colonel, you don't know seamen. Maconochie and I do. We know their feelings, what makes them tick. And I'm for a sea committal.'

'You mean you've decided, have you?'

Kemp nodded. 'Yes.'

'It wouldn't occur to you to ask the senior officer of the escort, eh?'

Kemp said formally. 'Colonel Harrison, I am the Convoy Commodore. I make my own decisions within the convoy itself and I do not propose to bother the senior officer of the escort with matters that don't concern him. In short, I'm not passing any bucks.'

'So you're going right ahead?'

'With the permission of the ship's Master, yes.'

'Righto, then, so long as you take the can. Meantime there's the question that I reckon all of you people want to know the answer to. And that is, what's to be done about my RSM, Treddle. Now, a little bird's been telling me something, something that got overheard. That bloke Pumphrey-Hatton. He's been opening his kisser over matters that are nothing to bloody well do with him. Now, I don't take anything from that dried-up old has-been nor do I take anything from seamen who know bugger all about the bloody army. So I want you to know that what is done about my RSM is my affair and no one else's, right? I make that decision for myself and I reckon I've made it. Pumphrey-Hatton needn't have bothered his arse, because I'd made it already.' He took a deep breath. '*Nothing*'s going to be done. We have a dead Nazi, and good on RSM Treddle's what I say.' He got to his feet, staring around truculently. 'That having been said, I'll say g'day to you all, gentlemen.'

He left the cabin. Kemp caught Maconochie's eye and gave a grimace. 'Honours even, I suppose. Got his own back . . . because we didn't go along with him from the word go.' He went on, 'They do have 'em in Australia! But so, I admit, have we.'

The departure of Colonel Harrison broke up the conference. Kemp, going back to the bridge with Maconochie, reflected that it was perhaps not so very surprising that Pumphrey-Hatton didn't appreciate the 'temporary gentlemen'. Kemp had learned that in civilian life, Harrison had been a car salesman. Probably a very successful one, if his pushing manner had originated in peacetime. And as for the RSM, Kemp was only too relieved not to have to interfere.

'A funeral, my dear. You remember – that German prisoner. It's necessary, you know.'

'It's upsetting,' Mildred Holmes said. 'Oh, I know he was a Nazi and may have helped to sink some of our ships, and that he was most dreadfully foolish to do what he did –'

'Well, then.'

She stuck to her point. 'No, Stephen, it's not a case of well, then. One can't help thinking of his family. Parents, possibly a wife and children . . . they'll all probably have heard he had been taken prisoner and will be thinking that at least he's safe from being killed. And now this. I call it very sad, even if you don't. I suppose soldiers see things differently.'

'You know they do, Mildred. Good God, you were a soldier's wife for long enough. A soldier's daughter too, as I said to that Northway woman, or was it Hench?'

'It wasn't either. You didn't say that.'

Holmes clicked his tongue. 'I think I said you came of a military family. Same thing.'

'It isn't the same thing,' she said in a rather high voice.

Her husband rustled irritably. 'Oh, don't be so . . .' He didn't go on; there had been a sound like a sob. 'Steady on, old girl, there's really no need to get so upset. Damn it, we're *fighting* the blasted Nazis, aren't we?'

'It's not just this – this funeral. It's everything about this voyage. The awful feeling that we might be sunk at any moment . . . and what's in store for us if we arrive –'

'*When* we arrive, Mildred. I've said so often, we're in good hands and we're going to be all right.' He added in what was intended to be a reassuring tone, 'You'll feel quite differently as soon as we pick up Ailsa Craig at the entrance to the Firth. Bring back happy memories. Remember the Turnberry Hotel? Golf, with good old Bill, first-rate course – Open standard, of course, same league as St Andrews, or Carnoustie, or Royal St George's, or Lytham St Annes –'

'Or Troon,' she put in, tongue in cheek.

104

'Oh, yes, Troon, of course. Remember the golfing week at Troon, back in '22 wasn't it – foursome with good old Bill and Arse-end Portlock and a feller called Bashy Longford? I often wonder what happened to Bashy Longford. Sherwood Foresters . . . said he'd once got a hole in one on the Old Course at St Andrews but I never quite believed him, he wasn't quite up to it.' Mildred would be all right now, he'd jollied her out of her mood, talking about old times. Nothing like old times and reminiscences. Mildred used to say that she might just as well have stayed at home when he went on his golfing weeks since she never set eyes on him all day, but of course that was a lot of tommy-rot. And she used to say she couldn't stand any more of good old Bill's laugh. It was certainly on the loud side, but still, it was jolly. He droned on now and never noticed that Mildred was crying.

The sea committal took place early next day, in the Morning Watch, the 0400 to 0800. Sharp on six bells Captain Maconochie went down from the bridge, with Kemp, to the after end of F Deck where Bosun Barnes had rigged a plank where a section of the guardrail had been temporarily removed. The body of the Nazi, sewn into canvas with fire-bars at the feet to ensure that the corpse would sink, was laid beneath a German naval ensign provided by Yeoman Lambert. Present were OC Troops, *Kapitan-Leutnant* Stoph, and an armed guard of the King's East African Rifles under the command of Sergeant Tapapa. Maconochie briefly read the words of the committal service, referring to 'our brother here departed', for there was no nationality in death, the plank was tilted and, with the engines briefly stopped so that the revolving blades of the screws should not suck the body down to be shredded into fragments, the canvas-shrouded corpse took the South Atlantic with a splash as *Kapitan-Leutnant* Stoph gave the Nazi salute.

After a decent interval, a matter of little more than a minute, Maconochie nodded to the bosun, who went to the sound-powered telephone and rang the bridge.

He spoke to the Officer of the Watch. 'From the Captain, sir. Engines to full ahead.'

The ship's halt had been very brief; she still had way on her and shortly after the telegraphs had rung on the bridge and had been repeated in the engine-room, the *Aurelian Star* was moving up to resume her station in the convoy. On the starting platform Chief Engineer French had just two thoughts: one more of the sods gone, and thank the Lord they were under engine power again. No one liked hanging about in enemy-infested waters.

Far to the north, a Morris Eight was parked in a road some distance xkaway from Chief Steward Chatfield's Southampton house, as was always the case when Cocky Bulstrode was making a night of it. A different street each time. No flies on Cocky Bulstrode, who as suspected by Chatfield was indeed a salesman, but not of furniture. Cocky Bulstrode was in the business of selling life insurance, being an agent of one of those insurance companies that sold door-to-door and made a weekly collection of premiums, mostly in small change. To accommodate this small change he carried a leather bag not unlike a schoolboy's satchel. At the time the German was being slid over the side of the *Aurelian Star*, and some twenty-four hours before the convoy was to heave-to outside Ascension Island, thus putting Cocky's hostess' husband at some risk of his life, this satchel hung by its strap from a hook behind the door of Chatfield's bedroom. In the double bed Cocky Bulstrode and Roxanne Chatfield lay, currently asleep but more or less still entwined. Both snored but were unable to hear each other. When one awoke, there would be a complaint.

It was Roxanne who woke first, and she awoke with a start that brought Cocky awake at almost the same instant so there were in fact no complaints.

Roxanne said, 'Oh, my God.'

'What's up, eh?'

'Nothing, not now. It's all gone. Nightmare,' she added in explanation.

Cocky always tried not to look at her first thing in the morning: her hair stuck up like the fuzz on a coconut and her breath smelled of too many fags, and she had no make-up on to hide the pallor. But he enquired about the nightmare nevertheless.

'My hubby,' she said.

'What about him?' He gave a light laugh. 'Not a nightmare that he'd turned up suddenly, was it?'

She shook her fuzz. 'No, not that. That he wouldn't ever turn up – not *ever*. He got sunk.'

'In the nightmare, love?'

'Yes. In that ship. The Germans had got him. Didn't have a chance. Down in the meat store, the refrigeration chamber he was, when them so-and-sos fired a torpedo at him. The door banged to, in the explosion like, and the door got a bit buckled. He was shut in, couldn't get out. He froze to death.' Roxanne shuddered. 'Ooh, it was that awful, it was reelly.'

'Sorry to hear it, love, very sorry. Only a dream, though. Best forget all about it now, eh?'

'I can't, it's still on my mind. It was really vivid, I see him go in, hear the door bang shut, hear the torpedo. I see him struggling like in vain, see his face, all cold and all twisted up with fear.'

'What you might call a frozen expression?' Cocky suggested, grinning.

She turned on him, fag breath and all, beat at him with small clenched fists. 'Don't bloody make a joke of it, it was reel. To me it was.' She added, turning away from him, 'Like an omen. Just like an omen.'

'No,' he said reasonably. 'Couldn't have been. Dreams are like that, daft mostly. Like I said – just forget all about it, love.' He cuddled her, for there was more he wanted before once again taking up his satchel from its hook and pounding what he called his book. But she stiffened in his groping grasp and said no, she didn't want it, not after that awful dream. She just couldn't. Not just yet, anyway.

'Tonight, love?'

'We'll see.'

'I'll come round anyway, usual time, all right?'

'All right,' she said in a voice that to Cocky Bulstrode seemed somewhat small, frightened even. 'I'm ever so worried,' she said. 'It's made me think, like. Anything can happen at sea, any time. Here one moment, gone the next. I never really thought about it like that, never. Not till now. I'd be all on my own, see. Lost. On me tod with a war on. Wouldn't I?'

Cocky was by nature cautious. 'Well . . .'

'That's what would happen. There'd be just you. I . . . I'd like to feel you were, well, around.'

'Yes,' he said. 'I understand, love. You can rely on me if the worst happened.' The worst, in Cocky's view, would be if hubby survived and came home when he wasn't expected, which could be very awkward indeed even though Cocky had a ready tongue. It would depend, of course, on what he and Roxanne happened to be doing at the time, just having a friendly drink, or – well. If it happened to be the latter then it wouldn't be funny. Cocky Bulstrode had seen photographs of Chief Steward Chatfield: he was big, a real heavyweight. Never, so far as Cocky knew, been a boxer but he certainly did have the build. It wasn't only Cocky's physical form that would be at risk, either: his insurance company had a reputation to keep up and wouldn't go much on agents who dallied with the clientele. Conversely, if hubby never did turn up, if he did get sunk like in the nightmare just ended, then Cocky might get stuck for life, which was definitely not his idea. Cocky was accustomed to roam with his book: Fareham, Cosham and down into Pompey where there were any number of lonely wives with husbands at sea, just like Southampton itself. No, he really wouldn't want a wife.

It might be prudent to stand off just a little. He might not turn up after all, come the evening. He could always plead pressure of work.

Having washed and dressed and had a good breakfast of Roxanne's ration of one egg and a rasher of bacon, plus toast and marmalade and *ersatz* coffee, he took up his moneybag, kissed Roxanne, circumspectly, in the hall and departed on his rounds, picking up the Morris Eight in the anonymous street a safe distance away.

In a different part of the United Kingdom worry of another sort entirely was taking place. In Kemp's home in Meopham not far from the port of Tilbury, peacetime home of the Mediterranean-Australia Lines' ships, Mary Kemp, lonely in the house now that John's old grandmother had died, waited for the telephone to ring and tried to control the shake in her hands. Early that morning there had been very bad news. A telegram had come from the Admiralty: one of their two naval sons, Harry, had been reported missing after his ship, a light cruiser on convoy escort duty in the North Atlantic, had been engaged and sunk by German aircraft as the convoy had come into the danger zone of the Western Approaches. 'MISSING BELIEVED DROWNED' the telegram had said. Waiting in despair until nine thirty when the Mediterranean-Australia Lines London offices would be open, she had spoken directly to the Chairman. Sir Edward had been very concerned: he would do his best to obtain more information from the Admiralty, where he had a number of contacts. He would telephone the moment he had any news.

So Mary waited. Waiting, she thought about the terrible state granny would have been in had she been still alive. Harry had always been her favourite, and he had been fond of her as well, her bedroom – she'd been bed-bound for years – always what he called his first port of call after arriving home from school or, more recently, on leave. Thinking of granny now, she found herself wishing her back alive so that they could be some comfort to each other. Loneliness was a scourge, the more so in wartime. As John Kemp, half the world away, had suspected, Mary missed even the peremptory thump of granny's walking-stick on the bedroom floor, the thump that announced some want or other to be instantly met. Granny had been a nuisance and a tremendous burden to a wartime housewife coping with rations and shortages of all manner of things and queues and bombs and a lack of help in the house, but she had been basically strongly supportive, kind and generous. She had also been someone to turn to when a couple of years earlier in the war another telegram had come, similar in content to this morning's, also announcing Harry missing presumed drowned. That had ended happily: Harry's destroyer in the Mediterranean had also been sunk whilst escorting a convoy, but Harry had turned up safe that time on the island of Pantellaria off the North African coast to become a POW and later had managed to escape.

The telephone didn't ring. Mary occupied her mind by writing out a list of chores for that morning: butcher to pay, rations to be bought there and at the grocer's, try for some fish, a pair of shoes to be soled and heeled, clean the kitchen range which used to be cleaned by Mary's version of Mrs Mopp but which wasn't any longer because Mrs Mopp had gone into munitions and was now rather hoity-toity . . . get her hair done because it was a mess, and see the local builder about some loose slates after a bomb had landed in a nearby field.

At a little after noon the telephone rang. There was, Sir Edward said, no further news.

'I don't need to tell you how very sorry I am . . . but you must not lose hope. I'm told by the Admiralty that there's every hope

Harry will have been picked up by another ship. It's just that up to the time I spoke to them, there hadn't been any lists available – naturally they have to wait for the full reports to come in.'

Sir Edward refrained from saying that, Harry's convoy having come under attack, there would be little likelihood of a sea rescue. But Mary said, in a dead-sounding voice, 'They never do stop to pick up survivors. I know that.'

'There are always exceptions, Mrs Kemp. It has to depend on the particular circumstances. I repeat, you must not lose hope. I really mean that. There *is* hope. You must believe me.'

She asked, 'Will my husband have been told? I'd really sooner he wasn't. Not while he's at sea, with so much to worry about.'

'I agree,' Sir Edward said. 'In fact he's not been told yet . . . the Admiralty has a human face, Mrs Kemp. They've considered the impact on a Convoy Commodore.' He cleared his throat. 'I did tell them . . . said I'd ask you –'

'Tell them not to tell him, Sir Edward, please. I – I'll do that myself when he gets home. That is, if I have to.'

Putting down the receiver, Mary Kemp went straight to the kitchen to start on the range. It was always better to keep busy. And of course there was always hope. Granny would have said the same.

After the sea committal the Nazi POWs were in a belligerent mood. They were accorded their exercise period as usual, under a heavier guard today, Sergeant Tapapa having reported that the prisoners were truculent whilst being escorted up from their accommodation.

'Sah!' he had reported to his Adjutant. 'They have called me unpleasant names and have only slowly and with menace obeyed my orders.'

'What sort of menace, Sar'nt Tapapa?'

'A waving of fists, sah.'

'But you were not struck?'

'Not struck, sah. Threat only, and noises. Loud voices, and some laughter at me, and things I did not understand.'

The Adjutant nodded. 'Very well, Sar'nt, I'll ask the RSM to add to the guard detail and I'll report what you've said to the Colonel.'

'Sah!'

110

'Carry on in the meantime. And watch it – watch carefully that the Germans don't try to get their hands on the men's rifles for instance.'

'Sah!' Sergeant Tapapa saluted and executed an about-turn that was as smart as any guardsman could produce. But he marched away an anxious man: the Germans had looked and sounded very hostile indeed, as though they were blaming him personally for the death of their compatriot. And, although he had not understood the words – and the riflemen under his command had understood even less, for none of them spoke even English – Sergeant Tapapa had known very well that the Germans had been jeering at the black skins.

In the office used for the trooping staff, the Adjutant of the rifles spoke to his RSM, asking for the guard to be strengthened.

'Very good, sir. Permanently, or just for this morning, Captain Harding?'

'Let's see how things develop, Mr Nunn.'

'As you say, sir.'

Harding asked, 'What's your view, Mr Nunn?'

'As to the Nazis, sir?' RSM Nunn was a very British RSM, seconded from the King's Royal Rifle Corps, the 60th Rifles. His back ramrod straight, he tweaked at the end of a waxed moustache and gave his opinion of the Nazis. 'Scum, Captain Harding, real scum. That cheering when the ammunition-ship blew up. It takes scum to do that, Captain Harding, sir.'

'Yes. But I think we shouldn't regard them all as scum, Sarn't-Major. Dangerous . . . prisoners, you know –'

'I'm aware of that, Captain Harding, very aware of that. The Nazis will be treated properly, scum or not scum, and we shall incur no complaints from those what regard the Geneva Convention as the equivalent of the 'Oly Bible or the blocks of stone brought down from the mountain by Moses. But I'll be keeping my ear to the ground, Captain Harding, sir, and my eyes front, back, and sideways.'

Harding concealed a grin. 'Meaning you expect trouble, Mr Nunn?'

'Trouble, sir, yes, that is what I expect. And now if you'll pardon me, sir, I'll see about giving extra backing to Sar'nt Tapapa 'oo's a good little bloke if black.'

The RSM marched away, left-right-left just as though on parade

111

at the Winchester depot of the 60th Rifles. Harding hoped he wouldn't be putting a big sergeant-majorly foot in it. RSM Nunn had lost a brother serving under General Auchinleck in the western desert – a Desert Rat, blasted by the guns of Rommel's Afrika Corps.

ELEVEN

The convoy had slowed some while earlier in order to accommodate the damaged cruiser, the *Okehampton* having been forced to reduce speed so as not to bring too much pressure of water on the torn fo'c'sle plating. She had reported some casualties; and the damage had included the rendering unfit for use of the two seamen's messdecks situated in the fore part of the ship. Kemp watched her progress from the bridge of the *Aurelian Star*.

'We've lost more time than we allowed for,' he remarked to Finnegan. 'We'll be around fourteen hours adrift on our ETA at Ascension.'

'Meaning we arrive after nightfall, sir?'

'Yes, exactly. I don't fancy hanging around with engines stopped in the dark hours. Nor do I fancy taking oil fuel at night. We'd need yardarm groups – too much damn light to home the U-boats onto us. That's not on.'

'Not on at all, I guess . . .'

Kemp grinned. 'Have another guess, sub?'

Finnegan lifted his cap and scratched reflectively at his forehead. 'Guess as to what, sir?'

'What we ought to do about it.'

'Simple,' Finnegan said. 'Make a signal to the senior officer, suggest the convoy and escort steam in circles till daylight, then start fuelling. How's that, sir?'

'Two minds with but a single thought, sub, to coin a phrase, apart from the circles. No reason why we shouldn't steam up and down in our present formation. I don't know why the senior officer hasn't thought of it for himself.'

'It takes a citizen of the good old USA, sir –'

'Come off it, Finnegan, it's my idea too. I'm going to stick my neck out.' Kemp turned. 'Yeoman?'

Yeoman Lambert came across. 'Yessir?'

'Make, from Commodore to cs23, in view of delay in forthcoming ETA suggest convoy and escort maintain formation under way after arrival and throughout dark hours.'

'Aye, aye, sir.' Lambert had been writing the message down on his signal pad. Moving away, he began making the senior officer's call sign on his Aldis lamp. There was a speedy acknowledgement from the cruiser. Kemp awaited for the reply. It came within a couple of minutes. Lambert approached the Commodore and read from his signal pad.

'Commodore from cs23 sir. Your 1436. Do not propose to accept delay involved. Ships will take fuel on arrival and leave soonest possible. Time of origin 1440, sir.'

'Thank you, yeoman.' Kemp blew out a long breath. 'Well, it's his decision . . . his responsibility too. He's taking a damn big risk in –' He broke off as the senior officer's signal lamp began winking again towards the *Aurelian Star*. Lambert made the acknowledgement, took down the signal, and once again read it off to Kemp.

'Commodore from cs23, sir. My 1440. Yardarm groups will not repeat not be used. Fuelling will take place with the least possible light.'

Kemp exploded. He said, 'Of all the world's constipated minds . . . the RN sometimes take the prize.' He added, 'Yeoman, just forget you heard that remark, all right?'

Lambert grinned. 'Cloth ears, sir, never heard a thing.'

Kemp nodded. 'And you, Finnegan.'

'Sure, sir, Commodore. In the United States Navy –'

'Save it, Finnegan, I'm not in the mood to appreciate the wonders of America.'

Some ten minutes later the flagship's masthead light went into action, making a general signal to all ships, repeating what had already been made to the Commodore. Kemp had the feeling that at least he had galvanized the senior officer of the escort into a decision, even though in Kemp's view that decision was quite the wrong one. Unless cs23 was in possession of information as to the disposition of enemy forces that had not been made known to anyone else.

*

114

'There's been a lot of signalling going on again,' Gloria Northway said, sitting at the bar. 'What's it all mean, Greg?'

Hench shrugged. 'How would I know?'

'You're a man. Or supposed to be. Men know about these things, I always thought. Like they're supposed to know about cars and railway timetables and choosing from menus.'

'What's the connection with naval signalling?' Hench asked acidly.

'Oh, I don't know. Forget it.' After a pause she went on, 'It's just that I'm scared, I suppose. In case you don't know, dearest Gregory, I'm a bloody bag of nerves. You wouldn't notice, I suppose.'

'I hadn't thought –'

'No, you wouldn't, would you? Men don't, do they?'

'I don't know.' Hench, somewhat out of his depth, took refuge in ordering more drinks from MacInnes. The usual in each case. The two passengers served, MacInnes turned away and began polishing glasses, keeping within earshot while he did so. He knew what Miss Northway was leading up to if Hench didn't. Perhaps Hench did, he couldn't be that insensitive, but preferred not to let on for reasons as aforethought by MacInnes himself. Miss Northway's next utterance left no room for doubt, in MacInnes' ears anyway.

'You know what the doctors recommend for women with nerves, don't you, Greg?'

'Well . . .'

'Right first time. Bloody brilliant! Look, we've been into this before. You know we have. It's about time you did something about it.'

Hench dithered, took a gulp at his whisky. He didn't feel in the least ready for a romp in the hay. Once again he temporized. He muttered into his glass, 'I don't know what you really want, Gloria, I always –'

'You know bloody well,' she said venomously, then raised her voice. '*You know bloody well I want to be, in your stupid phrase, taken advantage of.*'

Hench noted that the Holmeses had entered the lounge whilst Gloria's voice had been at its highest. He also saw them both turn and leave again. As they did so, Captain Mulvaney of the Australian Army came across, grinning. He put a hand on Miss

115

Northway's bare shoulder. As she turned to him in sudden surprise he said, 'Where I come from, that's to say along by the Murrumbidgee, a man doesn't need to be asked twice. Get me, bloke?' he added to Hench. 'Best make up your mind, hadn't you?'

Hench got to his feet, putting a hand on the bar to steady himself. 'The lady's no concern of yours,' he said thickly. 'I suggest you take your paw off her pronto.'

'You do, eh? And what if I don't? What happens then, bloke?'

Hench gathered himself, looked belligerent. 'I'll deal with you.'

'You and who else, eh?'

'I – well . . .' Hench looked around the lounge as though seeking assistance. He said, 'I'll hit you. Then there'll be a scene. For the adjutant of the trooping staff to be seen fighting . . . it'll be a matter for the ship's Captain as well as your own oc Troops.'

Mulvaney's voice was contemptuous. 'Just like a bloody pom, run to mummy.' He removed his hand from Gloria Northway's shoulder; she had made no move to remove it herself. 'Be seeing you, lady,' he said. Giving Hench a two-finger gesture, he turned away, grinning at the ex-planter's discomfiture. Hench finished his drink and demanded another. He had a bad shake in his fingers, MacInnes noticed, as he pushed the refill across the bar.

'Handled like a man,' Miss Northway said, her eyes glittering. 'I don't think.' She turned away and left the lounge. Her very walk told Gregory Hench that there was no invitation to him to follow her. In a way it was a relief; in another way it was not. In any case there was always the bottle. He downed the refill fast and asked for another. As he was drinking it he became aware of someone standing by his side. Brigadier Pumphrey-Hatton.

'Hench, isn't it?'

Hench nodded. 'Correct.'

'I heard some of that, Hench. Australians – a very primitive lot, very rough diamonds. Damn good in a fight. I expect you realized that. That man was a damn sight bigger than you, h'm?'

Hench stared wordlessly. What the devil was it to do with Pumphrey-Hatton of all people?

'Don't brood, Hench. That woman's not worth it, you must realize that. Don't overdo the drink, Hench.'

'I –'

'It's risky. On account of the flies.' Pumphrey-Hatton seized Hench's arm. 'Tell me frankly: have you noticed any flies since Simonstown? Fly-blows in the glasses?'

'No, I –'

'No more have I, thank God! But you never know. Just a friendly warning, Hench. Heed it for your own good.'

'Well, thanks –' Hench broke off; Pumphrey-Hatton was on the move again with his jerky walk. Hench shrugged, met the eye of the bar steward. MacInnes winked but said nothing. Hench reflected that it took all sorts; and he'd heard odd stories about the brigadier.

In the chart room in rear of the bridge, Kemp listened at 1600 to the BBC's Overseas news broadcast. There had been air raids over London during the night, the usual thing, and although there had been some damage in Clapham and adjacent districts a number, unspecified, of German aircraft had been shot down. There had been heavy fighting in the western desert, the 8th Army and the German Afrika Corps exchanging artillery fire and the armoured columns engaging. A convoy entering the Western Approaches had been attacked by enemy aircraft but this attack had been fought off, though not without some loss, a number of ships having sustained damage.

After the news there was a food programme. The role of the humble potato was being changed once again. Kemp remembered his wife saying that when there was a shortage of potatoes there were Government-sponsored propaganda broadcasts urging those who wished to preserve their figures not to eat potatoes; when there was a glut, then the eating of potatoes was advanced as an excellent and nourishing food with no weight-inducing qualities.

So much for propaganda.

And so much for the news broadcasts, which Kemp had largely ceased believing. Always so many enemy aircraft shot down, always the damage to British cities and ships and men played down. It was no doubt necessary in order to keep up morale. Or was it? The British public had already shown that it could take it. They'd taken Dunkirk, they'd taken the Battle of Britain. Right at the start of the war they'd taken the sinking of the liner *Athenia*, laden with women and children bound for the safety of the

United States, they'd taken the sinking of the battleship *Royal Oak* right inside the supposed safety of the boom at Scapa Flow; they'd taken the blowing-up of the mighty battle-cruiser *Hood*, largest warship in the world. And much else beside.

Nevertheless, the attack on that convoy in the Western Approaches nagged at Kemp. 'A number of ships had sustained damage.' What ships – merchantmen or naval escort? And how much damage? How many casualties?

Back on the bridge with Maconochie, Kemp forced the news broadcast out of his mind. The tones of Alvar Liddell, or Gordon MacLeod, or Bruce Belfrage, or Frank Philips or whoever it had been, faded. Kemp wasn't the only man in the world with sons at sea, sons at risk of their lives twenty-four hours a day, seven days a week. There would be very many fathers and mothers reading unpleasant things into that broadcast and all the other broadcasts that had gone on throughout the terrible years of war.

During the afternoon of the following day Kemp spoke on the Tannoy to all the passengers and crew, a brief and informative announcement to still rumour and speculation as issued by what was known at sea as the galley wireless.

'This is the Commodore speaking, with the approval of your Captain.' He paused, clearing his throat. 'At a little after dark tonight the convoy will heave-to off Ascension Island. Whilst stopped all ships will take oil fuel replenishments from two fleet tankers, naval tankers – RFA *Brambleleaf* and RFA *Oligarch*. This operation will naturally be conducted as speedily as possible but at this moment I'm not able to say precisely how long it will take since this has to depend on a number of factors, among them the weather, which at present happens to be fair.' Kemp didn't go into the other factors, which included any enemy presence and the difficulties of oiling at sea in darkness, which could lead to collisions. Nor did he add that on the previous day a wireless transmission from the Admiralty's Operations Room had indicated that the battleship *Duke of York* was adrift on her original time of departure from the Clyde owing to a union dispute over the handling aboard of an item of engine-room machinery by the ship's company, a job that should by rights belong to the Amalagamated Engineering Union or whatever. The battleship's rendezvous would thus be delayed – which fact Kemp now believed had swayed the senior officer's decision not to hold up the convoy overnight but to get the ships as far north as possible, as soon as possible, so as to bring them under the 14-inch batteries of the *Duke of York* before there was an encounter with the *Stuttgart*. He went on, 'I shall not disguise the fact that there is some danger in lying hove-to, but the exigencies of the convoy make this inevitable. Because of this possible danger, I intend to send the whole ship to boat stations for the period of refuelling. I know this will be uncomfortable to say the least, but the first concern of us all is the safety of all aboard. That is all. Except to assure you that you are in very capable hands under Captain Maconochie.'

He clicked off the Tannoy, saying a silent prayer that the lifeboats wouldn't have to be filled and lowered.

Instructions had already been issued by Maconochie and were now being put into effect throughout the ship. Chief Officer Dartnell, with the bosun, went round all lifeboats, inspecting their equipment – boats' bags, Verey lights, spare rudders, compasses, emergency rations – and seeing the falls in good running order, checking the Robinson's Disengaging Gear in each boat. Before arrival off Ascension all lifeboats would be ready for lowering to the embarkation deck with the gripes slipped and their crews standing by, and the Carley floats would be ready in their slides for instant release. In the engine spaces Chief Engineer French made ready for the taking of fuel into his tanks; Purser Scott and Chief Steward Chatfield made their arrangements, the Purser and his staff placing the ship's cargo manifest, passenger lists, Portage Bill and cash into leather bags ready to be taken to the lifeboats. Chatfield mustered his overtime sheets for the catering department and made them ready for fast removal if the worst should happen. With them he put his silver-framed photograph of Roxanne taken during a stay at Butlin's Holiday Camp in Skegness, Roxanne in a gay and happy mood, the happier because a redcoat had somehow got into the background, a redcoat, young and romantic, at whom she had made eyes frequently during their stay. Stowing away this reminder of times past, Chatfield wondered if that perishing Morris Eight would be round at his house that night. And what if the convoy got knocked off during refuelling? Was there someone already waiting to step into his shoes, take over his home, Roxanne and all?

Like Kemp, Chatfield tried to cast worry from his mind as he carried on with his duties, detailing his second steward to have hands ready to assist the masters-at-arms in ensuring that all cabins and other below-decks spaces were vacated when the bridge passed the order for boat stations, seeing to it that those of his department needed for the running-out of fire hoses were all on the top line. There were a hundred and one things to be seen to and thoughts of Roxanne's carryings-on receded.

TWELVE

As Ascension loomed through the night, the convoy reduced speed to ease its formation into the position where the ships would lie off to await the tankers. As a single flash came from the escort commander's masthead light, Kemp said, 'That's it, Captain. We're in position.'

Maconochie nodded. 'Stop engines,' he ordered.

'Stop engines, sir.' The Officer of the Watch pulled over the handles of the engine-room telegraphs. Bells rang in the wheelhouse, were repeated below in the engine-room. 'Engines repeated stopped, sir.'

'Slow astern both engines, wheel amidships.' Maconochie watched his bearings as the *Aurelian Star*'s headway came off. As the troopship began to ease astern, the final order was passed. 'Stop engines. Engines to remain on stand-by until further orders.'

When this had been passed below, Maconochie had a word with his chief engineer on the voicepipe. 'Here we wait, Chief. I can't say how long – there's no sign of the tankers yet, for one thing. I may need full power at any time and at short notice.'

'We'll be ready, sir. Ready for anything.'

'I know, Chief. And thank you.'

When the Captain had closed the voicepipe cover on the bridge, French left the starting platform and walked around on the greasy, slippery deck plates, checking here and there, watching the long, probing necks of the oil cans as the greasers kept the bearings sweet, felt the close heat that seemed to radiate from the very metal of the great shining steel shafts that, when in

121

motion, turned the screws . . . those shafts were idle now. How long for?

Every moment was a time of danger if the enemy should be anywhere around. But if he was, then surely he would be picked up on the radar or the Asdics. The Commodore had made the point earlier that the A/S screen would still be guarding the convoy. Until their turns came to lie alongside the tankers to take on fuel, the destroyers would be continually under way, circling the convoy and keeping a continuous watch on the Asdics. And if an echo was picked up, the ships would quickly be got under way. Except, of course, those that happened to have the tankers alongside when the lurking enemy was picked up.

'A matter of luck, that's all,' French said to his second engineer who had joined him in his tour of inspection.

'What's that, Chief?'

'Nothing really. Just thinking aloud.' French explained. 'A matter of luck that it's not us who get caught short.' He gave a brief laugh, one with no humour in it. 'We've always been a lucky ship. So far, anyway. We'll just pray it holds – that's all.'

The second engineer nodded but didn't comment. They both knew – or could guess intelligently – what it would be like to be torpedoed whilst alongside a laden tanker, taking oil fuel through pipelines that could hardly fail to fracture or tear away from the couplings. Explosion, fire, a searing blast from the tanker and they would emerge from the engine-room and boiler-rooms, if they emerged at all, into a world of flame, and a sea aflame as well, a sea beneath a carpet of burning oil into which it would be suicide to lower the lifeboats or rafts, assuming any were left intact.

Nobody wanted to die, that went without saying. But the second engineer happened to know that Chiefy French had a very particular reason for wanting to stay alive. The two of them were good friends, with shared confidences, and the chief had opened up about his family problems, needing someone to talk to, someone he could trust. He'd spoken about the sons, Alan and Billy, and the pending police court – shoplifting. Billy was the ring-leader and a right tearaway by the sound of it, and French's wife seemingly couldn't cope. If French should be killed, the family could disintegrate. Probably the Chief was visualizing that at this moment.

A very nasty worry on a night like this. The second engineer echoed the earlier thoughts of the Commodore: the Navy back at the Cape must have been like Harpic – clean round the bend –to have made the decision to bunker outside a port at night.

Once again the B deck lounge had been cleared for the reception overnight of the Germans. Once again those Germans were under guard of the native riflemen. But this time Sergant Tapapa would if required be backed up by a half-company of the Australian troop draft. OC Troops had agreed with Captain Maconochie and the Commodore that security was of more importance than having all the soldiers sticking rigidly to their allotted boat stations.

'Flaming Nazis c'd make real trouble,' Harrison had said in the orderly room. 'Watch the buggers like hawks, all right? But don't *you* be too bloody obtrusive, Sar'nt-Major,' he added to RSM Treddle. 'We don't want to *cause* trouble. Or give the Nazis the excuse to *say* we caused it. Understand?'

Treddle nodded. 'I'll act like a lovely, cuddly little bloody baa-lamb, Colonel. That do?'

Harrison grinned and clapped the RSM on the shoulder. 'Wolf in bloody sheep's clothing more like. Just keep the wolf hidden, that's all.' He added in an incredulous tone, 'Lovely, cuddly little baa-lamb my arse! Just don't look the part somehow. Tell you what, Sar'nt-Major. The rifles' RSM – he'll be, as he'd put it himself, on parade throughout the night. Let him do the high profile bit, eh?'

RSM Treddle said, 'Reckon he'll do that without bloody encouragement, Colonel. Bloke's a walking stuffed-shirt, as full of bullshit as you can get without being a bull's bum. Oh, beg pardon, I'm sure,' he added as RSM Nunn appeared in the orderly room doorway, his tight-lipped face indicating that he'd over-heard the closing remarks. RSM Treddle grinned cheerfully. 'No offence, mate, eh?'

RSM Nunn disregarded the overture. His pace-stick held rigid and precisely horizontal with the deck beneath his left arm, he crashed his boots and gave Harrison a magnificent salute. 'Sir! Reporting for duty as may be required, sir. I have the German prisoners in mind, sir. I –'

'Funny,' Harrison broke in with a straight face. 'We were just talking about you and the Nazis, Sar'nt-Major. . . .'

'Sir!'

'What was that?'

'Sir! I said sir, sir.'

'Oh, right. Well, good on you, Mr Nunn.'

'Thank you, sir.' RSM Nunn looked baffled. 'Sir! If I may be acquainted with your proposals for the night, sir, in respect that is to the Germans, sir.'

'Right you are, Mr Nunn, but I reckon I'll have to leave that to my sar'nt-major here. Me, I need to go to the bridge. A word with the Commodore.' Harrison was already moving for the door as he spoke. He paused on the threshold and waved a hand at Treddle. 'See you,' he said, and vanished. RSM Treddle returned the wave to an empty doorway and grinned at RSM Nunn.

'Bloody jack-in-the-box, I reckon 'e is. Dinkum bloke, though, no bloody bull, just like one of the ordinary diggers is Harrison.'

'Ha,' RSM Nunn said.

'Come again, mate?'

'I said ha, Mr Treddle.' RSM Nunn did not approve of warrant officers who spoke familiarly of their colonels, no more than he approved of colonels who were just like one of the ordinary diggers, whom RSM Nunn understood to mean the rank-and-file. It was not like that in the British Army. He rose and fell for a while on the balls of his feet, back straight, service cap very square on his head, peak well forward so that he had in fact to keep his back straight in order to see. 'If you would be so good, Mr Treddle, as to inform me –'

'Cut the bloody formality, mate, why not? I'm Jim. You, mate?'

RSM Nunn remained very still. There was a pause. 'I do not approve,' RSM Nunn said heavily, 'of the use of Christian names on, shall we say, early acquaintance or like on parade. Neither am I "mate". My name is Mr Nunn, Mr Treddle, and that, I am of the opinion, we would do best to stick with. I've no doubt I make my meaning clear, Mr Treddle?'

'As bloody crystal, Mr Nunn. Now, where were we, eh?'

'The matter of the night detail, Mr Treddle.'

'Dead right, Mr Nunn, so we were.' RSM Treddle grinned. 'If you'd care to come down off of your high bloody horse, mate, we'll get on with it. All right with you, is it, eh?'

*

124

'It may be cold, Mildred. The nights often are, you know that. If I were you I'd take a jumper.' Colonel Holmes added, 'It's going to be a long night at boat stations.'

'I do think it's so unnecessary,' Mildred said.

'Oh, no. We have to take on fuel.'

'I didn't mean that. Though why at night . . . What I meant was this business of being at boat stations all the time. We would be just as handy sitting comfortably in the lounge, wouldn't we?'

Holmes sighed. Women seemed at times to lose all sense, all contact with the world of war. 'Perhaps, Mildred, perhaps. But the Germans are being mustered in the lounge so none of the passengers can use it.'

'That's another thing,' she said. 'I call it very dangerous to have Germans –' She broke off as the Tannoy clicked on in the alleyway outside their cabin, and the Captain came on the air.

'This is the Captain speaking. All personnel are to proceed to their boat stations and remain there until further orders. I ask all civilian passengers to give priority in the alleyways and on the accommodation ladders to the troops. There is no urgency and no need for any rush. You will be kept informed throughout the night as to the progress of the fuelling operation. That is all.'

The Tannoy went silent. Holmes extended an arm to his wife. 'Come along, my dear. We're rather slower than most I'm sorry to say.'

'Why not do as the Captain said, and give the soldiers time to get to their stations, Stephen? The night's going to be long enough as it is, you said so yourself.'

'Oh, very well, very well.' Colonel Holmes sat down again while his wife searched through drawers for a woolly jumper. The old man gave an involuntary sigh: they were both too old for this kind of thing and one way and another Mildred was taking it pretty badly, he thought. Not like her; she was used to army life in both an active service sense and a retired one. Back in Mombasa they'd led an army-oriented life in so many ways, still stuck to the old routines, down to the club for coffee in the mornings, possibly a luncheon party, siesta in the afternoons, drinks as soon as the sun went down, dress for dinner and then after dinner perhaps bridge. Part of all that was the stiff-upper-lip tradition of Britons abroad. What Mildred needed really was a strong whiff of the real old times before the war, when everything had been jollity and security and, well, *British*. What would do wonders for her would be an evening with good old Bill and Arse-end Portlock, fun and games and a lot of army talk and reminiscences, but that was wishing for the moon of course.

Holmes gave it ten minutes during which time the progress of the troops could be heard: crashings and bangings of equipment along the alleyways and heavy boots clumping up ladders for the embarkation deck. Then they emerged from their cabin, two elderly people, both rather frail and hesitant in a crowd, liable to stumble and fall if pushed. Holmes found himself thinking once again of Arse-end Portlock, wondering if he was now as decrepit as he was and then remembering, with something of a shock, that Arse-end Portlock had been killed by a bomb at Paddington.

As the Holmeses reached the embarkation deck something large was seen approaching the *Aurelian Star*'s port side, coming in from aft. Mildred clutched at her husband's arm. 'What's that?' she asked.

Holmes looked. 'It's one of the tankers, my dear, that's all, nothing to worry about. They're evidently fuelling us first. The Commodore's ship, you see.'

'Here she comes, lads,' Petty Officer Ramm said. He and Petty Officer Biggar, Biggar for'ard and Ramm aft, were under orders, along with their gunnery rates, to assist the troopship's deck party with the handling of the fenders, wires and ropes as the big tanker manoeuvred alongside. '*Brambleleaf*,' Ramm said. 'Med Fleet before the war – seen 'er often enough.' He was all set to reminisce now, impress the hostilities-only men with his memory and his service. 'Commander-in-Chief, 'e was Admiral Sir William Fisher, flying 'is flag in the old *Queen Elizabeth*. The *battleship*, not the Cunard liner. Flag Lieutenant was a bloke called Duckworth . . . poor old Fisher died a year later, caught a chill taking the salute at the King's birthday parade on Southsea Common, when 'e was C-in-C Pompey. Buried off the Nab, along with a load of other admirals what 'ad gorn before. Coffin aboard the *Curacao*, light cruiser. An' what's the matter with you, may I ask, Able-Seaman Sissons?'

Stripey Sissons smirked. 'Department of useless knowledge, PO. Them days is over.'

'More's the pity, and take that grin orf your face, Able-Seaman

Sissons, or you'll be up before the Commodore on a charge of bleedin' impertinence, you'll see.'

'Sorry I'm sure, PO.'

Ramm grunted. 'You may know it all, Stripey, in fact you do, but there's them as can do with a spot of naval 'istory.' Ramm's tone altered. 'Right, lads, stand by now, *Brambleleaf*'s coming on and there'll be lines flying around.' He bent over the guardrail, checking the fenders. Stripey Sissons, standing by to take the first of the heaving-lines, thought about pre-war. True, it was over and done with, but there had been some good times. Stripey had seen a good deal of the world – West Indies, China-side, Singapore, Home Fleet in the days, back in the twenties, when it had been designated the Atlantic Fleet. But, looking back, his commission with the Mediterranean Fleet, also back in the late twenties, had been the most memorable. He hadn't been married then, which meant among other things no mother-in-law; and life when ashore from the battle-cruiser *Renown* had held plenty of promise. Nights in Alexandria, nights in Gibraltar and other places, most memorable of all the nights ashore in Malta. Down Strada Stretta, better known to generations of roistering British seamen as the Gut; plenty of booze in the many bars, plenty of women in the rooms above the bars, a wee bit sleazy but never mind, you could always see the quack when you got back aboard after dipping your wick. The RN surgeons had had any amount of experience in that branch of medicine, you should just see the queues outside the sick bays of the fleet, every morning . . .

Stripey's dreams of heaven were cut short when a heaving-line from the *Brambleleaf* whizzed through the air, the monkey's-fist at its end only just missing his head. Stripey, who was agile enough never mind his age, caught it expertly and began heaving it in, hand over hand, until the weight of the attached rope hawser came on and with the assistance of Ordinary Seaman Featherstonehaugh he struggled with it across the deck to place the eye over the troopship's bitts. When the eye was in position Stripey shouted 'All fast' and seamen aboard the tanker hauled in on the sternrope. When Petty Officer Biggar, up for'ard, had secured the headrope and the springs were hauled taut, the hands aboard the troopship were fallen out to stand by their guns, the two petty officers keeping an eye lifting on the securing lines.

127

On the bridge Maconochie and Kemp watched the lie of the RFA vessel closely. Maconochie, having the direct responsibility for his ship, would remain on the bridge throughout the operation. So would Kemp, though with the convoy hove-to he would be handy enough catching up on some much-needed sleep in his cabin immediately below the bridge, ready within half a minute if and when required. If there were U-boats in the vicinity, plenty of early warning would come from the guardships currently steaming up and down in protection of the convoy. But with the rest of the ship at boat stations he would not go below himself.

As the two of them watched, RFA *Oligarch* was seen approaching the ex-liner next astern of the *Aurelian Star*. As in the case of the *Brambleleaf* she already had her own fenders rigged along her starboard side to supplement those of the receiving ship. Also as in their own case there were no hitches. Aboard the Commodore's ship the oil pipelines were already being connected and shortly the discharge into the troopship's tanks would begin. Kemp took a look all round the assembly of ships, using his binoculars in a slow sweep. Luckily the weather had held; there was a flat calm and scarcely any swell, just enough to make it essential for all the wires and ropes to be watched closely in case there was any heave that could put enough strain on the lines to part them. Kemp knew that it would be an anxious time for the masters of the tankers. Very fast action would be needed on their part to prevent a collision if a heavy surge should happen to come whilst fuelling was in progress.

Brigadier Pumphrey-Hatton was at the same boat station as Colonel and Mrs Holmes. He was dressed in his khaki-drill uniform with a heavy khaki pullover beneath his cork life-jacket. He seemed distrait, nervous, walking up and down his section of the embarkation deck below the lifeboat hanging from the davits with steadying lines rigged fore and aft until such time as it had to be lowered for taking its passengers aboard.

He halted alongside the Holmeses.

He said, 'Ascension Island.'

'Er – yes, Brigadier.'

'Lucky it's close. If anything happens.'

'Yes, quite. Very handy. It might not have been.' Holmes gave a chuckle; he had made a joke of a sort.

Pumphrey-Hatton said irritably, 'What d'you mean, it might not have been? If we hadn't been here, neither would *it*. Stands to reason I'd have thought.'

'Yes, that's true.' Holmes felt bewildered, as though he'd possibly missed something of military significance, thereby showing his age. 'I take your point, Brigadier.'

'I'm glad to hear it, Colonel, very glad. It is necessary to make an assessment of any situation, an appreciation don't you know. Good practice. Always tell my chaps that. No doubt you yourself did in your day.'

'Er . . . yes. Yes, I did.'

'Which was your war, Colonel? South African – the Boers?'

Holmes felt shock. 'As a matter of fact, no. The Great War –'

'Ah. Well, same thing. You're all out-of-date now. In this one, you know. Agree?'

'I'm afraid I don't.' Holmes thought of good old Bill and Arse-end Portlock, who had both contributed to the war. 'I believe we do still have a useful role – or some of us do, some who are a little younger than I. I –'

'You're *disagreeing* with me?'

'Yes, I –'

'Don't, then.'

Holmes gaped. 'I beg your pardon, Brigadier?'

'You heard what I said. Don't damn well disagree with me. I happen to be right. There are too many damn disagreements and too many people not listening to complaints. I have had trouble with my bath water, did you know that?' Pumphrey-Hatton had pushed his face close to Holmes' and was staring belligerently. The old man took an involuntary step backwards, saying that no, he hadn't been aware of that.

'I spoke to that purser feller. Didn't do a *damn thing* about it! I told him my complaint was to be forwarded to the Captain for immediate action. Result, still no damn water coming through, either salt or fresh. You'd never think there was a war on. I shall represent it to that Australian – Harrison.'

'I see . . .'

'I doubt if you do. However – good luck to you. I hope you reach the Clyde, but I doubt if you will or your good lady either. If a convoy commodore can't regulate a damn bath, how in heaven's name was he ever given charge of a convoy?'

Pumphrey-Hatton turned sharply and walked away. Holmes shook his head in sheer bewilderment. It was unforgiveable for anyone to doubt their safe arrival home in front of largely scared civilians mustered at a time of danger at their boat stations. Holmes reassured his wife. 'Don't pay any attention, my dear. The man's as mad as a hatter. All that disjointed talk.' He shook his head. It was all very sad.

RSM Nunn was surveying the Germans assembled in the lounge beneath the blue police lights. He was doing so through the glass screen, from the deck outside. 'They appear docile enough, Mr Treddle,' he said, tweaking at his moustache.

'Could be deceptive, Mr Nunn.' RSM Treddle had lost the battle and had abandoned 'mate'. 'Can't always go by appearances, eh?'

'There's truth in that, Mr Treddle, that I don't deny.' RSM Nunn expanded. 'Take your lot, like. Very good fighters. Reliable in action.'

'Dead right they are. If they weren't, I'd be right up their arses. And don't get me wrong on that. You know what I mean. But so what?'

'So what, Mr Treddle?'

'So what, yes. I mean, I get the idea you were about to make a comparison. About appearances being deceptive, right?'

RSM Nunn, who had in fact been about to say that the Australians looked a right bunch, sloppily turned out and a sight too free-and-easy, refrained. It might cause offence since they were a touchy lot, especially if criticized by what they called pommies, or poms, which always put RSM Nunn in mind of a pomeranian dog. So he disregarded RSM Treddle's last query and instead drew attention to a POW lounging in a chair and smoking a cigarette. 'Tobacco, there,' he said, pointing with his pace-stick. 'Contraband! Passed by one of the ship's crew, I'll be bound. That must be dealt with, Mr Treddle.'

'Not by me,' RSM Treddle said at once. 'Now's not the time, mate.' That had slipped out past his guard. 'It can be investigated later, when they're back below. Not now. We don't want any trouble while they're up here, do we, eh?'

'Proper discipline must be maintained, Mr Treddle. I am aware of course that this is principally an Australian draft and that you personally are responsible to OC Troops. But if you will not take action then it is up to me. I shall speak to Sar'nt Tapapa.' RSM Nunn, replacing his pace-stick beneath his left arm, marched towards the entry to the lounge, his boots banging the deck, left-right-left, right arm swinging. Treddle shrugged; if old starcharse wanted to stir things up, it was his loss. Treddle himself had had his say, cleared his own yardarm as the poms put it.

RSM Nunn had reached the entry when the Tannoy came on from the bridge. Captain Maconochie announced a contact by the A/S screen. Boat stations were now for real. To give point to his words and to alert any passenger or crew member who might have gone below in defiance of orders, the alarm rattlers sounded throughout the ship.

THIRTEEN

Maconochie called the engine-room. 'Disconnect, Chief. How much have you taken?'

'Around three-quarters full –'

'We'll resume later if all goes well. Meanwhile I'm casting off the tanker.' Maconochie banged the voicepipe cover down, then went at the rush to the port bridge-wing. Using a megaphone he called across to the RFA master. 'I'm casting you off, Captain. Hope to see you again when the panic's over.' He used the megaphone again to call down to his own decks. 'Unberthing parties stand by fore and aft. As soon as the pipeline's disconnected, cast off all ropes and wires from *Brambleleaf*. Tend all fenders as she goes.'

He met Kemp's eye. 'Just what I feared,' Kemp said, his face set hard. The naval command in Simonstown had made a boob that might cost the convoy very dear. He watched as the tanker slid away astern, her twin screws sending up a kerfuffle between the ships that helped to keep them apart. Along the troopship's decks the fenders were hauled back aboard. In charge of the naval party aft, Petty Officer Ramm was more outspoken than the Commodore had been.

'Bird-brained admirals, that's what, don't know there's a war on, half of 'em.' He paused, noting the tremor of the deck and the surge of water astern. 'Under way already – and thank God for it. Bridge didn't take long to get moving, I'll say that for 'em. I tell you –' He broke off suddenly. There had been a sharp crack from for'ard, followed a moment later by two more. 'Now, what the hell was that, eh?'

Featherstonehaugh said, 'Rifle fire, PO –'

'God give me strength, *Featherstone*haugh, I bloody know that, thank you very much! What I meant was who and why, and I reckon it's them bloody Germans. You and you,' he said to Leading Seaman Purkiss and the OD, 'get up to the bridge, at the double, stand by the Oerlikons. And remember, no firing without orders.'

Ramm was aware, as Featherstonehaugh started for'ard, of a kind of glitter in the OD's eyes and he remembered the lad's dad had been knocked off by the Nazis.

RSM Nunn had gone into the B deck lounge, pace-stick beneath his arm, cap on square as ever, very regimental, to sort out the crime of smoking and contraband. He had halted just inside the door from the open deck and had used his parade-ground voice.

'Now what's all this, then? That man there.' The pace-stick had been pointed. 'Smoking by POWs is not permitted, the more so as POWs do not have access to tobacco! Right! Now, extinguish that dog-end, that man, and then we'll see.'

He waited. The Nazi blew a long trail of smoke, grinning. Then he reached into a pocket and brought out a packet of cigarettes. He handed this to the man next to him, who took one and lit up. RSM Nunn's eyes bulged with anger. 'Matches,' he said in a loud voice. 'Likewise not permitted. Well?'

'Not well, British pig,' the first smoker said calmly. 'The fat murderer Churchill smokes cigars. We smoke cigarettes. The monster Churchill is also a pig.'

RSM Nunn advanced a few paces. 'Do you know what you are saying?' he enunciated. The speaker seemed to have good English but he might simply be mouthing what he'd learned back in his own country. He had to be given a chance.

'I know what I say,' the German answered. 'I speak of the mad Churchill, who is a wicked warmonger and will shortly be made to answer for his crimes against the Third Reich and the German people.' Then he stiffened to attention, clicked his heels, raised his right hand in the Nazi salute and said, '*Heil, Hitler.*'

This was echoed by the whole POW contingent.

'Right,' RSM Nunn said. 'That does it. I'm going to 'ave your guts for garters.' Armed only with his pace-stick, the Regimental Sergeant-Major advanced, pushing his way through the

133

Germans, who were now jeering and cat-calling, fast becoming an undisciplined mob.

'Sar'nt Tapapa,' RSM Nunn called.

'Yes, sah!'

'Where the devil are you, man?' Sergeant Tapapa was so far invisible.

'Here, sah.' Sergeant Tapapa appeared in the doorway to the open deck, looking frightened out of his wits.

'Get your men in here, Sar'nt Tapapa, you booby, with bayonets fixed and a round up the spout. Then follow my orders very closely, all right?'

'Yes, sah –'

'Right! First thing. Send a man to the orderly room and the bridge to report the state of affairs. That done, come up alongside o' me with your revolver ready. No one's to open fire, however, till I give the word. Or one of the officers does if they 'appen to get here in time. Now then, got that, have you?'

'Yes, sah!'

'Right, get to it, then. *Pronto!*'

RSM Nunn stood his ground stolidly while the mêlée went on around him. Within half a minute he was joined by the native riflemen, their black faces gleaming in the blue police lights that were the only illumination.

Harrison had gone at once to the bridge, where he was joined by Colonel Carter of the Rifles. They conferred with Maconochie and the Commodore.

'The situation's electric, I reckon,' Harrison said. 'I took a gander. My adjutant's gone along to take charge in the lounge. I reckon that RSM of yours,' he added to Carter, 'has kind of gone loony or something, bellyaching about a bloke smoking –'

'Mr Nunn's a first-class warrant officer,' Carter said crisply, 'but we'll not go into that now.' He turned to Kemp. 'In my opinion, sir, the POWs should be marched back below right away. My riflemen are in control so far but that may change quite quickly. I believe the Germans'll take a chance that no one's going to open fire, and try a break-out.'

'We certainly don't want shooting,' Kemp said, 'but I'll not have anyone shut down below when we're likely to come under attack at any moment. I –'

'There's civvy passengers at risk, Commodore.' This was Harrison. 'Me, I go along with Carter.'

'No,' Kemp said firmly. 'Those Germans are not going to be put below. To do that . . . it's not in the tradition of the sea –'

'For Jeez' sake,' Harrison cut in, 'balls to tradition, in a situation like this. What we –'

Kemp rounded on him. 'I have given an order, Colonel Harrison, and you will obey it. I'm giving another order and it's this: the Germans are to be made to understand that they wouldn't have a hope if the riflemen or your Australians were ordered to open fire. They must be told quite clearly that if they don't calm down, the order to open fire *will* be given – though I hope to God it doesn't come to that. And now, gentlemen, go away and carry out my orders and leave me to do my job – which concerns the safety of the convoy as a whole against possible attack.'

The soldiers turned away and went down the ladder, their faces saying clearly that they considered the Commodore to be entirely wrong. It was soon after they had left the bridge that the sound of rifle fire came from below. Kemp, awaiting further reports from the A/s screen and worrying about the state and readiness of the merchant ships as they got under way, shut his ears to it. The soldiers would have to cope. It was their job to guard the prisoners. And undoubtedly, on the face of it, the regimental sergeant-major had stuck his neck out rather too far. Kemp cursed the involvement of prisoners-of-war; he was a seaman, with a vital job to do, not a pongo or a warder.

He found himself wondering how Pumphrey-Hatton would have reacted, had he still been OC Troops.

Kemp had a feeling the brigadier might have made a better fist of it than Harrison. Pumphrey-Hatton was, after all, of the old school of military thought, and part of his code would be at least a degree of chivalry towards a defeated enemy, though in all conscience the *Aurelian Star*'s prisoners-of-war didn't appear to regard themselves as defeated. But in any event Pumphrey-Hatton's attitude would be very different from Harrison's; Harrison was brash.

As it happened, Pumphrey-Hatton was already involving himself. He had been startled by the sound of what he took to be revolver fire followed by rifle fire, quite a number of rounds, coming from the deck above. He had at once left his boat station and had climbed fast to B deck. There was a shindig coming from the lounge and he had seen that some of the big square ports had been shattered, no doubt by the rifle fire. He found Captain Mulvaney outside the main door.

'What's going on?' he asked.

Mulvaney told him. 'Bloke smoking. One of the black NCOS fired his revolver on the RSM's order and that did it, I reckon. There was a riot and the blacks fired over the Nazis' heads. I reckon –'

'Where is OC Troops?'

Mulvaney gave a jerk of his head. 'In there. Sorting it out or trying to.'

'Ask him to come out on deck.'

Captain Mulvaney pushed his bush hat back from his head. 'Now look,' he began in a tone that suggested he was speaking to a child. 'You don't want –'

'Kindly refrain from telling me to look, Captain Mulvaney, and from telling me what I don't want. Go and fetch Colonel Harrison. That is an order.'

'You've got no authority that I know of –'

Pumphrey-Hatton's voice rose. 'I am a brigadier of the British Army and I have given you an order. You will disobey it at peril of a Court Martial. Do I make myself clear, Captain Mulvaney?'

Mulvaney glared, muttered something indistinct, then swung away sharply and went into the lounge. A few moments passed and then he returned with OC Troops.

Harrison was tight-faced. 'You listen to me, Brigadier. I –'

'On the contrary. You will listen to me.' Pumphrey-Hatton's tone was crisp and authoritative, his curious manner and his preoccupations with trivia seeming to have vanished. 'I may not be OC Troops any longer, but I have experience that, if I may say so, you lack. The whole ship is now faced with a very difficult situation, as you must realize. I have had experience of dealing with German prisoners in the western desert – Eighth Army, also under Australian command in Tobruk.' He paused. 'A day or so ago you asked my advice as to the duties and so on of OC Troops. I now apologize for my abruptness. I am asking you to allow me to handle this situation . . . on your behalf.'

Harrison's mouth opened and then closed again. He was still angry, wishing to tell the old geezer to stuff his advice and not act as though he were God. But something was stopping him. A riot that could now be held only by gunfire, a riot that could end in the killing of prisoners-of-war under the protection of the Geneva Convention would for sure rebound on him as OC Troops. He might just as well keep his trap shut and let Pumphrey-Hatton take at least some of the blame afterwards. He glanced at his adjutant, whose face told him he was keeping out of it so far as he could, then he turned back to Pumphrey-Hatton.

'Righto,' he said grudgingly. 'Advise away if you want to.'

Pumphrey-Hatton asked, 'Is the German officer, *Leutnant* Stoph, in there?'

Harrison said he was.

'Have him brought out. And the regimental sar'nt-major who I understand is involved. The rifles' sar'nt-major.'

'Too bloody right he's involved –'

'Just have him brought out, Colonel Harrison. And then we shall all shift up to A deck, rather than conduct proceedings in the view, and possibly in the hearing, of the prisoners.'

Harrison, fuming, gestured to Mulvaney. The Australian captain turned away and went back inside the lounge, returning after an interval with *Kapitan-Leutnant* Stoph and RSM Nunn, plus native escort. They all climbed to A deck, whence Pumphrey-Hatton had already gone. RSM Nunn slammed to attention in front of the brigadier with much banging of boots and a quivering salute. In rear of Stoph stood one of the riflemen with his bayonet fixed and his eyeballs rolling.

'Now then,' Pumphrey-Hatton said briskly, addressing the German officer. 'I understand there is a complaint.'

'There is much of a complaint,' Stoph said.

'You will address me as sir, or as Brigadier.'

'I will not address you as sir,' Stoph said superciliously.

'I see. Then I have to say that I am disappointed in you, *Kapitan-Leutnant* Stoph. Also surprised. I take you for an officer and a gentleman. For a professional seaman rather, perhaps, than let us say one of the *Gestapo* or the SS.'

There was no response from Stoph, who stood looking disdainfully at Pumphrey-Hatton, his tall body as straight as that of the RSM.

Pumphrey-Hatton went on, 'I believe there is a German Grand Admiral named Stoph, who retired from your service before the war. A Prussian, with a Prussian's code of honour.'

'My uncle, yes.'

'Then may I say that were I a prisoner, I would address your uncle as sir, or as Admiral,' Pumphrey-Hatton said mildly.

There was another silence. Then Stoph said, 'I understand. I shall therefore address you as Brigadier.'

Pumphrey-Hatton smiled. 'Good! A small but important point of etiquette is settled, and we can talk about your complaint. We can talk, too, about what is currently taking place in the lounge. Your complaint is to do with smoking, as I understand?'

'My complaint is to do with harassment over one of my men observed to smoke, *Herr* Brigadier.'

'Yes, I see. Not perhaps harassment but the establishment of discipline and the safety of the ship, upon which we all depend, your men included, *Kapitan-Leutnant* Stoph. I don't see it as any occasion for the sort of trouble that seems to have erupted. Do you?'

Stoph's eyes shifted. 'Perhaps no.'

'H'm. Sar'nt-Major?'

'Sir!'

'A word from you would help, Sarn't-Major.'

RSM Nunn stared at a fixed point over the brigadier's head. 'There was words, sir. Provocative words, sir, as to Mr Churchill who was referred to as being a pig, also as being a monster, sir. Also as being mad, sir. Such arose, sir, on account of my stopping the man smoking.' Nunn paused. 'The cigars, like, sir, see.'

'The cigars, Sarn't-Major?'

'Mr Churchill's, sir.'

'Really. Sarn't-Major . . . if you were a prisoner in Germany . . . I wonder what you might say about Herr Hitler?'

RSM Nunn lifted a hand and tweaked at the ends of his moustache. 'Yes, sir. I get your meaning, sir. Perhaps I was over-hasty, sir.'

Pumphrey-Hatton nodded. 'A little give-and-take, Sar'nt-Major, that's the thing. A storm in a tea-cup, I rather fancy.' He turned to Stoph. 'If the rifles are withdrawn, *Kapital-Leutnant* Stoph, have I your word that your men will quieten down and remain obedient to orders for your own safety while the convoy is in danger?'

Stoph hesitated, but only for a moment. Then he said, 'You have my word, *Herr* Brigadier. I thank you.'

Pumphrey-Hatton nodded again and turned to Colonel Harrison. 'Now it's over to you again, Colonel. I trust I've been of some assistance.'

He went away with his odd, jerky walk. He felt he'd settled something, defused a tricky and dangerous situation. Now he had other matters back on his mind and once the convoy was safe from possible attack he would make representations in the proper quarter. Really, these days it was one damn thing after another and just before going to his boat station he had discovered that the tank beneath the wash-basin in his cabin had not been properly emptied by his steward, a residue of water being left after his last wash. These things all added up to a very serious lack of discipline throughout the ship, as dangerous in its way as the Germans.

Pumphrey-Hatton had started down the ladders to the embarkation deck and his boat station when he heard more firing, this time heavier as though from one of the close-range weapons, the Oerlikons mounted in the bridge-wings or on monkey's-island above the wheelhouse.

As *Kapitan-Leutnant* Stoph had been ordered back down the ladder to B deck he had slipped on a greasy patch. He had lost his balance, pitching sideways and knocking RSM Nunn off his feet. A trigger-happy gunnery rate at the starboard bridge Oerlikon had, without waiting for orders, opened fire in a short burst, evidently taking the incident as an attack on the RSM. The bridge personnel had been taken off guard and had reacted too late. As the burst ended, Kemp himself seized the man and wrenched him bodily from the straps. The rating was Ordinary Seaman Featherstonehaugh.

One of the Oerlikon shells had taken an escorting native rifleman in the left shoulder; another had hit *Kapitan-Leutnant* Stoph, who was lying on the deck. The rest of the burst had gone harmlessly aft.

FOURTEEN

Petty Officer Ramm, hearing the Oerlikon in action, had gone at the double to the bridge. He saluted the Commodore.

'Sounds like trouble, sir,' he said breathlessly. He looked at Featherstonehaugh, standing quietly in the bridge wing. Again there was something funny in the OD's eyes. Or could have been the moonlight streaming across the bridge into his face.

'Trouble's right,' Kemp said. 'This man fired without orders. Sub-Lieutenant Finnegan will make the charge and carry out a preliminary investigation once the convoy's in the clear and he'll be brought before me subsequently. Until then, he's to be held in arrest.'

'Aye, aye, sir. Where's he to be placed, sir?'

Kemp hesitated. He had no wish to place any man in cells at sea, still less so in current circumstances. He said, 'Contact the Purser, Ramm. There's always a cabin or two kept empty for emergencies of one sort or another.'

'Aye, aye, sir.' Ramm saluted again. 'Right, Featherstonehaugh – about turn, quick march, down the ladder.' He added to Kemp, 'I'll send up a replacement right away, sir.' He clattered down the ladder close behind the OD. When he reached the bottom he said in a low voice, 'What d'you want to go and do a thing like that for, eh, lad? Bloody daft.' Then, quickly, he said, 'Don't answer that. Forget I asked. You're what they call *sub joodyce* now.'

The rifleman was in a bad way as reported to OC Troops by the medical officer. The shoulder was shattered and there had been a

140

serious loss of blood plus some ancillary injury to the head on the left side. Emergency surgery would need to be carried out and it was too early yet for any positive prognosis. The German, Stoph, was not badly hurt: nothing beyond a graze to the right upper arm beneath some torn clothing. He had been concussed by striking his head on a mushroom ventilator when he'd fallen and he would be kept under guard overnight in the sick bay for observation.

Soon after the doctor's report had reached the bridge a series of explosions was heard away on the convoy's starboard beam.

'Depth charges,' Kemp said. 'And a perfect night for attack. Has that rating been fixed up, Finnegan?'

'Yes, sir, I guess so. When the attack is over he'll be accommodated in a cabin on F deck, armed sentry on guard outside. Meantime he's back on the after three-inch. Petty Officer Ramm's acting as watchdog. I gave that the okay, sir, all right?'

Kemp nodded. 'Sensible, Finnegan.'

There was a grin. 'Trust the US Navy, sir, Commodore –'

'Stop boasting, Finnegan, and watch out for torpedo trails.'

'I'll do that thing, sir, Commodore.'

'Which I take it is American for aye, aye, sir.'

'You bet it is,' Finnegan said.

'In that case,' Kemp said heavily, 'it's time you learned English, young man.'

Finnegan grinned again. They understood one another well enough. The explosions continued, growing more distant. Half an hour later there was a blue flashing lamp from the senior officer of the escort. Yeoman Lambert reported, 'Enemy losses believed to be three U-boats, no losses to convoy or escort. Have broken off action.'

Kemp said, 'Thank God for a good result. Tell the guns'-crews, Finnegan. They can stand down but remain handy. Yeoman, make to the senior officer from Commodore, propose to resume fuelling.'

Over the next fifteen minutes the convoy resumed its formation for completion of taking bunkers, turning back through 180 degrees for Ascension Island.

Finnegan thought ahead to his forthcoming session with Ordinary Seaman Featherstonehaugh, which would take place next forenoon. He had no liking for that task; he, as well as Kemp,

141

knew the rating's recent history. If the Nazis had killed his, Finnegan's, dad he would very likely do the same thing if he got the chance. But the moment that line of thought entered his mind, he conscientiously dismissed it. That would be prejudging the case: there was so far absolutely no evidence that Featherstonehaugh had been aiming for *Kapitan-Leutnant* Stoph.

Nattering whilst the ship was once again taking oil fuel from the *Brambleleaf*, Petty Officer Ramm did what he shouldn't have done which was to discuss what had happened with Petty Officer Biggar. He had no qualms about prejudgement. 'Avenging his dad,' he said firmly. 'Stands out a mile. Bloody rotten shot, that's all.'

'Took 'is chance, like.'

'Wouldn't you?'

Biggar scratched his head. 'Dunno. Maybe.' He thought for a moment. 'Yes, I just might, I s'pose. But only when I knew I was going to get away with it. I'm not that bloody daft.'

Ramm nodded. Himself, he didn't believe the OD had a hope in hell of getting away with it. His dad – circumstantial evidence they would call that. Ramm wondered what the penalty would be; and pondered on what Biggar had said. In the last war, so it had been rumoured, officers on the Western Front, officers who'd been rotten bastards to their men, had on occasion taken a shot in the back during an advance on the Jerry trenches. It was different at sea: Featherstonehaugh had been much too indiscreet. Daft, really.

Kemp paced the bridge while the interrupted oiling continued, and the tanker, having completed fuelling the *Aurelian Star*, moved off the troopship's side and proceeded to the next of the waiting ships. Kemp had much on his mind, not least the stupid action of Ordinary Seaman Featherstonehaugh. To go into action without orders was bad enough; to project gunfire towards a prisoner-of-war, unarmed and giving no trouble, was conduct of the worst kind. Featherstonehaugh could say goodbye to any prospect of a commission. Kemp would be immensely sorry about that; but there were no two ways about it. It was, however, not that alone that now weighed heavily with the Commodore. Kemp was in a fair way to blaming himself for both Featherstonehaugh's predicament and the injury to the native rifleman

None of this would have happened if he had heeded the opinions of Colonel Carter and OC Troops that the POWS should be taken back to their quarters below.

He had perhaps been obstinate.

He paced on, his face set into hard lines. No use having regrets now; what was done was done and that was that. But his self-recrimination could be reflected in the view he would be taking of Featherstonehaugh's action when the rating came up before him. He must not allow that either. Whatever he, Kemp, might have done, Featherstonehaugh's action stood on its own demerits.

Kemp, as he came to Finnegan hunched in the starboard wing of the bridge, stopped his restless pacing. He said, 'Your investigation, Finnegan. The shooting.' He paused. 'First thing after dawn action stations, Finnegan. I want all this settled soonest possible.'

The shooting had naturally reacted on the civilian passengers. Mothers had become extra protective of children, in most cases holding them tight. The children themselves were scared. They knew there were Germans aboard, and they had mostly heard scary tales about Germans from fathers who had fought in the trenches of the Western Front in the last war. Germans were Huns, warlike, ferocious as the giants and ogres and hobgoblins in Grimm's Fairy Tales. The nanny of one of the children had said they had horns like devils, and forked tongues that went out and in like serpents. They spitted children on their bayonets, and roasted them over fires like the fires of hell that would burn them up one day if they didn't say their prayers.

One small boy, known to the Holmeses back in Kenya, voiced some of this in a loud whisper to a girl of about his own age and was overheard not by his mother but by Colonel Holmes, who intervened.

'What nonsense, Billy. Whoever told you that?'

The boy looked up at him round-eyed. 'Nanny did.'

'Then Nanny had no business to. Nanny's quite wrong, Billy.'

'Nanny's never wrong,' the boy stated firmly. 'Mummy said so.'

'Really.' A matter of discipline, of course. You always stood by your NCOs in front of the soldiers. Holmes cleared his throat. He said, 'Certainly Nanny is always right when, for instance, she

143

says it's time to go bed, or . . . er . . . things like that. She really doesn't know very much about the Germans, Billy, take it from me.'

The boy stared him in the eye. 'Nanny knows all about witch doctors.' Nanny, of course, would have been black. The boy went on, 'She says they push red-hot needles into your eyes.'

'The witch doctors are –'

'No, silly, the Germans.'

At this point the small girl started crying and gave a shriek for her mother. Mother appeared from the lee of the boat's falls, together with Billy's mother, who said she hoped Billy wasn't being a pest but she knew he would be all right with the Holmeses. 'Come along, Billy –'

'The boy's no trouble, Mrs Moriarty,' Holmes said. 'But he has some strange ideas about the Germans –'

'That's Nanny,' the mother said. 'She's rather alarmist.' The children were gathered up and removed. Alarmist, Holmes remarked to his wife, was scarcely the word for such horror stories. Modern mothers, he said, didn't pay half enough attention to their offspring, leaving them too much to their nannies. Then he remembered his own childhood days. What with boarding school and Nanny, he'd scarcely seen his own mother, just an hour a day after tea before he and his younger sister were gathered up and returned willy-nilly to the nursery. But that had been before the Great War when Germans had not yet become monsters, were indeed quite socially acceptable since their Kaiser was a grandson of the Queen-Empress . . .

Farther along the embarkation deck Gregory Hench was comforting Gloria Northway. She had become almost hysterical when she'd heard the rifle fire, more so when the short burst from the Oerlikon was heard. Hench had put a protective arm around her and she had snuggled. She was snuggling still; Hench felt he had stolen a handy march on the Australian, Mulvaney.

Brigadier Pumphrey-Hatton received a message from the Commodore: Kemp's compliments and he would appreciate it if Pumphrey-Hatton would find it convenient to come to the bridge. Pumphrey-Hatton would. He went up immediately. Kemp said, 'I just wanted to thank you, Brigadier. I understand you defused a very nasty situation.'

'Potentially nasty, yes. Tact – that's all. The Australians are no tactful. No more was that RSM – but RSMs are seldom renowned for tact, excellent fellows though they are. I'm glad to have been of service. Well, that's in the past, or I hope it is. I'd like to take the opportunity of drawing your attention to my wash-basin . . .'

Pumphrey-Hatton had indeed been of service; Kemp listened patiently to the woes of the wash-basin and the bath water and a recap of the electric fan and the flies. It took quite a while and when Pumphrey-Hatton had left the bridge Kemp shook his head in bewilderment as to how the brigadier's finicking could possibly add up with the firm way in which he appeared to have taken charge of the German problem. Of one thing, however, Kemp was determined: when his voyage report went to the Admiralty after arrival in the Clyde it would contain a glowing report of Pumphrey-Hatton's action for forwarding to the War Office. It might do the man some good in whatever he was due to face in London. In spite of all Kemp hoped very much that it would.

When Pumphrey-Hatton, leaving the bridge, moved aft to take a look astern at the rest of the convoy, many of the ships still awaiting one or other of the tankers, he came face to face with Leading Seaman Purkiss.

He stopped, drawing himself up. Each stared into the other's eyes. It was Purkiss who looked away. Pumphrey-Hatton said, 'You're the damn blackguard who struck me in Simonstown. Don't attempt to deny it. I recognized you instantly. What have you to say about it before I call the master-at-arms and have you placed in arrest?'

Purkiss swallowed, and remembered an important tenet of life on the lower deck, this tenet being that however bleak the prospect you never admitted to anything. You let the buggers prove it for themselves. Since, when an officer was involved, you were going to be found guilty anyway, you couldn't lose out by taking a chance that just might come off, however unlikely. So he pulled himself together and answered smartly.

'Never set eyes on you, sir. 'Cept in the distance like, sir. Not at close quarters, what I'd 'ave 'ad to be to clock you one, sir.'

'I said you were a blackguard. Name?'

'Purkiss, sir, leading seaman –'

'Now you're a liar as well, Leading Seaman Purkiss. Two crimes I make that. However, with the convoy in possible danger

145

and the likelihood of action stations, I shall leave the matter until the situation changes.'

Pumphrey-Hatton marched away. Purkiss let out a long breath and wiped the back of a hand across his forehead. Then he went for'ard in search of Petty Officer Biggar.

Biggar was worried but said, 'He'll have a job on his hands to prove it. Just you and me. So we stick together, no perishing admissions. His word against two of us. Look on the bright side, Purkiss. Make out it's a case of mistaken identity.'

'But you said earlier, 'e'd recognized you too, PO.'

'Yes, that does complicate it sure enough. I'll think of something . . . I still say, stick to what we says is the facts, all right?'

'All right,' Purkiss said gloomily. He was in deeper than Biggar; all Biggar had done was to do sod all when as a PO he should have taken action, made a report. A different matter from a Court Martial offence. Biggar might lose his rate, he, Purkiss, would not only lose his rate but his freedom as well for an indefinite period. Could even be six months or more in a civvy jail, like say Barlinnie in Glasgow on arrival in the Clyde. Striking an officer was about the worst thing you could do, short of desertion. Purkiss wasn't too sure what powers of punishment the Commodore had; he could no doubt punish summarily or by warrant but if the punishment was more than ninety days there might have to be reference to a higher authority such as the Flag Officer in Charge, Greenock, and God only knew what an admiral might inflict.

Next morning, a day of fair weather and calm seas and no further contact reported from the destroyer escort, Ordinary Seaman Featherstonehaugh was brought out from the cabin where he was being held and was taken under escort to the port side of the Captain's deck below the bridge. With Petty Officer Ramm in attendance, acting as naval master-at-arms, the routine was gone through as it would be aboard a warship.

Ramm gave the orders as the OD was marched in by Leading Seaman Purkiss, to whom the proceedings were by way of a rehearsal for his own arraignment.

' 'Alt, off cap.' Ramm turned to Finnegan. 'Ordinary Seaman Peter Ewart Featherstonehaugh, official number P/JX 187153, sir.

Did at 0123 hours of this day, open fire with the starboard side bridge Oerlikon without orders to do so.'

Ramm stood back. Now it was over to Finnegan. Ramm wondered if subby was going to lean over backwards to favour a rating who was in for a commission and whose old man had been an officer. It should prove interesting. Finnegan, however, had had further words with the Commodore. Kemp had stated the obvious: the charge was an extremely serious one and could turn out even more serious if the native soldier should die. The man was still on the danger list according to the doctors. Thus Finnegan was to do no more than bring out the basic facts. He was not to allow Featherstonehaugh to incriminate himself along the lines of possible motive.

He asked Featherstonehaugh if he had anything to say as to the charge.

'Only that I did open fire, sir.'

Finnegan, standing with his hands behind his back, nodded. So much was indisputable. He addressed Ramm. 'Petty Officer Ramm. Were instructions given that there was to be no firing without orders?'

Ramm temporized. He had no wish to harm Featherstonehaugh. He said, 'It's standing orders, sir, always is, that fire is never opened without orders.'

'Yes. But more precisely, Petty Officer Ramm. On this occasion. If you follow me.'

'Yes, sir,' Ramm said reluctantly. 'Before sending the ack-ack crews to the close-range weapons, sir, I issued the order for no firing unless specifically ordered.'

Again Finnegan nodded. 'Featherstonehaugh, were you or were you not, aware of this order?'

'I was, sir.'

'And was it,' Finnegan asked, knowing the answer, 'countermanded by anyone on the bridge?'

Featherstonehaugh shook his head. 'No, sir.' He paused briefly. 'I opened fire, really without thinking, when I saw the trouble on A deck.'

'Right,' Finnegan said. It would be as well if the OD offered no further evidence at this stage. Finnegan said, 'Commodore's report,' and nodded at Ramm. 'Carry on, please, Petty Officer Ramm.'

147

'Aye, aye, sir.' Ramm saluted. 'Commodore's report, on cap, salute the officer, about turn, double march, down the ladder, fall in on A deck.' Finnegan watched him go, feeling immense sympathy for what must be Featherstonehaugh's state of mind. Slowly, he climbed to the bridge. He found Kemp in his usual place, standing in the starboard wing, body braced against the guardrail, using his binoculars to scan the seas and the ships moving along sedately, the shepherd watching his flocks by night and day. Finnegan saluted the turned back.

'Commodore, sir?'

'Yes, Finnegan.' Kemp turned round, lowering the binoculars to the limit of the codline preventer. 'Well?'

'Placed in your report. Full admission.'

Kemp gave a short laugh. 'Obviously! Nothing further?'

'He opened fire without thinking, sir. What I'd call an automatic response, I guess. Do the same myself.'

'We're not considering hypothetical situations, Finnegan, or what you would do.' Kemp paused. 'What's your opinion?'

Finnegan shrugged. 'Guy's honest and straightforward, I guess. And if he did aim for the kraut . . . well, killing krauts is what the war's all about. Isn't it?'

'Not prisoners-of-war, Finnegan. Clear your mind on that, for God's sake! And don't get sentimental –'

Finnegan's eyes widened. 'Me, sir? Sentimental?'

'Yes, you, sir. Sentimental. Sympathy doesn't come into this . . . though God knows I do understand.' Kemp's mind was with his two sons, serving the King at sea as he was himself. If one of them should be killed, and he had a Nazi in his sights, POW or not . . . he couldn't be sure what his reaction would be. Probably responsible enough; he was too old, too accustomed to command, too experienced in controlling his feelings to let those deep and instinctive feelings get the better of him. But a younger man, a much younger and more callow man, might respond quite differently and in that category he had to place his own sons. Either of them, given a similar set of circumstances, might have been in Featherstonehaugh's shoes. Once again, as Finnegan stood there waiting for him to go on, Kemp forced the mental images from his mind. He was jumping the gun. Featherstonehaugh, he reminded himself for the tenth time, very likely had had no such intention.

He looked at his wrist-watch. He was about to tell Finnegan that he was going below to his cabin for five minutes when a rating came up the bridge ladder and approached with a signal form in his hand. 'Cypher from Flag Officer Gibraltar, sir.' He passed it over. Kemp glanced at it and handed it to Finnegan.

'Prefix Most Immediate, Finnegan. See to it at once.'

Finnegan went below to get his decyphering tables out of Kemp's safe. He was back on the bridge within twenty minutes with the plain language version. Kemp read, CS23 repeated Convoy Commodore, German raider Stuttgart reported in position 30 degrees east 22 degrees 25 minutes north, course south, estimated speed 25 knots, now disappeared into fog. Time of origin 0933 GMT.

Kemp called to Maconochie and went with him to the chart room, where Maconochie noted the positions of his own ship and the raider. Laying off the distance between, he said, 'Around 200 miles ahead. Closing speed . . . forty knots. A little over two days.'

'And then that's it,' Kemp said. 'That's it – and no word of the Duke of York.'

Commodore and Captain went out to the open bridge. Nothing was said between them, but Kemp's mind was racing. The heavy guns of the Stuttgart . . . the convoy had nothing to match them. All would now depend upon the arrival of the Home Fleet battleship from Scapa Flow. If she failed to turn up, the convoy would be decimated. The only heavy ship the convoy had was the Vindictive, due shortly to detach to her Freetown base. No doubt she would be ordered to remain, but her guns too would be no match for the Stuttgart.

Kemp and Maconochie waited now for messages from the senior officer of the cruiser escort. In the meantime there was a tacit agreement that it was as yet too soon to warn the passengers as a whole. The report would of course be communicated to OC troops, but it was to remain strictly in the confines of the orderly room until Kemp broke silence throughout the ship.

149

FIFTEEN

The orders had come quickly from cs23: the convoy would alter
course north-westerly in the hope of bringing the ships to the
westward of the *Stuttgart*'s estimated course. With luck, they
would stand clear of the raider, then alter again to make the
rendezvous with the *Duke of York*. As they made their northing
there might be an aerial reconnaisance by the enemy long-range
Focke-Wulfs and if they were picked up then the *Stuttgart* would
inevitably be homed onto them. If there was an encounter the
convoy would be scattered on orders from the Commodore, and
the escort would stand and fight to the last, putting themselves
between the enemy and the valuable troopships and cargo
vessels. In the meantime *Vindictive* would detach in accordance
with previous orders: she had reported to the senior officer of the
escort that she had insufficient oil fuel in her bunkers to remain at
sea beyond Freetown, not having fuelled off Ascension since she
had intended taking on fuel at her Freetown base.

Kemp cursed, but said, 'Fortunes of war, Maconochie. We've
all been relying on the *Duke of York* turning up before we met the
Stuttgart.' He paused, then turned to Finnegan. 'Exercise guns'
crews, Finnegan, till they drop.'

'I'll do that, sir. But they can do the drill in their sleep by
now.'

Kemp grunted. 'I'm glad to hear it. If we scatter, they'll be all
we've got.'

Captain Mulvaney, having promulgated Colonel Harrison's
orders for engagement to the Australian company commanders,

150

went below to fulfil an engagement of his own. He tapped at Gloria Northway's cabin door.

She was irritable. 'What's been keeping you?' she asked.

'Routine. Work. Not like some.' Mulvaney had sealed lips by order, though he failed to see the point. All aboard were going to have to know sooner or later, unless the Commodore intended saying nothing at all if they managed to evade the *Stuttgart*. Maybe there was sense in that.

He threw his bush hat onto a chair and stripped off his khaki-drill jacket. Miss Northway watched him sardonically. She said, 'Don't bother with the trousers.'

He stared, trousers waistband already slackened. 'Eh? What 'you mean, don't bother with the trousers?'

'What I say. Something's happened.'

'What's bloody happened?'

'Don't sound so damn truculent, and don't make out you're that dumb. Men who come from whatsit, the Murrumbidgee, didn't come down with the last shower. Or that's what you once said.'

Mulvaney ticked over. 'Bloody hell, girl, so that's it, eh?'

'That's it,' she said. 'Sorry, but there it is. Time of the month and all that.'

'Bloody sudden,' Mulvaney said angrily.

'That's the way it goes. Caught on the hop.' She added, 'There'll be other times before we get to the Clyde, don't worry yourself.'

Captain Mulvaney resecured his trousers, put his tunic on again, took up his bush hat and stormed out of the cabin. Bloody women, he thought, they're all the same, lead you on and then go and get the curse. Or maybe she hadn't; maybe she'd just changed her mind . . . but he didn't think she had. Captain Mulvaney from the Murrumbidgee was a real man and women didn't turn real men down. Not in his experience. But she should have got her dates worked out better and not got him all worked up in anticipation. That rankled. Sod the woman.

He didn't see Gregory Hench at the end of the alleyway when he stormed out of Miss Northway's cabin, but Hench saw him very clearly and it gave him a jolt. Hench had intended going himself to Gloria's cabin. He'd had a sudden feeling things might turn out all right and he'd meant to take advantage before that particular urge subsided.

151

Now he turned away. It *had* subsided. He knew he would be n⸱
match for Mulvaney. After that sighting, he simply couldn't. H⸱
went instead to the B deck lounge and ordered a large whisky.

Brigadier Pumphrey-Hatton's mind nagged away at th⸱
wretched matter of the two ratings involved in the fracas at th⸱
Cape, men of whose names he had made a note on recognizing
them. He had yet to decide what to do about them. Currentl⸱
they were probably laughing at him behind his back. Meanwhile
having observed the extra gun-drills currently in progress, h⸱
had another ground for complaint, since he realized the signifi
cance of the drills as the Commodore's assistant stood by th⸱
exercising, sweating crews with a stop-watch in his hand. Th⸱
closing-up, the opening time after time of the breech-block, th⸱
thrust of the ram as an imaginary projectile and charge wer⸱
loaded, the shouts of the petty officers as the breech-blocks wer⸱
slammed shut and the gunlayers swung onto imaginary target⸱
. . . the repeated exercising of the misfire procedure, for ancien
naval guns were prone to misfires at critical moments . . . it al
had the unmistakable sound of much urgency. To Pumphrey
Hatton urgency meant only one thing: the German raider wa⸱
believed to be in the vicinity.

And he had not been informed.

As a matter of courtesy he should have been. The Commodor⸱
and OC Troops were slighting him. He began to tremble as tha
realization came to him. He might have no official standin⸱
aboard the *Aurelian Star* but he remained a brigadier of the Britis⸱
Army on active service and as such he was not going to b⸱
disregarded.

He stalked away towards the orderly room, shaking, his ange⸱
boiling up inside him. On the way he passed the entry to the ⸱
deck lounge. He hesitated, then turned back. He went inside
went to the bar, where he stood in preference to sitting like ⸱
lounge lizard on a stool. He felt vaguely unwell. Not gin today
'Brandy,' he said to the bar steward. 'Courvoisier.'

'No Courvoisier, sir. Only Van der Humm.'

'Damn. All right.'

'Coming up, sir.' MacInnes turned away. Pumphrey-Hatto⸱
became aware of a person on a stool nearby.

This person wished him good morning.

'Good morning. Hench, isn't it?'

'That's right, Brigadier.'

'I remember. Told you not to overdo the drink. And that awful woman. No good to you at all, Tench.'

'Hench –'

'Don't damn well argue. I'm sick and tired of being damn well disregarded.'

Hench gave a laugh. 'Snap.' He sounded bitter.

'What?'

'Snap. So am I. Fed up with being –'

'Ah. You, too? That woman?'

'Yes,' Hench said viciously.

The Van der Humm arrived. Pumphrey-Hatton took it, examined it closely, then knocked it back and demanded another. He said, 'I did tell you. If you can't take advice, then you've only yourself to blame. I think I also said, don't do anything silly. Remember?'

'No,' Hench said.

Pumphrey-Hatton shook with anger. 'Damn stupid,' he said in a high, almost hysterical voice. 'I . . .' His voice tailed away and suddenly he seemed to crumple. He slid to the deck, knocking over a stool. The Van der Humm spilled over his uniform, the glass broke.

Hench stared. 'My God,' he said. He remained as though rooted to his stool. MacInnes came round the bar, asked Hench for assistance. Hench didn't react; it was old Colonel Holmes who came across and helped MacInnes to carry the limp form to a settee. MacInnes felt for a pulse. 'Alive,' he said. 'I'll put out a call for the doctor.'

Yeoman of Signals Lambert had happened to look in at the w/t office when the leading telegraphist was picking up an overseas broadcast from Germany. The tones of the broadcaster were nasal. 'Lord Haw-Haw,' Lambert said. 'Stand by for a laugh, eh?'

William Joyce, British subject, traitor who spread propaganda for Adolf Hitler, trying to undermine the morale of the home front, had long been dubbed Lord Haw-Haw. Earlier in the war he had constantly asked the question over the air, 'Where is the *Ark Royal*?' in reference to Britain's newest and largest aircraft carrier, the inference being that she had been sunk and the British

153

public had not been told by a cowardly Admiralty. In fact, though she had later been sunk by submarine attack a little east of the Gibraltar Strait, she was at the time of Lord Haw-Haw's queries very much in being. That had been one of Lord Haw-Haw's boobs; but mostly he had been extraordinarily accurate in his war news. It was supposed that he had any number of informers inside Britain who made clandestine radio contact with Berlin, men and women who described with deadly precision the air attacks that had been made the night before. Lambert himself had heard Lord Haw-Haw speak of local damage, Pompey damage: Haw-Haw had told Britain of the massive attack by the *Luftwaffe* on the Royal Naval Barracks in early 1941, when the petty officers' block had been demolished by a land mine, with more land mines smashing onto the parade ground and the air raid shelters beneath. Lambert had heard him speak of a terrace in Arundel Street that had taken a direct hit and had mostly gone up in flame and rubble. Lord Haw-Haw had spoken of the demolition of Palmerston Road in Southsea, of the total destruction of what had been Handley's Corner. Lord Haw-Haw had known his stuff. He had said in that peculiarly offensive nasal tone, 'The naval officers of the Portsmouth base and their families will never again dilly-dally over coffee and biscuits in Handley's cafe next to the china and glass department nor use the old-fashioned lift like a mobile parrot's cage . . .'

To naval personnel serving overseas such a broadcast would have struck home very forcibly. And it had been the same all over the country. The result could have been devastating, could have impressed people with the perspicacity of Germany's all-seeing eye, could have made them fearful of their own neighbours. But that had never happened: Lord Haw-Haw had become a comic turn even though he was known to speak the truth on most occasions. He had become compulsive listening, enlivening many an evening of short rations and a huddling in thick clothing over almost non-existent fires in winter. He was as popular as Tommy Handley in It's That Man Again, as popular as Much-Binding-In-The-Marsh.

'What's he on about now?' Lambert asked.

The leading telegraphist put a finger to his mouth. Lambert listened.

'. . . told me by, let us say, a little bird. Are you listening, down here in the South Atlantic?'

Lambert stiffened, stubbed out a fag-end in a handy ashtray. Lord Haw-Haw went on, 'Are you listening, Commodore Kemp? Are you still acting the good shepherd of your convoy aboard the *Aurelian Star*, bound for the Firth of Clyde, and home? If you are listening I have, I'm sorry to say, some bad news for you.' There was a pause. 'Your son, Sub-Lieutenant Harry Kemp, has been drowned at sea when his ship was sunk by action of one of our U-boats. . . .'

Lambert's face had gone white; he listened for a moment longer, but Lord Haw-Haw had gone on to other matters, describing the fate of more than a hundred people, men, women and children, in a cinema in south-east London that had taken a direct hit the night before.

'I'll be buggered,' Lambert said in a voice little above a whisper. 'That's bloody horrible.'

The leading telegraphist said, 'Typical, is that. Will the Old Man have heard?'

'Not on the bridge, no. I wonder . . . will somebody tell him?' The answer was a shrug. 'Wouldn't care for the job myself, 'eo.'

'Nor me neither. I'll have a word with Mr Finnegan, see what he thinks – leave it up to him. He and the Commodore, they seem to understand one another.' Lambert paused. 'I reckon he'll *have* to be told, and you know why as well as I do. That Haw-Haw . . . he knows where we are, what our orders are for the Clyde. You know what that means, eh? What with the bloody *Stuttgart* and all . . .'

'. . . eart attack,' Dr Grant said succinctly. He stood up. 'Get him down to his cabin,' he said to MacInnes. 'I'll treat him there. He'll pull through, I believe, it's not too serious.' He added. 'Can you rustle up a couple of hands with a Neil Robinson stretcher?'

'Yes, sir. Leave it to me, sir.'

'Sister Forman'll go with the stretcher party.' MacInnes got on the phone to the second steward, and two men came up within the next couple of minutes, carrying a stretcher. Pumphrey-Hatton was carried below, the ship's nursing sister walking beside him along the cabin alleyways. Outside in the lobby was

Petty Officer Biggar, and Biggar happened to see the face in the stretcher as the party came past him, out of the lounge door to head for the ladder down to the accommodation decks. Biggar moved away thoughtfully and went in search of Leading Seaman Purkiss, who was having a smoke by the guardrail aft, it being stand-easy.

He retailed what he had seen.

Purkiss gave a low whistle. 'May let us off the 'ook, PO.'

'Yes. If he 'appens to kick the bucket, that is.'

'How did 'e look, eh?'

'White. Or sort of parchment. Face gone all thin like.'

Purkiss nodded. 'Not too good?'

'No, I'd say not. So here's hoping, eh? Looks like the good Lord'll provide.'

Purkiss clicked his tongue. 'That's bloody blasphemious, PO.'

'Much you care, eh? And don't be bloody impertinent, all right?'

Finnegan came up the ladder to the bridge. Kemp asked, 'How's the invalid now, Finnegan?'

'Haven't enquired, sir. But I guess he's okay. The doc didn't seem worried, so Sister Forman said.'

Kemp grinned. 'So you did make some sort of enquiry? If only as an excuse to chat up the nursing sister.'

Finnegan didn't comment; there was a formality about his manner. He began to fidget and said, 'Commodore, sir.'

Kemp raised an eyebrow. 'Well?'

'I guess . . . well, if I could have a word.'

'With me?'

'That's so.'

'Here I am,' Kemp said impatiently, 'so go ahead.'

Finnegan hesitated, not meeting Kemp's eye now. He said, 'In your cabin, sir?'

Kemp frowned. 'In my cabin? What have you been up to, young Finnegan?'

'Nothing, sir. It's not me. But I guess it's – it's important.'

'Oh, very well, if you must.' Kemp called across to the Officer of the Watch that he would be in his cabin if required, then went down the ladder with Finnegan.

*

Pumphrey-Hatton, given a sedative, slept for some hours. When he awoke, Sister Forman was sitting by the side of his bunk. Jane Forman was a cheerful girl with a placid expression that the uncharitable called cow-like. Her figure tended to stoutness. Being cheerful, and seeing the signs of life as the patient's eyes opened and he stared around somewhat vacantly, she spoke brightly.

'How do we feel now?' she asked.

Pumphrey-Hatton focussed. 'I don't know how *you* feel, my good woman. I feel bloody.'

'That's only to be expected. We'll feel better soon, won't we?'

'How the devil do I know?'

'Because I say so.' Sister Forman had been put out by being addressed as 'my good woman'. She went on, 'Now we'll make you all comfy, shall we.' She lifted Pumphrey-Hatton's head gently and fluffed at the pillow, straightened the sheet over the recumbent body. 'There. That's better, isn't it?'

Pumphrey-Hatton said disagreeably, 'Will you kindly tell me what's wrong with me?'

'That's up to Doctor,' she said in a reproving tone. 'He'll be along just as soon as I tell him we've come round –'

'Oh, for God's sake, woman! Kindly remember I'm singular, not plural. *I've* come round. *We* haven't. And I've had a heart attack. Haven't I?'

Sister Forman busied herself at the wash-basin. 'Well,' she said. 'P'raps Doctor will say that, I don't know. But we're – you're doing very well so there's no need to worry about –'

'Oh, go away, woman, and fetch the doctor.'

'Oh, very well.' Looking hurt Sister Forman left the cabin. Pumphrey-Hatton glared after her. He disliked being fussed over and he disliked nurses; they were a bossy, interfering bunch. And he had no intention of finishing the voyage in his bunk. Confined to his cabin he would be angered beyond measure by his electric fan and his wash-basin, and there might well be flies in the vicinity of the equator, and he had yet to deal with his attackers, Biggar and Purkiss. He felt groggy when he tried to sit up, and he broke out in a profuse sweat. But that nurse woman had said he'd feel better soon. One had to assume she knew her job. When he felt better he would get up and that would be that, nurse or no nurse, doctor or no doctor. After a while, staring at the deckhead, he saw a fly. Worse than a fly: it was, he believed, a bluebottle. He couldn't have that. By the side of his bunk was a magazine, a very old copy of the *London Illustrated News*. He reached out and rolled it up.

Sister Forman was reporting to Dr Grant that her patient had woken up and seemed likely to prove a difficult and very rude man, when Pumphrey-Hatton, standing on his bunk and feeling groggier than ever but flailing away at the bluebottle, if such it was, suddenly clutched at his chest and fell, landing in a heap on the cabin deck.

The news went quickly round the troopship, together with Dr Grant's theory of what had happened, reconstructing from the rolled-up magazine, the continuing presence of the bluebottle on the deckhead, and the well-known antipathy of the brigadier towards flies and such.

'Killed by a blue-arsed fly,' Leading Seaman Purkiss said in something like awe that Petty Officer Biggar's thoughts had borne fruit so quickly. 'Would you bloody well believe it, PO?'

'It's fact, anyway. You don't speak ill of the dead, I know that and respect it like. But I can't deny it's a relief. Almost like it was meant to 'appen. Providence, see?'

In the chart room aboard the *Stuttgart* a conference was being held. Present with the Captain were his navigating officer, the gunnery and torpedo officers and the radar and communications officers.

The *Stuttgart* was now within twenty-four hours' steaming of the northbound convoy. Captain von Bellinghausen's face was formidable as he outlined his plan of attack, emphasizing with blows of his fist on the chart table the great glory that would accrue to the Third Reich and to his ship's company if an important troop convoy was successfully attacked. A number of Iron Crosses of the Military Division were likely to be awarded.

'I propose to open fire the moment the convoy is sighted, gentlemen,' Captain von Bellinghausen said. 'The first point of aim is to be the ship of the Convoy Commodore – the *Aurelian Star*. At the same time as I open fire with my heavy batteries the escort will increase speed towards the convoy.' The raider was accompanied by four destroyers, one on either bow, one ahead nd one astern acting as rearguard. 'They will go in amongst the hips of the convoy and will fire their torpedoes. We must naturally expect opposition from the convoy's escort, but as you now, gentlemen, the British escort has no battleship, whilst its ight cruisers have no armament that can match our eight-inch atteries.' He paused, seeing that his gunnery officer was nxious to speak. 'Yes, Schürer?'

'The British battleship *Duke of York*, Herr Kapitan. Is she not –'

'There has been a signal a matter of minutes ago from the Naval Command in Wilhelmshavn, Schürer. The sailing of the *Duke of York* was delayed. So very British a delay – a dispute with their rade unions. We in Germany are fortunate that our Führer has ever in Germany permitted such stupid disputes. *Heil, Hitler!*'

The dutiful chorus of *heils* came. Von Bellinghausen continued. The British battleship is believed to be currently no closer than ve hundred miles westward of Cape Finisterre. We shall not be othered by her, and we shall destroy the convoy. When that has een achieved, then we shall head at once, but not directly, for Germany. There will be many warships searching for us, but we hall set our course westwards towards the vicinity of Venezuela nd then head east and north for the Denmark Strait. There will e dangers but we shall overcome them – with the assurance that he Reich has God on its side. God and our Führer, gentlemen, annot be defeated.'

There was a lengthy dissertation on the various technical details f navigation and ship-handling after the attack, talk about equent alterations of course and other ways of evading the ritish who would be bent upon a swift revenge. Von ellinghausen refrained from drawing any comparisons between he sinking of the British battle-cruiser *Hood* and the subsequent wift pursuit and destruction of the mighty *Bismarck*; there was othing to be gained from gloom. The *Stuttgart* was going into the ttack and afterwards she would steam safe home to glory and hat was all about it.

When the conference broke off the various heads of depart- ents went about their duties to their parts of ship. In the big urrets the gunner's mates put their guns'-crews through their aces for the hundredth time; the torpedo crews were exercised me and time again aboard the *Stuttgart* and the destroyers of the scort. In the engine-rooms extra checks were made of the propelling machinery and all bearings were examined and given an injection from the oil-cans. The telegraphs were checked dummy runs to ensure that orders from the bridge were transmitted to the starting platform without delay due to any mechanical fault. All the electrics were checked and double checked throughout the ship. Every man worked at the peak of efficiency. The honour of the Third Reich was the guarantee of that; a notable blow was to be struck, hammer-like, at Britain and the monster Churchill to the glory of the Führer and his so-victorious Navy.

Next morning, after dawn action stations had been fallen out the final accolade reached the *Stuttgart*: a cypher had been received in the main receiving room deep below the ship's armoured belt. Captain von Bellinghausen, when this signal had been de-cyphered, read it himself to all his ship's company over the internal broadcasting equipment.

'May God be with you,' von Bellinghausen read in a voice that shook with the emotion of the moment, 'in your so splendid bravery and loyalty to the Third Reich that will last a thousand years.'

It was from the Führer himself. The ship rang with cheering.

SIXTEEN

Finnegan left the Commodore's cabin, went into the pantry next door and spoke to Kemp's steward. 'Commodore's had bad news, I guess, Horton. Wouldn't hurt to take him in a whisky.'

'Commodore doesn't drink at sea, Mr Finnegan –'

'I know. Just this once, all right?'

Finnegan went back to the bridge, had a word with the Officer of the Watch. Captain Maconochie was in the wheelhouse, using the voicepipe to the engine-room. Finnegan moved into Kemp's position in the starboard wing of the bridge. He was very concerned about the Commodore. Kemp had said little, had seemed to be in a state of shock. That was far from surprising. Finnegan had stressed that since the name was known, Harry Kemp must have been picked up and that anyway the word had come only from Lord Haw-Haw, who could be, probably was, wrong. But Kemp had known all about Lord Haw-Haw's curious ability to get at the facts. He'd heard that from his wife among others. On leave once, Mary had told him that Lord Haw-Haw had announced, after German aircraft, chased by Spitfires, had ditched some bombs over a nearby village, that a certain Mrs Brampton, address given, had had her house taken out by a direct hit. Mrs Brampton, Lord Haw-Haw had said, had two daughters named Lilly and Lucy who attended Queen Anne's School in Caversham, Reading. Mrs Brampton had been killed but her husband Tony, who worked in the Bank of England, had been away for the night and was safe. Lord Haw-Haw had added, as a sort of throw-away line, that Mrs Brampton's bridge-playing friends would miss her.

Mary had been one of the bridge addicts and had known just how correct all the details were.

Kemp, standing by the square port of his cabin and staring out across the troopship's fore decks, hadn't moved when Finnegan had asked in embarrassment if there was anything he could do. Finnegan had had to repeat the question.

'Thank you, Finnegan. No.'

Finnegan had then left him alone with his thoughts and his anguish.

Within the next quarter of an hour Kemp was back on the bridge. His face, very pale, was set into hard lines that deterred any expressions of sympathy. The only reference he made to the broadcast from Germany was made obliquely to Maconochie.

'There seems a likelihood that the *Stuttgart* is homing onto the convoy, Captain. We could be in action at any time after about the next twelve hours. Before that happens, we'll need to carry out a sea burial. Pumphrey-Hatton. I shall attend, of course.'

Maconochie nodded. 'I suggest the afternoon watch. Three bells.' He paused: currently this was a fraught situation. He said, 'I'll have the bosun informed.' Bosun Barnes would have to see to the preparations, the plank, the Union Flag, the canvas shroud, the bearer party. Bearers were, it seemed, on the Commodore's mind as well.

He said, 'We'll have to liaise with Harrison. Or Carter – or both. The bearer party must come from the military.' His tone was expressionless. 'Pumphrey-Hatton . . . a difficult man but very much a soldier. I'm wondering if he'd prefer a native guard or an Australian one. I believe he'd have preferred the rifles. Same sort of traditions as a regiment from home.' Kemp half turned his head. 'Finnegan?'

'Yes, sir, Commodore?'

'Take soundings. We don't want to hurt any feelings.'

Finnegan went below and made contact with both colonels. The sea committal was carried out as planned at three bells in the afternoon watch. The bearer party was provided by the riflemen, Colonel Harrison being only too glad to spare his Australians the duty. It was, however, the Australian padre who conducted the service with both Kemp and Maconochie in attendance. Among the immediate attendance were Colonel and Mrs Holmes

162

Mildred had been reluctant; she disliked funerals and there was something extra about a funeral conducted in the midst of possible terrible danger to them all; but Holmes had insisted. It was their duty: the late brigadier had been one of themselves.

During the short service it was observed that the Commodore had tears in his eyes. By this time all aboard knew the reason why. Mildred Holmes remarked *sotto voce* to her husband that Lord Haw-Haw ought to be shot.

'After the war,' Holmes said, 'he will be.'

The absence of the heavy cruiser *Vindictive* had made itself felt once she had detached for the Freetown base. There was a naked feeling, a feeling of being exposed. The biggest warship now left was the escort carrier *Rameses* and she hadn't a great deal of speed and manoeuvrability, and her guns were not of heavy calibre – her Barracuda torpedo-bombers and her Seafire fighters, the naval equivalent of the land-based Spitfires, were her armament. They might well be called upon. Before the light faded that afternoon, they were. A signal was flashed to the Commodore from the senior officer of the escort, informing him that *Rameses* had been ordered to fly off one of her Barracudas to spot ahead, searching out the oncoming German raider. If contact was made, the Barracuda would refrain from attacking and would return to the carrier to make its report. *Rameses* would then fly off her full squadron and the convoy would deviate westwards in an attempt to stand clear of the *Stuttgart*. It would be up to the Commodore thereafter if and when he ordered the merchant ships to scatter.

'Always a tricky decision,' Kemp said. 'There's danger either way. You can stay and maybe form a compact target, or you can risk being caught without the escort. So we'll play it by ear when the time comes.'

There was another point to be considered now: the signalling between the Commodore and the escort would have been noted from the troopship's decks and obviously the flying-off of aircraft from the carrier was going to be very plain to see. Kemp said, 'The time's come to give them the facts, Captain.'

Maconochie agreed. Kemp, as signs of activity were seen on the carrier's flight deck, went to the Tannoy in the wheelhouse. His words were brief and to the point. 'This is the Commodore speaking. *Rameses* is about to fly off aircraft on a spotting mission.

Troops must not crowd the starboard side to watch, since to do s⌐
would bring us too heavy a list.' He paused, cleared his throa⌐
His voice was unaccustomedly husky. 'It is believed the Germa⌐
raider is coming down upon the convoy from the north. You ma⌐
all be sure I shall take avoiding action in good time once th⌐
Stuttgart's position is known. I am expecting to rendezvous wit⌐
HMS *Duke of York* shortly.'

That was all; 'shortly' was but a hope. Kemp believed th⌐
battleship to be still well to the north. It was perhaps too much t⌐
hope that she would intercept the *Stuttgart* before the latte⌐
picked up the convoy. But if by some chance she did, then her b⌐
guns should make short work of the German.

Within the next ten minutes a lone Barracuda was seen to b⌐
taking off from the carrier. The sound of its engines was hear⌐
aboard the *Aurelian Star* as she cleared the flight deck and gaine⌐
height, heading north to seek out the enemy. Gregory Henc⌐
heard it from his stool in the B deck lounge, the stool to which h⌐
seemed anchored. Miss Northway heard it as she came up fro⌐
her cabin to take a walk on deck and worry about the immediat⌐
future. She was looking for Captain Mulvaney but failed to fin⌐
him amongst the troops thronging the upper decks. In the loung⌐
she joined Hench: any company was better than none. Hench sa⌐
gloomily, nursing a double whisky just provided by MacInne⌐
He looked up as Gloria Northway joined him. He said, 'Speakin⌐
again, are we?'

'Don't be stupid. And don't sulk. You've been sulking eve⌐
since –' She broke off, realizing what she'd been about to revea⌐
not that it mattered all that much.

'Ever since what?'

'Nothing, nothing, Greg.'

'Ever since that loud-mouthed Australian screwed you.'

She laughed. 'He didn't, as a matter of simple fact.'

'Oh, yes?'

'Yes. I mean no, it's a fact he didn't. He turned up at the wron⌐
time.'

'Wrong time?'

'Oh, don't you be thick too. Anyway, he seemed offended an⌐
took himself off. Now he's sulking too, I think.'

Hench had ticked over. He said, 'In a few days' time he won⌐
be.'

'Maybe not,' she agreed. 'That is, if we're still around. You heard the Commodore's broadcast, I take it?'

He nodded, and ordered another large whisky and a gin for Gloria – why not? He might as well lose with a good grace, especially if they were all going to die within a day or so. He said, 'Nothing we can do about it. Except wait and see.'

'And pray.'

He jeered. 'You, pray?'

'I'm going to, Greg,' she said seriously. 'I may not be used to praying and I'm darn sure God won't be rating me very high, but . . .'

'But what?'

She took the gin from MacInnes and sipped. Then she said, 'I heard one of those Aussies talking, Greg. He said there are no atheists in a fox-hole. I think he was right.'

Hench didn't answer; he stared down into his whisky, into the comforting amber glow. Maybe that was his God. If you were going to die, what better way to go than pissed as a newt so you felt no pain? He signed a chit for another large Scotch.

Below decks, others worried about the prospects for a safe arrival in the Firth of Clyde. The Holmeses worried, though the old colonel tried not to show it. It was, of course, Mildred whom he worried about rather than himself. He was a soldier. Death in action was always on the cards for a soldier from the moment he left Sandhurst or his regimental training depot. A wife was different. But if one of them was left – either one – what would become of the other? Holmes couldn't begin to visualize life without Mildred. Love and companionship apart, he would be lost. He couldn't even boil an egg – had never had to. Servants in pre-war Britain, native houseboys in Africa . . . life on his own in England would be insupportable. And Mildred, if she was left and he had gone? Of course it was easier for a woman, women were domestic creatures anyway and they could cope better. But she would be in a financial mess, only a widow's pension to live on, a pittance when based on his service pay of so many years before when the pay of officers had been itself a pittance.

After the Commodore's broadcast Holmes put his arms around his wife and held her close. He told her that he loved her; she said she knew that though it had been a long time since he'd said so;

165

and she loved him. She said quietly, 'If you go, Stephen, I shall follow you. I mean that.'

'Oh no,' he said. 'No. Don't think about it, my dear. It isn't going to happen. Commodore Kemp –'

'He's not God,' she said. Holmes could think of no adequate response to that.

Once again Chief Steward Chatfield was gathering up his overtime sheets and other documents concerned with payments and stores requisitions. Never mind a sinking if it came, the Superintending Chief Steward ashore in Liverpool would demand all relevant bumph. Life – or death, come to that – was like that, you always had to show a chit.

The photograph of Roxanne went in with the bumph; she would be nicely cushioned by the stewards' overtime. Chatfield was still worried about that Morris Eight as he prepared to face German gunfire and maybe leave Roxanne a widow though possibly not a sorrowing one. Chatfield's mind switched to his home: all his furniture, his bits and pieces, things that had come down from his mum and dad, from his grandparents too. Things that in many cases had not appealed to Roxanne. The stuffed owl beneath a glass dome that had been his dad's pride; the reproduction of a painting, *The Monarch of the Glen*, in which an antlered stag on a mountain-side stared arrogantly at a bit of Scotland; an antimacassar, pink and blue stitching, that his gran had laboured over for hours; a chocolate tin that had been presented by Queen Victoria to his uncle along with all the other troops on active service in the Boer War; a po that his dad had bought in Arundel and was said to have been used by Queen Victoria on one of her visits to the Duke of Norfolk at Arundel Castle. It was now in Chatfield's parlour, in use as a receptacle for a pot plant. Things like that, all treasured, though not by Roxanne. Roxanne didn't like what she called antiques; she was all art deco, modern stuff. Now, if he went, the stuffed owl and all the rest would no doubt pass to the sod he still didn't know was called Cocky Bulstrode. Either that, or it would all be chucked out as junk.

It was a nasty thought, with the bloody *Stuttgart* no doubt all set to blow the *Aurelian Star* out of the water. It wasn't bloody right. Wasn't bloody right at all. Chief Steward Chatfield reflected on the air raids on Southampton. Maybe a bomb would sort out the Morris Eight. The Lord, Chatfield understood, moved in a mysterious way and in so doing was wont to sort out the good from the bad. Chatfield had always been an honest man. Well – more or less; he was, after all, a chief steward and perks were perks, anyone knew that.

Within minutes of the returning Barracuda's approach to the carrier's round-down and its hook being caught by the arrestor wires stretched across the flight deck, Kemp had been informed by the lamp flashing from cs23's bridge that contact had been made with the *Stuttgart*, which was approximately seventy-five miles ahead of the convoy's track and steaming south at an estimated 25 knots. While Kemp and Maconochie conferred with Chief Engineer French and the officers of the trooping staff, the torpedo-bomber squadron took off from the *Rameses* and headed north on their killing mission. Kemp was reserved as to their chances.

'The German's got fairly massive ack-ack,' he said. 'And Barracudas aren't all that manoeuvrable. We'll still be very vulnerable.' Already the convoy had altered away from the raider's track, steaming west-nor'-westerly and maintaining the zig-zag against possible U-boat attack. 'We may be lucky and miss her – it's a chance either way. We may come inside radar range, in which case she'll home onto us, but –'

'Are you going to scatter the convoy, Commodore?' This was oc Troops. Kemp shook his head.

'Not yet, Colonel. Time enough for that when we get a further report from the aircraft.'

'Not much time surely? Closing speed, what, 40 knots or so? She'll be on us within a couple of hours.'

'Yes, I know. If she finds us. But she'll be engaged by the escort, don't forget. The escort's the only screen we have and I have to consider that.' Kemp's face was grey with tiredness and anxiety: he could be making the wrong decision, he was always aware of that. But there were the risks inseparable from any scatter order, the over-riding risk that individual ships on their own could become easy prey to a U-boat . . . the whole idea behind the convoy concept was that there was safety in numbers. Not always, though; and it was Kemp's responsibility to decide.

167

As the conference broke up, Kemp thought suddenly about Featherstonehaugh, whom he had yet to see. It wasn't fair on anyone to keep him hanging on but certainly now was not the time. Once the threat from the *Stuttgart* was over and done with, the matter would be a first priority.

The reconnoitring aircraft had not approached within range of the *Stuttgart*'s AA armament; but she had been spotted by the German lookouts shortly after the radar had picked her up on the screen. Captain von Bellinghausen was not unduly worried: the presence of a carrier with the convoy's escort had been known but von Bellinghausen had full confidence in the ability of his anti-aircraft gunners to deflect any bombing or torpedo attack. Those gunners would put up a virtually impenetrable shield of lead and shrapnel, and the British would go down like ninepins.

Nevertheless, it was plain that the British convoy would now know for certain of the presence of the *Stuttgart*; therefore it would be necessary to re-think the situation, just a little, in order to outwit the enemy. Von Bellinghausen tried to, as it were, insert himself into the mind of the British commander. The British were a wily race; where the German, or at any rate the Prussian, mind was straightforward and forthright, the British mind twisted and turned so that it was very difficult indeed to determine what they might be expected to do next . . .

Captain von Bellinghausen spoke to his navigating officer. 'Clearly the British will alter course.'

'*Ja, Herr Kapitan.*'

'In which direction would you expect them to alter, Friske?'

Friske said confidently, 'To the east, *Herr Kapitan*, in order to remain closer to the shore of Africa. There is the British base at Freetown in Sierra Leone –'

'You believe they may run for Freetown, Friske?'

'It is possible, yes, *Herr Kapitan*.'

Von Bellinghausen stalked his navigating bridge; he was deep in thought. There was truth in what Friske had said, but von Bellinghausen was doubtful. If to run for the safety of the Rokel River and its filthy native Kroos in their deplorable dug-out canoes with persons defecating over the sides was what the British would think that he, von Bellinghausen, would think . . . then their duplicity would have to be matched by his own wits.

The British might in fact move westerly while the *Stuttgart* moved easterly and then he would miss his prize.

It was a quandary, but not for long. Von Bellinghausen made up his mind. 'Friske,' he said, 'we alter course south-westerly. I believe the convoy will attempt to escape on a north-westerly course, hoping to outflank us and then to make their rendezvous with the battleship from Scapa Flow.'

'*Ja, Herr Kapitan.*' The navigating officer bent to the voice-pipe and passed the orders to bring the *Stuttgart* onto what was to prove a closing course with the convoy.

SEVENTEEN

The convoy had increased speed to the west-nor'-west, each ship managing to squeeze out the extra three knots that was the most Chief Engineer French could extract from his own engines. More than that and they would rattle to pieces, he had told the Commodore, might even be at risk of shearing the holding-down bolts, he had added – which was an exaggeration but not so far from the truth all the same. The ship had been continuously at sea from the beginning of the war and never enough time in port for a full engine-room overhaul.

On the bridge Kemp and Maconochie, as the sun went down in a brilliant scene of orange and green, scarlet and purple over the shores of South America far to the west, maintained an unbroken vigil of the horizon behind the ship. Their binoculars searched for the first signs of the enemy: the masts and then the funnel, indicating a ship as yet hull-down . . . and then the emerging upperworks, the bridge and the gunnery control tower, then the heavy fore batteries of the raider. The *Stuttgart* had the legs of them; once sighted, the uneven battle would be joined at once, starting with the cruisers of the escort. The destroyers and the aircraft carrier had altered to take them onto a course to intercept the enemy, while the cruisers, remaining with the convoy, stationed themselves between the merchant ships and the bearing from which the raider might be expected to appear. If the raider was sighted the cruisers would make smoke, laying a screen to hide the convoy and confuse the aim of the German gunnery controllers.

It wouldn't really help much; but it was all that could be

done. And if the German did appear, then Kemp would scatter the convoy.

The *Stuttgart* was sighted by the lookout at the foremasthead just before the sun, with a farewell blaze of colour, dipped below the horizon, sending a shaft of blinding golden brilliance across the water and silhouetting the ships against the backdrop.

Kemp said, 'Make the executive, Yeoman.'

Yeoman Lambert doubled to the signal halliards and hoisted the ready bent-on flag signal for the convoy to scatter. A few moments later thick black smoke began rolling from the cruisers' engine-room uptakes as the stokers in the boiler-rooms opened the taps to send a surge of oil fuel into the furnaces.

Two minutes later, invisibly to the ships behind the smoke-screen, there was a series of flashes as the German batteries opened.

Aboard the *Aurelian Star* and the other troopships, all hands except those required at their action stations – the naval guns'-crews, the ship's officers and engineers and those needed to man the pumps and fire hoses and so on – had been assembled at their boat stations and the embarkation deck was filled with troops and the civilian families. Gregory Hench had been prised from his bar stool by the Chief Officer, the latter making his rounds of the ship before reporting to the Captain that all crew and passenger spaces had been cleared.

Except, so far, for Hench.

'Out on deck, Mr Hench.'

'I'm all right here, thank you very much.'

'Don't thank me,' Chief Officer Dartnell said. 'The bar's shut down, or have you not noticed?'

'I've noticed.' Hench waved an arm, indicating three glasses of whisky lined up. 'Precautions.' He gave a belch.

Dartnell said, 'Out. That's an order.'

'And I,' Hench said indistinctly, 'am a fare-paying passenger. All right?'

'All wrong,' Dartnell answered crisply. He laid hold of Hench's shoulders and lifted him bodily from the stool. 'Fare-paying passengers cease to exist as such in an emergency. And when I say out, I mean out. *Out!*'

Hench made a disoriented swipe in the direction of the

171

whisky glasses. 'And you can leave those behind,' the Chief Officer said.

As, under propulsion, Hench went through the door to the open deck there came a distant whine, one that grew quickly louder as it made its approach, not more than a matter of feet above the *Aurelian Star*'s mastheads. On the bridge, the officers and ratings ducked instinctively. As a moment later Kemp straightened he heard an explosion, saw a gigantic burst of flame from a ship steaming away south on his port beam. Finnegan was at his side. '*Buckfast Abbey*,' he said. 'Dry cargo, foodstuffs mostly.'

Kemp levelled his binoculars. 'Fore part gone,' he said tautly. 'She won't make it . . . looks as though the hit was aft of the collision bulkhead. I'll give her three minutes. And God damn Hitler.'

It was in fact a little over three minutes before the freighter began her plunge. The Master had signalled that the German shell had smashed away the collision bulkhead and his pumps were unable to cope. With her fore part shattered, the *Buckfast Abbey* went down bows first and then, as the waters spread aft throughout her length, she settled briefly. Kemp saw men trying desperately to launch a lifeboat, but before the boat could be got into the water the ship went lower very suddenly and the boat, still on the falls of the davit, went down with her. Kemp saw men struggling in the sea until there was a blast of steam from her engine spaces, followed by a dull internal explosion and then she had gone.

In the meantime, the *Stuttgart* continued firing, the shells coming closer.

Hench was more than three parts drunk. He lurched about, bumping into the other passengers at his boat station. He seemed scarcely aware of the gunfire. He was by the after fall of his allotted lifeboat when the *Aurelian Star* was hit aft, a shell taking the after deck-house above the engineers' cabin alleyway. The deckhouse crumpled and fire started. The after gun's-crew were blown flat. Petty Officer Ramm was caught by a flying jag of red-hot metal that sliced through his neck. The head rolled grotesquely, fetching up against the ready-use ammunition locker. Stripey Sissons lay apparently lifeless, with both legs blown away and blood gushing from the stumps. As the rest of the gun's-crew stirred, Leading Seaman Purkiss got groggily to his feet and looked around. He saw the PO's head, and retched. Then, taking a grip, he said in a shaking voice, 'Right. I'm in charge now. Back on the gun, those that can. You, Featherstonewhat's it. Take over gunlayer.'

'Me?' Featherstonehaugh was dazed.

'Yes, you. I don't feel so good.' Suddenly, Purkiss went down flat on the deck, groaning in agony. Featherstonehaugh got down beside him. There was a spreading patch of blood from the leading seaman's stomach. The face was deathly white. Featherstonehaugh shouted at the top of his voice towards the embarkation deck, shouted for medical assistance, then went back to the gun. As a bright moon came out and beamed through the clearing smoke he could see the *Stuttgart* bearing down on the scattering ships of the convoy. She was still out of range of the troopship's inadequate, out-dated armament. Not that it mattered; Featherstonehaugh saw for the first time that the barrel was twisted into a cat's cradle and the whole mounting was tilted sideways.

On the bridge the orders had gone down for the fire parties. As the medical orderlies provided by the Australians arrived aft with Neil Robinson stretchers, a party of seamen dragged the hoses to the burning remains of the deck-house and began playing on the flames. Featherstonehaugh, in the absence of any orders, doubled for'ard to back up the crew of the fore three-inch. And Gregory Hench, whose drunken clumsiness had pitched him over the guardrail when the German shell had hit, drifted helplessly astern to wallow in the South Atlantic until a fin, slicing through the water, found him and turned for the kill. His screaming end was seen from the decks. One of those who witnessed it was Gloria Northway, though at the time she didn't know it was Hench. She gave a low, keening sound at the sheer moonlit horror of it and collapsed in a faint at the feet of Captain Mulvaney.

Kemp said, 'The German's making short work of the Barracudas, Finnegan. Four down.'

'That's right, sir. I –' Finnegan broke off as another of the cargo vessels was seen to be hit aft, a tearing explosion that had almost certainly damaged her rudder and screw. As if in confirmation the freighter swung, and began turning in a circle until she slowed to a stop. A minute later Kemp saw a flash of flame and billowing smoke from the German: one of the cruisers had scored a hit just for'ard of her bridge.

As the smoke cleared Kemp was able to see the damage: the shell had taken one of the heavy gun-turrets and the gun-barrels had drooped as if weary of action. That turret wouldn't be firing again; and one of the searchlights on the German's bridge seemed to have been put out of action in the blast.

'One up to us, sir!'

Kemp nodded. There was a glimmer of hope; if the cruisers could put more guns out of action . . . but where, in Heaven's name, was the *Duke of York*? After the raider had been sighted, wireless silence on the part of the convoy and escort had no longer been relevant and the troopship's wireless room had picked up the signals from the escort commander, indicating that the convoy was under attack. If the *Duke of York* was anywhere in the vicinity, she would surely be steaming towards them at maximum power. In theory at any rate she should show with her massive gun power at any moment.

In theory . . .

By now reports were coming in from aft: the fire was coming under control. There was no significant damage below decks. As yet there were no further hits on the convoy; the *Stuttgart*, with that one turret out of action, was being closely engaged by the escort. But, as Kemp was about to use the Tannoy to give what reassurance he could to the troops and civilians, two of the cruisers, *Marazion* and *Lydford*, were hit. *Marazion's* bridge was taken fair and square, and the director on the foremast came down mast and all on the wreckage. *Lydford* was hit on the starboard side amidships. There was a burst of smoke and flame and she took an immediate list.

Kemp felt drained of all emotion. First his son, then the possible – probable – loss of an entire convoy. And all he could do, with his popgun armament, was to stand by helplessly and watch it all happen. Or he could do the other thing, the heroic thing, and emulate Captain Fogarty Fegan of the armed merchant cruiser *Jervis Bay* and close the enemy with his popguns barking – they couldn't be said to roar – in selfless but doomed defence of his convoy. Should he?

174

It was a hard decision but an inevitable one: no. Fogarty Fegan had had no troops embarked. No civilians, no women and children. Because of them, Kemp had to stand off and await the arrival of the *Duke of York*.

Old Colonel Holmes was doing his bit. He asked permission of Purser Scott, in charge of his boat station, to absent himself so that he could circulate and talk to the riflemen in whose regiment he had served for so long, and so long ago. He spoke Swahili and he had been a familar figure, latterly as a guest, around the KEAR depot for longer than he cared to remember. So he walked, a little stiffly because of his age, among the assembled riflemen. He spoke to Sergeant Tapapa and the other NCOs, assuring them that help would arrive, that the German devils would not win and that they were in the safe and capable hands of men who knew the sea, who had sailed it all their working lives in peace and in war. He spoke to Regimental Sergeant-Major Nunn, asking if the native troops were likely to believe what he had said.

'Sir! Yes, sir, I believe they will. You are a respected gentleman, Colonel Holmes, sir, what I might call a father figure to them lot. With respect, sir.'

Holmes laughed gently. 'Yes. I'd sooner be a brother, Mr Nunn, but of course we all grow old.'

'Sir! That's a fact, sir.'

'I only hope I'm not letting them down. Giving them a false appreciation of the situation.'

'I'd say, sir, it's the only line you could have took. They want to be, well, fortified like, sir.' Nunn was standing as if on parade, ramrod-straight, immaculately turned out, Sam Browne gleaming with spit-and-polish, inevitable pace-stick at the correct angle beneath his left arm. He was, Holmes thought, almost a caricature of himself, of any pre-war warrant officer. Nunn went on, after clearing his throat rather noisily, 'Sir, if I may be so bold as to ask, sir, what do you think of the situation? Between ourselves like.'

Homes pondered for a moment, then asked, 'You don't want any devil-talk, I take it?'

'Me, sir? Oh no, sir, which is why I enquired like –'

'Yes, quite. Well, Mr Nunn, I rather think you know the answer for yourself, without my underlining it. Don't you?'

175

'I think I do, sir, yes. May I take the opportunity, sir, of asking you to take my respects to Mrs Holmes, sir. And my respects to you of course, sir. It's been a long association, sir.'

'Yes, indeed it has, Sar'nt-Major.' Holmes held out his hand knowing that this was the RSM's way of saying goodbye in case there was no other opportunity. The RSM executed a difficult manoeuvre. Grasping his pace-stick even tighter, he slammed his right hand to a quivering salute, brought it down to shake that of Holmes, saluted again, then brought the hand down to the 'attention' position at his side, fingers clenched, thumb in line with the seam of his trousers.

Holmes said rather sadly, 'Don't give up hope, Mr Nunn. And God be with you.'

'Sir! And with us all, sir.'

Holmes turned away before the RSM could see that his eyes were becoming moist.

All the while the distance between the scattering ships of the convoy was becoming greater, but still the raider seemed to be stalking the Commodore's ship, one of the biggest prizes of the attack, probably unaware that the troopship carried German prisoners-of-war.

Finnegan remarked on this. 'If they don't know, that's surprising. Seem to know everything else about us.' Having spoken, he wished he'd kept his big mouth shut: the Commodore would have got the reference. But all Kemp said was that they probably did know but were disregarding the facts.

'War, Finnegan. I dare say we'd do the same. In war, you kill because that's what you're there for. You can't afford to be squeamish.'

Finnegan didn't respond. He knew he would hate to be killed by his own side. But of course the Old Man was right. You couldn't afford to be choosy. Hundreds of thousands of civilians on both sides had been and would continue to be killed in the air raids, another thing to be accepted as inevitable. It had become a dirty war.

Kemp said, 'Go below, Finnegan. Let me have a report on the prisoners.'

Finnegan went down the ladders to B deck. All seemed well and was reported so by Captain Mulvaney who was also checking on orders from oc Troops. 'Well but restive,' the Australian said. 'Buggers cheered when we took that hit.' His voice was savage but he said, 'Reckon it's natural really. Tell you one thing: I'd bust a gut laughing if a Nazi shell landed in the bloody lounge.'

'Not for long you wouldn't. If that happened, the shell'd be likely to plough right down through the ship's innards. We haven't got armoured decks.'

'Too right, bloke, too right. Maybe I'll send a negative on that thought, addressed God.' Mulvaney frowned, dug into a nostril with a finger. 'That old bloke. Know who I mean? Dug-out colonel –'

'Yes.'

'Weird old geezer, been gassing away to the troops, all about how safe we're going to be. Like hell we are! I'd say we don't have a snowflake's chance in hell, that's what I'd say. How about you, eh?'

Finnegan said, 'Fifty-fifty. We just have to stay afloat till the *Duke of York* turns up.'

Mulvaney jeered at that. 'Which she won't. Not in time, anyway.'

Finnegan went back to the bridge, giving the Commodore the report as ordered.

The attack was kept up throughout the night hours. The *Stuttgart*'s escorting destroyers had moved in quite early on, weaving at speed past the depleted British escorting force, coming in with their torpedo-tubes ready. Two more of the merchant ships had been sunk by those torpedoes, but the destroyers hadn't had it all their own way. The DEMS gunnery crews aboard the merchantmen had scored a couple of hits on the bridges of destroyers that had closed the convoy unwisely, and some damage had been done, one of the enemy vessels turning in a wide circle as her bridge personnel were blown apart, and ending up slap across the rearing bows of the Commodore's ship. The German had been sliced in half by those heavy bows, 24,000 tons of steel moving at full speed had been too much for the thin sides and she had gone down in two separate halves that for a brief time had banged their way down the *Aurelian Star*'s port and starboard sides. There had been further torpedo sorties by the

177

Barracudas from the carrier, engaging the German ack-ack and helping to keep the raider at a distance from the scattered merchant vessels by blowing a hole in the stem just below the waterline, thus forcing the ship to reduce speed. But the end for the Barracudas came when a German shell smashed away the carrier's bridge superstructure and another penetrated her starboard side and fractured her aviation spirit pipelines rigged ready for refuelling when the aircraft landed on. The *Rameses* went up with a deafening roar, an envelope of flame, and a shower of debris some of which spattered down on the decks of the *Aurelian Star*. The airborne torpedo-bombers were left without a base, left to fly around aimlessly until their fuel ran out and they were forced to ditch.

Pessimism, as a fiery dawn came up, had gripped the bridge of the *Aurelian Star*. Though slowed, though harried by the British destroyers, the *Stuttgart* now looked set to obliterate the whole convoy. The fleeing ships could be picked off one by one. At intervals through the night shells had come close to the Commodore's ship, close enough to send heavy spray flinging over the decks, drenching the guns'-crews and the troops at their boat stations. One hit had taken the foremast fair and square, and the smashed remains had come down across the bridge, by some miracle injuring no-one but the lookout in the crow's nest, smashing the woodwork of the wheelhouse and chart room. The ship's carpenter and his mates were working to clear away the debris when an urgent shout came from the yeoman of signals.

'Ship hull down, sir, bearing red one-oh. Looks like a battleship, though I can't be sure yet, sir.'

A miracle? Kemp ran for the vertical ladder from the bridge to monkey's-island before realizing monkey's-island was no longer there. He turned back to the yeoman of signals. He said, 'The moment she's within signalling distance, make the challenge without further orders.'

'Aye, aye, sir.' Lambert went on watching, feeling the shake in his hands, the nervous tension building up: that battleship, if such it proved to be, could be the *Duke of York*. It could equally well be a German.

Cocky Bulstrode, in the evening of that same day, was in

Portsmouth on business. He had a prospect, a chap he'd met quite casually in a pub in Southsea, the posh part of Portsmouth. The pub was the India Arms in Castle Road. He'd subsequently worked on this contact, getting his confidence by exchanging confidences of his own, possibly indiscreetly but then Southampton was quite a fair distance from Pompey. Cocky had discovered two things: one, that his contact was a man with tastes similar to his own, i.e., the man liked a little on the side and they'd had a quiet giggle over this, sort of comparing notes of conquests. Two, that his prospect – Alf Smith by name – was a civvy working as a technician in an Admiralty department, situated in Fort Southwick on Portsdown Hill just behind the town. This department was concerned with wireless telegraphy and the receipt of codes and cyphers together with non-secret messages. Neither Cocky nor Alf had ever discussed this, neither of them being spies nor having any interest whatsoever in information that was none of their business; but on the evening of Cocky's visit to Alf's home to sew up a life insurance policy, Alf came across with some information that was very relevant indeed.

'You did say, Mr Bulstrode,' he whispered when his wife had left the parlour to make a cup of tea, 'you did say you had a, well, bit of stuff in Southampton?'

'That's right, Mr Smith, yes.'

'Wife of the chief steward of a ship called –'

'The *Aurelian Star*, yes.'

Alf looked round: the parlour door was still shut fast. 'Convoy under attack, South Atlantic. Commodore's ship, this *Aurelian Star*. Big losses believed but no ship names given. Anyway, not that I overheard.' Alf paused, and gave Cocky Bulstrode a nudge in the ribs with an elbow. He also winked. 'Could leave the coast clear, eh, Mr Bulstrode?'

'Er . . . yes. Yes, indeed, and I'm much obliged.' Cocky was in something of a mental whirl; his worst fears could possibly be about to be realized. He concluded his business as quickly as was decently possible and then, with the signed contract in his money bag he returned to the Morris Eight and drove back to Southampton but not to Roxanne Chatfield, whom in any case he hadn't visited since she had become possessive, going to the pub to avoid her incessant telephone calls. Now he wouldn't be seeing her again, not ever. Much too risky to a man who valued his freedom and his spare cash.

'Acknowledged, sir. Correct reply.'

Kemp breathed easy: the battleship was not German. He said, 'Get her signal letters, Yeoman.'

Lambert was using his signal lamp again when there was a startling yell from Finnegan. The battleship was now coming into view through his binoculars. 'Oh, gee . . . oh, gee whiz . . . oh, daddy-oh!'

Kemp swung round. 'I beg your pardon, Finnegan?'

Finnegan gave a yelp, a sort of war-whoop. 'It's the good ole United States Navy! It's the *North Dakota*! Oh, gee . . .'

Kemp grunted. 'Custer rides again,' he said. He levelled his binoculars. The Captain of the *North Dakota* was evidently a man of quick understanding and quicker decision. There was a flash followed by billowing clouds of smoke as the American's for'ard turrets opened and moments later, as the great projectiles winged across the seas between, big spouts of water rose around the *Stuttgart*. The *North Dakota* was seen to swing so as to bring all her guns to bear, and then she opened in the form of a broadside. Salvo after salvo; and when the range and deflection came spot on the German blew up in a shattering roar, split from stem to stern as her magazines opened her up like a sardine tin.

One of Kemp's first duties was to have Ordinary Seaman Featherstonehaugh brought before him officially. The proper formalities were gone through. Kemp listened and then pronounced; the situation had been eased by the shot native now being on the way to recovery. 'I have good reports of you, Featherstonehaugh. You had a nasty experience at the after gun . . . and Petty Officer Biggar reports that you stood up to action well enough.' He paused. 'I propose – there being no evidence to the contrary – to accept your own story. I accept that you acted instinctively to put a stop to what looked like a breakout. On that score the case is dismissed.' He paused again. 'The fact remains, however, that you fired without orders to do so. That is a very serious charge and one that should normally be beyond my powers to deal with summarily. However, I propose to use my discretion and allow you the likelihood that you acted in the instinctive way I've referred to already. Now, I can't say what view the members of the Admiralty Interview Board will take in regard to a potential officer who acts without orders, but I suppose there's a chance they may remember Lord Nelson . . . as for me, I propose to stop your leave for fourteen days.'

Featherstonehaugh had looked much relieved as well he might. But, as Kemp began the task of rounding up the convoy's surviving ships and shepherding them back into their formation, he had plenty to ponder. Had he handled the matter wrongly? Had he risked backing a potential officer who might impetuously lead men into unnecessary danger, an officer who at some vital moment might make the wrong decision? Well – that was in the lap of the gods now. He, Kemp, had made his own decision and that was that. But the affair still nagged at his mind as, some twelve hours later, they picked up the *Duke of York* and exchanged signals, after which the *North Dakota* detached to resume her original course; Finnegan was still cock-a-hoop about the arrival in the nick of time of the US Navy . . . feeling half inclined to shut him up, Kemp decided to allow him his natural enthusiasm. They had indeed been given salvation.

When some fourteen days later the convoy picked up Ailsa Craig, the great seagull-whitened rock at the entry to the Firth of Clyde, Kemp's heart was heavy. Within hours now he would be at anchor off the Tail o' the Bank, off the town of Greenock where news might be awaiting him, where there would be a telephone available to reach Mary. This could be the worst landfall of his career. When Maconochie brought his ship to anchor later that morning, the Commodore's lips were moving in silent entreaty to his God. Throughout the ship, throughout the remains of the convoy, many other people had their worries, the worries that would come home to them when they disembarked. Old Colonel Holmes and his wife, taking their leave a little later of the Commodore, had a defeated look. They had seen Greenock town, dour and grey under a leaden sky with a hint of lashing rain. So very different from East Africa. They left the ship aboard the tender for Prince's Pier, where they bought third-class railway tickets for austerity and obscurity and a sort of obliteration of so much of their past. Miss Northway had tagged onto Captain Mulvaney, who was determined to ditch her as fast as possible though she didn't know this because he had promised faithfully to call her the moment he got leave to London. Chief Engineer French, when Maconochie rang down Finished With Engines, was worrying about the mail that would probably give him news of what the magistrates had done to his two boys. And Chief Steward Chatfield, who though he didn't know it had nothing to worry about now, was mentally attaching a bomb to the Morris Eight.

There were a number of letters for Commodore Kemp: an Income Tax demand, a tailor's bill, letters from both his sons posted some while ago . . . two from Mary, one from the Chairman of the Mediterranean-Australia Lines. No telegram from the Admiralty. Hopes rose. He opened his wife's letters first. One told him the first news, and that there had been no confirmation either way. The second was very brief: would John please telephone as soon as he possibly could after arrival? Reading that, Kemp went very white. There was no telephone connection when at anchor; that privilege was reserved for the flagship buoy. Kemp went ashore to RN headquarters and used a telephone to his home. The second letter from Mary had warned him. His hand shook so badly that he could scarcely hold the receiver steady when the confirmation of the bad news came. The German Admiralty had reported Harry picked up alive; but he had died shortly after, presumably from exposure or wounds received.

Kemp would be home the following night; that was the fastest he could make it, there being unavoidable convoy matters to attend to and an obligatory visit to the Admiralty on the way south.

First there was something else: the bar of the Bay Hotel in nearby Gourock: the Naval Officers' Club in Greenock would scarcely do. He had a need to get drunk. He wouldn't go the whole hog; but the pain had to be eased.